T0205108

the idea *of* you

the idea *of* you

robinne lee

st. martin's griffin · new york

THE IDEA OF YOU. Copyright © 2017 by Robinne Lee. All rights reserved. Printed in the United States of America. For information, address St. Martin's Press, 175 Fifth Avenue, New York, N.Y. 10010.

www.stmartins.com

Designed by Anna Gorovoy

Names: Lee, Robinne, date, author.
Title: The idea of you / Robinne Lee.
Description: First edition. | New York : St. Martin's Griffin, 2017.
Identifiers: LCCN 2017004299| ISBN 9781250125903 (softcover) |
    ISBN 9781250125910 (ebook)
Subjects: LCSH: Man-woman relationships—Fiction. | Divorced women—Fiction.
    | Rock groups—Fiction. | Singers—Fiction. | BISAC: FICTION /
    Contemporary women. | FICTION / Romance / Contemporary. |
    GSAFD: Love stories.
Classification: LCC PS3612.E348527 I34 2017 | DDC 813/.6—dc23
LC record available at https://lccn.loc.gov/2017004299

Our books may be purchased in bulk for promotional, educational,
or business use. Please contact your local bookseller or the Macmillan Corporate
and Premium Sales Department at 1-800-221-7945, extension 5442,
or by e-mail at MacmillanSpecialMarkets@macmillan.com.

First Edition: June 2017

20   19   18

For Eric,
who has loved me best

acknowledgments

My heartfelt gratitude goes out to so many who accompanied me on this journey.

My agent, Richard Pine, who fell in love with this story the second it crossed his desk, and who generously shared his brilliance and expertise. I feel so lucky to have had such an enthusiastic champion in my corner! His assistant, the invaluable Eliza Rothstein, for her keen input. And everyone at InkWell Management.

My supremely talented editor, Elizabeth Beier, who believed in the magic of Solène and Hayes and made it possible for me to share them with the world. My copy editor, Mary Beth Constant, who has an exquisite eye for the finest detail. Danielle Fiorella, who designed a mesmerizing cover. Nicole Williams, for keeping everything organized. Brittani Hilles, Marissa Sangiacomo, Jordan Hanley, and the rest of the exceptional team at St. Martin's Press.

My team of beta-readers: My sister, Kelley, for always being my first and most appreciative; Colette Sartor, Lisanne Sartor, Laura Brennan, Aimee Liu, Gloria Loya, and the incredibly supportive, accomplished women of the Yale Women L.A. Writing Group; Monica Nordhaus, for insisting I accompany her to the AMAs and for opening doors; Hope Mineo, Colleen Cassidy Hart, M. Catherine OliverSmith, and Dawn Cotton Fuge (my expert on all things British), for reading, for listening, and for being there when I needed to cry; and Mary Leigh Cherry, whose art world expertise was essential to creating Solène's universe.

My support system: My friends who were sounding boards and who encouraged me to tell this story: Louise Santacruz, Emily Murdock, Carrie Knoblock, Michelle Jenab, Julie Simon, Kate Seton, Mia Ammer, and Meghan Wald; my fellow Joy Luckers, especially Denise Malausséna, for tweaking my French; Bestie Row, for enduring my crazy, with an extra-special thank you to Amanda Schuon, for the phone call; my fellow writers on a mission: Jennifer Maisel and Dedi Feldman; my FB family, for answering so many random questions—from Scotch to seaplanes and everything in between. Collectively, they are better than Google.

My darlings, Alexander and Arabelle, who allowed me the time and freedom to write around their crazy schedules, and never once lost their patience with me.

My mom and dad, who have always been the biggest fans of my writing.

And above all, my extraordinary husband, Eric, who when I joked, "I'm thinking about leaving you for a guy in a boy band," responded, "That would make a great book," and in doing so, gave me the gift of a lifetime. (Thank you, Sweet.)

And lastly, my most favorite muse. I might have still written this story had I never seen his face. But I doubt it would have been as enjoyable.

All the love,
Robinne

the idea *of* you

las vegas

I suppose I could blame it all on Daniel.

Two days before my planned getaway to Ojai, he showed up at the house in a tux with our daughter, Isabelle, in tow. He'd left the car running in the driveway.

"I can't do the Vegas trip," he said, thrusting a manila envelope in my hand. "I'm still working on the Fox deal and it's not going to close anytime soon."

I must have looked at him in disbelief because he followed that up with:

"I'm sorry. I know I promised the girls, but I can't. You take them. Or I'll eat the tickets. Whatever."

An unopened package of Da Vinci Maestro Kolinsky brushes was lying on the entry table, alongside a set of thirty-six Holbein watercolors. I'd spent a fortune at Blick stocking up on materials for my artist retreat. They were, like the trip to Ojai, my gift to myself. Forty-eight hours of art and sleep and wine. And now my ex-husband was standing in my living room in formal black tie and telling me there'd been a change of plans.

"Does she know?" I asked. Isabelle, having retreated immediately to her room—no doubt to get on her phone—had missed the entire exchange.

He shook his head. "I haven't had time to tell her. I thought I'd wait and see if you could take them first."

"That's convenient."

"Don't start, okay?" He turned toward the door. "If you can't do it, have her call me, and I'll make it up the next time the group's in town."

It was so like him to have a Band-Aid for everything. To walk away from commitments guilt-free. Would that I had acquired that gene.

Isabelle and her two girlfriends had been counting down the days to see the band August Moon, a quintet of handsome lads from Britain who sang pleasant pop songs and drove tween girls mad. Daniel had "won" the tickets at the school silent auction. Paid some formidable amount to fly four to Vegas, stay at the Mandalay Bay, and attend the concert and a meet-and-greet with the band. Canceling now would not go over well.

"I have plans," I said, following him out into the driveway.

He slipped around the back of the BMW and withdrew a cumbersome bag from the trunk. Isabelle's fencing equipment. "I assumed you would. I'm sorry, Sol."

He was quiet for a moment, drinking me in: sneakers, leggings, still damp from a five-mile run. And then: "You cut your hair."

I nodded, my hands rising to my neck, self-conscious. It barely reached my shoulders now. My act of defiance. "It was time for a change."

He smiled faintly. "You're never not beautiful, are you?"

Just then the tinted window on the passenger side rolled down and a sylphlike creature leaned out and waved. Eva. My replacement.

She was wearing an emerald-green gown. Her long, honey-colored hair twisted into a chignon. There were diamonds dangling from both ears. It wasn't enough that she was some youngish, stunning, half-Dutch, half-Chinese star associate at the firm, but that she was now sitting in Daniel's 7 Series in my driveway looking every bit the princess while I was dripping sweat—now, *that* stung.

"Fine. I'll take them."

"Thank you," he said, handing over the bag. "You're the best."

"That's what all the boys say."

He paused then, screwing up his aristocratic nose. I anticipated a response, but none was forthcoming. Instead he smiled blandly, leaning in to do the awkward divorcé cheek kiss. He was wearing cologne, which he'd never done in all his years with me.

I watched him make his way over to the driver's side. "Where are you going? All dolled up . . ."

"Fund-raiser," he said, getting into the car. "Katzenberg's." And with that, he pulled away. Leaving me holding the baggage.

I was not a fan of Vegas: loud, fat, dirty. The underbelly of America convened in one garish skid mark in the desert. I'd visited once, years before, to attend a bachelorette party that I was still trying to forget. The smell of strip clubs and drugstore perfume and vomit. Those things linger. But this was not my adventure. This time I was just along for the ride. Isabelle and her friends had made that clear.

They spent that afternoon running circles around the resort on a quest to find their idols, while I followed dutifully. I had become accustomed to this: my passionate daughter trying any- and everything, setting her mind and forging her way. Isabelle and her American can-do spirit. There was trapeze school and figure skating, musical theater, fencing . . . She was fearless, and I loved that about her, envied it even. I liked that she took risks, that she did not wait for permission, that she followed her heart. Isabelle was okay with living outside the lines.

I was hoping to convince the girls to visit the Contemporary Arts Center. It would have been nice to squeeze some real culture into the weekend. To imprint something worthwhile upon their impressionable minds. I'd spent countless hours trailing my mother through the Museum of Fine Arts in Boston as a child. Following the click of her Vivier heels, the scent of the custom-made fragrance she bought every summer in Grasse. How knowledgeable she was to me then, how womanly. I knew the halls of that museum as well as I knew my third-grade classroom. But Isabelle and her cohorts had balked at the idea.

"Mom, you know at any other time I would say yes. But this trip is different. Please?" she'd implored.

They'd come to Vegas for one reason only, and nothing would thwart their mission. "Our lives begin tonight," Georgia, with the silky brown skin, had proclaimed on the flight in. Rose, the redhead, agreed, and the three quickly adopted it as their mantra. No expectation too high. They had their whole lives ahead of them. They were twelve.

The meet-and-greet was at six o'clock. I don't know what I was expecting exactly, something slightly elegant, civilized, but no. They crammed us into a fluorescent-lit holding room in the bowels of the arena. Fifty-odd worshippers in various stages of puberty: girls in braces, girls in wheelchairs, girls in heat. Wide-eyed and smitten and on the verge of combustion. It was at once beautiful and desperate. And it pained me to realize that Isabelle was now part of this tribe. This motley crew searching for happiness in five boys from Britain whom they did not know, could never know, and who would never return the adulation.

Several parents were scattered throughout. A select swath of Middle America: jeans, T-shirts, practical shoes. Faces pink from a brutal introduction to the Vegas sun. It dawned on me that I would be lumped in with these people. "Augies," as the media had dubbed the fandom. Or, worse yet, an "Augie Mom."

The girls were beginning to fidget when a side door opened and a hulking bald man with a neckful of laminated passes entered. "Who here is ready to meet the band?!"

Shrieks pierced the air, and I suddenly remembered that I'd forgotten my earplugs in the hotel room. Lulit, my business partner and confidante in all things worth confiding, had mentioned it yesterday at the gallery, told me I'd be crazy to step into a stadium of Augies without a pair. Apparently, she'd once attended a concert with her niece. "The boys are adorable, but my God, the fans are loud."

Beside me Isabelle's entire body had begun to shake.

"Excited?" I squeezed her shoulders.

"Cold." She shrugged it off. Ever the aloof one.

"The guys are going to be five more minutes," the hulking man continued. "They'll stay for about twenty. I need you all to form a line up here to the left. You'll each get your turn for a quick hello and a photo with the group. No selfies. Our photographer will take the pics, and you'll be able to download them later online. We'll provide you with the link. You all get that?"

It seemed so impersonal. Certainly there were better ways Daniel could have spent his money. I was thinking, as they steered us into line, that I was overdressed in Alaïa sandals and out of place. That I was pulled together and polished and that once again, for better or worse, I stuck out. This, my father's mother had explained to me on numerous occasions, was my birthright: "You are French, at your core. *Il ne faut pas l'oublier.*" There *was* no forgetting it: my

Frenchness. And so I resisted being grouped in with these women, but at the same time I was keenly aware of their selflessness, their patience. The things we did for our children. What kind of mother would I be to begrudge Isabelle this moment?

And then they entered. The five of them. There was a groundswell and audible swooning, and Rose let out a little yelp like a puppy that had her tail stepped on. Georgia threw her a look that said, *Get it together, sister,* and indeed Rose did.

They were young—that was my first thought. They had dewy, fresh skin, as if they'd been raised on an organic farm. They were taller than I'd expected, lean. Like the swim team at Brown. Only prettier.

"Now, who is who?" I asked, and Isabelle shushed me. Right.

We migrated to where the boys were positioned before a banner with the August Moon logo: big yellow letters across a gray backdrop. They seemed happy, giddy even, to be mingling with their fans. A mutual love affair. The way they hammed it up for the camera and put the awkward adolescents at ease, the way they flirted with their older fans—sly, but not crossing the line—the way they engaged the tweens and charmed the mothers. It was an art. They'd nailed it.

When we were next in line, Isabelle leaned into me. "Left to right: Rory, Oliver, Simon, Liam, and Hayes."

"Got it."

"Don't say anything embarrassing, okay?"

I promised her I wouldn't.

And then it was our turn.

"Well, hullo, lasses!" Simon bellowed, eyes wide, arms outstretched. He had an impressive wingspan. Isabelle had mentioned on the plane that he'd rowed crew in boarding school. "Step right up, don't be shy!"

The girls did not need a second prompt. Georgia lunged into Simon's arms, and Rose sidled up next to Liam, the baby of the bunch, he with the green eyes and freckles. Only Isabelle hesitated, her eyes darting back and forth. Eenie, meenie, miny . . . Quite the candy store.

"Having a hard time deciding?" The tall one on the far end spoke. "Come, come stand near me. I don't bite, I promise. Now, Rory, Rory might bite, and Ollie's unpredictable, so . . ." He smiled this dazzling smile. Wide mouth, full lips, perfect teeth, dimples. Hayes.

Isabelle smiled and made her way in his direction.

"Ha! I win! I win . . . What's your name, love?"

"Isabelle."

"I win Isabelle!" He flung his arm over her narrow shoulders, protective-like, and then glanced over to me. "And you must be the big sister?"

Isabelle laughed, covering her mouth. Her features delicate, like a little bird. "That's my mom."

"Your mum?" Hayes raised an eyebrow, holding my gaze. "*Really?* All right then. *Isabelle's mum.* Do you want to join us for the picture?"

"No, I'm fine. Thanks."

"You sure? Promise to make it worth your while."

I laughed at that. "I'd like to see you do that."

"I'd like to *show* you." He smiled, bold. "Come on. You'll want something to commemorate our wild night in Vegas."

"Well, when you make it so appealing . . ."

The first photo I have of myself with Hayes is of the nine of us, in the basement of the Mandalay Bay. He has one arm draped around me and the other around Isabelle. I'd ordered two copies. In time Isabelle would destroy hers.

"I'm impressed you flew out here just for us." The guys were in full conversation with my brood, making the most of our ninety seconds. Liam was asking Rose about our trek to Sin City, and Simon was touching Georgia's hair.

"I love these curls."

"Do you?" Georgia gave as good as she got. She'd benefitted from an older sister.

"That's quite an indulgence, flying in for the day." Hayes was engaging Isabelle, leaning on her shoulder like a big brother. Like he'd known her all her life. I knew inside she was dying.

"Two days," she clarified.

"It was a gift from her father," I volunteered.

"'Her father'?" He looked over to me. There was that raised eyebrow again. "Not *your husband*?"

"He *was* my husband. Now he's just her father."

"Well . . ." He paused. "That's serendipitous, isn't it?"

I laughed. "What does that mean?"

"I don't know. You tell me."

There was something about him in that moment. His ease. His accent. His cocksure smile. Disarming.

"Next!" Our time was up.

He humored us again at the end of the meet-and-greet. When everyone had taken their requisite photos and the group was signing autographs, we filtered over to him amidst a sea of moving bodies. Fish swimming upstream. All around us there was collective squealing and swaying and "Hayes, can I touch your hair?" But my group was holding it together. It might have been that jaded L.A. thing: that they were used to seeing the likes of the Beckham boys at the local park, or "Spider-Man" in the carpool lane at drop-off. It took a bit more to faze them. They were, despite all their exuberant canvassing of the resort that afternoon, surprisingly poised.

"I'm really loving the *Petty Desires* album. It's deep on so many levels," Georgia gushed.

"Yes," Rose chimed in. "Such clever lyrics. I love 'Seven Minutes.'"

"You like it, do you?" He glanced up from where he was signing a T-shirt.

"It's like . . . you've really tapped into our generation. You speak for all of us." Isabelle flipped her hair, an attempt at flirting, but the awkward pursed-lipped smile belied her youth. There were braces under there. Oh, sweet girl, in time . . .

She had my face. Large almond-shaped eyes, pouty French lips, a fair olive complexion. Her hair thick, brown, almost black.

I watched Hayes take the girls in. His eyes moving from one to another, amused. I imagined he was used to this. Finally, he landed on me.

"Where are you ladies sitting?"

The girls rattled off our seat numbers.

"Come backstage after the show. I'm going to have someone come and get you on the floor. Don't leave." He looked to me then. Piercing blue-green eyes and a mass of dark curls. He couldn't have been more than nineteen. "All right?"

I nodded. "All right."

There was something mind-bending about emerging from an intimate conversation with a member of the biggest boy band of the last decade and being thrust into an arena with twelve thousand of his shrieking fans. There was a shift of equilibrium, a disconnect. For a moment I lost sense of where I was, how I'd gotten there, what my role was supposed to be. The girls were buzzing with excitement and rushing to find our floor seats, and I was spiraling. I was not prepared for the onslaught: the roar, the pitch, the energy level of so many adolescent girls at the peak of arousal. That this, all of this, could be for the boys we'd just left in the basement seemed inconceivable. They were bewitching, yes, but still flesh and blood.

The screamfest started before the guys hit the stage and continued without pause for the next two and a half hours. Lulit had been right. It was at a decibel level that was near impossible to get used to. Particularly for a woman pushing forty.

The year I turned sixteen, I saw the New Kids on the Block at Foxboro Stadium during their Magic Summer Tour. A handful of us went for Alison Aserkoff's birthday. Her father had finagled floor seats and backstage passes. It was loud and unwieldy and not typically my thing. Boy bands were not part of the prep school culture. We grew up listening to the Stones, U2, Bob Marley. Music that never got old. So five working-class boys from Dorchester, Mass., should theoretically not have had any appeal.

But there was something there. The rush, the hormones, the heat from the stage. The idea that they were longed for and lusted after by so many made them exponentially more appealing. And for a brief moment I thought I could let myself go, in the madness. But then I realized how indelicate that would seem, how unbecoming. And I remembered who I was supposed to be, at my core. And whatever wanton adulation might have occurred I stopped before it could take root. Well before the encore at the New Kids concert.

A near quarter-century later, it was threatening to play out again.

Despite the noise and the hormones coursing through the Mandalay Bay, the band put on a great show—although whether a group could truly call themselves a band if they didn't play instruments was unknown to me. Rory stroked the guitar for a handful of songs, and Oliver sat down before the piano once or twice, but other than that, the only instrumentation came from the accompanying backup band. Mostly the guys sang and jumped about onstage like young virile pogo sticks. There was lots of roughhousing and clowning around and very little choreography, but the fans did not seem to mind.

"I love them! I love them! I love them!" Georgia proclaimed after a rousing rendition of "Fizzy Smile," the titular track from the band's first album. There were tears streaming down her doll-like face, and her curls had begun to frizz in the humidity. "They touch my *soul*."

Rose was clearly in agreement, shrieking every time Liam walked the extended platform that brought him within feet of us. Isabelle was in her own trance, singing and swaying deeply with the music. They were a happy bunch. And in that moment, I forgave Daniel for welshing as he often did, because his flounder had gifted me the opportunity to witness the girls' rapture. One could not put a price on that.

Like clockwork, a burly black man wearing credentials arrived at our section just as the band exited the stage after the final encore. Hayes had kept his promise.

"Is one of you Isabelle?"

I barely made out what he was saying through the incessant hum in my ears, the sense of conversing underwater. But we followed him to the gate, where he presented each of us with wristbands and all-access lanyards.

No words were spoken on the long walk backstage. I suspected the girls did not want to ruin the moment, to be woken from the dream. Their expressions were expectant, serious. They could barely look at one another for the excitement. *Our lives begin tonight.*

I got the impression that the security guard was used to this, plucking young girls from the audience to hand-deliver to the band. For a moment I feared what we might be getting ourselves into. Where was he taking us exactly? And at what point might I be liable for child endangerment? Because certainly handing over a trio of twelve-year-olds for consumption would constitute some sort of misdemeanor, if not felony. No, I would not let them out of my sight. This was Vegas, after all.

But as we entered the after-party it became apparent that my worries were unnecessary. Girls for consumption seemed few and far between: a couple of unrecognizable models, the Dane from the *Sports Illustrated* swimsuit issue, a reality star, and an actress from the new Netflix series. Other than that, it appeared to be family and close friends: a bunch of Brits and industry types and a hand-ful of well-behaved, lucky young fans. It felt decidedly safe.

Eventually the band emerged, freshly showered, hair damp and void of product. There was applause and whistles and the pop-popping of champagne. And I had to wonder if this happened every night. This sort of self-congratulatory celebration. Isabelle and her friends wasted no time flocking to Simon and Liam at the party's core. Composure regained, they were once again on a mis-sion. I wasn't certain what that mission was exactly: "Make said member of August Moon fall in love with me" sounded about right, and yet surely they must have realized that was highly unlikely. As it was, Rory was chatting up the swimsuit model in a corner. Beanie pulled low on his brow, hands jammed deep into his pockets, forc-ing the waist of his black jeans lower than their already ridiculous latitude. The incline of his head and his body language conveyed all: he had claimed her.

Oliver was deep in conversation with what I took to be a record exec—some guy in a gray shiny suit who might or might not have been hitting on him. He was the most elegant of the group. Wil-lowy and thoughtful with hazel eyes and golden hair. The type I would have fallen in love with in college only to discover he was gay. Or far too profound to be interested in an art history major. Either way, he would have broken my heart.

And then there was Hayes. Holding court like Simon and Liam, but in a manner that seemed more deliberate, intense. From my vantage point on the far side of the room, where a writer from *Vanity Fair* was chatting me up, I could see Simon goofing off and Liam being young, both captivating their fans. But Hayes was harder to read. Hayes's attention appeared sincere. Even from a distance, his conversation with his sycophants seemed earnest.

It wasn't until thirty minutes or so later, when I'd almost pol-ished off a glass of Perrier-Jouët and extricated myself from the writer, that Hayes approached me in the corner.

"Well, hello, Isabelle's mum . . ."

"It's Solène."

"So-lène . . ." He took his time with it. "Like, 'So, lend me some money and I'll pay you back'?"

I laughed. "Exactly."

"So-lène," he repeated. "I like that. It's French? Are you French?"

"My parents are. Very."

"So-lène." He nodded. "I'm Hayes."

"I know who you are."

"Yes. Fancy that." He smiled this half smile, the left side of his mouth turning up at the corner, putting precious dimples into relief. His mouth was too big for his face—wide and unapologetic. But he had dimples, and what might have been arrogance came across as endearing. "Are you enjoying yourself?"

"I am, thank you."

"Good." He stood there, grinning, arms folded across his broad chest. He was doing that thing that tall guys sometimes do, copping a very wide stance to bring him closer to my eye level. "Did you like the show?"

"It was . . . entertaining."

His smile widened. "You didn't like it."

"It was surprisingly loud," I laughed.

"No one warned you? I'm sorry, Solène."

There was something about the way he kept saying my name: raspy voice, unwavering gaze, the roll of his tongue. It felt . . . intimate.

"I was warned, just not enough, clearly. Your fans are—"

"Excitable."

"That's one way of putting it."

He laughed, tossing back his head. He had a beautiful jawline. "They're a wild bunch. Next time we'll get you headphones."

"Next time?"

"There's always a next time." He said it with a straight face, but there was something there that gave me pause.

"How old are you, Hayes?"

"Twenty."

"Twenty," I repeated, and then downed the rest of my champagne. One gulp. Well, at least that was better than nineteen.

"Twenty." He bit down on his bottom lip and smiled.

Right then would have been a good time to excuse myself. Collect the girls and call it a night. But I could see the expressions on their faces from across the room. Simon was patting Georgia's hair again, and Liam was showing off his breakdancing moves, and the euphoria was palpable. We'd been there less than an hour. Pulling them now would be cruel.

"You're thinking about leaving, aren't you?" Hayes's voice drew me back in. "Please don't. I'm going to get you another drink."

"No, I'm good, thank you."

"Rubbish. It's Vegas." He winked before taking the empty flute from my hand and heading over to the makeshift bar.

There hadn't been many since Daniel: a series of dates with one of the dads from Isabelle's fencing team and a two-month dalliance with the TV writer from my spin class. Neither had been consummated. Once they'd threatened to go beyond casual flirtation, I'd closed up. I'd shut down. And while three years of accidental celibacy had been oftentimes miserable, I was not going to jump into bed with a rock star barely half my age because he'd winked at me at an after-party. I was not going to be a cliché.

Before I could fully plot my exit, Hayes returned with another glass of bubbly and a bottle of water for himself. His hair had dried into an enviable mop of silken curls. There were blogs dedicated to Hayes's hair—this I would learn later—but there in the belly of the Mandalay Bay, I resisted the urge to touch it.

"So, Solène, what is it that you do when you're not attending August Moon concerts?"

"You are amusing, Hayes Campbell."

"Ha. You know my last name . . ."

"Yes, because I live with a twelve-year-old girl."

"But not your ex-husband?"

"Not my ex-husband, no," I laughed. "I could be your mother, you know."

"But you're not."

"But I could be."

"*But you're not.*" He held my gaze, smiling his half smile.

I felt it then, that little flip-flop in the pit of my stomach that told me that whatever this twenty-year-old was doing, it was working.

"Are you going to give me that glass? Or did you just bring it over here to tease me?"

"To tease you," he laughed, and took a sip of my champagne before handing it over. "Cheers."

I stood there, staring at him, not drinking. Enjoying it. "You're bad . . ."

"Sometimes . . ."

"Does that work for you?"

He laughed then. "Mostly. Is it not working now?"

I smiled, shaking my head. "Not as well as you think it is."

"Ow, that hurts." His eyes darted across the room then, searching. "Oliver!"

Oliver looked up in our direction. He was still being cornered by the guy in the shiny suit and seemed eager to have an out. I watched as he excused himself and made his way over to us.

"Ol, this is Solène."

"Hi, Solène." He smiled, charming.

The two of them stood peering down at me, equally tall, equally confident. And for a moment I wished I hadn't worn flats, because even at five foot seven, among these boys I felt small.

"Tell me, Ol, could Solène be my mother?"

Oliver raised an eyebrow, and then took an extended moment to look me over. "Most definitely not." He turned to face Hayes. "And your mother is a very beautiful woman . . ."

"My mother *is* a beautiful woman."

"But she doesn't look like this."

"No, she doesn't." Hayes smiled.

Oliver's eyes were arresting. "What are *you* doing slumming in *Vegas*?"

I took a sip of champagne then. Game on. "I got roped into attending an August Moon concert. You?"

They were both quiet for a second. Hayes laughed first. "And a brilliant wit, to boot. Ol, you can go."

"You just invited me to the party, mate."

"Well, now you're being uninvited."

"Hayes Campbell. Doesn't play well with others," Oliver said, deadpan.

"I just saved you from the wanker in the bad suit. You owe me."

Oliver shook his head before extending a graceful hand. "Solène, 'twas a pleasure, albeit brief."

Albeit brief? Who *were* these guys? This rakish quintet. Clearly Isabelle and the other umpteen million girls around the world were on to something.

"'Doesn't play well'?" I asked once Oliver had departed.

"I play very well. I just don't share."

I smiled up at him, taken. His face, like art. His mouth, distracting. And that which crossed my mind was not all pure.

"So," he said, "tell me about you."

"What do you want to know?"

"What are you willing to share with me?"

I laughed at that. Hayes Campbell, twenty, and making me sweat. "As little as possible."

He smiled his half smile. "I'm listening . . ."

"So you are." I took a sip from my glass. "Where to start . . . I live in L.A."

"Are you from there?"

"No. The East Coast. Boston. But I've been there for a while now, so . . . it's home, I guess. I own an art gallery, with my girlfriend Lulit."

"Girlfriend?" He raised an eyebrow.

"Not that kind of girlfriend."

He smiled, shrugging. "Not that I was judging . . ."

"Just that you were fantasizing?"

He laughed, loud. "Did we just meet?"

"Do you want to know more or not?"

"I want to know everything."

"We own an art gallery. In Culver City. We sell contemporary art."

He let that sit there for a second, and then: "Is that different from modern art?"

"'Modern art' is a broad term that covers about a hundred years and encompasses many different movements. Contemporary art is current."

"So your artists are all still alive, I gather?"

I smiled. "On most days, yes. So . . ." I was going to need more champagne. "What is it *you* do when you're not attending August Moon concerts?"

He laughed at that, crossing his arms over his chest. "I'm not sure that I remember. This has kind of consumed the last few years of my life. Touring, writing, recording, publicity . . ."

"You write your own music?"

"Most of it."

"That's impressive. You play piano?"

He nodded. "And guitar. Bass. A little saxophone."

I smiled at that. Clearly I'd been underestimating boybanders. "Do you ever just go home and do nothing?"

"Not often. Do you?"

"Not as much as I'd like."

He nodded slowly, sipped from his water, and then: "What does it look like? Your home?"

"It's modern. Clean lines. Lots of midcentury furniture. It's on the Westside, up in the hills, overlooking the ocean. There are walls of glass, and the light is always shifting. The rooms change, at dawn, at dusk. It's like living in a watercolor. I love that." I stopped then.

He was standing there, staring at me in a way that he probably should not have been. He was so ridiculously young. And I was someone's mother. And in no world could this lead to anything good.

"Wow," he said, soft. "That sounds like a pretty perfect life."

"Yeah. But for—"

"But for the ex-husband," he finished my thought.

"Yeah. And everything that comes with that."

As if on cue, Isabelle skipped up to us, wide-eyed and happy. "Mom, this is the best party *ever*! We were talking about it, and this is even better than Harry Wasserman's Bar Mitzvah."

"Not Harry's Bar Mitzvah?" Hayes had snapped out of wherever his thoughts had taken him and returned to teen idol mode.

She blushed, covering her mouth. "Hiiii, Hayes."

"Hiiii, Isabelle."

"You remembered my name?"

"Lucky guess." He shrugged. "What's Liam doing over there? Is he showing you how he does the worm? You know I taught him everything he knows, right? Shall we have a worm-off? Liam!" Hayes called across the room. "Worm-off! Now!"

I could sense Isabelle bursting out of her skin when Hayes threw his arm around her shoulders and began leading her away. "Excuse us, Solène. There's a competition to be had."

The sight of the two of them, my awkward daughter and the comely rock star, making their way across the room was so bizarre and ironic, I had to laugh.

Hayes was in his element. In no time, he'd become the center of attention, lying prostrate on the floor, psyching himself up for the competition, his bandmates and fans swarming around him. While Liam's wiry frame and jerky moves might have made him the more natural dancer, Hayes was far more captivating. There was a grace to him, sliding across the floor in his black jeans and boots. His feet kicking high up into the air, lifting his hips intermittently off the ground. Arm muscles straining with each thrust. A sliver of abdomen peeking out from beneath his thin T-shirt. He was such a vision of virility, it almost felt dirty to watch.

There was hooting and whistling, and when Hayes finally rose from the floor, Simon grabbed him in a man-hug. "This lad right here!" he howled, his blue eyes wide, his blond hair standing on end. "Is there nothing he can't do?!"

Hayes threw back his head and laughed, hair in disarray, dimples blazing. "Nothing." He beamed. But at that moment his eyes caught mine and the charge was so strong, I had to look away.

We left shortly after the "worm-off." When a lithe, questionably legal brunette had situated herself atop Liam's lap, and Rory's lips were on the neck of the swimsuit model in the corner, and at least half a dozen of the crew had slipped out and then reappeared glassy-eyed, I figured it might be a good time to get the girls out of there. The *Vanity Fair* writer was long gone.

"We've had such a lovely time. Thank you for inviting us."

We had congregated by the door, Rose wilting, Isabelle yawning, Georgia's hair growing to impressive proportions.

"I can't convince you all to stay longer?"

"It's late and we're flying out in the morning."

"You could change your flight."

I could feel my eyes narrowing, some involuntary tic I must have picked up from my mother.

"Right, okay, so that wouldn't be a good idea," he backpedaled.

"Probably not. No."

"This was the best night ever," "Brilliant," "Epic," the girls all said at once.

"Glad you had fun." Hayes smiled. "We'll do it again sometime, yeah?"

There was unanimous agreement from my entourage.

"So, um . . ." It was he who was stalling, eyes searching, fingers running through his poufy hair. "What did you say the name of your gallery was? You know, should I ever be in California and desire some contemporary art . . ."

"Marchand Raphel." I smiled.

"Marchand Raphel," he repeated. "And you would be—"

"She's the Marchand," Georgia volunteered.

"Solène Marchand." His smile widened. His teeth were decidedly un-English. Big, straight, white. Someone had spent good money on those teeth. "'Til next time, then?"

I nodded, but the seed had been planted. If I hadn't had the girls . . .

And then, completely aware of what I was suggesting and with surprisingly little hesitation, I laid the bait: "There's always a next time."

bel-air

He called.

Five days after Vegas, there was a message on my voicemail at the gallery. His voice: elegantly raspy with that darling British lilt. "Hello, Solène. This is Hayes Campbell. I'm in Los Angeles just for a few days. Was wondering if you'd be up for grabbing a bite."

I must have listened to it five times.

Hayes Campbell. On my voicemail. For all his coy and calculated charm in Vegas, I was genuinely taken aback. I did not expect the follow-through. And what had passed as harmless flirtation in the underbelly of the Mandalay Bay seemed suddenly lurid in the Southern California light. *Grabbing a bite*. With a twenty-year-old. From a boy band. Under what circumstance might that ever be construed as acceptable?

I tried to push it to the back of my head and get on with my work. But it remained there all day. Subtle, enticing, like the last piece of chocolate in the box put away for safekeeping. A little gift I was holding onto for myself. I didn't even share it with Lulit. And with her, I shared quite a bit.

We'd met fifteen years earlier in New York at Sotheby's exclusive training program. Lulit stood out to me in a class of exceptional people. Sylphlike brown limbs, lyrical Ethiopian accent, a love for Romare Bearden. I adored the way she used her arms when she talked, about art in particular: "Basquiat is so *angry*, the teeth never fit in the mouth!" "Dead sheep in a box isn't art! Add some bread, it's *dinner*."

She'd only just received her BA from Yale and I had already completed my master's when we met, but we shared a sensibility for contemporary art and the desire to be a part of something thrilling and unexpected. We found it in L.A.'s burgeoning art scene.

It was Lulit who'd come up with the idea of only representing female artists and artists of color. She'd spent three years in Sotheby's contemporary art department following our program. I'd done a year at the Gladstone Gallery before Daniel and I moved to L.A. We'd been married all of five months before I got pregnant with Isabelle and surrendered everything that had made me *me*. When Lulit arrived on the West Coast, spirited and ready to change the art world, I allowed myself to be swept up in her zeal. Marriage and motherhood had started to deaden mine. "Let's shake things up a little, yes?" she'd exclaimed over sushi at Sasabune. "You know, white men are so overrated."

At the time, I was spending my days tending to a willful twenty-month-old while Daniel was out billing 2,800 hours; I was inclined to agree. Within a year, Marchand Raphel was born.

The day that Hayes Campbell left a message on my voicemail, we sold the final piece of our current show. Argentinean-born art-

ist Pilar Anchorena was known for her arresting mixed-media col-
lages. Contemplative works in vibrant colors, always offering some
commentary on race or class or privilege. Not for those seeking
tame, pretty pictures, but catnip for the advanced collector.

Together with our sales director, Matt, and gallery manager,
Josephine, Lulit and I toasted with a bottle of Veuve Clicquot. One
sweet moment of accomplishment before tending to the logistics of
our May show.

In the late afternoon, when the others had gone, I locked myself in the office and took a bite of my metaphorical chocolate. "So,
you tracked me down, did you?"

"I did." Hayes's gravelly voice filled the phone.

"Very resourceful."

"I have an assistant . . ."

"Of course you do."

"Her name is Siri. She's quite good at her job."

I laughed at that. "Well played, Hayes Campbell. What can I
do for you?"

"Oh dear"—he cleared his throat—"the first and last name.
Kiss of death."

"How so?"

"Far too formal."

"What would you like me to call you?"

"Hayes will do."

"Hayes will do what?" I laughed. "I kid. I'm sorry. It's been a
long day." I stole a glimpse at my watch. I had forty-five minutes
before I had to pick up Isabelle from fencing. It would take me anywhere from twelve minutes to an hour to get there. L.A.

"Let me take you to dinner." It was a statement, not a question.

Dinner? I had been thinking more along the lines of a Starbucks.
Maybe Le Pain Quotidien . . .

My pulse quickened. "I can't . . . tonight. It's short notice and I
don't have a sitter." This was a half-truth. Isabelle didn't need a
sitter. She was twelve. But dinner seemed too official. Too much of
a *thing.*

"Maybe drinks tomorrow," I offered as a concession, and then realized my faux pas. He was not yet twenty-one.

It did not seem to faze him. "Can't tomorrow. We're playing the Staples Center."

"Oh." Yes, of course. The Staples Center. He'd said it so matter-of-factly. No conceit. Like Daniel announcing he had to work late on a deal. "Well, that won't work then, will it?"

"No," he laughed, this throaty laugh that made him sound older than twenty. Or so I wanted to believe. "Kind of have to show up for that. How about lunch then?"

I had a client lunch scheduled for Friday. I told him so. "Breakfast?"

He couldn't. The band was booked on a couple of morning shows. I threw out Saturday and Sunday as dinner options, and he declined. They were playing four nights at Staples and then heading up to the Bay. I tried to imagine how many screaming girls it would take to fill the Staples Center four times over, but I couldn't begin to wrap my head around it.

"Why don't we just do this the next time you're in town, Hayes?"

"Because I want to see you now."

"Well, we can't always get what we want, can we? Or do the usual rules not apply to you?"

He laughed at that. "Are you going to make me beg?"

"Only if it's something you feel you need to do."

I did not know why I was leading him on. It was absurd. Perhaps if I'd been a bolder person, if I hadn't cared what people thought of me, I could have entertained the idea of a fling with a twenty-year-old boybander. But I wasn't, and I did, and so maybe the thrill was in just *knowing* that I could. We would have lunch and be done with it.

The line was quiet, but something told me I still had him.

"All right," he said. "I'm begging. Lunch. Tomorrow. *Please.*"

I glanced at my watch again. I was going to be late for Isabelle. It would not be the first time. She'd be waiting for me in the gym, amidst the clinking of metal and the whir of the fans and the high-pitched hum of the scoring machine. The coaches yelling in Russian. My little bird in that foreign space. She was surprisingly okay with it. And to me, she never looked more graceful than when she was competing. Controlled, powerful, elegant.

"Fine. Lunch tomorrow," I agreed. "I'll move around my schedule."

Canceling a client lunch was irresponsible, but I attempted to rationalize it. The client was an old friend of Daniel's from Princeton. He wasn't going anywhere. Plus I had the satisfaction of having just sold out a show. So what if I played hooky for an afternoon?

"Yes!" Hayes made some little cheering sound, and I imagined his smile at the other end of the line, dimples and all. "Let's do the Hotel Bel-Air, shall we? Twelve-thirty. I'll handle the reservation."

Of course he would pick someplace fancy and terribly romantic. *Grab a bite*, indeed.

"Hayes," I said before he hung up the phone, "this is just lunch."

He paused for a moment, and I wondered if he'd heard me. "Solène . . . what else would it be?"

He was there when I arrived. Tucked away in one of those recessed alcoves against the far side of the restaurant's terrace, backed by a wall of glass and a view of the gardens. I expected him to be late, strolling in—all bewitching smile and rock star swagger. But he was punctual, early even. And the sight of him sitting there, in a gray-and-white-print button-down (was that a Liberty floral?) and tidy hair, told me he'd made an effort. He was poring over the menu and spinning his Ray-Ban Wayfarers between his thumb and forefinger when we approached. The maître d' had taken one look at me and—with "Ms. Marchand, I presume"—escorted me to my unlikely date.

Oh, to have captured the expression on Hayes's face when he glanced up to find me. Like Christmas morning. Joy, surprise, promise, and disbelief rolled into a singular moment. His blue-green eyes brightening and wide mouth giving way to a dazzling smile.

"You came," he said, standing to greet me. He seemed even taller in the daylight. Six foot two, I guessed . . . maybe three.

"Did you think I wouldn't show?"

"I thought there was a chance."

I laughed, leaning in to graze his cheek. An art world air-kiss. Relatively low on the intimacy level.

"I don't imagine you're the kind of guy who gets stood up often."

"I'm not the kind of guy who begs for dates either. There's a first for everything." He smiled, stepping aside and allowing me access to the booth.

"This is okay, I hope? It wasn't until after I made the call that I realized I had no idea where Culver City was and whether I was asking you to trek from the other side of the world to meet me. Turns out nothing is close in L.A. . . ."

"That's true. But no, it's fine."

"Okay, good. Because it's a beautiful space. Feels like being on holiday," he said, looking out over the terrace bathed in its perfect California light. Potted fruit trees and palms, white tablecloths adorned with purple Dendrobium orchids, boughs of fuchsia bougainvillea spilling in through the slats in the roof.

"Yes, it's enchanting. It's the Rockwell Group."

"Pardon?"

"Rockwell Group. They did the redesign of Wolfgang's restaurant. Lovely flow of indoor and outdoor spaces. Won a bunch of awards. And there's a great Gary Lang in the dining room. Painted concentric circles. Aggressive. Unexpected."

Hayes turned his attention back to me, the left side of his mouth curling into a smile. "Aggressive circles? That sounds sexy."

I laughed. "I suppose. If you're into that . . ."

He was quiet for a second, watching me. "I love that you know so much about art."

Oh, little boy, I wanted to say, *if I could show you the things I know.*

"Tell me what you told the maître d'," I said instead. "How was he able to identify me?"

Hayes opened and closed his mouth a couple of times before shaking his head in laughter. "You're tough."

"Tell me."

"I told him . . ." He spoke softly, slowly, leaning into me. "I told him I was meeting a friend, and that she had dark hair and haunting eyes and would probably be dressed very well. That she looked like a classic movie star. And that she had a *great* mouth."

I sat there, still. "Is that figurative or literal?"

"The mouth?"

"Yeah."

"Both."

He was so close to me then I could smell the scent on his skin. Some sort of sandalwood or cedar. And lime. It threw me. The way he looked at me threw me. This was not the plan. Not that I had one, really. But it certainly wasn't to be turned inside out by this boy five minutes into our date. We hadn't even ordered drinks.

"What are you thinking?" He smiled that disarming smile.

"I want to know what your intentions are, Hayes Campbell."

"What are *your* intentions? Did you come here to sell me art?"

"Maybe."

"Hmm . . ." he said, without breaking eye contact. "Well . . . I came to buy whatever you're selling."

In that moment, it didn't matter how old he was or how many fans he'd amassed. In that moment, he had me. And I realized that just *knowing* that I could have a fling was not going to be enough.

He nodded then, as if sealing some unspoken pact, and turned his attention back toward the dining room, waving his hand in the air. "Shall we order?"

"How's Isabelle?" he asked once the waiter had departed.

"She's fine. Thank you."

"What'd she say when you told her we were having lunch?"

"I didn't."

Hayes raised an eyebrow in my direction. "You didn't?" He smiled.

I was not proud of this. Keeping secrets.

"Well, that's *telling.*"

That morning, for Isabelle's breakfast I had prepared a bowl of hot chocolate. Like I'd done when she was little, like my mother had for me, like her mother for her. And with it came a flood of memories: summers in the South of France, on the terrace beneath the pines, the hot chocolate accompanied by *baguette et confiture*, the smell of orange blossoms and the sea. And always most comforting on the mornings when I'd been kept up half the night by the mistral winds rattling the shutters, monsters breaking in.

"*Chocolat.*" Isabelle's eyes had lit up on entering the kitchen. "Is it a special occasion?"

I'd frozen before the stove. Was it that obvious, my guilt?

She'd wrapped her thin arms around me and squeezed. "You never make it anymore. Thank you."

"Are you laughing at me?" I asked Hayes now.

"Nawww . . . I would never do such a thing." He had interlaced both hands behind his bonny head and was reclining on the banquette. There was something lovely about how comfortable he was in his skin. How at ease he was with his body. He owned it. He was happy with it. Boys were so different from girls.

"How's your *mum*? What'd she say when you told her we were having lunch?"

"Ha!" Hayes threw back his head and let out a deep belly laugh. "You're good."

"You have no idea." I had not meant to say it out loud, but there it was.

"Did you . . . ? You're *flirting* with me."

"I'm sparring. I'm not flirting."

"Am I to know the difference when I see it?"

"Don't know. Depends how bright you are."

He sat up then, erect. And then, without a hint of guile, he said: "I like you."

"I know you do."

"Hayes!" Some guy in a suit was approaching the table. Suits were a rarity in Los Angeles. Nine times out of ten, a guy in a suit was an agent. Five times out of ten, he could not be trusted. So said Daniel.

I noted a quick look of annoyance wash over Hayes's features before he turned to see who was summoning him. And then like that, he turned on the charm.

"Heeeyyy."

"Max Steinberg. WME."

"Of course, I know exactly who you are. How are you, Max?"

"How are *you*? Tour's going amazing, isn't it? We're all really stoked. I'm coming by Staples tomorrow night. Bringing a couple of my nieces. They couldn't be more excited. And I caught you guys on *Jimmy Kimmel* last night. They're just eating you up . . ."

Jimmy Kimmel? Was that before or after our phone call? Hayes had not mentioned it. I opened my mouth to say something and then stopped.

"It went well, yeah."

"They *loved* you. Everyone loves you. That new ballad, 'Seven Minutes.' Great. And great banter. Hi, I'm Max Steinberg." The suit leaned over to shake my hand, having finally acknowledged my presence at the table.

"Max, this is Solène Marchand."

Max cocked his egg-shaped head, trying to place me. "You with Universal?"

"No."

"42West?"

I shook my head.

"Solène owns an art gallery in Culver City."

"Oh . . . Nice." He did that thing Hollywood people did when they learned I wasn't in the industry: he tuned out. "Well, okay, I won't keep you.

"Hayes, good luck tonight, buddy. We'll see you tomorrow. I'll have two squealing teenagers with me. But I guess you're used to that, huh? Just girls . . . everywhere . . . Enjoy it." He winked. "Solène, nice meeting you. If you two haven't ordered yet, get the halibut. It melts in your mouth."

"So, Max Steinberg . . ." I said once he was out of earshot.

"Max Steinberg," Hayes chuckled. "I'm sorry, that was rude. That 'girls' comment was completely unnecessary . . . I don't know what he was thinking."

"I don't know that he *was*," I said. "I find in this town men don't even *see* women over a certain age. And if they do, they register them as either 'mom' or 'business.' I'm guessing he thought I worked for you. Which should show you just how inappropriate this is."

Hayes's mouth was agape. "I don't even know what to say to that . . . I'm sorry."

"Yes, well, good thing this is just lunch." I smiled. "Right?"

He didn't say anything then. Just sat there looking at me with an inscrutable expression etched into his features. I had the impulse to reach out and stroke the side of his youthful face, but already I was mixing my messages.

"What are you thinking, Hayes?"

"I'm still processing."

"It's okay. It's not too late to turn back."

Just then the waiter arrived with our plates.

The second we were left alone Hayes turned to face me. "Look, I'm not going to ask you how old you are because it's impolite, but I want you to know there's very little you could say that's going to deter me. And I really don't give a damn what people like Max think. If I did, I wouldn't have asked you here. So no, in case you're wondering, I'm not turning back."

"Okay."

"Okay?"

"Okay," I repeated.

"Good. Cheers."

"Thirty-nine. And a half."

Hayes lowered his glass of Pellegrino, revealing a huge smile. "Okay. I can work with that."

Dear God, what was I getting myself into?

"So," he began, not two minutes into his grilled jidori chicken, "how did your 'very French' parents end up in Boston?"

I smiled. He'd remembered. "Academia. My father's an art history professor at Harvard."

"No pressure there."

"None," I laughed. "My mother was a curator."

"So it's the family business, art?"

"Sort of, yes. And you? Is this your family business? Was your dad a Beatle?"

"A Rolling Stone, actually . . ." Hayes laughed, the corners of his eyes crinkling. "No, nothing could be further off the mark. Ian Campbell is a very highly respected QC, Queen's Counsel. I'm descended from a long line of highly respected people. On both sides. And then somehow something went wrong."

"Something in the water in Notting Hill?"

He smiled. "Kensington. Close. Yes, perhaps. I came out singing. And writing songs. They were not amused."

He shifted then, and his leg rubbed up against my bare knee—casual, but there was no mistaking it. For a moment he left it there, and then just as casually he drew it away.

"Did you attend Harvard?"

"I went to Brown. And then Columbia for a master's in arts administration."

"Did that piss the professor off?"

"A bit." I smiled.

"Not as much as blowing off Cambridge to start a boy band, I bet."

I laughed. "Is that what you did? Did someone put you together?"

"*I* put us together, thank you very much."

"Seriously?"

"Seriously. Does that impress you? I'm going to print up some calling cards: Hayes 'I Put the Band Together' Campbell."

I laughed, setting down my fork and knife. "So how did you manage that exactly?"

"I went to Westminster, which is this pretty posh school in London where half your year ends up going to Oxford or Cambridge. And instead of that route, I decided to convince a couple of mates who I'd sung with there to join me in forming a group. We were initially supposed to be more of a pop band, but we kept losing our drummer. And Simon's bass sucks . . . and we all wanted to sing lead," he laughed. "So it was quite a bit of an interesting start. But we were lucky. We were really, really, *truly* lucky."

His eyes were dancing. He was so comfortable, animated, happy.

"Is that all stuff I can find online?"

"Um, probably. Yes."

"Hmm." I returned to my omelet. "Tell me something I can't find online."

He smiled then, leaning back in his seat. "You want to know all my secrets, do you?"

"Just the big ones."

"The big ones? Okay." He was fingering his lower lip. I assumed it was an unconscious habit, but it worked wonders in drawing attention to his ripe mouth. "I lost my virginity to my best friend's sister when I was fourteen. She was nineteen at the time."

"Whoa . . ." It was both horrifying and impressive. "What . . . What did you look like at fourteen?"

"Kind of like this, but shorter. I'd just gotten my braces off," he laughed. "So, you know, instant swagger."

"Fourteen is so young." I was doing my best not to picture Isabelle. Fourteen was around the corner.

"I know; it was naughty. *I* was naughty."

"*She* was naughty. Nineteen? I assume that's not legal in England."

"Yes, well, since I spent two years hoping and praying it would happen, I didn't exactly rush to file charges." His smile was salacious. "Anyway, you're not going to find that on the Internet, and if it ever got out it would ruin everything: friendships, the band—"

"The band?" It clicked. "Whose sister did you sleep with? Who's your best friend, Hayes?"

For a moment, he didn't speak, just sat there tugging on his lip, debating. And then, finally: "Oliver."

He reached across the table for his Ray-Bans and placed them on his face.

The waiter arrived to clear our plates. Hayes declined dessert but ordered himself a pot of green tea. I did the same.

"Was it only once?"

He shook his head, a mischievous grin playing over his lips.

"Who else knows?"

"No one. Me. Penelope . . . that's her name, Ol's sister. And now you."

It hit me, the weight of what he was saying.

"I need to see your face," I said, reaching for his glasses. He surprised me by grabbing both my wrists. "What?"

He did not speak, lowering my hands to the banquette between us. He'd hooked his thumb inside the double leather band of my watch, and then slowly, deliberately, rubbed it against my pulse point.

"What?" I repeated.

"I just wanted to touch you."

I heard my own breath quicken then and knew that he'd heard the same. And there I sat, transfixed, while he stroked the inside of my wrist. It was decidedly chaste, and yet he may as well have had his hand between my legs, the way it was affecting me.

Fuck.

"So," he said after several moments had passed. "Did you come here to sell me art?"

I shook my head. Was this how he did it? The seducing? Subtle, effective, complete. They had rooms here, didn't they?

He smiled, releasing my wrists. "No? I thought that was your intention, Solène."

I loved the way my name sounded in his mouth. The way he savored the *en*. Like he was tasting it.

"You, Hayes Campbell . . . You are dangerous."

"I'm not really." He grinned, pulling off his sunglasses. "I just know what I want. And what's the use in playing games, right?"

Our tea arrived just then. It was a flawless presentation. A still life.

"You're on tour," I said once we were alone again.

"I'm on tour," he repeated.

"And then afterwards, you're where? London?"

"I'm in London, I'm in Paris, I'm in New York . . . I'm all over."

I took a moment to collect my thoughts, gazing out the window at the greenery. Nothing about this made sense. "How is this going to happen?"

Hayes slipped his hand beneath the table, grabbing mine on the banquette again, curling his finger inside my watchband. "How would you like it to happen?"

When I didn't say anything, he added: "We can make it up as we go."

"So I just meet you for lunch when you're in L.A.?"

He nodded, biting down on his bottom lip. "And London. And Paris. And New York."

I laughed, looking away. The realization of what I was agreeing to sinking in. The arrangement.

This was not me.

"This is insane. You realize that, right?"

"Only if someone gets hurt."

"Someone always gets hurt, Hayes."

He said nothing as he slid his fingers in between mine, squeezing my hand. The intimacy of the gesture threw me. I had not held a man's hand since Daniel's, and Hayes's felt foreign. Large, smooth, capable; the coolness of an unexpected ring.

I shifted in my skirt, legs sticking to the leather cushion. I needed to get out of there, and yet I did not want it to end.

We finished our tea like that: fingers entwined on the banquette away from prying eyes, and the knowledge that we'd made a promise.

When the bill was paid, the maître d' returned to our table. He asked if everything had been to our satisfaction. And then, very matter-of-factly, he said, "Mr. Campbell, I regret to inform you, it appears someone got wind of your whereabouts and there are a few paparazzi awaiting you out front. I apologize. They're not on the premises, but they are just across the street from the valet. I wanted to give you fair warning, should you want to stagger your exit."

Hayes took a moment to digest the information and then nodded. "Thank you, Pierre."

"What does that mean exactly?" I asked once he'd departed.

"It means that unless you want to be on all the blogs tomorrow, you should probably leave before me."

"Oh. Okay. So now?" I reached across the banquette for my Saint Laurent tote.

He laughed, pulling me back into him. "You don't have to go this very moment."

"I should, though."

"Here's the deal," he said. "If we *don't* walk out of the restaurant together, we risk looking guilty. But if we walk to the valet together and the cameras catch us, we risk looking guilty to a much larger audience."

"So it's a game?"

"It's a game." He slipped on his sunglasses. "You ready?"

I began to laugh. "Remind me how I ended up here again."

"Solène"—he smiled—"it's just lunch."

If I'd managed to forget Hayes was a celebrity during our near two-hour meal, there was no ignoring it when we walked across the terrace of the Hotel Bel-Air restaurant. All six feet two inches of him, in black jeans and black boots. Heads turned and eyes widened and patrons gestured among themselves, and he seemed not to notice. He'd grown accustomed to tuning them out.

In the walkway, just before we reached the bridge, he stopped me, his hand on my waist, familiar. "You go on, and I'll pop into the lounge for a bit."

That seemed wise. Not that I couldn't sell Hayes being a potential buyer to inquiring friends. I just wasn't sure I could sell it to Isabelle.

He seemed to realize how close he was standing and stepped back, his fingers loosening slowly.

"Thank you," he said, "for coming today. This was perfect."

"It was." We stood there for a moment, at arm's distance, feeling the undeniable pull.

"Isabelle's mum," he mouthed, smiling. I wasn't sure if he was relishing the moniker or the thought.

"Hayes Campbell."

"I can't kiss you here." His voice was low, raspy.

"Who said I wanted you to?"

He laughed at that. "*I* want to."

"Well, that's problematic, then, isn't it? You should have chosen a more secluded place."

Hayes cocked his head, his jaw falling slack. "Excuse me?"

"I'm just messing with you," I laughed. "This was lovely."

"Because if you want, I could get us a room . . ." He grinned.

"I'm sure you could."

"I just thought you were a respectable lady."

"Only sometimes." I leaned into him then to kiss his cheek. Not an art world air-kiss, but the chance to press his skin against mine, breathe in his scent, and lock it in my memory. A little like stealing. "Thank you for lunch, Mr. Campbell. 'Til next time . . ." And with that, I turned and walked off toward the unassuming paparazzi.

new york

There was no definitive plan. We'd parted without making specific arrangements; I went back to my full life, and he to his. And yet almost immediately, I found myself wanting to see him again.

He called from the road, every three days or so, beckoning. "Come to Seattle, Solène . . . Meet me in Denver, Solène . . . Phoenix . . . Houston . . ." And each time I declined. We were swamped at work: opening our May show for conceptual painter Nkele Okungbowa, prepping our pieces to be shown at Art Basel. Isabelle had the school play. Much as I wanted, I could not just hop on a plane at his whim and allow myself to be whisked away. I had responsibilities. I had priorities. I had concerns about how it would look.

But in mid-May, it all came together nicely when the Frieze New York art fair fell on the same weekend August Moon was scheduled to do the *Today* show. The trip had been on my calendar for months, and the realization that I would have the satisfaction of seeing Hayes without the moral dilemma of flying across the country for that sole purpose felt like a win. This I was able to rationalize. Even to my daughter.

I picked her up from school the Friday before, and she was still riding high from her performance in *A Midsummer Night's Dream* earlier that week. "Scott, the drama teacher at the Upper School, came up to me in the hall and said he couldn't remember when last he saw a more compelling Hermia. He said that! To *me*!"

She was gushing as I pulled out of the carpool area. Her smile bright, eyes dancing.

"That's great, peanut. You *were* compelling. You were very, very good."

"Yeah, but you *have* to say that because you're my mom. Oh, and Ella Martin, her brother Jack played Lysander. She's a junior and she's like beautiful and smart and everyone loves her, and she congratulated me."

"That's awesome," I said, drinking her in. Her long hair, wild, free. "How'd the algebra quiz go?"

"Blech." She stuck out her tongue. "Torture. I'm never going to be good at math. Clearly, I didn't get Daddy's gene."

"Sorry," I laughed.

"It's not your fault. Well, maybe a little bit." She smiled. She was syncing her iPhone with the car stereo, thumbing through her various playlists while I navigated the traffic on Olympic. Eventually she found what she was looking for.

A piano intro began, vaguely familiar, melancholy. She leaned back in the seat, closed her eyes. "I love this song. I love this song so much."

I did not need to ask. The vocals kicked in, the voice deep, raspy, unmistakable.

"'Seven Minutes,'" she said. "Hayes has the sexiest voice ever . . ."

I could not say anything for fear of giving myself away. We sat there quietly, Hayes filling the space between us. *Will you catch me if I fall?* I could feel my face growing hot, his thumb on the inside of my wrist. My thoughts, indecent.

"Is my fencing tournament in San Jose next weekend?" Isabelle sat forward, breaking the spell. "Who's taking me, you or Daddy?"

"Daddy. I'm in New York next week for Frieze. Remember?"

She sighed, sinking back into the seat. "I'd forgotten."

"I'm sorry."

"You're always gone—"

"Izz—"

"I know, I know. It's work."

I reached over the console then and squeezed her hand. "I'll make it up to you. Promise."

New York was a dance, coordinating our itineraries so that Hayes and I might steal a few hours together. He was in midtown. I was staying in Soho, but commuting up to Randall's Island for the fair. We were not exhibiting this time around, so I'd come alone to meet with clients while Lulit held down the fort at home. There were business lunches and festive dinners and few opportunities to fraternize outside of work. But Hayes's schedule made mine look like child's play.

It was his grandeur, in a town as big and bustling as Manhattan, that affected me in ways I did not expect. An album promo plastered across the side of a city bus. The band's image looming large in Times Square. The occasional tween sporting the now-familiar *Petty Desires* tour T-shirt. Hayes's face greeting me at random turns. At once lovely and unsettling.

On Friday morning, I'd met Amara Winthrop, a former classmate who was now working with Gagosian's camp, for an early breakfast at the Peninsula. I'd arrived fifteen minutes late, apologizing profusely for the abominable traffic. "Oh please," she'd said, waving her hand. "It's Friday. It's the *Today* show. I should have warned you. I think that British boy band is playing. It's madness out there. Latte?"

It hadn't dawned on me until that moment that when Hayes had mentioned doing the show, he was talking about performing before close to twenty thousand in the middle of Rockefeller Plaza. That the ripple effect of him and the group singing alfresco on a Friday morning in midtown would affect me and a million others attempting to negotiate our morning commutes. I'd had this naïve idea that if I just ignored his celebrity, I would become immune to it; that it might cease to exist for me. I was wrong.

We had made tentative lunch plans. I was to meet him at the Four Seasons after spending the morning up at Frieze. He'd warned me it might be hectic, but nothing could have prepared me for the onslaught of fans surrounding the entrance of the hotel. It appeared to be some three hundred of them, swarming, swooning, waiting for a glimpse of their idols. Augies clutching photos and cell phones. Paparazzi convened and at the ready. There were barricades erected on both sides of the main entrance and the opposite side of the street. At least a dozen of the band's security milled about, dressed in black with identifiable lanyards. Another seven or so guards in suits blocked the hotel's entrance. And half a dozen or so of New York's Finest. My heart was racing as I exited the Uber car. As if I'd somehow caught the girls' excitement by my proximity. These fans were older than Isabelle and her brood. More impassioned, more determined. And being near them left me with a feeling I could not quite articulate. Along with the rush and the nerves, there was a sensation not unlike fear.

I had no problem walking into the hotel. Hayes had said I wouldn't. That hotel security would assume I was a guest and not question my being there. I was the right age and socioeconomic background, and I imagined most groupies did not wear The Row. Regardless, he'd had one of the band's detail meet me in the lobby: Desmond, a stocky redhead who greeted me with a little bow before escorting me to the elevators and up to the thirty-second floor. I could only imagine what he thought my visit might entail, but if he assumed anything improper, he did not let on.

There were two additional security detail on Hayes's floor, strolling the corridors. Perhaps this was what it felt like to have an audience with a head of state. Or clearance at the Pentagon. I'd begun to sweat.

At the end of the hall, Desmond withdrew a key card and opened the door to Hayes's suite. I was not prepared for the commotion within. The room was cluttered with floral arrangements and fruit platters and mini-bottles of Pellegrino, although no one seemed to be eating. There was a young South Asian guy, all business, wheeling and dealing on his cell phone; two PR-type women congregated on a sofa, texting madly; a wardrobe lady holding suit jackets in both hands and giving orders to her assistant in a British-by-way-of-Jamaica accent; the aforementioned assistant traipsing back and forth to the bedroom with numerous shopping bags; a nattily dressed fellow plunking away on a laptop at the desk; and in the midst of it all: Hayes. His eyes met mine from the far side of the living room where he stood, arms outstretched, Jesus-like, while the wardrobe woman wrestled him into one of the jackets.

"Hi," he mouthed. His lips parting into that megawatt smile.

"Hi," I mouthed back.

Heads turned then, the entourage not so furtively checking me out. I was trying to read their looks without being read. No easy feat.

"Everyone, this is my friend Solène. Solène, everyone," Hayes announced.

There were genuine smiles from the stylists and a nod from the guy on the phone, but there ended the hospitality. The laptop fellow was dismissive, and the sofa women were surprisingly cold. The fact that my role there had already been assessed and discredited was startling. This was precisely what I had dreaded.

It struck me then that I could not have looked like a typical groupie, and for them to dismiss me so summarily, it was quite possible that Hayes Campbell had a "type."

"I'm sorry, it's just going to be a few minutes more," he said.

"No problem."

"I don't like this shirt, pet. Maggie, check the Prada bag in the bedroom and see what shirts they sent over."

"What's wrong with this shirt?" Hayes made a face. "Beverly doesn't like my shirt."

"I'm not crazy about the fit." Beverly pulled at the extra material on his sides, drawing the shirt tight across Hayes's abdomen, revealing his narrow waist. "See all this. You don't need all this. I can take it in, but let's see if something else fits better."

"We have a fancy dinner tonight," Hayes explained, "at the British Consulate General's residence. That's all, right?" He turned toward the women on the sofa.

"That's all." The blonder of the two smiled. "I'm emailing you the itinerary now. Along with your notes about Alistair's charity."

I was right: they were PR girls. Well-dressed, well-accessorized thirty-something women with matching Drybar blowouts. This was how I suppose Max Steinberg saw me. Perhaps he had not gotten the memo about Hayes's type.

"I like the cut of this suit on you, but not the shirt," Beverly mused. "Maggie!"

The wardrobe assistant emerged from the bedroom holding two dress shirts. Beverly looked them over quickly, grabbed the one on the right, and instructed Hayes to remove his clothes.

Hayes peeled off the trim suit jacket and unbuttoned his shirt before grabbing option no. 2. For a prolonged moment he was there, shirtless, in the middle of the living room. The others were consumed with whatever it was they were doing, but I could not resist the temptation to ogle. He was a vision: smooth, creamy skin; broad shoulders; taut abs; sculpted arms. Flawless. So this was what twenty looked like. That sweet spot between adolescence and the moment things begin to unravel.

"Perfect," Beverly announced when he was done buttoning the replacement shirt. "You need to stick with the Italians, pet. They cut for a slimmer build. Maggie, be a love and get me the skinny tie on the bed."

I watched Beverly as she fussed with her muse. Arranging his collar, smoothing his lapels, tying his tie. Like a mom . . . if Hayes were to have a forty-something Jamaican mom.

"All right. I'm happy with this. I'm leaving a pair of dress shoes for you in the bedroom."

"Can't I just wear my boots?"

"No," Beverly, Maggie, and the nattily dressed fellow on the laptop said in unison.

"Absolutely not," one of the PR women added.

Hayes laughed, and then his eyes narrowed, sly. "I'm wearing my boots."

Beverly made some disapproving clucking sound with her mouth as she and Maggie began assembling their various wardrobe and shopping bags. "Leave the things hanging in your closet and I'll make sure to press them before tonight. I'll send someone up later to polish your boots."

"Thank you, Bev. Ooh, whose suit is that?"

"That one is for Oliver."

"How come Ol gets all the dandy suits? Maybe I want to be a dandy. Is he wearing a bow tie? I want a bow tie."

"You want a bow tie now?"

"Maybe."

"*Lawd Jeezum.*" Beverly's Jamaican was coming out.

"I know, I know . . . I'm swagger," he laughed, turning to find me in the corner. "Solène, did you know I was 'swagger'? That's my official archetype. Lest you think we were interchangeable. That's what you think when you see me, right? You think, 'Oh, he must be the swagger one.'"

I laughed at that. As did all the other women in the room. Hayes and his loyal subjects.

The business guy who had been consumed with his phone call

up until then let out a little whoop, calling our attention. "You, my friend, are going to owe me big-time."

"TAG Heuer?" Hayes asked.

"TAG Heuer. Hi, I'm Raj. Pleasure." He leaned in to shake my hand before turning back toward Hayes. "Yes, they're sending over someone at three o'clock with several watches. You're to choose one appropriate for this evening. And then another more casual for every day."

"Well done, Raj," laptop fellow said.

"This could be huge, Hayes. If they offer it to you, you can't say no," the darker of the blondes said.

"Yes, but isn't it off-brand?"

"It's off August Moon brand. It's not off Hayes Campbell brand."

Hayes was doing that thing where he pulled at his lower lip, pensive. "I just think it's kind of elitist. I mean fourteen-year-old girls aren't buying TAG Heuer watches."

"They are in Dubai." Laptop fellow again.

"You're reaching beyond fourteen-year-old girls, mate. That's the whole point. You're expanding your brand. You're redefining yourself. You're not going to be in a boy band forever."

Hayes turned to me then. He was so dashing in his suit. Were these people ever going to leave? "They want me to do an ad campaign for TAG Heuer. Solo. What do you think?"

All eyes were on me then, and I assumed they were wondering if and why my opinion should matter. "Who else has done them?"

"Brad, Leonardo," Raj said.

"Who's shooting it?"

"They have a couple of people they use for all their projects. Very competent, impeccable work, but not celebrity names."

"So he can't request Meisel or Leibovitz or Afanador?"

"I'm sorry, what is it you do again?" The fellow at the laptop stopped plunking.

Hayes broke into one of his half grins then. "Solène owns an art gallery in L.A." He sounded almost boastful. "I trust her taste implicitly."

I would have laughed at him had he not been staring at me so intensely. So much for secrets.

"Well," I said after a charged moment, "if it's good enough for Brad and Leo . . . go for it. Give them swagger."

"I missed you." Not long after the entourage had parted and Hayes had changed out of his suit, we found ourselves on the sofa. Alone.

The heightened energy of his celebrity had dissipated in the absence of those whose job it was to fawn and dote and cater. As exhilarating as the fame aspect could be, there was something appealing about him not having to be "Hayes Campbell, pop star." Something raw, naked, accessible.

"It's only been two weeks," I said.

"For you it's been two weeks. For me it's been ten cities." He reached for my hand then, sliding his fingers between mine. Suggestive.

"Well, if that's how you're measuring time—"

"Ten cities . . . What, thirteen shows? Three hundred fifty thousand screaming girls . . . who were not you."

"No. I've never been a screaming girl."

"Well, we'll have to change that, won't we?"

God, he was good. The ease with which he slipped in these little lines: seemingly innocuous, but loaded.

The side of his mouth was curling up in that way that I had come to adore. "What are you smiling at, Solène?"

"Nothing," I laughed.

"I know what you're thinking."

"Do you?"

He nodded, his free hand reaching up to finger my hair. I could smell whatever fragrance it was he had put on his skin. Wood and amber and lime. "You're thinking, 'God, I could really use some lunch right now.'"

"Yes. Exactly. That's exactly what I was thinking."

For a moment he did not speak, and I could hear my heart pounding in my chest as his thumb traced the side of my jaw. So faint I might have imagined it.

"Okay . . . Let's go out and get something to eat."

He'd already crossed the room before I registered what was happening. "Outside?"

"Yeah. There's a great sushi place not far from here. Do you like sushi? We can walk, it's such a beautiful day," he called from the closet.

It dawned on me that, sheltered in the Four Seasons fortress, he was probably not aware of the commotion he had caused on Fifty-seventh Street. "Have you seen what it's like out there?"

He returned from the bedroom then with a pair of black boots in hand. The infamous boots, I gathered. "What? Are there a lot of fans? All right, so I'll have Desmond take us over in a car then—"

"It's not a matter of not walking, it's . . . I don't think you can leave the building." The idea of trying to get through that throng accompanied by one of the objects of their desire terrified me.

"It's really that bad?" His eyes searched mine before he made his way over to the window. But the window did not open and there was no way at that angle that he could see the street.

"Well, that's crap," he said, tossing the shoes aside. "They followed us over from Rockefeller after the show. Swarming the cars. Complete insanity." He turned back to me. "I'm sorry . . ."

"Don't be."

"I *really* hate being locked up in here . . . All right, so, plan B, then? Room service? Bloody hell, that sounds not romantic at all."

I laughed at that. "Were you trying to do romantic?"

"I was giving it a shot. Unless . . ." His eyes widened then. "Come with me." He grabbed my hand, leading me toward the bedroom. Romantic, indeed.

I followed him into the room, past the bed and a wardrobe trunk marked AUGUST MOON/H. CAMPBELL, and out onto a large terrace. Spread before us was an unobstructed view of Upper Manhattan and Central Park in all her spring glory. A green oasis under a clear blue sky.

"So . . ." He squeezed my hand. "Lunch? Here?"

"Lunch here would be divine."

Hayes wasted no time calling up our order, and then joined me at the railing, drinking in the view, the smell of spring, the sun. There was something so comfortable about being near him in that space. Bumping up against his tall frame. His closeness, now familiar.

"What would happen if we blew off the rest of the day and spent it together?"

"Your management would not be happy. And my partner, less so."

"But think of the fun we could have." His eyes lit up. They'd gone from green to blue in the sun. Mutable, like water. "Getting into trouble. Running amok in New York . . ."

"It's not like we could leave. You're like . . . *Rapunzel* up here. Locked away in your castle . . . with all your *hair* . . . Hayes Campbell, the new-millennium Rapunzel."

"Rapunzel of the Four Seasons . . ." he said.

We laughed.

For a moment, he held my gaze and I felt that distinct rush. The realization that this attraction had ceased to be just physical. That somewhere I'd crossed over. That I liked him.

"When I was ten, I came here for the first time with my parents. We stayed in a hotel in Times Square and we visited the Statue of Liberty and did all these touristy things. We went to see Ground Zero and they were just starting to build again . . ."

I realized that this, what he was talking about, was only ten years ago. That I was living in Los Angeles by then, still somewhat happily married, and with a two-year-old. Our references were so far off. When the Towers came down, Hayes would have been in the equivalent of the third grade.

"There was this one afternoon," he continued, "that we spent up in Central Park. Just walking around. And there was so much going on. These huge Latin families picnicking and playing music. People roller-skating. Blokes playing football . . . soccer. It was so alive and full of energy and *happy*. And I remember feeling it was wicked that for one afternoon I was a part of that.

"I was talking to Rory this morning, and I was telling him how brilliant it was to lose a day walking in Central Park because he's never been. He'd never been here before the group. But then I realized, *we can't do that.* I can't do that anymore. He may never have the opportunity to do that. Which is weird, yeah? It's a trade-off . . ." He was quiet for a moment, looking out toward the greenery. His stunning profile. His beautiful bones.

He turned in my direction suddenly, pressing his back up against the railing. "I'm rambling, aren't I? Sorry. I just get going sometimes and—"

Hayes's lips were still moving when I kissed them. This warm, wide, inviting pool that beckoned. I could not resist the bait. His youth, his beauty. And everything, everything about the moment, was wonderful.

"Oh-kay," he said when he finally allowed me to pull away. "I didn't see *that* coming."

"Sorry. I just . . . Your mouth."

"Really?" He smiled. "It wasn't the hair?"

I began to laugh.

His large hands circled my waist, drawing me into him. "It wasn't me waxing nostalgic about my childhood holidays? Because this one time we were in Majorca . . ."

"Shut up, Hayes."

"You know this means I win, right? Because I held out longer."

"I didn't know it was a competition."

He shrugged. "I didn't know it *wasn't*."

"That's because you're twenty."

"Yes, well . . . You seem to like that." He stopped talking and leaned in to kiss me again. Deliberate, intense. God, I had missed this. This exploration of someone new.

Eventually, he withdrew, a grin plastered across his exquisite face. "Soooo, lunch?"

Our meal passed all too quickly. Time bending and behaving in unpredictable ways. And him, sucking me in.

"Where'd you spend your childhood holidays? France?"

"Mostly." I was watching his finger trace the lip of his glass. He had barely touched his sandwich. "Christmas in Paris with my dad's mom. And summers in the South with my mother's family."

"Are they still there?"

"My grandparents have all passed away."

"I'm sorry . . ."

"It's okay. It happens when you get to ninety."

He smiled then. "Yes, I suppose that makes sense."

"I have cousins in Geneva. I don't see them as often as I'd like."

"That's not entirely a bad thing," he croaked, his voice still hoarse from the morning's show. "Mine serve as a brutal reminder that I'm not doing something more noble with my life."

I smiled. "You still have time."

"You'll remind my parents of that, won't you? Not that they're not proud. I do think they're genuinely proud. But I believe they see this as a temporary thing. Sort of 'Oh, Hayes and his little pop group. Isn't that nice?' "

"The burden of being an only child . . ."

"Yes. Sole bearer of all their dreams. Utter torture."

I smiled at that. And yet I understood. If I calculated the time and energy Daniel and I had put into Isabelle thus far, cultivating this extraordinary person—French-immersion toddler programs, private school, fencing lessons, sleepaway camp, ballet, theater, all of it—I imagine it might be a bit of a shock if she decided to quit school and run off to join the circus. (Despite the fact that we'd footed the bill for trapeze lessons.)

"What?" He'd pushed away the dismantled turkey club and was reclining in his chair. "Your expression tells me you're siding with them."

"Not *siding* exactly . . ."

"But?"

I laughed. "I'm a parent. We have expectations. This is not to say I never went against my parents' wishes, or went after things solely for me, because I did. And some of it I lived to regret and some of it I didn't. But I think you kind of have to do that. That's what growing up is all about."

He was quiet for a moment. "What did you live to regret?"

"Getting married at twenty-five . . . which isn't *ridiculous*, per se, but for me it was too young . . ."

"Is that why it didn't last?"

"Partly. We were young. *I* was young. I was still figuring things out: who I was, what I wanted. And ultimately we wanted different things. I don't think it was anyone's fault. We're just really different people."

He nodded. "What is it you want, Solène?"

I hesitated. There was more than one way to interpret the question. "What everyone wants probably: to be happy. But I'm still defining that for myself. I had to *redefine* myself. Because I didn't want to be just 'Daniel's wife' or 'Isabelle's mom.' I wanted to go back to work, and Daniel did not want that."

"Did you resent him?"

"Eventually. And still . . . I don't want to be put in a box. I want to do things that feed me. I want to surround myself with art and fascinating people and stimulating experiences . . . and beauty. I want to surprise myself."

Hayes smiled then, slow, knowing. "It's like unfolding a flower."

"It's what?"

"You, revealing yourself. You, who vowed to share as little as possible."

I sat there for a moment, not speaking.

"That sounds totally corny, doesn't it?" His cheeks flushed. "Okay, pretend I never said that."

I laughed then. "Okay."

Hayes walked into the crowded bar at the Crosby Street Hotel looking every bit the "swagger one." Tall and slender in his impeccably cut suit and coiffed hair. Turning heads, per usual. We'd made plans to meet late that night after my dinner and his gala at the British Consulate. He offered to make the trek down to where I was staying in Soho. I did not doubt he would keep his word, but still there was something about his showing up when he said he would that thrilled me.

"I know why you chose this place," he said, sidling up to me on the candy-striped banquette tucked away in the back corner.

"Do you?"

It was dark, moody, with multicolored globed lighting fixtures hanging from the ceiling.

He nodded. "The art. That humongous *head* in the foyer. What is that? Is that Martin Luther King?"

I started to laugh. "No. You're funny. It's a Jaume Plensa."

"A who? A what?" He was loosening his tie.

"Jaume Plensa. Spanish sculptor. He's quite good."

"It's a little unsettling is what it is."

He had a point. The sculpted head stood about ten feet high in the hotel lobby. It was slightly too large for the proportions of the space, which made it all the more arresting.

"And the dogs. There's like a pack of wild dogs out there made of paper. Papier-mâché dogs."

"Justine Smith. She's British."

"Figures." He was wriggling out of his suit jacket and paused then to take me in. "Do you know all that off the top of your head?"

I nodded. "I've been doing this for a long time. Plus, I've stayed here before."

"Ha." He seemed to slow down, allowing the high of wherever he was coming from to settle. His attention zooming in on me. "You look stunning."

"You're not so bad yourself."

"God. Wow."

It was new, my Jason Wu. Purchased especially for this trip. Oyster sequined tank and an ivory pencil skirt. Paired with Isabel Marant heels. Sexy, because I knew I would be seeing him. And because—if I was being honest with myself—I wanted to leave him wanting more. I wanted to torture him.

"I can't even believe you're with me," he laughed, unbuttoning his cuffs, rolling up his sleeves.

"Why do you say that?"

"Because I'm like this *kid*. And you are clearly not. And I mean that in the most flattering way possible."

"Okay, don't ever bring that up again."

"Okay." His hands reached for the cocktail menu. "Are we drinking?"

"That was the plan."

I watched him peruse the menu. Unlike Daniel, he did not need to squint, even in the half-light.

Our server showed up eventually. I chose a tequila-peach-chili-pepper concoction. And without the slightest hesitation, Hayes ordered a Laphroaig 10. Neat. The server, male, midthirties-ish, did not bat an eyelash.

"Scotch?" I asked once he'd left the table. "What are you? Sixty?"

Hayes laughed, running his hands through his hair, mussing it strategically. He'd been deconstructing since he arrived. I wasn't certain what he was going for. Elegantly disheveled, perhaps.

"I find in America they're less likely to ask me for ID if I sound like I know what I'm talking about. And," he added, "I like the taste. Earthy."

He allowed that to sit in the air. And then he smiled, coy.

"You are trouble."

"I thought you knew that . . ."

"How would I? One of your many blogs? Tumblr?"

He laughed. "Oh, don't read those, those are rubbish. Promise me you won't read those."

"I have no desire to," I said. I should have added "again." It would have been more truthful.

That first night after our lunch at the Hotel Bel-Air, while the boys were jumping around onstage across town at the Staples Center, I had locked myself in my bedroom and Googled "Hayes Campbell." The search revealed thirty million matches, which did not seem fathomable to me. And so I hit refresh. Twice. And then over the next three hours consumed half a bottle of Shiraz while wading through site after site of all things Hayes: news items, photos, videos, blogs, fan fiction, odes to his hair.

The entire time, Isabelle had been just across the hall on the phone with her friend, oblivious to her mother going down the rabbit hole. Face-first.

But here, in the intimacy of a hotel bar, I didn't feel any of the anxiety I had while searching the Internet. I did not feel as if I were sharing him with his twenty-two million Twitter followers. Here, tonight, in this space, he was mine. He'd made that clear.

"You're not wearing your watch," he said. We were two drinks in and the crowd had thinned somewhat. The music had mellowed, atmospheric trip-hop.

"I'm not."

His hand had slipped down between the two of us and encircled my wrist. "Where is it?"

"Upstairs."

"I've come to depend on your watch."

"It's not TAG Heuer."

"No. It's Hermès," he said.

"Wow. You're good."

He smiled, his thumb stroking my pulse point. "I've gotten very good at watches lately."

I didn't say anything for a moment. Just sat there, allowing myself to be hypnotized by his touch. When his hand moved from my wrist to my thigh, I flinched. "Watches, huh?"

"Watches."

"What else are you good at?"

His eyes widened then, and he let loose one of his sly smiles. "Is that a trick question? All right, I'll have a go. Football, I mean soccer . . . Tennis . . . Downhill skiing . . . Chess . . . Foxhunting . . ."

At that, I laughed. "Foxhunting?"

"I was just seeing if you were paying attention." His fingertips slipped beneath the hemline of my skirt, grazing my knee. I was paying attention, all right.

"Rowing . . . Squash . . . Badminton . . . Poetry . . . Break-dancing . . ."

"The worm?"

"The worm," he laughed. "You remember that, do you? I think I won you over with that." His fingers were moving over my skin, sensual.

"I don't know. 'Won me over' sounds a little strong." I uncrossed my legs and watched as his hand found its way between my knees. He had large, beautifully wrought hands, long fingers.

"You were interested."

"Maybe."

"You're interested now."

I nodded. My heartbeat had begun to accelerate. I took the liberty to finish what little was left in my glass. He leaned into me. But he did not kiss me, I assumed because we were not alone. Because there was another couple two seats over, and a room half filled with strangers—most certainly with cell phones. It was probably for the best.

"Your turn, Solène. Tell me what you're good at."

"Watercolors. French. Ballet."

"Ballet?" His hand had migrated north, his fingers pressing at the inside of my lower thigh.

"I used to do ballet. I was good."

"Why'd you stop?"

"Wasn't good enough."

"Mm." He nodded, fingers mounting. "Go on."

"Umm . . ." I was losing focus. "Running. Cooking. Pilates. Spinning."

"I'm trying to picture you doing all those at once . . ."

I laughed, uneasy, under the spell of his touch. Trembling, intoxicated, wet.

"I sing. Did I say that? How'd I bloody forget that?" he chuckled. "I sing. I'm quite good. I write songs. I perform. I'm good with people. I like kids."

"I don't think you should be talking about liking kids with your hand up my skirt."

He smiled his half smile. "Is it up your skirt?"

"It's up my skirt enough."

"Do you want me to stop?" He started to withdraw.

I grabbed his wrist. "No."

He leaned forward then and kissed me. His mouth soft, smoky from the Scotch; his tongue supple. It was brief, but he'd made his point.

His fingers persisted, the pressure alternating between soft and strong. "You know what else I'm good at?"

I nodded. Slow.

"Okay." He smiled. "Shall we get a room?"

"I have a room."

"Shall we go to it, then?"

"No."

He laughed. "Do you not trust me?"

"I don't trust *me*."

"I won't let you do anything you don't want to do. Promise."

I couldn't help but laugh. "I'm not going to have sex with you, Hayes Campbell."

"Awww." He dropped his head. "Are we back to the first *and* last name?"

"That's who you are, isn't it?"

"Yes, but that's more like the *idea* of me than . . . Never mind," he trailed off. "Look, we don't have to have sex, we can just cuddle." He'd said this with his right hand wholly between my thighs. That he wasn't touching my underwear was a calculated tease. *Cuddle*, my ass.

"Okay," I said, my breathing labored. "Here's the plan. We're going to go upstairs. We're going to fool around. We're *not* going to have sex. And you're *not* going to spend the night. Deal?"

"Deal."

The rooms at the Crosby Street Hotel were finely done: individual, warm, eclectic. Unexpected patterns juxtaposed in soothing colors. Dressmaker mannequins as art. The light was low when we entered, the mood inviting. Fitting for a tryst.

"I like this," Hayes said, laying his jacket neatly over the arm of the sofa and stooping to remove his boots.

"You're getting awfully comfortable."

"Am I not allowed to be? Is that not part of the deal?"

I laughed at his inquiry. He was clearly more used to this than I. Being physically and emotionally naked before someone whose middle name you did not know. I did not want to calculate how often he did this.

"Last bit." He smiled, emptying his pants pockets onto the coffee table. An iPhone, a wallet, lip balm, and a pack of gum. Noticeably absent: a condom. Or perhaps it was in his wallet. Or his jacket pocket. I was overthinking this.

"I want to see the view. Do you want to see the view?" I stalled, making my way across the room and opening the curtains, unveiling the floor-to-ceiling industrial windows. There was something extraordinary about Manhattan at night: twinkling lights and indigo sky.

I stood there for a moment, my hands pressed against the cool panes, wondering how I'd ended up here with the boy from Isabelle's posters. And what that would mean for our relationship going forward. She would hate me, and yet still . . .

"You nervous?" Hayes approached me from behind, his hands running the length of my arms.

"No," I lied.

"Don't be nervous, Solène. It's just me."

Yes, that was precisely the problem.

His closeness, which had felt so reassuring on the balcony at the Four Seasons, felt reckless here. I was suddenly aware of his height, his power. The fact that maybe I was no longer in charge.

He sensed it. His fingers slipped in between mine, holding my hands while my nerves settled. And then, when enough time had passed, he wrapped his arms around me, drawing me in closer. I could feel him—all of him—pressed up against my back.

"Hiiii," he said, and I laughed. "You good?"

I nodded, meeting his eyes in our reflection in the glass. "I'm good."

"You sure?" He leaned forward then and kissed my bare shoulder.

"Sure."

"Good." He kissed me again, and again. And again. His mouth moving over my shoulder, toward my neck, to the crook just behind my ear. He breathed me in, and I could feel it in my toes. His mouth, his tongue, his teeth on my flesh. His hand moving up over the sequins of my top to stroke my throat, angling my head toward his. He smelled of soap and Scotch, and he tasted . . . warm. I turned to him, devouring his mouth. And oh, the feel of his hair in my hands: thick and smooth and substantial. I probably pulled on it a little too hard.

We moved to the bed.

Hayes seated himself on the edge and had me stand in front of him. "I just want to look at you," he said. We stayed there, my hands in his hair, his hands at my hips, running to and fro over the material. "God, you are so unbelievably sexy."

I leaned over to kiss his dimples. They had been beckoning since the Mandalay Bay. The mileage he got out of a muscle flaw . . . "I bet you say that to all your fans' mums."

He laughed, his hands sliding down over my ass, along my thighs, to the hem of my skirt. "Not so much, no."

I could feel the coolness of his rings at the back of my knees, teasing. I had not planned how far I'd intended this evening to go. I wasn't certain if there was a protocol for postdivorce sex. Second date? Third? I assumed the etiquette was different than it was in one's twenties. The need to be respected in the morning seemed less dire. Maybe none of that mattered anymore. Maybe it was all about the thrill. And surely rock stars played by different rules. We were pioneers out here, Hayes and I. Forging new territory. Making up shit as we went along.

"You know," he said, his hands rising, hot against my skin, "I find this skirt really flattering. Truly. But I think I would like it better on the floor."

I laughed then. "Well, that would be convenient, wouldn't it?"

He nodded, his mouth finding mine.

"But actually," I continued, "I'm more interested in seeing what you can do with the skirt still on."

Hayes laughed, tossing back his head. "I appreciate the challenge."

"I knew you would."

He undid his tie and tossed it across the bed before lying on his back. "Come here," he ordered. I obeyed, only pausing to remove my heels with their bondage-like ankle strap. Tonight they'd earned their keep.

Hayes hoisted me atop himself with ease, and I quickly became aware of just how inconsequential my clothing was. It did not matter that I was still wearing my skirt. I could sense his solidness beneath me, the breadth of his chest, the tightness of his stomach. His thighs . . . Jesus fuck, was that his dick?

"Oh."

"Oh?" he repeated, smiling. He had one hand in my hair, the other cradling my jaw, his thumb moving over my mouth.

"Oh, that's *you*," I laughed.

"I hope it's me. I mean, I hope someone else didn't come up here in my stead."

"In your 'stead'?" I licked his thumb. "I love how proper you are."

"Do you? Because I can do this proper thing all night long. Or I can stop . . . What do you want, Solène?"

"I want you to show me what you're good at."

He nodded, his lips curling into a smile. And then, with little effort, he rolled me onto my back. For a moment he hovered above, his dominance palpable. "Just let me know when you want me to stop."

My pulse had once again begun to rush. His fingers were tracing my jawline, my lips. "God, I love this mouth," he said before moving on to my neck, pausing at the hollow, and then continuing down over my breastbone and across the fabric of my top. His touch was measured—light, but deliberate. And when the back of his hand grazed over my breasts, I heard myself inhale. His own breathing was shallow, his mouth near my ear enticing. His fingers skimmed the underside of my arm and I shuddered. That he could make something so innocent feel suggestive was a skill.

In no time, his hand was between my thighs again, forcing my skirt up north of my knees. "I'm not taking it off," he said. But at that point it didn't matter. I would have let him.

He shifted above me, his mouth melting into mine. His hips pinning me to the bed. His fingers titillating.

"Do you want me to stop?"

"No."

"You sure?" His voice was low, raspy. His hand had reached my crotch, and by then I was so wet it was hard to discern where my panties ended and I began.

"Yes."

"Not taking these off either," he reassured me, his hand stroking the thin material. "I'm not even going to push them to the side . . . And I'm *still* going to make you come."

————

He kept his word.

I don't know where I got the idea that someone his age would be overeager or inept, or that a person in his position would be used to being indulged and thus inadequate at returning the favor. But Hayes dispelled every myth. And he did so with one hand tied figuratively behind his back. The way he touched me: unhurried, focused, exact. He knew precisely what he was doing. His movements accelerating and then slowing down, repeatedly, taking me to the brink and then stopping, teasing, over and over and over again. His fingers pushing inside of me, his thumb massaging my clitoris, his pressure intense, and all this *through* my underwear. God bless him.

I came. And it was so unbelievably powerful, for a moment I thought I might black out. There, in Hayes Campbell's arms, in room 1004 of the Crosby Street Hotel.

For a long time I lay there, shaking. My limbs numb from pleasure; my mind reeling, unable to digest the magnitude of what I had just let happen. What, if given the opportunity, I would let happen again. I'd been so intoxicated. By his smell and his taste and his touch. By his breath in my ear and his Scotch on my tongue and his fucking fingers. And the illicit thought that he was barely an adult and I had not let that stop me. That it had not stopped him.

And then I had the sobering realization that I could not remember the last time I had come with someone else in the room. The very idea that I had denied myself that for so long struck me. Hard.

And there, still in his arms, my mind began to race and I fought it. I did not want to think about the repercussions just then. I did not want to think about Isabelle, or Daniel, or how this would look to my clients or the other mothers at the Windwood School (dear God!). I wanted to bask in the glow for a little while longer. Savor this present from him.

But the thoughts were there, right below the surface.

"Are you happy?" he asked, once my breathing had calmed. Not "Are you good," or "all right," or "okay." *Are you happy?*

I nodded, trying to find my voice. "Yes. Very."

"Good."

"I can't wait to see how you play badminton."

"Sorry?" He paused for a moment and then it clicked. "Yeah," he laughed, "I might be a little better at this than I am at badminton."

"Luckily for me . . ."

"Luckily for you, yes."

We lay there for a moment, curled up in each other, taking in the quiet of the room. It felt a little like magic to me, this in-between time. This shared moment. But I could feel it rising again, the thoughts, the guilt, the panic. Mounting. And I could not stop it.

"Oh God, what have I done?" I heard myself say. "This was just supposed to be lunch. Jesus. What am I doing here with you? You could be my *kid*. This is so wrong. You're *twenty*. And you're like a rock star. What the fuck am I thinking?"

Hayes sat up beside me, his eyes wide. "Are you serious?"

I was as surprised as he was by the verbal diarrhea. Even as it poured out, I recognized that it was very American of me, and that my mother would have scoffed. "Kind of, yes."

"What? Are you feeling guilty now? You were happy two seconds ago. *Very happy.*"

"I can't believe I let you do that. I'm sorry. That was totally inappropriate of me."

"Were you *forcing* me? Did I miss something? We both wanted this," he said, sounding every bit the rational one. The adult in the relationship.

I glanced up at him then, all disheveled in his wrinkled Prada shirt and his hair sticking out in fifty-one directions and his eyes tired and the slightest hint of stubble shadowing his jaw, and the thought occurred to me that he was a man.

I needed a moment.

"Don't mind me. This is just my postorgasmic freak-out."

He laughed. "Is this going to happen every time? Because if I know that I'll just plan ahead."

I smiled then. "No. It won't. It shouldn't."

"I'm serious, Solène. I can't . . . You cannot freak out like this. I don't do well with women who freak out. I pegged you differently."

"You *what?*"

"Fuck. I'm sorry. I just . . ."

"Come here." I reached for him.

"Fuck," he repeated, lying back beside me.

He was quiet for a moment. And then: "Once, when we were in Tokyo, there was this girl who . . . Never mind. I don't want to talk about it. Just promise me you're not going to go crazy."

"Okay." I smiled. "Promise."

He jumped up again. "And I checked in with you, right? I asked if you were okay. Several times. Right?" He sounded uncertain.

"Yes, you did."

"I just want to make sure I'm not losing my mind."

It was fascinating to see his anxiety. The things that tormented him. I couldn't begin to imagine what life for him and the other guys in the group must have been like. Not knowing whom to trust, and worried that at any time something could be used against them. I assumed there was probably much at stake.

"And don't let the rock star rubbish get to you," he said, lying down again. "Because it's not real, it's crap. It's like this *idea* and it's not who I am and . . . I'm always going to be real with you, okay?

"Fuck, it's late," he said, glancing at his watch. "I have a six a.m. wake-up call. Which is in three and a half hours. And I've been up since four. God, I just want a bloody break."

"Is that the watch?"

"Yeah. What do you think?"

"Nice."

"It's kind of sleek, isn't it? This one is the Carrera . . . Carrera Calib-something . . . I don't remember. It's late."

"It's a good-looking watch."

"I think it's too sleek for me," he said, slipping it off his wrist. "It's fancier than I usually am. Here, you try it."

I let him put the watch on me. It was stainless steel: clean, masculine, elegant.

"Wow, that looks good on you. Keep it."

"No, thank you."

"I'm serious. It looks good on you and I'm probably never going to wear this one. They gave me two others. Just keep it."

"I'm not keeping your watch," I said, handing it over.

"Okay, just borrow it, then."

"Hayes, I'm not the woman who's going to accept gifts like this from you. Thank you, but no."

"Don't think of it as a gift. I'm lending it to you. If you borrow it, it kind of ensures that you'll have to see me again."

"You still want to see me again? Even after I freaked out on you?"

He nodded, a lazy smile spreading across his wide mouth. "Yeah. Because you have to return the favor. And I'm too exhausted to let that happen now."

I started to laugh. "Really? So we're going to do this again because I *owe* you?"

"Yes," he laughed, sitting up and inching across the bed. "And because I have lots more things I want to do to you, I'm just too knackered to think of them."

I sat up and watched him collect his belongings, zip his boots, smooth his hair, reapply his lip balm.

He made his way back over to the bed to kiss me. "This was fun," he said, slow, sensual, his eyelids heavy. "I really like you."

"I really like you, too."

"Thanks for giving me the pleasure."

"Ditto."

On the way out of the room, he stopped and placed the TAG Heuer atop the stenciled credenza in the corner. "I'm going to be in the South of France next month. You can return it to me there."

And then he was gone.

côte d'azur

I knew I would go. The way he'd dangled it in the air . . . like candy.
This sweet, sweet lure. The way he'd phrased it. As if I did not have
a choice. The way it fit into my schedule. Easy.

I had the gallery's travel agent make the arrangements: a quick
detour to Nice following Art Basel. I lied to Lulit and told her I
was visiting family. I lied to my family and told them I was meeting clients. I tried to be honest with myself. It was just physical, this
arrangement. Carnal. Nothing more, nothing less. And knowing
that, I thought, would allow me to enjoy the ride.

I should have been able to pull it off: sex without guilt, sex without shame, sex without expectation. The French had been doing it for centuries. It was in my DNA. Surely, I could tap into that part of me that had yet to surface. Three days on the Riviera with a beautiful boy and no strings attached. I would not overthink it. I would go and have fun, and then return to my life. And no one would be the wiser. It had been three years. I deserved this.

The week before I left for Switzerland, Isabelle and I spent the weekend in Santa Barbara. Just the two of us, at the Bacara Resort, catching up on some mother-daughter time as I'd promised. She was heading off to Maine for summer camp at the end of the month and would be gone until mid-August. As it did every year, the pending separation weighed on me. The idea that she would return to me forever changed, in some small way or another. Time eluding us both.

Late in the afternoon on Saturday, we laid out a blanket on a promontory overlooking the ocean, and set out to capture the view in watercolors. It had become something of a ritual for us, painting side by side. I dreaded the day she would outgrow it.

I watched her as she painted in broad, sure strokes, confident in her artistry. Her nose screwed up in concentration, her French pout. Her long hair knotted at the base of her neck, secured with a pencil, like I used to wear mine in school. For all her independence, she was still my mini-me. We had marveled at that when she was small. Those first few weeks home from the hospital when everything was new and full of wonder. Daniel and I would lie in bed cocooning her and gazing at her features, her every little movement. Discovering what was mine and what was his and what was decidedly Isabelle's. Falling in love with her, and each other, anew.

"Do you think you'll ever get married again, Mom?"

It came out of nowhere. The big questions always did.

"I don't know, peanut. Maybe . . ."

She was quiet for a moment, filling in her sky.

"Why? What made you ask?"

Isabelle shrugged. "I just wonder sometimes. I don't want you to be lonely."

"Lonely? Do you think I'm lonely?" I laughed, uneasy. "I've got you."

"I know, but . . ." She stopped to look at me. "I just want you to be happy."

I was not sure where all this was coming from. In the beginning, I'd spent a great deal of time letting her know that I was all right. That the divorce was best for all of us. That Daniel and I would be happier people apart, and how that, in turn, would make us better parents. It took much consoling and eighteen months of therapy, but lately the topic hadn't reared its head.

"I *am* happy, honey," I said, returning to my makeshift easel. "I have everything I need."

It sounded truthful.

She watched me for a while. Scrutinizing my horizon, the meeting of violet and cerulean. And then: "I think Daddy's going to marry Eva."

It was a kick to the gut. "Why do you say that?"

She shrugged, noncommittal.

"Did he say something to you?"

"I think he's feeling me out," she said.

I sensed it: the familiar tightness in my chest. It had been years, but there it was, that thick, heavy feeling of something lost. "Why? What did he say to you?"

She shrugged again, looking away. I could see her struggling to make this easier for me.

"Isabelle?"

"He said that you would always be my mother. No matter what happened. That nothing would ever change that."

She'd said it flatly, with little emotion. But it was all there.

"Oh."

We sat for a moment, neither of us speaking, lost in our thoughts. The sound of the waves. The sun flaring white on the water.

"I just thought it sounded like he was trying to prepare me for something. I thought you should be prepared, too."

It stayed with me, Isabelle's concerns. I did not bring it up with Daniel because it wasn't my place. But it felt a bit like waiting for the other shoe to drop. And so I left for Europe with a little bit of a hollow in my heart. The one that I thought had mended. And I tried my best to forget it was there.

Hayes and his bandmates were staying at a fabulous villa on the Cap d'Antibes. They were there for only a week before heading up to record at some state-of-the-art studio in Saint-Rémy-de-Provence. This was a luxury, he'd conveyed, as more often than not they found themselves recording in hotel rooms in between shows. Hayes and Oliver and occasionally Rory doing the bulk of the songwriting with their producers at odd hours of the night; the boys laying vocal tracks in their makeshift studio, mattresses propped against the walls for acoustics. No rest for the weary.

In the time since I'd last seen him, they'd wrapped up the North American leg of the *Petty Desires* tour, spent two weeks decompressing at home, and were gearing up for their next album. It was a machine, he'd explained. They were milking them, twelve months a year, to feed a growing fandom that seemed to not be able to get enough of these five boys.

"There's like a clock ticking. An expiration date," he'd said, late one night on the phone from London. "I think they're afraid we're going to grow hair on our chests and our fans are going to just up and disappear. So they're trying to get as much money out of us as they can now. But really we could use a break. Take That are working on yet another album, and the New Kids are still doing cruises and they're in their forties. They still have die-hard fans. But they both took breaks."

"Do you want to still be doing this in your forties?" The idea seemed absurd.

"I don't know. I think I just want to do it until it's not fun anymore. Sometimes I think that could be sooner rather than later. But then, look at the Rolling Stones. They're still having a heck of a good time."

August Moon was *not* the Rolling Stones. But I did not want to be the one to tell him that.

The Monday morning after the closing of Basel, I flew directly to Nice and barely had time to unpack and shower at my hotel in Cannes before Hayes sent a car and driver to retrieve me. I'd rejected his offer to stay at their villa, not liking the impression it gave, but I'd agreed to join him for the afternoon.

The estate of Domaine La Dilecta was breathtaking. Iron gates rolling back to reveal a rambling drive, acres of lush lawn, a sizable guesthouse, a majestic villa perched atop the hill—stark white against an azure sky. I could get used to this, rock star living.

He was standing there beneath the portico. Tall and slim-hipped, in head-to-toe black and Wayfarers. His jeans, skinnier than mine.

"So . . ." I said, stepping out of the car. "This is you?"

He smiled, leaning into me. Oh, the smell of him. "This is *us.*"

"It's not a bad pad you've got."

"Yeah." He shrugged. "Thirty million records will do that for you. Welcome. No bags?"

"I told you: I'm not staying."

"Right." He smiled his half smile, dimples beckoning. "No pressure."

He took my hand then, leading me into the house, through the foyer, and up the stairs to the main floor, past room after oversized room. The architecture was Art Deco, the décor ornate. Not particularly my style, but impressive nonetheless.

"So all is well in Basel?"

"All is well in Basel."

"Did you sell a plethora of art?" He smiled. His skin was bronzed, kissed by the Riviera sun.

"A plethora of art." My laugh echoed over the marble floors.

It had been a week of wining and dining and posturing in a variety of languages: English and French and Italian, a smattering of German and Japanese. Lulit had bemoaned the fact that, despite the three Ivy League degrees between us, it still came down to the length of our skirts, but we'd stuck to our mantra—*Go. Sell. Art. To rich white men*—and sold out our entire booth at the fair.

"This place is massive."

Hayes and I had happened into a drawing room. There was a baby grand piano in the center, and he ran his fingers over the keys as we walked through. The motion was simple, and yet the melody he'd produced was so pure, it stayed with me.

"You have to see the rest of the grounds," he said as he continued across the space. "The record company's treat. A little 'Well done, lads! Have a spot of fun and then back to work, all right? But if you're inclined to do some writing in the interim, we won't stop you.'"

He threw open a set of doors, opening onto a grand terrace, revealing the yard in all its vast verdant glory. A bit of a ways down there was a sizable pool, a handsome pool house, and way, way beyond the rolling hills and the horizon of trees, there was the Mediterranean.

The two of us stood for a minute, soaking it in. I could barely make out a few bodies prostrate on the lounges poolside. But other than that, it felt like we had the place to ourselves.

"So," Hayes continued, "we're here for a few more days, and then we head into the studio to work on *Wise or Naked*."

"*Wise or Naked*?"

"The new album."

"Oh. So which one are you?"

He laughed. "Which one would you like me to be?"

"Ideally, both."

"Ha! That's a flirt, not a spar."

"You're getting good at this."

"I have an exceptional teacher. Come meet our friends."

I followed him down to the lawn and across the wide expanse of grass. "Where is everyone?"

"Liam and Simon took the boat out to go jet-skiing with Nick and Desmond, a couple of our security guys. Oliver is playing tennis down at the courts with Raj. Trevor and Fergus, also security, are in the gym. And Rory . . . I think Rory is taking a well-deserved nap." He laughed at that.

And then I understood.

Lying out by the pool were three young, sublimely formed females in various stages of naked. If I hadn't had a heart-to-heart with myself about being comfortable with the fact that I would likely be twenty years older than all the other eye candy offered on this trip, I might have reacted differently. I might have run back to my hotel. Back to L.A. But I'd rationalized it shopping for swimsuits at Barneys. And on the flight to Switzerland. And again, just now, in the drive over from Cannes. I was here because Hayes wanted me to be. And being near forty and having birthed and nursed a child did not change any of that.

Hayes proceeded to introduce me to their guests. In one corner, Oliver's girlfriend, Charlotte: a porcelain-skinned, bikinied brunette who'd separated herself from the others with the aid of an oversized sun hat and an iPad. She smiled up at me from her place in the sun, sipping Vittel and cracking pistachios with the finesse of a duchess.

And in the other corner, the French girls, Émilie and Carine. I'd mistaken them for twins, but Hayes disabused me of that notion. They were locals, friends of Rory, delightfully pretty and ridiculously young, in matching black bikini bottoms. And sunglasses.

"Ça va?" I nodded toward them. I'd grown up summering with girls like this. I had only stopped being intimidated once I'd realized that the particularly aggressive mixture of competitive tanning, cigarettes, and Bordeaux caught up with them at around age thirty-two. But I could appreciate them for all their nubile beauty now. I assumed Hayes could as well.

"*Avez-vous du feu?*" the one with the slightly more perfect breasts asked.

"*Non, desolée. Je fume pas.*"

"*Tant pis, alors.*" She tossed her blonde head.

Hayes called to me from the far side of the pool. Someone had set up a lovely spread: crudités, fresh fruit, a selection of chilled drinks. "Rosé?"

"What? No Scotch?" I made my way over to him.

"When in France . . ."

"So your friend Émilie—"

"Rory's friend," he corrected me, pouring the wine.

"Rory's friend. She just *vous*-ed me."

"So?"

"So I'm guessing she thinks I'm your mother. Or that I work here."

"Really?" he said, handing me a full glass. And then, before I could take a sip, he grabbed my head in both his hands and kissed me firmly on the mouth. "Well . . . she doesn't think that now."

Somehow I'd managed to forget how wonderful his mouth was. Soft, enticing. "You should probably do that again. Just to be sure."

"Just to be sure," he repeated. And then he obliged me.

When he eventually pulled away, I could feel the girls' eyes on us. Even Charlotte, who was still cracking pistachios.

"Not that that wasn't fun," he said, soft, "but you probably shouldn't care what she thinks.

"Come." He grabbed his glass. "Let's go for a walk."

"The French girls, what are they? Twelve?" I asked once out of earshot.

He laughed. "Eighteen."

"You know that for a fact?"

"Desmond checked their IDs."

I paused for a moment, making sense of it. "Is that what Desmond does? Does Desmond check IDs?"

Hayes smiled. "No one on the premises under eighteen. That's the rule."

I couldn't help but laugh. "No one asked for *my* ID."

"I vouched for you. Come here." He took my chin in his free hand and kissed me. "*Twelve* . . ." He laughed.

"They look twelve to me."

"Isabelle is twelve. Isabelle is not *that*. Yet."

I gave him one of my best withering looks.

"I'm kidding. Isabelle will *never* be that. She's going to go from twelve straight to sixty. No stopping in between."

I looked back toward the pool then. One of the girls was oiling the other's back. Was this real life? "Aahhh, France . . ."

Hayes smiled, wide. "It's like a gift."

"I imagine it is. I imagine being in a boy band is like a gift as well."

"Sometimes." He sipped from his glass.

"Only sometimes? When is it not a gift?"

"When the woman you're trying to impress reminds you that you're in a boy band."

"Touché," I said. We were making the trek across the lawn down toward the south corner of the property. "Are you trying to impress me?"

"Was that not apparent?"

"I'm here, aren't I?"

"But you didn't bring any bags."

"I've got *this*." I smiled, proffering my purse: the Céline hobo bag in chamois, perfect for everything but holding a change of clothes.

"Does it have a toothbrush in it?"

"You're bad—"

"If not, I'm not interested."

"You would fuck me even if I didn't bring a toothbrush."

Hayes stopped in his tracks, pushing his sunglasses up on his head. "You just used the f-word."

"Imagine that . . ."

"I have been. For two months now," he admitted. "You realize this changes everything, right? I was trying to be a gentleman, but why bother?"

I smiled, swilling the wine. "I like that you're a gentleman."

"You, Solène Marchand, are very complex. Which I find incredibly appealing."

"Like unfolding a flower?"

It took a moment, and then he remembered, smiling. "Like unfolding a flower."

A sudden glare of light ahead caught our attention, and Hayes and I looked up to see a golf cart careening toward us from the direction of what I assumed were the tennis courts. Rory was at the wheel, Oliver beside him, long legs outstretched on the dash, and Raj was seated on the bench in the rear. They made for quite a sight. Bronzed youthful skin, chiseled features. Like they'd rolled out of the pages of a catalog . . .

"'Ello, chaps!" Rory called, bringing the cart to an abrupt halt alongside us. "Where are you two off to? Hi, I don't believe we've met. I'm Rory."

"Solène."

"*Enchanté,*" he said in a thick Yorkshire accent. He had a lopsided grin and random tattoos on his arms, and still I could see the appeal. The dark hooded eyes, the leather necklaces, the scruff on his otherwise youthful face.

"You *have* actually," Hayes intervened. "In Las Vegas."

"This year?"

"How was Switzerland?" Oliver asked, which threw me. We hadn't spoken since that evening at the Mandalay Bay and here he knew my itinerary. It made me wonder how much these boys shared. My mind flashed back to the Crosby Street Hotel. What, if anything, had Hayes told him?

"Switzerland was lovely, thank you."

He smiled, nodding slowly. I could not discern what was going on behind his gold-rimmed aviators.

"Good to see you, Solène." Raj waved. In a polo and madras

shorts, he seemed decidedly less business wunderkind and more sixth boy band member.

"Are you guys coming from the pool? Are the twins still there?" Rory raised an eyebrow.

"They're not twins, you know, mate. They're not even sisters," Hayes laughed.

"Let me have the fantasy, man."

"Simon, Liam, and the others are on their way back," Raj said. "The match is at six. Benoît is grilling lobster. We can eat at eight. And Croatia and Mexico won't start until ten."

I felt like they were speaking in code. "What match?"

"Netherlands and Chile," Hayes said. And when my expression indicated that I'd registered nothing, he added, "The World Cup."

"Oh. Right."

"It's going to be a hell of a match," Oliver said. "I hope you'll stay."

"We haven't decided what we're doing yet," Hayes said, wrapping his arm around my waist in a manner that struck me as possessive. "We'll let you know."

"All right, we're off!" Rory announced.

"Nice watch," Raj called back as they peeled out.

Hayes laughed. "She's keeping it warm for me. I can only wear one at a time!

"We don't have to stay," he said once we were alone again. "It's going to be loud and crazy, and if you'd rather not, I certainly understand. We can go out for dinner. Or we can go back to your hotel, or . . . whatever makes you most comfortable."

There was something about Hayes when he was being polite that was such a turn-on. The idea that no matter how famous he was he had this breeding that would endure.

"You know what? Why don't we go to your room?" Even as I said it, I could feel my face flushing. It was not like me. But none of this had been. I was *redefining*. This was me trying to enjoy myself. This was me trying not to care.

His eyes widened. "Now?"

"Yes. Now. Why? Is it not tidy?" I smiled up at him.

"Oh . . . it's *tidy*."

"Well, good then."

"I just thought you wouldn't want to . . . see it . . . so early in the day."

"Well, we're just looking at it, right?" I said, polishing off the rosé.

"Yep." He nodded, all dimples. "We're just looking at it."

It didn't take long to trek back to the house and up to Hayes's suite. It was, like everything else at Domaine La Dilecta, lavishly decorated: an eclectic mixture of furniture, various objets d'art, trompe l'oeil on the walls.

"So this is where the magic happens," I said, tossing my bag on an armchair in the corner. There was a sunken alcove off the main room, bright with magnificent wraparound views.

Hayes laughed, setting down his wine. "Magic? No pressure or anything."

"None at all. Goodness, it's like Versailles in here."

"I think they were going for a *thing*."

"A *thing*?" I approached him.

"A *thing*," he repeated, reaching out for my waist and pulling me into him. "You are so fucking beautiful."

"You said the f-word."

"You started."

"Maybe." I flinched. His fingers had found their way beneath the hem of my blouse and were surprisingly cool against my skin.

"Are my hands cold? Sorry," he said, but he did not remove them.

I stood there, breathing him in. Wondering at how effortlessly he managed to span my waist, making me feel fragile, breakable almost. His thumbs tracing over my bottom ribs, and alternately fondling the material of my shirt.

"I like this top," he said.

The blouse was white, sleeveless, sheer in some places, ruffled in others, and altogether very feminine. I felt like a girl in it, which is admittedly why I'd bought it for this trip. So that I would not look like someone's mother.

"Are you just going to stand there counting my ribs, or are you going to kiss me?"

He smiled at that, his eyes decidedly green. "You like me kissing you."

"Well, I did come all this way . . ."

"I thought you came to return my watch."

"You want it back?"

He shook his head. "I just want to look at you for a moment."

"You've been looking at me for over an hour."

"Yeah, but before I was trying not to be obvious about it. Come here." He led me over to the daybed against the far wall and pulled me onto his lap.

I could feel him through his pants. Oh, the wonders of twenty.

"You want to be kissed, Solène?" His hands were in my hair, pushing it off my face, cradling my neck.

"Yes." I nodded. "You think you can handle that?"

"I'll see what I can do."

We had not been at it for five minutes when I was distracted by a series of calls coming in to my phone. I could hear it vibrating in my purse. Across the room, in the chair, while Hayes's mouth was on my neck, his hands up the back of my blouse. I attempted to ignore it.

The calls then switched to the text signal, one after another. I pulled away from him for a moment, trying to do the math. What time was it in Los Angeles? Boston?

"Do you want to get that?" His hands were on my breasts, over my bra, his thumbs rubbing my nipples through the sheer material. Black, silk, ridiculously overpriced, purchased expressly for this trip. *Getting that* was the last thing I wanted to do.

the idea *of* you   77

Eight twenty-five a.m., I registered. Eleven twenty-five Eastern.
"No."

"You sure?"

"I'm sure."

"Okay." He smiled and slowly lifted off my blouse. "Hiiii." That
face.

"Hi, yourself."

His finger hooked beneath the shoulder strap of my bra, before
running down over my breastbone and dipping inside the demi
cup. Teasing. He looked up, as if to check in with me, before pushing the material to the side and lowering his head. My breath
caught, his tongue on my nipple. Fuck fuck fuck. What was it about
being with him that made me feel as if everything were happening for the first time?

My fingers entwined in his hair as he unhooked the clasp and
cupped my breasts in his hands.

"God, everything about you is perfect," he said. It was precisely
what an almost forty-year-old woman wanted to hear about her
breasts.

I was reveling in the smell of his hair and the feel of his mouth
when I heard it again, my phone. Dammit.

I waited for two more text alerts before I attempted to stop him.
"Hayes . . . Hayes."

He lifted his head, slow.

"I should probably make sure that's not an emergency."

He nodded, his eyes holding mine as he completed removing
the bra and placed it beside him on the bed. "Go," he said, coy.
"But come back to me."

There were three missed calls and voicemails from Isabelle. Followed by five texts:

Where are you?
Please call me!!

It's urgent!!!
Mom!!!!!!!
Mommy!!!!!

Shit.

"I'm sorry. I have to take this. It's Isabelle."

He was reclining on the daybed, arms clasped behind his lovely head, long legs hanging off the edge. "Do what you have to do. I'll wait."

She answered in a tizzy. Frenetic, which was not typical of her behavior.

"Heeey. What's happening?"

"Why aren't you here?"

"Because, honey, I had to come for Basel. You know that. Is everything okay? What's going on?" I had this feeling in the pit of my stomach that it had happened, that Daniel had proposed. And that I was going to have to be strong for her, six thousand miles away and topless. And that I was going to have to lie and tell her that it wasn't going to change anything, even though deep down I knew it would. And that Hayes was going to be witness to it all.

I folded my arm across my "everything about you is perfect" breasts and prepared for the worst.

"You should be here." She'd begun to cry. "I *need* you."

"Izz . . . what happened?"

"I got my period."

I sank into the armchair then, relieved. "Izz, that's great. That's *wonderful*. Congratulations!"

"It's not wonderful. You're not here."

"I know, honey, I'm sorry. But we thought there was a good chance it was going to happen this summer when you were in Maine anyway." This was me trying to deflect the fact that I was an absentee mother out gallivanting in the South of France with rock stars while my daughter was experiencing her first true coming-of-age milestone. I sucked.

She was quiet for a moment. I was staring out at the lawn, the long drive winding down the hill, so much green.

"It got on the sheets," she whispered.

"It's okay, you can wash them. Use cold water. But do it now, okay. Don't wait."

"And I don't have any, like, stuff here."

"We'll take care of that. Where's Daddy?"

"He's out running."

"All right. He can swing by the drugstore before work."

"I'm not *telling him.*"

I could feel her getting worked up again over the phone. "Isabelle, he's your father."

"He's a *guy.*"

I smiled at that, looking over into the alcove. A guitar case was propped up against the far wall. Hayes was in the same position on the daybed, eyes closed. I wasn't sure if he was sleeping or just lying very still, listening. "Honey, he's your dad. He's not just a *guy.* I promise."

"No, I'm not telling him." She paused. "*You* tell him."

"Okay, I'll tell him—"

"No, don't tell him."

I laughed. "Where's Eva?"

"In the shower, I think."

I hated going this route. I hated knowing that she would be the one to hug her first, to share knowing looks and nudges and traipse with her through the aisles of CVS in search of Always with Wings. Like some chummy big sister or cool aunt and not the intellectual property tramp who was fucking her father. But it was not to be avoided.

"Do you feel comfortable talking to Eva?" I asked.

She was quiet for a moment. "I don't know. I guess . . ."

"She's not a guy."

"She's not my mom."

That hurt and felt good at the same time. "I'm sorry I'm not there, Izz. Truly. I'm sorry. I love you."

"I love you, too. Hurry up and come home, okay?"

Just then a black Range Rover came pulling up the drive followed by two smaller cars. Simon and Liam were back. The thought arose that maybe they could see into this window.

"I'll see you Thursday, in Boston. And we'll celebrate. Promise."

"Okay," she sighed. "Have fun. Don't work too hard."

The last bit was like twisting the knife.

"*Bisous*," she said.

"*Bisous*."

"Everything okay?" Hayes asked when I sat beside him on the bed.

"Yeah."

"Girl stuff?"

I smiled, nodding. "She would *die* if she knew you knew."

"I won't tell her then." He reached up to stroke my hair, his movements slow, lethargic.

"Your friends are back."

"Yeah. The match is starting soon."

"I don't think this is going to happen right now," I laughed, awkward, my arms still across my breasts. "I'm sorry."

"Don't apologize." He smiled. "It couldn't be avoided. I'm sorry for Isabelle that you weren't there."

I felt my chest tighten then, and for a second I thought I might cry. "I'm sorry, too."

"Come here." He pulled me onto him. "Come lie down with me for five minutes. Before the madness . . ."

"The madness?"

He nodded. "There's always madness."

Hayes was right. There was a certain level of madness. Simon and Liam were *loud*, crazy. They'd returned from their jet-ski outing with two girls. Apiece. I wasn't certain whether they'd just met them or they were prior acquaintances. I did not want to ask. But I had this moment of "What the fuck am I doing here?" followed by

"Where are these girls' mothers?" And I felt an intense need to chaperone them all.

Much later, when I had the gumption to ask Hayes if it was typical of his bandmates to entertain two women at a time, he laughed, amused. "No. Usually they're interested in one and the other is a friend or sister who tags along for moral support. A wing woman, if you will. Except for in extreme cases . . . like Rory. Or . . . Ibiza."

For those who cared, the Netherlands v. Chile game was a nail-biter. For me, it was an opportunity to down rosé and oysters on the terrace while the others hooted and hollered and yelled indecipherable Britishisms in the salon.

When the match was over and Netherlands had triumphed, the gang descended on the lobster spread and then, after, engaged in an impromptu soccer game and frolicking on the lawn.

"Do you have everything you need? Are you all right?" Hayes insisted on checking in every ten minutes or so. He'd swept his hair back with a headband and changed into a jersey and shorts to play, and there was something so boyish about him that it almost felt wrong. Almost.

"I'm fine. Watching you and your friends have fun."

"All right." He kissed me, the sweet smell of sweat on his skin. "Let me know when you stop being fine, all right?"

At some point in the evening, Rory headed up to the terrace with the French sister wives and a guitar and began serenading them. By the time he launched into a startlingly good rendition of "Hotel California," the lot of us had joined him, Simon and Liam chiming in with some impressive harmonies. I felt like I was in college all over again. Except these guys actually got paid to do this. I drank in the moment: Cap d'Antibes on a balmy June night. Close to ten and the sky a pale orchid, the immense stretch of green, the smell of the sea, the wine, and "a lot of pretty, pretty boys . . ."

I chose not to stay for the second match. Hayes insisted on driving me back to my hotel but did not press to come upstairs when I pled exhaustion.

"Come with me to Saint-Tropez tomorrow," he said. "We'll have lunch." We were sitting in his Bentley Continental cabriolet, a rental, in a parking space on the Croisette, a few doors down from the Hôtel Martinez. Stalling. "It's just going to be a handful of us on the boat. Much less madness."

"I don't mind the madness."

He smiled, reaching out to finger my hair. "I do. You were stellar. We're a lot to take on, I know. I promise tomorrow will be different."

"Did I say I didn't have a good time? If I didn't want to be here, I wouldn't be here."

"I didn't really give you a choice," he laughed.

"I always have a choice, Hayes."

He let that sit there for a moment. "God . . . It's really too bad you're so knackered. It would be nice to finish what we started . . ."

"If you were to come upstairs now, you'd miss all of the Croatia-Mexico game."

"Somehow I think it would be worth it."

I took his hand from my hair then and held it to my mouth, inhaling new car leather. "I will . . . see you . . . tomorrow," I said, and kissed his palm. Twice.

He grinned, his head reclining on the headrest. "Now you're just teasing me."

"Tomorrow," I repeated.

"So you'll come to Saint-Tropez?"

"I'll come to Saint-Tropez."

Not that I couldn't have enjoyed a day alone decompressing from Art Basel at the hotel's beach club, downing Campari and orange juice and luxuriating in all that was good about Cannes in its off-season. But that was not the purpose of this trip.

And I was reminded of that again, sailing through the sapphire waters of the Mediterranean under a cloudless sky. The jagged coastline bathed in Riviera light stretched out alongside us, offering up lush pines and terra-cotta rooftops. The extravagance of endless Moët & Chandon Rosé Impérial aboard a sixty-three-foot crewed yacht. The indulgence, the beauty—made all the more so with him.

It was just us, Oliver, Charlotte, Desmond, and Fergus. The others had opted to drive the Grande Corniche to Monaco and take their chances in the casinos for the day. And so, as Hayes had promised, it was tranquil. We took our time getting there, drinking in the sun and the views. And when we passed Saint-Raphaël, the town where I'd spent every summer from one to twenty-one, I felt not just a little nostalgic.

Hayes and I separated from the others in Saint-Tropez, sharing a quiet lunch on the Place des Lices and strolling the narrow cobblestoned streets. It was almost like having him to myself. And the dozen or so times he was stopped to pose for a picture, he was so gracious and his fans so adoring, I could not begrudge them the moment.

It became apparent that this, whatever it was we were doing, would never truly be just the two of us. So long as he was in August Moon, Hayes was someone I would share with the world. And I understood then why it was so important to him that I separate Hayes from Hayes Campbell.

"How do you do it?" I asked. "How do you always say yes?" We were leaving Barbarac, a gelateria, where we had been stopped by a Belgian family with two teenage girls. Hayes had obliged them with photos and autographs while I attempted to be inconspicuous, selecting gelato flavors until they were done.

He shrugged then, licking his cone. "I figure that a gesture that might take two minutes out of your life could be a much more significant moment for someone else. So you kind of don't want to ruin it for them."

I peered over at him: backwards baseball cap, sunglasses, dimples. That he was this sensitive, conscientious soul only sweetened the deal.

"What are you thinking?" He smiled. "You want a lick of my ice cream, right?"

"Yes," I laughed. "I want a lick of your ice cream."

The plan was to meet up with the others on the boat at four. England was playing Costa Rica at six o'clock, and the guys did not want to miss it. We had just exited Rondini, the handmade leather sandal boutique, where I'd purchased matching pairs for Isabelle and myself, and were heading down Rue Georges Clemenceau when Hayes stopped short at the corner in front of Ladurée.

"Fuck."

"What? Did you forget something?"

"Fuck," he repeated.

And then I saw it. The dock where we'd moored was swamped with photographers: ten to fifteen paparazzi with massive cameras and two dozen cell-phone-laden tourists.

"Where the bloody hell did they come from?" He grabbed my hand and turned me back up the narrow pedestrian street and into Rondini again.

"I'm sorry, Solène. So much for a holiday . . ."

I watched him whip out his iPhone and text Desmond, while the salt-and-pepper gentleman who'd assisted me before asked in French if everything was okay.

"*Oui, pas de problème, merci. On attend quelqu'un.*"

Hayes's tall frame filled the space in the tiny boutique, and after a minute or so, he took a seat on one of the few chairs and pulled me onto his lap. The intimacy of the act rattled me. There were only a handful of others in the store, but the light was bright and we were in front of the shop window and it just felt *public*.

I tensed.

He sensed it immediately, burying his face in my hair. "I love it when I can feel you getting nervous," he whispered.

I opened my mouth to respond, but nothing came out.

"Don't worry, Solène. No one knows you here."

He had a way of getting inside my head. Of knowing what I was thinking at the same time I was thinking it. It was possible he was that way with everyone. But I liked thinking it was just with me.

Desmond and Fergus showed up at the door shortly with a plan. They swooped in like MI6. Fergus grabbing me and our many shopping bags, Desmond taking Hayes. The strategy was to escort us separately. Hayes would arrive at the dock first and stop to take photos with civilians, luring them away from the stern of the boat. And when his presence was causing a large enough commotion, Fergus and I would board together. It wasn't clear if we were supposed to be a couple or part of the general entourage. I suppose in the end, it didn't matter. So long as I did not show up on TMZ.

The plan worked. And poor Hayes got stuck doing the celebrity thing for fifteen minutes, while Oliver, Charlotte, and I popped another bottle of Moët belowdecks.

"He must really like you," Oliver said, completely straight-faced as he poured my glass. "I mean to sacrifice himself like that."

I was not certain how to respond.

"Sometimes this business sucks," he said. "And sometimes it's really grand. To Hayes"—he lifted his glass—"for taking one for the team. Cheers!"

On the ride back to Antibes, we stopped for an impromptu swim near the Massif de l'Estérel. The water was a magnificent hue, and that half hour the six of us spent splashing about with the red volcanic mountains looming overhead was superlative.

Hayes and I lay on the sun pads at the fore of the boat for the remainder of the trip. His skin—bronzed, smooth, warm to the touch—was perfect. I told him so.

"Let's go back to your hotel," he said softly, his fingers tracing across my back.

"I thought you wanted to watch the match."

"I do want to watch the match. But I want to go back to your hotel room more."

I laughed, pushing myself up on my elbows. "What do you think is going to happen when we get there?"

He shrugged, his fingers playing over the ties of my bikini top, teasing. "You tell me."

"We could cuddle." I leaned in to kiss him. His lips tasted of salt, of sun. He offered up his tongue and I took it.

"Cuddling sounds good," he said when we'd parted. "Naked."

Desmond dropped us off at the Hôtel Martinez and we made our way through the sleek lobby as quickly as possible. My heart was already racing. Up in the elevator, down the hall, fighting with the key card. He grabbed it from my hand, stopping me.

"Full disclosure," he said. "You should probably know . . ."

I braced for the worst. HIV, herpes . . .

". . . I brought my toothbrush." He smiled, coy. "But I'd let you fuck me even if I hadn't."

Inside, the late-afternoon sun was streaming through the French doors, bathing the large room in Provençal light. Artists' light. Cézanne, Picasso, Renoir. A light worth capturing. It felt decidedly appropriate.

"That's not a bad view," Hayes said. Mediterranean blue as far as the eye could see, the hills of the Massif de l'Estérel in the west.

I agreed, setting down my bags, slipping off my sandals, easing into the soft of the carpet.

"You know what else I brought?" He smiled, reaching into a canvas bag he'd lugged over from the boat and withdrawing not one but two bottles of Moët. "I assume we're going to be here for a while."

Hayes opened the champagne while I fetched glasses from the minibar.

We toasted, and drank. He poured more. I made a point of turning off my phone, and then made my way over to the windows to draw the sheer curtain, diffusing the light. He came up behind me, like before, in the hotel room in Soho. And with his finger he traced the faintest of lines over the curl of my ear, down the back of my neck, across my shoulder, and along the length of my arm. I could feel myself stiffening, anticipating his mouth, his kiss, his breath at the side of my face. But they did not come. Instead, his hands worked their way down the sides of my lace sundress to the hem just above my knee. His fingertips flirted with the skirt before stealing underneath. I could hear myself breathing, could hear him breathing behind me, the room otherwise quiet. His hands ascended to my hips, and then, without hesitation, peeled off the bottom of my swimsuit.

"Um . . . This doesn't feel anything like cuddling."

He turned me to face him then, taking my glass and setting it to the side. "And it's not going to either."

"You lied to me, Hayes Ca—" I caught myself.

He smiled. "Maybe." And then, with seemingly little effort, he lifted me and carried me over to the bed. "You're not going to freak out, right?"

"It depends how good you are."

"I'm going to be very good," he said, sliding me back on the duvet.

In that moment, when he hiked up my dress and descended between my legs, the realization that this was indeed happening struck me as absurd. There had probably been many before me, and there would be many after, but in that moment, it was just me. And for whatever reason I was plucked from the sea of nameless, faceless women who would have willingly shared Hayes Campbell's bed, and brought to this place, to this precise instant, to engage in this act.

His mouth was moving up along the inside of my thigh, his tongue tracing lazy circles. His movements slow, maddening. And at the moment when I thought he would land, he aborted his mission and moved to the other thigh. Like a cunnilingus flyby. I must have pulled on his hair because he laughed, raising his head.

"For someone who only wanted to cuddle, you're awfully impatient."

"I just wanted to make sure you knew where you were going."

"You want to draw me a map?" He smiled. Those fucking dimples.

"Do you need one?"

"I don't know . . ." He lowered his head and ran his tongue slowly, explicitly over my clitoris before looking up at me. "Do I?"

My heart all but flipped out of my chest. "No. No, you're good."

"Yeah. Can I do this my way now?"

I nodded, my fingers still wrapped in his hair.

He took his time. His mouth moving at the inside of my thigh again, higher, closer. His tongue teasing. And then he stopped and waited, hovering, letting me feel his breath. I didn't dare move. And at the point where I thought I could no longer bear it, he dove in. His tongue dipping down so low it was essentially at my ass, and then ascending in one fluid motion over the opening of my vagina and up to my clit. He did it again. And again. And again. And each time was so unbelievably wonderful and thorough, I felt like I had no secrets left. Hayes, unfolding me with his mouth.

At some point he paused again, waiting, breathing, knowing what it was doing to me. That he could be so in control at his age boggled the mind. I felt myself rising off the bed to meet him when he stopped me with the palm of his hand.

"I'm not going anywhere, Solène," he said. His voice low, raspy; his fingers playing over my lips, slipping inside.

I watched him. The light creating a soft halo around his beautiful head. He returned his mouth to me and I heard myself moan. The deftness of his tongue. But even if he hadn't known what he was doing, the sight of Hayes Campbell with his head between my legs was an image worth holding on to.

It didn't take very long. His mouth, his fingers, sublime. This was not his first time. And the way he held me down when I came, wrapping his arms around my legs and refusing to pull away even during the "StopStopStopStopStop," was such a fucking turn-on that I thought I would implode.

"Are you happy?" he asked before I was even capable of speech. Climbing up beside me, wearing me on his face.

I nodded, wiping his cheeks, kissing him, tasting myself.

"Well, I guess my work here is done then." He smiled, rolling onto his back.

"If you leave now, you might be able to catch the second half of the match."

"You're making jokes, I see. I suppose that's better than freaking out."

"I'm still freaking out. Just on the inside," I said, positioning myself on top of him.

"What are you saying to yourself?" His hand moved up to my head, his fingers playing in my hair.

"I'm saying, 'Wow, that alone was worth the flight to Europe.'"

"Really?" He smiled. "Are you thinking it was worth a first-class ticket or just economy?"

"That . . . that was worth flying private." I reached down to pull up his T-shirt, exposing his abs, allowing my hands to run over his taut skin, his defined muscles, the crease that ran diagonally from his hip to his groin.

"Wow. That's like a hundred-thousand-dollar orgasm."

"At least."

"I'm flattered. Maybe I can auction those off? eBay?"

"Do it for charity," I said, forcing his shirt up farther, admiring the breadth of his chest, the russet color of his nipples. "Look, you have a Saint-Tropez tan."

"A what?"

"There's this old suntan oil, Bain de Soleil. They had these great commercials in the eighties and . . ." I laughed suddenly. "And you were not yet born."

"I wasn't."

"Pity." I managed to remove the rest of his shirt. His skin: so flawless, soft, like a baby's. "You are so ridiculously beautiful," I said, and almost immediately regretted it. I didn't want him to know that I was falling. If indeed that's what this was. I could indulge him with sexy, witty banter, but hesitated to go beyond that. It was like prep school all over again. He who guards his feelings wins.

"I feel the same about you," he said. "I like everything about you."

I was quiet then, tracing my fingers over his face: his chin, his jaw, his mouth. Saying more, I thought, could affect the order of things. The arrangement.

I kissed him, letting my hand traverse his firm stomach and land somewhere just north of his swim trunks. My fingers slipped in between the elastic waist and his skin, and he flinched. And in that instant I was reminded that he was twenty.

There is this moment that every woman knows, when she reaches into her date's pants for the first time and is not sure what's going to come out. And she says a little prayer to the penis gods and hopes that she will be pleasantly surprised. And for me, it hadn't happened in a long time. But I was amazed to see the same anxiety was there. As in grad school, as in college, as in one memorable summer in Saint-Raphaël. That second of holding my breath and extending my hand . . . and the way that Hayes filled up my palm was a very good thing.

"Hiiii," he said, and I laughed.

"Hi, yourself." I took my time, freeing it from his trunks, admiring the way it lined up straight, thick, landing just above his belly button. "Mr. Campbell. This is a really nice dick."

"You're making me blush," he laughed, tipping his head back. His jawline from this angle was well-defined, exquisite, like art. His beauty, like a gift that kept revealing itself.

"Sorry," I said. "I just thought you should know."

He was quiet when I took him in my mouth. His hands playing in my hair, gentle. His body tense beneath me. I could still smell the sunscreen on his torso, taste the salt on his skin. This sweet boy.

It did not seem so long ago that the girls and I had flown to Las Vegas. When I could not pick him out of a meet-and-greet lineup. When he was just a pogo stick on a stage amidst a sea of girls losing their minds. And now here we were.

"I don't know your middle name," I said, pausing.

"Sorry?" His breathing was fast.

"I just realized I don't know your middle name."

Hayes screwed up his face, puzzled. "Is that a requirement of yours or something?"

"If you're going to come in my mouth, yes."

"Really?" he laughed. "Seriously? Philip."

"Philip," I repeated. It was so charmingly English. "Of course it is."

"So is that it? Do I pass?"

"With flying colors."

It happened relatively quickly, which I suppose was a good thing. To wield that kind of power. His breath coming in short, shallow spurts, his hands gripping my skull, his moans deep and sporadic; to realize that I'd done that. Especially having *not* done it in so long. And to someone whose idiosyncrasies I did not yet know. Like riding a bike.

He shuddered beneath me, his warmth filling the back of my throat. Familiar.

After, when his breathing had returned to normal and I was curled up beside him, my head buried in his neck, he said: "Tell me something, if I'd told you my middle name in Las Vegas, would this have happened then?"

I laughed at that. "What do you think?"

"Because you could have found it on the Internet. It would have saved me a lot of wooing."

"I like the wooing."

He was quiet for a moment, his fingers running over my ribs. "I like wooing you."

The thought crossed my mind that this could be dangerous. Not the ill-advised sex with the just-out-of-his-teens pop star, but the cuddling. The lying there, drinking in his scent, watching his chest rise and fall, allowing myself to bask in my own happiness. I could fall in love this way.

"May I ask you a question?" he asked. It was not his usual starter. "Is Daniel the last person you slept with?"

His query threw me. "Are you lying here thinking of Daniel?"

"I'm lying here thinking of you."

The sun was shifting, casting the room in a pale pink hue. Like being inside a shell, a watercolor. I wanted to hold on to the moment, paint it.

"Yes . . . Does that change things for you?"

He shook his head, his fingers moving over the material of my dress. "No. So long as you're all right with this."

I probably should have asked him to define "this" exactly. It might have saved us a lot of confusion and heartache.

"I'm all right with this," I said instead.

"You sure?"

I nodded.

"Let me know if that changes," he said.

He took his time peeling off my dress, untying my bikini top, kissing and caressing every inch of me. My shoulder blades, my breasts, the dip at the base of my back, my hip bones, my knees, the insides of my wrists. He was so tender, so complete in his lovemaking. Someone had taught him well.

"Is there anything you have that I should know about?" I asked. He had fetched a condom from the canvas bag and was opening the wrapper.

"Other than a few thousand psychotic fans?" He smiled. "No."

"Only a few thousand?"

"Who are genuinely psychotic? Yes," he laughed. "Anything *you* have that I should know about?"

"A twelve-year-old daughter who will disown me when she finds out what I'm about to do," I said, watching him roll on the condom. Condoms. Right. God, it had been a long time.

"I won't tell her if you don't."

"Good. I won't tell your fans."

In that final minute, with Hayes above me, and my mind clear, I recalled an earlier conversation. "So this is just lunch. Right?"

He hesitated, and then smiled. "It might be more than lunch."

That first moment of entry was everything. And after three years of nothing and ten years of Daniel—who was lovely, but definitely *not* Hayes—it was transcendent.

He was slow and gentle, and I knew immediately why he'd asked about my ex. Because he'd managed to make me feel like a virgin in his hands, in a way that I had not expected. I wanted to tell him that he need not be so delicate, but I was kind of enjoying it. I was kind of enjoying everything. The weight of him, the size of him, the smoothness of his back, the firmness of his ass . . . all of it. I didn't even care that it hurt. Part of me wondered why I had waited so long. Perhaps what I had waited for was him.

We lay there, after, bathed in fractals of light, watching dust particles dance in the air, spent, happy.

"It's a pity I don't smoke," I said eventually, "because I could really use a cigarette right now."

"I have gum."

"Gum?"

"Yes." He rolled over, to fish through his trusty tote bag. What *didn't* he have in there? "Solène, may I offer you a stick of post-coital gum?"

I laughed at that. "Why, yes, Hayes, I would love a stick of post-coital gum."

"We should hashtag that. #stickofpostcoitalgum. Now trending."

"Yes, your twenty-two million followers would love that."

He stopped. "You know how many followers I have?"

I felt as if I'd been caught knowing something I was not supposed to know. Information that might have been valid for mass consumption by his fans, but not general knowledge to those who knew him personally. It was tricky, this celebrity thing.

"Do you follow me?" he asked.

I shook my head. "I follow about two hundred people. And they're all in my industry."

"Huh," he said, watching me and doling out his postcoital gum. Hollywood, a French brand. So apropos.

"Would it be weird if I followed you?"

"I don't know. Maybe."

He lay back then, interlacing his fingers with mine, holding our hands up toward the light. "Then again, I pursued you rather earnestly, so maybe not."

"Rather," I repeated. "My very posh Hayes."

"Yes, well . . . It worked." He looked over to me and smiled, one of his huge disarming smiles. "Because if you had told me that night in Las Vegas that I'd be lying here with you, naked, in a hotel room, in the South of France, in two months' time . . . I would have told you, 'No, it will probably take three.'"

I couldn't help but laugh.

"I can't even fuck with you properly," he laughed, rolling into me. "You've totally thrown me off my game."

"I know you too well."

"Already, right? That happened surprisingly fast."

"Don't go falling in love with me. Hayes Campbell."

"I'm not gonna fall in love with you. I'm a rock star. We don't do that."

"You're a boy band member." I smiled, fingering his hair.

His eyes widened and his mouth formed this perfect O. I assumed he was going to scold me, but then he stopped himself, his face settling into a wry smile. "Well," he said, "I guess all bets are off then."

west hollywood

"I met someone."

It was late on Wednesday, the following week, and Lulit and I were winding down our June show. We had the long holiday weekend ahead of us, and the install of July's joint exhibit, *Smoke; and Mirrors*. But in that dead period, coming down from the Basel high, the gallery was relatively quiet and I thought it might be the right time to broach the subject of Hayes.

"What? No. Who? When?" Lulit shut the office door. Matt and Josephine had already gone for the day, so I don't know from whom she was hiding exactly.

"You have to promise me you won't judge."

"Judge? Why would I judge? He's not an actor, is he? Please say no."

I smiled at that. "No. But possibly worse."

"Worse than an actor?" She was leaning against the wall, her long arms crossed before her narrow frame. "What? An artist?"

We both laughed—a shared joke. Artists: dashing, brilliant, crazy. We'd both gone down that road before and vowed never to return.

"Do you remember in the spring when I took Isabelle and her friends to Vegas to the August Moon concert?"

She nodded. I could see her focusing, trying to follow the thread. There was no way she could have predicted the direction in which it would go.

"Well, I kind of met one of the guys . . ."

"One of which guys?"

"The August Moon guys."

Her eyes widened. "The *boys*? The *boys in the band*?" Coming out of her mouth it sounded dirty, wrong, possibly illegal. "I am going to need some wine. I'm going to the kitchen. You stay right here."

She returned shortly with two glasses and a bottle of Sauvignon Blanc. "Start at the beginning. Don't leave anything out."

And so I recounted the story of Hayes. Right up through the thirty-six hours we'd spent locked in the hotel room in Cannes. Only stepping out at dusk on Wednesday to walk the Croisette and dine at La Pizza because I insisted we get some fresh air. But he'd have been just as content to stay in our lair and fuck.

"Is he the cute one?" she asked now.

"Aren't they all?"

"No, I mean the *sexy* one."

I must have made a funny face because she followed that up with "The *really* sexy one."

"The swagger one?" I smiled.

"Yes! With the dimples?"

"Yes. That's mine. The swagger one."

"Holy fuck," she said, sitting on the floor with the bottle. She rarely cursed. "That is pretty impressive."

"Thank you."

"Does he know you could be his mother?"

"Yes," I said. Lulit was not one for sugarcoating things. "And apparently he's okay with that."

"Is *Isabelle* okay with that?"

I swiped the glass of wine she'd poured and downed a mouthful, Hayes's watch sliding over my wrist. "Isabelle doesn't know."

I still hadn't told her. Not during the overnight at my parents' in Boston; not during the nearly three-hour drive up to Denmark, Maine; not when she emptied her backpack and placed the framed photo from the meet-and-greet upon a shelf beside her bunk. And there he was: smiling wide, hugging us both, shaming me from the confines of a five-by-seven.

"Oh my God, you met them! I love them! I saw them at the Garden," one of Isabelle's bunkmates, a sporty brunette from Scarsdale, had said. "We were on the floor. Who's your favorite?"

Isabelle had shrugged, noncommittal. "I don't really have a favorite."

Thank God.

"I love Ollie." The bunkmate's eyes had gone all googly. "I know people say he's gay, but I loooove him."

People said he was gay? This was news to me. Although it might have been my initial impression, I'd rethought it when he mentally undressed me in Vegas. For a split second I considered telling the bunkmate that, but then decided it was best not to engage at all. At that point, I excused myself and stepped outside the cabin.

"I don't imagine she's going to take it very well," Lulit said to me now.

"I was waiting until I knew what it was that I was telling her."

"That you've made an arrangement to meet Swagger Spice in various cities around the world and have sex with him." She'd said it with a wry smile, but the reality of it deflated me.

"I'm going to need a better explanation than that."

She was quiet for a moment, contemplating. "Is he kind?"

"Kind? Yes."

"And you like him? Not all the hoopla that accompanies him." She waved her arms in the air—her gesture for "hoopla," I gathered. "But *him*."

I nodded.

"And he makes you happy?"

"Very."

She smiled then, easy, her brown eyes squinting. "Then I don't think it's a bad thing. You deserve to be happy, Solène. Go get your rock star."

"Thank you." I did not need Lulit's approval, per se. I'd already decided that I would not be thwarted regardless of her opinion. But it was nice to know I had it.

"You're welcome," she said, rising from the floor. And then as she was heading back into the gallery, she added, "I assume there are others."

"What?"

"Other women . . ." She had said it offhandedly, but boy, did it land.

I had not assumed so. I assumed there were several before. I assumed there would be several after. But I had not allowed myself to imagine that there were others concurrently. And the realization that I had not even considered it made me suddenly ill. When? How? Where was it happening? Was he flying them to the cities that I'd declined? What was it: Seattle, Phoenix, Houston? And who, who were they?

"Did that not cross your mind?" Lulit's voice jarred me. "Solène, he's twenty. He's in a boy band. There is like pussy falling from the sky. And every time he steps outside, it's raining."

My forehead suddenly felt clammy, my throat dry. The walls had begun to bend.

"I think I'm going to be sick." I pushed past her, rushing to the toilets in the rear of the gallery, where I promptly threw up my Sauvignon Blanc and the salad from lunch.

"Are you okay?" She was standing at the bathroom door, a concerned look on her face.

"No."

"You're not pregnant?"

"God, no." I was laughing even as the tears were running down my face.

She stood watching me while I washed my hands, rinsed my mouth, and made myself presentable. And then, when I could, I faced her again. "Fuck. I like him."

Lulit began to laugh.

"It's not funny."

"Oh, sweetie." She embraced me. "This is *good*. You haven't liked anyone since Daniel. And you haven't liked Daniel in years."

"That's true," I laughed.

"I think Hayes could be a nice distraction for you. Just don't mistake it for more than it is . . ." She sounded so levelheaded, like my mother. "And use a condom . . . always."

The following week, Hayes came to town for a series of meetings. He arrived late on Wednesday, but I would not see him until the following night. "I have an early dinner, but I'll rush," he'd said on the phone. "I can come to your place."

"I don't think that's a good idea," I'd said. I was still perturbed about the conversation I'd had with Lulit: the possibility that I was one of many.

"You don't want me to see where you live? What are you hiding over there? Another boy band?"

"Yes. You've found me out. I've got the Backstreet Boys in the attic."

He paused for a second and then began to laugh. "The Backstreet Boys? How old are you again?"

"Shut up, Hayes."

"You sure you don't have the Monkees over there as well?"

"I'm hanging up."

"Chateau Marmont. Tomorrow. Nine o'clock. I'll leave a key for you at the desk."

On Thursday, I met Daniel for lunch at Soho House. I dreaded the place. For all its aesthetic appeal, I couldn't help but be aware of everyone checking everyone else out, calculating one another's box office, posing, judging. The air of self-importance. Daniel had joined when it first opened despite my many pleas, and conducted almost as much business there as he did at his firm in Century City. He called it a necessary evil of being an entertainment lawyer. But I knew that deep down he enjoyed it.

I was already planning my escape as I made my way down the narrow corridor to the rooftop restaurant. The walls famously covered with black-and-white Polaroids from the club's photo booth, various members having immortalized themselves for posterity. Many of them drunk.

Daniel had birthday gifts for Isabelle that he wanted me to deliver Parents' Weekend. I was okay with the handover, but I feared he was going to use this opportunity to inform me about him and Eva. It was just like him to choose someplace public and impersonal where he could avoid any show of emotion.

I spotted him immediately, staked out at his favorite table in the southeast corner of the room. It really was a beautiful space: wicker lanterns dotting mature olive trees, potted herbs and floor-to-ceiling windows offering up the best of West Hollywood and the Sunset Strip. And my ex-husband.

He was buried in a *New York Times*. It was one of the things I still liked about him. That he hadn't given over completely to the digital age, that he didn't have to fill his silences with an iPhone.

I'd begun snaking my way in Daniel's direction when a large table near the koi pond in the center caught my eye. There were eight of them, loud. I did not recognize the faces in my line of sight, but the back of one head struck me as familiar. And then I heard the laugh.

My chest tightened. I had ceased to breathe, inching around the perimeter of the table. And as I arrived on the opposite side he raised his head, his eyes meeting mine. The two of us, paralyzed.

"Hi."

"Hi." Hayes's lips curled into a wide smile. "What are you doing here?"

"Meeting . . . I'm meeting . . . someone . . ." I was tripping over my words. I could not even register the others at the table. It was just him and me. In this space. And yet I was painfully aware that I could not touch him. That people would talk, that people would judge.

He stood, pushing his chair back.

"No, don't get up . . ."

"Where are you sitting?"

I gestured vaguely toward the corner.

"I'll come say hi."

I nodded, and then remembered the rest of the table. "Excuse me. Sorry to interrupt."

There were two women, three men I did not recognize, one who looked familiar, and seated beside Hayes was Oliver, whom I had somehow managed to overlook.

"Hi."

"Solène." He smiled. I'd last seen him when we got off the boat in Antibes, when I was smelling of salt and sun and high on champagne and the promise of what was to come. A world away.

I excused myself and made my way over to Daniel, but from that moment on, my mind was elsewhere. We talked about the necessary things: Isabelle, the weather. My back was to Hayes. I was out of his earshot, but I could *feel* him. And just knowing he was there put me on edge. Especially in the presence of my ex.

"Are you okay? You seem distracted," Daniel said, sometime after we'd put in our order. He was, as usual, impeccably groomed—smooth skin, chiseled jaw, not a hair out of place—the years had been good to him.

"I'm fine."

"Work?"

"Work is fine. We have a show going up Saturday."

"Which artist?"

It was nice of him to ask because I didn't think he cared.

"It's a joint exhibit. Tobias James and Ailynne Cho."

"Well, that should be good. Oh, before I forget . . ." He reached down and handed over two tiny shopping bags: one from Barneys, the other from Tiffany. "For the birthday girl."

"*Two* fancy gifts? Wow."

"Thirteen is a big year," he said, sipping from his Evian. And then: "One of them is from Eva."

He had my attention then. "Which one?"

"Barneys."

Which begged the question: "Why is Eva buying Isabelle a gift from Barneys?"

"It's not that big a deal, Sol."

"It is."

"It's like a little ring. It's not a big deal."

"A little ring from Barneys can be a very big deal, Daniel."

He sighed, turning to look out the window, the southern view. "Let's not do this here. Okay?"

Our food arrived then, and we dropped the subject. He asked about my parents, Isabelle's bunkmates, what I thought of the conflict that had just erupted in Gaza. There was a time when this was not so hard, finding things to say. When we were young, and kind to each other.

That first spring in New York when we were in love and we whiled away hours in Central Park, studying in Sheep's Meadow and drinking in the lilacs in the Conservatory Garden. He was so tall and brilliant and sure of himself, and he quoted Sartre and Descartes and that was all I needed.

I had just finished my kale salad when Hayes strode up to our table. Suave and gallant in full swagger mode. A printed white shirt, top three buttons undone, skinny black jeans, roguish hair. The polar opposite of Daniel in his gray Zegna suit and a tie I did not recognize but I assumed Eva had something to do with.

"Fancy seeing you here." He smiled.

"Yes. Imagine that."

"Hello, I'm Hayes." He reached over the table to shake Daniel's hand.

"Daniel, this is Hayes. Hayes, this is Daniel."

"Daniel. *The* Daniel?"

"*The* Daniel, yes," I laughed nervously, and Daniel threw me a peculiar look.

"Daniel, Hayes is . . . um . . . Hayes is . . ."

"Hayes is a novice art collector who is very impressed with this woman's knowledge of Fauvism," he said, dimples shining.

I sat there for a second, drinking in the deliciousness of the moment. Daniel, trying to figure it out.

"All right, I'm going to let you get back to your . . . *meeting*. And we'll touch base later."

"Sounds good." I smiled, casual.

I watched as Daniel watched Hayes make his way across the room. Heads turning, members murmuring, par for the course.

"Who is that?"

"A client."

"Looks familiar. Is he an actor?"

"No." I did not elaborate further.

"Ford!"

My interrogation was cut short by the approach of Daniel's longtime friend, fellow entertainment attorney Noah Feldman. Noah was magnetic, kind, sincere, a rarity among Hollywood types. I'd lost him and his lovely wife in the divorce. Along with their three kids. It hurt.

"Feldman!" Daniel greeted him.

"*Solène*. This is a nice surprise. How are you guys?"

"Good. How are *you*? How's Amy?"

"Fine, great. She got a writing gig." His eyes lit up.

"I know. I saw on Facebook."

"It's a pretty big deal. I mean we don't see her anymore," he laughed, "but she's happy. And I'm happy that she's happy."

I smiled. Of course he was. What a novel idea: a husband supportive of his wife's work. A wife that did not fit in a box.

"See those *Transformers* numbers?" Noah directed at Daniel.

"Fucking Michael Bay . . ."

"Fucking Michael Bay . . ."

My phone buzzed then on the table. The guys continued talking shop, and I took the opportunity to glance at the incoming text.

Daniel?????????!!!!!

I snatched the phone and hid it in my lap to respond.

Fauvism???

Shot in the dark.
Meet me in the lavvy in 5 min?

Ha!

Absolutely not.

Fuck.

I looked up. Daniel and Noah were still talking.

"I don't think that deal's going to close," Noah was saying. "Ryan's got one foot out the door."

"Where'd you hear that?"

"Weinstein."

I returned to my texting:

Later . . .

☺
You look beautiful, btw.

Ditto.

Hayes was still winding up his lunch meeting when I left. We locked eyes as I crossed the room, and the moment was so intense I almost reconsidered his lavatory proposal. But in this clubby place where everyone knew everyone, it was far too risky. He inclined his head and smiled. It was enough.

I was making my way back through the dark, narrow corridor when Noah came up behind me on his way out.

"So . . ." he said, low, "Hayes Campbell. Nice."

"What?" I turned to look at him in the shadows.

He smiled. "Your husband might be oblivious, but I'm guessing that's how he lost you in the first place."

I stopped, under the gaze of a thousand Polaroids. Stunned. What had he seen? Heard? Fucking Soho House.

"Don't worry," he said, "your secret's safe with me."

Hayes was late. He'd texted no fewer than half a dozen times from his dinner, apologizing. I'd had instructions to go to the front desk at the Chateau Marmont and ask for an envelope that the general manager, Phil, would have put aside for me under the name Scooby Doo, which was apparently Hayes's alias.

"Scooby Doo? Is that a joke?" I'd asked when he first told me via phone. "Scooby?"

"Hey, it's Mr. Doo to you."

But forty minutes later, when I was still alone in the somber suite, I was becoming restless. I'd already itemized his closet: two pairs of boots, one pair of sneakers, six dress shirts, two suits, four pairs of black jeans. All high-end (Saint Laurent, Alexander McQueen, Tom Ford, Lanvin) and smelling faintly like Hayes. That woodsy, amber, citrus scent that he owed to Voyage d'Hermès. The fragrance I'd learned during our romp in Cannes. I did not open his drawers, or riffle through his bags, or his toiletries, or the leather journal he'd left on the night table. Because that, I thought, would be crossing the line. But the closet—in which I had hung tomorrow's dress and placed my shoes—the closet was fair game.

He arrived shortly before ten. Ravishing and apologetic. He was wearing a dark suit, white shirt partially unbuttoned, no tie, and just the sight of him filling up the doorway was enough. I wanted him. And even though I'd spent the past week doubting him, and being angry with myself for not clarifying the boundaries of this arrangement, the moment he stepped over that threshold none of that seemed to matter. I had come there for a reason, lest I forget.

"Hi," he said, making his way across the room to me.

"Hi, yourself."

He stooped before where I was lying on the couch, took my head in both his hands, and kissed me. Like I'd wanted to be kissed. His lips were cool and his breath was sweet and his mouth was wonderfully familiar. And he was twenty. And I didn't give a damn.

"I'm sorry I'm late." His thumb was rubbing over my lips. "Are you hungry? Thirsty? Did you order room service?"

"I'm good."

"You sure?"

I nodded, watching as he peeled off his suit jacket, and pulled off his boots, and removed the various accoutrements from his pockets: iPhone, wallet, lip balm, gum. Now all recognizable as Hayes paraphernalia.

"How was dinner?" I asked.

"Long."

"And your day?"

"Long," he grunted. "We're doing a movie. Like a hybrid between a documentary and a bunch of tour footage. A rockumentary, if you will. Or a popumentary"—he smiled—"because it's *us*. Anyway, just a lot of meetings about when they're releasing it and all the promos they have to do and when they want to be able to release the new album and then schedule our next world tour. And it's all happening sooner than you would think possible. And I'm fucking tired. I'm really fucking tired." He sat down beside me on the sofa, reclining his head.

"I'm sorry," I said, reaching for his hand.

"I hate complaining about it, because it feels like I'm being unappreciative and I'm not. I know how lucky we are, how lucky *I am* . . . I know that I'm living this dream life and I don't want to be this bastard who's like whining, but we could all use a couple of months of just doing nothing. And if they continue to stuff us down these fans' throats, they're bound to lose interest. Right?" He looked to me then, sincere.

"I don't know. I kind of like having you stuffed down my throat."

His eyes grew wide. "You're naughty. Come here." He pulled me into him, my head on his shoulder, legs over his lap. "Wherever did I find you?"

"Vegas." I smiled. "So is there nothing in your contract that addresses vacation time?"

"Vacation time. What a quaint idea. Most groups get months of downtime with the natural ebb and flow of putting out an album and supporting it, touring, and then the time it takes to gear up to do another one. We just don't have that luxury."

"So you're just beholden to the record company?"

"We're beholden to our management first, and they run a very tight ship." His hand was in my hair, comfortable. "Oh, Graham says hello, by the way."

"Who's Graham?"

"Graham, with our management company. He was at lunch today. You met him in New York."

It clicked then, the nattily dressed laptop fellow from the Four Seasons. The one who could not have been more dismissive. I'm sure he was surprised to find me still in the picture.

"Speaking of lunch . . ." Hayes raised his head up from the couch. "Daniel!"

"Daniel. Yes. So that's Daniel."

"Wow. So *lunch* with Daniel?" There was more than a hint of suspicion.

I laughed at that: the idea that I would entertain anything with my ex-husband ever again. "Trust me, it was just lunch."

"I've seen your 'just lunch.' I've been on the receiving end of your 'just lunch.'" He smiled. "It's not always 'just lunch.'"

"With Daniel, it's just lunch," I said definitively. "I'm going up for Parents' Weekend at Isabelle's camp at the end of the month and he wanted to pass on a couple of gifts for her birthday."

He let that sit there for a moment, and then, satisfied: "How *is* Isabelle?"

"She's fine."

"What did she say when you told her about us?" His hand was on my knee, beneath the hem of my linen skirt. It had started.

"I didn't . . ."

"You haven't told her?" His eyes widened, huge blue-green pools. "What are you waiting for?"

"The right time. I was dropping her off in the wilderness for seven weeks. I didn't think it was appropriate to lay that at her feet before heading out the gate. 'By the way, I'm fucking one of the guys from your favorite band. Have a great summer!'"

He was quiet for a minute, thoughtful. "'Fucking'? Is that what we're doing?"

I paused. "Well, not right this moment. But I'm guessing soon, yeah."

He nodded his head, slow. "And what about the in-between times? When we're not having sex and we're just enjoying each other's company. Like now. What do you call that?"

It felt like a test. "Friendship?"

"Friendship," he repeated. "So we're just friends?"

"I don't know. That depends."

"Depends on what?"

"On how many friends you have . . ."

He nodded again, weighing his response. "I have a lot of friends," he said slowly. "Most of them I'm not fucking."

I didn't say anything.

"What is it, Solène? What is it you *don't* want to ask me?"

"I want to know if there are others."

Hayes took his time responding. "Right now?"

I nodded.

He shook his head. "There are no others."

"What does 'right now' mean to you exactly? Today? This evening? This week? What does that mean?"

He took a moment too long to formulate his answer.

"You know what? Never mind. I don't want to do this to you. I don't even know that I want to know."

"Okay," he said, slow, careful.

"You're trying not to hurt me."

He nodded, biting his lip.

"Fuck."

"I'm trying not to *mislead* you," he said, soft, his hand moving in my hair. "I just want to make certain we're on the same page."

"Hayes, I haven't done this in a while. I don't even know what the page looks like."

He chuckled at that, kissing the top of my head. "It looks like this, Solène. We get together when we can, and we really, really, *really* enjoy each other's company. And I wouldn't say we were just fucking."

I took a moment to process that. "Are you doing that with anyone else?"

"*That?* Right now? No."

"Right now this week?"

"Right now this month. Does that work for you?"

I nodded. "If it changes, will you let me know? I'm not going to lose my mind, I just want to know."

"If it changes, I will let you know."

He kissed my head again, and I could feel him breathing me in. So much lay in what we were not saying.

"What'd you do while I was gone?" he asked. His hand had found its way back to my knees, rings cool against my skin.

"Went through all your stuff. I sold your underwear for ten thousand dollars on eBay."

"Only ten?"

"Turns out fourteen-year-old girls don't have that much money."

"They do in Dubai." He smiled, his fingers traveling farther up my skirt, prying open my thighs. "Are you splitting the proceeds with me?"

"I wasn't planning on it."

He laughed then. "Somehow that doesn't seem fair."

"Life isn't fair."

"It's not." He'd arrived at my underwear, the tips of his fingers tracing over damp cotton. "You know how I know that? Because tonight I get to have you . . . and no one else does."

"You'd better earn it. Hayes Campbell."

"I always do."

It might have been the ghosts of the Chateau Marmont, and the feeling that wild things had happened there. It might have been the fact that we'd been separated for two weeks. It might have been my sudden determination not to be replaced. But that night, although Hayes might have had another word for it, we fucked like rock stars.

He was thorough and intense and insatiable. And the third time he handed me a new condom package to open, while he simultaneously disposed of another, I paused.

"Do you never need recovery time? Ever?"

He smiled, shaking his beautiful head. "I'm twenty."

I tried to remember what sex with Daniel was like in the beginning, and sex with my two boyfriends in college, and sex with the boy from Saint-Raphaël, all who were in the realm of twenty, and while I could remember the appetite, I did not recall this level of stamina. But maybe that was just me getting older.

"You tired?" he asked, taking the condom from me and slowly rolling it on. Just watching him do that was a turn-on. Hayes, with his dick in his hands.

"Yes. But don't let that stop you."

He laughed. "Do you want to stop? We can stop, Solène." Even as he was saying it, he was lifting me by the hips, hoisting me above him, determined. Round four.

He took his time guiding it in. Eyes peeled to mine, teeth sinking into his bottom lip, hips rising. "Just say the word and we can stop."

"Really?" I smiled.

"Really." His hands moved up over my hips and around to my ass. "Although, I'm no expert, but . . . it feels to me like you don't want to stop."

"Is that what your dick is telling you?"

"Fu-uck." He started to laugh. "I think I might love you."

"Don't say that."

"I'm just putting it out there as a possibility."

I stopped moving then, folding into him, close. "Not even as a joke."

"Okay," he said, serious.

"You're trying not to mislead me, remember?"

"I like you." I kissed him, deep. "A lot. But as long as you're fucking other people, you're not allowed to make jokes about being in love with me."

"I'm sorry." His hands had moved to my hair, holding it out of my face.

Neither of us spoke for a moment. And then: "Are you angry with me?"

I shook my head, rising up off his chest, moving on top of him again, not wanting to lose this precious thickness. His gift that kept giving. "Does it feel like I'm angry?"

He smiled, even as his breath was quickening, his hands cupping my breasts. "I'm not sure. I can't read you."

I didn't respond, but the thought went through my head that maybe it was better that way.

When it was over and I lay on top of him, feeling the layer of sweat between us and drinking in his four-times-over postcoital scent, he held me, tighter than he ever had, and said nothing.

In the morning Hayes blew off an appointment with his trainer and chose to come with me to the gallery instead. "I want to see what you do when I'm not with you," he'd said at some point during our debauched night. He'd uttered it at a moment in which its meaning could have been taken in a variety of ways. But when we awoke, he made himself clear. "So it's Take Your Lover to Work Day, right?"

I had an unexpected surge of nerves driving down La Cienega with him in the front seat of the Range Rover. The idea that I had his life in my hands, this irreplaceable commodity, and that should anything happen to him on my watch I would be forever culpable. It was like driving with Isabelle as a newborn all over again: the pressure, the fear.

It is likely I had never seen Lulit's eyes as wide as when I walked into the gallery with Swagger Spice. I had not warned her or the others. It was the day before our July opening, and I knew they'd be swamped with detailing the show. I did not want to give her something else to think about until he was already there.

Her jaw dropped and she moved to fix her hair, which was in a perfectly messy topknot. She was in jeans and no makeup and she was still flawless. Her enviable brown skin that would not age.

"You've brought . . . *company*."

"I have." I smiled, wide. A whole conversation transpired between us then without a word spoken. "Hayes, this is my partner, Lulit Raphel. Lulit, Hayes."

"So this is the famous Lulit. It's a pleasure. I've heard plenty about you." Hayes's voice sounded particularly deep in the cavernous space. Gravelly. As if he'd been up eating pussy until four in the morning. Which, indeed, he had.

"Lovely to meet you, Hayes."

"God, this space is brilliant." He began walking around, admiring the layout, the art. The juxtaposition of Cho's atmospheric images and James's emotional landscapes. Both abstract, more metaphoric than literal. Smoke and mirrors.

"You want a guided tour, or you want to wander on your own?"

"I want to wander first."

"Okay, I'll be in the office. It's toward the back, off to the right."

Matt popped his head out from his office in the rear, and Josephine exited the kitchen as I was approaching.

"Who is that?" Matt raised a wily eyebrow. "Client? This early?" It was not quite ten.

"Potentially," I said.

Josephine headed out toward the reception desk, sipping from her mug of green tea, and then very quickly turned around and headed back to us. "Holy shit, is that Hayes Campbell? Is he a client now?" Josephine was twenty-four.

"Who's Hayes Campbell?"

"Only like the hottest guy in the hottest band. In the *world*. Where have you been?"

"In my thirties, clearly." Matt smirked. "What band, now?"

"August Moon," Josephine whispered. "Holy shit."

"The boy band? Those adorable posh boys from Eton . . ."

"Only one went to Eton," Josephine said matter-of-factly.

"Who went to Eton?" I asked.

"Liam."

"He did?" This was news to me.

"Yes. And the others all went to a posh school in London. Except for Rory, he's the bad boy."

"You know all their names?" Matt asked.

"All whose names?" Lulit joined us in the kitchen and made a beeline to the espresso machine.

"August Moon. Our newest client is from August Moon."

Lulit threw me a seemingly casual look, and I shrugged in response. She understood: she was not to say a word.

"Well, I'm going to offer our boy band visitor some Pellegrino," Matt said, grabbing a small bottle from the fridge. "We're being rude here."

"Forget it, you're not his type." Josephine swiped the bottle from him.

Matt was stocky, sardonic, Korean-American, male. I doubted highly he was Hayes's type.

"He only dates older women. Don't you watch *Access Hollywood*?"

She started out of the kitchen and then suddenly stopped, swiveling around, her eyes landing on me. "*How* do you know him exactly?"

Lulit pressed the button on the espresso machine just then, filling the space with a welcome roar.

"He's a client."

I barely had the time to process all that Josephine had said—who knew she was such a wealth of boy band information?—before Hayes came looking for me. I could hear them in the hall: Lulit making introductions, Hayes's not-enough-sleep voice, Matt and Josephine sounding not at all like themselves.

He popped his head into the office eventually. "Hi. I'm looking for the boss lady."

"There are two of us here."

"I'm looking for the one I came with." He smiled, sly, sliding the door shut behind him. "This is a cool space."

Lulit and I shared the oversized box. White walls, cement floors, like the rest of the gallery, except the lighting here was warmer and there were personal touches throughout.

"Is that Isabelle?" He came up behind me, admiring the photos on my desk. Two of Isabelle: one as a toddler, dressed as a ladybug for Halloween; the other at age seven, a snapshot taken on the Vineyard, my little bird. And a black-and-white of me, captured by Deborah Jaffe, one of our photographers, at her opening earlier that year. Close up, in profile. I'm laughing and my hair is still long.

"I like this." Hayes lifted it from the desk. "Solène Marchand," he said softly.

"We are not having sex."

"I . . . wasn't expecting us to . . ."

"No, I don't mean now, I mean in general. They cannot know that we are having sex." I pointed to the door.

Hayes's expression was contrite. "But Lulit knows, right?"

"Lulit knows. The others do not. And we're keeping it that way. And later you can tell me why you only date older women."

"Who said that?"

"*Access Hollywood* apparently."

Hayes followed me around the gallery while I gave him a brief overview of the exhibit. The work of the two artists, how they were similar, how they were not. How Ailynne worked with film and created ethereal nature stills by experimenting with depths of field and focus. And how Tobias's prints were done digitally, playing with shutter speed and then further manipulated in post. How his captures managed to look like the world flying by at sixty miles per hour. Both artists' works: blurred, evocative.

He was quiet for the most part, attentive, like a young student. His hands clasped behind his back, his face open. I imagined this was what he looked like at his posh school. Minus the skinny jeans, of course.

"How do you find them? Your artists?"

"Different ways. Some we plucked straight from grad school and have been with us since we first started. Tobias was at CalArts. Ailynne came over recently from a smaller gallery."

"I really like this one," he said, pausing in front of a large James print. A moody seascape, at once peaceful and aggressive.

"It's very masculine."

"Is it?" Hayes cocked his head. "What makes it masculine?"

"The energy, the mood, the colors. It's just a feeling I get."

"I thought water was feminine."

"I think art can be whatever you want it to be." I reached out to grab his hand and then remembered where we were and who he was, and so quickly retreated, crossing my arms.

He laughed softly. "What are you so afraid of? You ashamed of me?"

"I'm not ashamed of you."

"You don't want your friends to know about us."

"I don't want my *employees* to know about us."

He leaned into me, suggestive. "They're going to figure it out. And then you're going to have to admit that you like me. And then maybe you'll realize that's not such a bad thing. Boy band and all. I want this. I'm going to buy it."

He pulled away from me, stepping to the middle of the room for perspective, while I pondered what he'd said.

"They'll ship it to London?"

"They will."

"Do you like it?"

"I do."

"Do you love it?"

"I like it a lot."

"Is there anything here that you love?"

I nodded. "In the front room, in Gallery 1."

"Show me."

He followed me to the Cho piece that I most coveted. An image so blown out it appeared almost translucent. Sunlight in a garden, and the vague silhouette of a woman, nude, her features blurred and indeterminate, lying in the grass, bleeding into the atmosphere behind her. A faded anemone, the one certainty in the foreground. *Unclose Me*, it was titled.

"This . . ." he said, tugging on his lip, pensive. "This is what you love?"

"This is what I love."

He nodded, slow. "What do you feel when you look at it?"

"Everything."

His eyes caught mine then, and he held my gaze and smiled. "Yeah."

He did not stay for long. He had meetings starting at twelve and scheduled throughout the afternoon, and that evening he boarded a plane to London. I would not see him for a few more weeks. And each day was agony.

the hamptons

Visiting Day at Isabelle's camp was the last weekend of July. In the early years, Daniel and I would go together, a forced show of solidarity. But eventually that ended. And now I handled drop-off and Parents' Weekend, and he did the pickup. The arrangement seemed to work best for all parties.

My parents made the trip with me in Daniel's absence. We'd drive up together from Cambridge and stay in a quaint B&B not more than an hour from the camp, each time exploring some hitherto unchartered territory. Strolling in Ogunquit, scouting small galleries in Portland. It was the one time I felt most like a daughter, when all the other labels and the weight of them seemed to fade. I welcomed it.

On that Saturday, we spent a leisurely afternoon in Boothbay Harbor. Following a fish-and-chips lunch, we popped into a very local gallery and just as quickly popped out.

"Beh," my father grunted in that very French way of his. "Blown glass and lighthouses."

After thirty-six years in Harvard's art history department, my dad was almost as much of an institution as the department itself. He had opinions on such things. He'd met my mother when they were both students at the École du Louvre in Paris, the two sharing an intense love of art. He: European modern and contemporary. She: American. In the late sixties they'd arrived in New York, where he earned his Ph.D. at Columbia before they eventually settled in Cambridge. There was much they embraced about the U.S., but they were never going to *not* be French.

"We're in a tiny little seaside town, Dad. What were you hoping to find?" I asked. "Koons?"

"What I am always hoping to find," he said, stroking his once-roguish beard. "Someone who goes against the grain. Who doesn't seem to care what everyone else thinks."

"Ha!" I said. This from the man who did not speak to me for a week when I chose Brown over Harvard. Who cried actual tears when I moved to the West Coast. And who, in the three years since the end of my marriage, had to repeatedly stop himself from saying "I told you so."

"He thinks you are beautiful and he thinks you are smart," he'd surmised about Daniel, that first weekend I'd brought him to Boston, when we had been dating for seven months. "But he has no real appreciation for what you are passionate about, who you are on the inside."

It had angered me when he said it, but much of it turned out to be true.

"Your father is full of contradictions in his dotage," my mom contributed, clutching his arm. "*C'est vrai, Jérôme?*"

"I always said this, 'not to care.' But I also said, 'Be respectful.' Yes?" He angled his head in toward my mom, and she stood on her toes to kiss his brow. All these years later, they were still in love.

"The best artists, they are like this. You don't shock just to shock. You create beauty, you create art. You don't do it for attention."

I made note of that as we negotiated the narrow sidewalk. My father and his digestible morsels of art critique.

As we approached the intersection at the corner, a family of five made their way in our direction. The youngest, a girl of about nine, caught my eye immediately. There was no missing her August Moon shirt.

My heart was audible in my chest. I had made great efforts not to think about him constantly, and yet here he was coming toward me via some tween's printed jersey. Hayes's face plastered over where her left breast would one day be.

"Do you know that girl?" my mom asked when we'd passed them in the crosswalk.

"No."

"*Tu en fais, une tête!*" she said. Rough translation: That's an odd face you're making.

"Sorry," I said. "It happens."

"Sometimes, you give away everything on your face." She frowned. "It is when you are least French."

This, from my mother, was not a compliment.

I had made the decision that I would tell Isabelle about Hayes that weekend. Not everything in its entirety, but—as the experts suggested when teaching one's child about sex—just as much as she needed to know.

It was after lunch, and we were winding our way down toward the lake, surrounded by mature maples and pines, the smell of summer in New England. My parents had wandered up to the stables to see the horses, and for the first time that day it was just the two of us. Isabelle had been so excited to show us all that she'd mastered in her short time there (zip-lining, waterskiing, tennis), that I'd had to wait for her to settle a bit before bringing it up.

"So," I said, as casually as I could muster, "wanna hear something really cool?"

"Did you meet someone?" she asked. We were approaching the boathouse, and only a handful of other campers and their parents were in sight.

"Did I *meet* someone?"

"Yeah, like a guy, a boyfriend. I was hoping that's what you were going to say."

I stopped. I could feel my face flushing. Oh, that she was so close. And that this was what she wanted for me. Although certainly not with *him*. "No. No boyfriend. Something you'll think is much cooler. Guess who my new client is?"

Her eyes grew wide. "Taylor Swift? Zac Efron?"

"Cooler than that."

"Cooler than Zac Efron?" She looked at me, doubtful, and then: "Oh my God, oh my God . . ."

I waited for it to register.

"Barack Obama?!"

"Yes," I laughed. "He called and said he needed something special for the Oval Office. No, not Barack Obama. In what world would that happen?"

"Ours," she said, "because we shouldn't put limits on ourselves. Remember?"

I smiled at her then. It was something I had said often. I was pleased to see it had stuck.

"Hmm." She was twirling her new ring around her middle finger. The gift from Eva was a thin Jennifer Meyer creation. Gold with emeralds in a circle pavé setting. Delicate, simple . . . easily five hundred dollars.

"Is it? Is it . . . ?" Isabelle's voice grew very tiny, as if saying it any louder would kill the possibility. "August Moon?"

I smiled, nodding. My gift to her. "Hayes Campbell."

Isabelle's entire body seemed to alight from within. She had

Daniel's blue eyes. But my hair, my nose, my mouth . . . "Oh my God! You saw him? He came to the gallery?"

"Yes, yes."

"Did he remember you? Did he remember *us*? Did you remind him that we'd met?"

"Yes," I laughed. "He remembered us. He remembered *you*. He sends his regards."

"Oh my God—"

"Stop with the 'Oh my Gods'—"

"Sorry. I love him. Did you tell him I love him? No, you wouldn't do that. Did you?"

"No," I said, uneasy. We'd begun walking again, the pine needles crunching beneath our feet. "I wouldn't do that."

"Are you going to see him again? Do you think he'll come back to the gallery?"

"I'm not sure," I said. This was a lie. I'd already made tentative plans to see him the following weekend. I did not like lying to her. It was time to change the subject.

"So how's the sailing going?"

"Good. Really good. I can take the Sunfish out by myself now."

"That's great, Izz."

"Yeah. Even better, I can get it back in," she laughed, referencing a mishap from the previous summer. It was a great big belly laugh: happy, unaffected, carefree. The laugh of a girl on the brink of all things good.

Dear God, what kind of animal was I?

They were spending the weekend in the Hamptons. The boys were in New York for two weeks, finishing up their album. They'd been in the studio round the clock. Hayes, longer than the rest. While the others typically laid their tracks and left, he tended to linger during the sessions. ("They're singing my words," he relayed. "I feel like I have a vested interest in making sure they don't fuck it up.") They were exhausted, but they had three days off and they wanted out of the city. Dominic D'Amato, one of the heads of the record company, had offered up his place in Bridgehampton, and Hayes insisted that I join them.

"I don't want to infringe," I'd said on the phone Monday night when I was back in Los Angeles from Maine.

"You're not infringing, you're coming as my guest."

"I know. But I would feel uncomfortable with your record exec there—"

"He won't be there. They're in Ibiza for the week. Everyone is in Ibiza this week. I think Diddy's throwing a party. Which means the Hamptons will be quiet."

I paused, deliberating. I so wanted to see him, but I wanted it to be just us. I wanted to hole up in a hotel room with him somewhere and forget the rest of the world existed. "And the madness?" I asked.

"No madness. It's just me and Ol and Charlotte. The others are heading down to Miami."

I was quiet for a moment, and he jumped on it. "Good. It's decided then. My assistant, Rana, is going to call you and arrange your ticket. She'll get it all sorted. I'll see you Friday."

I took the red-eye, because I didn't want to lose another full day of work. Like all galleries, we were closed on Mondays, but I was blowing off Friday and Saturday, and I did not feel wonderful about it, despite Lulit's understanding.

"Go and have great sex and come back and tell me what it was like," she had said.

"You have an *amazing* husband," I reminded her.

She did. A doting husband, no kids. Exactly the way she wanted it.

"Which is great for like five years, and then it's just the same guy," she laughed. "I mean I love him to death. But it's the same guy. Go. Have fun."

Hayes was staying in one of the sky apartments at the London in midtown. A massive suite high above everything with stellar views of Central Park. He'd already departed for the studio by the time I arrived, and I made my way past the forty or so fans camped outside at nine a.m. and to reception, where I met up with Trevor, one of their security. Trevor was formidably tall and not easy to miss. He wasn't as bulky as Desmond, Fergus, and Nick, but Hayes had said he was some sort of Krav Maga expert, and at six foot seven, he was certainly intimidating. He waited for me while I picked up the key card for "Scooby Doo's" suite and accompanied me in the elevator to the fifty-fourth floor.

The doors rolled open, and standing in the corridor before us in full workout gear and with large headphones hanging from his neck was Simon. Even without an accompanying entourage or screaming fans, he was remarkable. Tan and blond and athletic with deep blue eyes and razor-sharp cheekbones. If Hayes was swagger, and Oliver was dandy, and Rory was the bad boy, then Simon Ludlow was definitely the David Beckham one.

"Hey." He appeared to recognize me, extending a strapping arm to hold the doors as Trevor filed out with my bags. "You just getting in?"

"Yeah. Red-eye."

"Ooo, brutal. Sorry."

"Are you not in the studio today?" I asked.

"They don't need me until eleven. I'm heading down to the gym." This he directed at Trevor. "I'm meeting Joss there. It should be fine."

Joss, Hayes had told me, was one of their trainers.

"Ring me if anything comes up," Trevor said.

"Will do."

Simon was only a couple of inches shorter than Hayes, but broader and clearly capable. It seemed bizarre to me that these guys would need bodyguards. As if a slew of thirteen-year-olds lying in wait could conceivably overwhelm them. But then I recalled that morning at the Four Seasons and the terror I'd felt; perhaps it was possible.

He stood in the frame of the elevator doors for a moment longer, as if he were trying to remember something. "How's your daughter?" he said, finally.

"She's fine. Thanks."

"Good." He smiled. "Good. Right. Have fun in the Hamptons."

"Have fun in Miami."

"Oh"—his smile widened—"we will."

I wasted no time showering and climbing into Hayes's unmade bed. Left on the pillow, on hotel stationery, was a handwritten note:

Sorry I'm not there to greet you. Feel free to keep my bed warm. Back after 1. —H.

His penmanship was surprisingly neat. All that posh schooling. Perhaps it had been spanked into him. I smiled at the thought and curled up in the linens, reveling in the smell of his sheets, his pillow, his life.

It was the feel of him that awoke me. The inexplicable sense that the atoms of the room had rearranged themselves somehow. For a moment I was not sure where I was or how long I'd been sleeping, but finding him there, seated at the foot of the bed, watching me, filled me with such an intense happiness I was immediately fearful of it.

"Hi." He smiled. "Nice nap?" His hair was standing on end, his youthful skin poreless in the soft blue light of the room. And I was once again overcome by his beauty.

I nodded. "You have a very nice bed."

"It's much nicer with you in it."

"That's what all the boys say."

"Really?" He raised an eyebrow. "And what about the girls?"

I laughed at that. "There haven't been too many girls."

"Pity. You don't know what you're missing."

"I think it's too early for this conversation."

"Too early in the day or too early in our relationship?"

"Both."

He glanced down at his watch, one of the preferred TAG Heuers. Masculine, mature. "All right, that's fair."

"Are you going to come here and kiss me, or are you going to spend my entire visit at the other end of the bed?"

"That depends . . . What are you wearing under there?"

"Tank top. Underwear."

"Hmm. That's going to be a problem."

"Is it?"

"We've bumped up our departure time. We chartered a seaplane. It leaves in an hour. The car's on its way. I'm going to kiss you, but I'm going to show incredible restraint and not get into that bed. Do you think you can handle that?"

"I don't know. You're awfully irresistible when you're being obnoxious."

"You," he said, inching toward me.

"Me?"

"You." He kissed me, slow. He tasted like mint. Stick of postcoital gum. "You. Are going to have to wait."

"Fine," I said, peeling back the Italian sheets and heading across the room to the bathroom. It was a sheer tank, La Perla panties. "So are you."

There was an art to traveling with the band. A calculated series of staggered entrances, exits, timed departures. There was no walking out onto the street and flagging a cab, not with two hundred girls swarming the exterior of one's hotel. Someone—there were more security guards than I could keep track of—took our bags down ahead of time. Hayes and I rode down to the lobby with Trevor, where we met up with Oliver and Charlotte, and were then escorted out. Charlotte and I first, one after the other. Trevor leading us, a handsome black guard pulling up the rear. There were girls lining barricades on both sides of the entrance and across Fifty-fourth Street. All manners of dress, all complexions, loud. They did not seem fazed by the fact that it was ninety degrees and unbearably humid, the joy of New York in the summer.

They identified Charlotte immediately, which surprised me. I had not realized she was such a fixture in Oliver's life. She smiled and waved faintly beneath her wide-brimmed hat, ever the duchess in training. And they, in turn, were surprisingly respectful: "Hi, Charlotte!" "How are you, Charlotte?" "Charlotte, you look beautiful!" "I love your dress!"

They ignored me.

It was probably for the best.

When we were ushered into the waiting Navigator, I allowed myself to exhale. "You handled that quite well."

"This isn't bad. Paris . . . Paris is bad. Girls running in the streets and paparazzi on scooters. The roads are narrow and there's nowhere to go and you fear for your life. They're particularly aggressive there. Anytime you're walking eight security deep and it's not enough . . . it's a problem." She said it so casually it struck me as odd. But then I thought: one would have to be terribly nonchalant to be in a relationship with one of these guys and put up with this madness on a regular basis. Or, perhaps, insane. I was not sure I was either of those.

The volume outside of the SUV rose considerably, and I looked out to see two more security emerging from the hotel. Oliver was in tow. He had a slow gait and a sly smile, and the way he walked with his hands in his trouser pockets was so effortlessly elegant and entitled, I could feel my eighteen-year-old self swooning. He was prince-like in his demeanor. As if he were strolling the grounds of Kensington Palace, engaging his subjects, and not holding court at the London. And in that moment he reminded me of a young Daniel, right down to the aristocratic nose. How I had loved him. Controlled, powerful, elegant. My Princeton fencer. Ol stopped to take a few photos, and all I could hear was "OliverOliver-OliverOliver" until the pitch changed and there were incoherent shrieks and I knew without even looking that my date had exited the building.

It was strange to see Hayes from this perspective. The way he smiled easily and turned on the charm. Perfect teeth, dimples, his long torso angling over the barricades to fulfill every selfie request and hug. Like a demigod. They swayed and scrambled and screamed "Iloveyou Iloveyou Iloveyou." "Hayes, here. Hayes, over here. Over here, Hayes!" "Hayes, I love you!" And my heart broke for every one of them.

And it broke a little for me.

And then the doors were opening and they were filing into the car, Desmond and Fergus accompanying them. When they shut the door, Trevor banged thrice on the side of the SUV and our driver pulled out.

"All good?" Hayes turned back to check on me. There was lipstick on his face, a frosty pink that I would never have worn on one side, a deep plum on the other.

I gave him a thumbs-up from the third row, and he winked in return.

"The adventure begins." He smiled.

Three dozen or so girls were following the Navigator. Running alongside us as we headed east on Fifty-fourth. Banging on the doors each time we slowed, holding up their phones, pleading for the guys to roll down the windows.

"Is this okay? Are we okay?"

"We're okay. They can't see you."

But it did not feel okay. The panting, painted faces pressing up against the window, desperate, deranged. Was this what his life was like? *All the time?*

"You get used to it," Hayes said, as if reading my mind. "And this is nothing compared to Paris. You'll see."

"Or Peru," Oliver tossed over his shoulder.

"Oh God, Peru," Hayes laughed. "Desmond, remember Peru?"

Desmond looked back from his position in the front seat and grimaced. "Fucking crazy bastards."

Somewhere around Fifth Avenue we lost the last of the fanatics and then proceeded down to Twenty-third and the FDR Drive unscathed. But my mind was still on Paris and the promise Hayes had made.

It took us forty-five minutes to get to Sag Harbor via seaplane. The flight out was calm, the skies clear, and the views traversing Long Island's North Shore sublime. Sprawling mansions and fields of green, the colors vibrant and exaggerated like a David Hockney. He held my hand the entire trip, squeezing it at times, and the gesture seemed so natural and comfortable, one would have thought we were an established couple and not two mismatched people navigating an illicit arrangement.

I smiled to myself at one point during the ride, somewhere over Sands Point.

"What's so funny?" he asked, leaning into me close, his nose buzzing my neck.

"I could be your mother."

"You find that amusing now, do you?"

I nodded. "Just a little."

He smiled, wry. "I'm going to make you forget that . . . if it's the last thing I do."

The house in Bridgehampton was a sprawling nine-thousand-square-foot shingle-style manse on 3.3 acres of manicured lawn, complete with pool, pool house, tennis courts, a putting green, formal gardens, and home theater. Naturally, it was fully staffed. We would want for nothing.

But what impressed me most was the D'Amatos' contemporary art collection: Cy Twombly, Kara Walker, Damien Hirst, Takashi Murakami, Roy Lichtenstein. I found myself salivating at every turn. Furthermore, it was well curated. Not cluttered or intention-ally ironic, but all coexisting beautifully. Each piece allowed to breathe in its own space. The D'Amatos not only had taste; they had restraint.

"What's the wife's name again?"

We were in our bedroom, an airy suite with views overlooking the putting green and the stretch of lawn extending to the pool. On the far wall, above the sitting area, was a framed pigment print of Kate Moss, taken by the legendary Chuck Close.

"Sylvie . . . Sylvia . . . One of those. Do you want me to introduce you?" Hayes was lying on the chaise longue, watching me unpack.

"I'd like that. Yes."

"Where is she getting her art?"

I did a quick mental compute. "Mainly Gagosian, and probably some auctions."

"Like that?" He nodded toward the Moss photo.

"No. That's Chuck Close. He's with Pace in New York. She probably bought it from them or at auction."

"Is that Kate Moss? She looks weird."

"It's the process he uses," I explained, "like a daguerreotype. The way you can see every pore on her face. Age spots that the naked eye probably can't even pick up yet." I made my way back across the room to the closet.

The Close piece was haunting. Mostly because Kate was my age. She couldn't have been more than thirty in the photo, and yet I could see everything that she would become. Everything that I, *we*, probably already were. I wondered if Hayes could see it, too. The opposite of youth.

"I used to love her as a wee lad."

"Yes. Well, who didn't?"

"Come here," he said. It was the way he said it. I knew that we'd stopped talking about Kate. That we'd stopped talking about art.

I made my way over to him, and he extended a languid arm, his hand wrapping around the back of my thigh, beneath the hem of my dress.

I did not speak as his fingers moved up my leg, arriving at my underwear, slipping beneath the fabric. "Hiiii."

"Hi." I smiled.

"I missed you."

"That's . . . apparent."

He nodded, his fingers moving against me. "It's been three weeks. That's like decades in the music industry."

"I imagine it is," I said. But I could not imagine it was as he was saying it. Had he not been with *anyone*? Or just not with me?

I was quiet for a moment, listening to him breathe, listening to my heart beat, watching his hand move beneath my dress. Possessing me.

The bedroom door swung wide open suddenly, and Fergus was standing there at the threshold, his bald head buried in a pile of magazines. Hayes's arm was back at his side before I could even register what was happening.

"Hey, mate, we picked these up for you," Fergus said, finally looking up. "Sorry. Door was ajar." He stepped into the room and very casually tossed a handful of magazines onto the credenza before turning and leaving. As if he hadn't just walked in on us.

"We should probably lock that," Hayes said, calmly.

I nodded. "We should."

It was hours before we left the room.

I had the thought that, regardless of how unconventional or ill-fitted the two of us together seemed, the chemistry was like nothing I'd ever experienced. And by the way he responded to me, it appeared that for him it may have been the same.

He lay there at one point, staring at the ceiling.

"What?" I asked, my fingers tracing his ample mouth. "What are you thinking?"

"Just . . . I don't know. I don't want to say the wrong thing again."

"Okay."

He reached for my hand then, stilling me, his eyes intense. "This thing . . . us . . . It's more than I expected."

I hesitated, not wanting to misread the moment. Something had shifted. "Yeah," I said, "for me, too."

We went for a walk before dinner. Down the winding tree-lined drive and out onto Quimby Lane.

"So I'm going to do the TAG Heuer thing," he said, his fingers entwining with mine.

"Really? That's good."

He shrugged. "Expanding my brand, right? Life outside of August Moon . . ."

"You're not thinking of quitting the band?"

"No. I couldn't . . . Not now . . . No. It's *my* band. I can't leave them. Contractually or otherwise . . .

"And all this." He waved his free hand in the air, gesturing at our surroundings: massive hedges hiding estates, endless green. "All this stuff that kind of falls into your lap. All this is because of them. *Us*. I'm not ready to end us.

"When Ol and I first started writing music together, we never imagined this. We fancied ourselves a modern-day John and Paul. But really we were just a couple of posh toffs sitting around our parents' country homes writing songs about love and loss and things we hadn't actually experienced because we were thirteen." He laughed then, trailing off.

I squeezed his hand but said nothing.

"How's Isabelle doing?"

"Good. I told her."

He stopped, his eyes wide. "No fucking way."

"I told her you were a client, so . . . not exactly everything."

"Not anything at all actually," he laughed.

"Baby steps . . ."

We began walking again, east, toward where the road dead-ended.

"So, a client, huh?" he said, after a minute. "I'm afraid to see what you do for your friends."

"What was it you said? 'I have a lot of friends. Most of them I'm not fucking.'"

"Did I say that?"

"You said that."

"Hmm." He smirked.

"Yeah, well . . . I'm not fucking any of my friends."

"Just me?" He squeezed my hand.

"Just you."

We had dinner at the house. The D'Amatos' chef—they had two: one they'd taken with them to Ibiza, and a second they were kind enough to leave with us for the weekend—prepared a paella feast that we downed on the back patio beneath a lilac sky. The conversation flowed, lubricated by endless pitchers of sangria. Oliver and Hayes held court, regaling us with stories from their travels and school and growing up in London. They'd shared such a long, entangled history, and they seemed to speak in code, like something out of Hogwarts:

"We were playing football on Green, and it was Fifth Form."

"No, we were Lower Shell that year, because Simon was Upper."

"Right. And our headmaster said never in the history of the school had he seen such hooliganry. He was quite cross. Not even during the Greaze."

"We won the hooliganry award. Unofficially."

This, I was able to detect, was regarding an incident that had happened at school and not with the band, but it was difficult to keep it all sorted. And each time the others got the joke and I didn't, I felt decidedly American.

Desmond had a raunchy sense of humor and peppered the discussion with sordid tales from the road, mainly the antics of Rory, which were easy enough to follow. Fergus had an infectious laugh, but spoke little. And Charlotte sat, taking it all in, a sweet smile on her delicate face. She clung to Oliver's hand. And every once in a while she would look over to me, shake her head in feigned annoyance, and toss off something wry, like: "You'd think they'd tire of talking about themselves?"

When the sky was finally dark, around nine o'clock, and Desmond and Fergus had retired to watch a movie in the subterranean theater, the four of us relocated to the sofas and sat gazing at the stars, enjoying the breeze blowing in from the ocean mere blocks away. Oliver lit up a cigarette. The figure he cut, reclining—legs crossed in white trousers, linen shirtsleeves rolled to his elbows, golden hair pushed back off his brow—brought to mind another era. Like something out of a Fitzgerald world, if not Gatsby himself.

"I plan to lie by the pool and do nothing all weekend. And not sign one fucking autograph or write one tweet. Is that okay with everyone?"

"It's a real tough life you lead, HK," Hayes said, wrapping an arm around my shoulders. He occasionally called Oliver by the initials of his last name, Hoyt-Knight. And there was something about that that I found old-boy-ish and sexy.

"Yes, well, someone has to do it. And I brought three books, and I intend to crack at least one. Which I am sure is a hell of a lot more than those blokes are doing in South Beach."

Hayes glanced at his watch. "I'm guessing they're about three mojitos in, apiece. And they've got ten models with them."

"Where are they staying? Soho House?"

"Yeah. Watch." He pulled his iPhone from the pocket of his shorts and began texting. "How. Many. Models. Do. You. Have. With. You. Right. Now."

"We have to do something absolutely mad so we can prove we had more fun." Oliver flicked his cigarette between his thumb and forefinger. Charlotte tossed me one of her exasperated looks.

"I *am* having more fun," Hayes laughed.

"Really?" I turned to him. "You wouldn't rather be with ten models in South Beach?"

He looked at me for a moment, not speaking, one eyebrow raised. And then finally: "Do you not know me?"

"I do. I was just . . . teasing."

He leaned into me so that the others could not hear. "I wouldn't rather be anyplace else. Than here. With you."

"Ditto."

His phone buzzed in his hand. "Eleven!"

"Fuck!" Oliver laughed.

"Yes, I don't know how you're going to have more *fun* than that," Charlotte said, straight-faced.

Oliver furrowed his brow, snuffed out his cigarette, and then pulled her onto his lap. "Charlotte, you know me. Models are like toffee. They often seem like a great idea, especially on holiday. But once you get them in your mouth, you remember that they're cloyingly sweet and they stick to your teeth. Plus they've no nutritional value whatsoever . . . But they're certainly very pretty in the window."

It is likely I had never heard anything more perfect.

We laughed for a long time.

Hayes excused himself at some point and went inside, and when he reemerged five minutes later he had a bottle of Scotch in one hand and two glasses in the other. He was laughing to himself as he traipsed across the patio.

"What?" Oliver asked.

"Simon sent another text. He said, 'We had eleven models and seven of them just left with Rory.'"

"Ha!"

"Wait, I have to read it to you," he snorted, placing down the Scotch and pulling out his phone. "'Liam was totally gutted and I had to remind him that he only has one dick . . . He thinks it might be Rory's tattoos and now he's considering getting one.'"

"Tell Liam he mustn't forget where he comes from." Ol smiled. "And to not fret if his type is not appreciated in South Beach, because it still has value in Courchevel."

"'We are this close to becoming a joke.'"

"How old is Liam?" I asked.

"Nineteen. God, that's priceless."

"Only two glasses?" Oliver sat up and began pouring the drinks with Charlotte still on his knee. Laphroaig 10. Neat.

"My hands are only so big, and I didn't want to break Mrs. D'Amato's crystal. Just double pour it and we'll share."

"*Mrs. D'Amato?*" Oliver mocked him. "She's like in her forties, mate."

"Great," I said.

"Sorry," Oliver said.

"But she looks like a Mrs. D'Amato. You don't look like a Mrs. D'Amato," Hayes explained.

"What exactly does a Mrs. D'Amato look like?"

"Like she's done stuff to her face." He gesticulated. "She's like frozen things and puffed things up. Your face isn't anything like that. Your face—"

"Your face is perfect," Oliver interjected.

It was more than a little awkward.

"Thank you."

Hayes spun to look at him. "Yes, Oliver. Thank you . . . And your face is perfect as well, Charlotte," he added, pointedly.

Charlotte smiled, trying to make the best of the situation. "Thank you, Hayes. For noticing."

"Bloody hell, I was just paying a compliment," Oliver laughed.

Hayes held his gaze for a moment and then shook his head, as if he did not know what to make of him. "All right," he said, grabbing one of the glasses, "we're going for a walk. Don't follow us."

We trekked down across the lawn to the far side of the pool and installed ourselves on one of the lounges.

"I'm sorry about that. That was weird, right?"

"No weirder than Liam only having one dick."

He laughed. "God, I love your humor."

"I love hanging out with you. Thanks for inviting me. I'm glad I came."

"I'm glad you came, too. And it *is* perfect . . . your face."

I kissed him then. "Yours, too."

We lay there for a bit, side by side on the lounge, kissing, and it felt like high school, innocent and pure.

He stopped at one point, reaching for the Scotch and taking a long sip before offering it to me.

"I'm not really a Scotch person . . ."

"How do you know? You weren't a boy band person either, and now look at you. You're like knee-deep."

I laughed at that.

"You're worse than knee-deep. You're like up to your chin."

"Fine." I allowed him to serve me. It was hot going down, smoky, like all the goodness of the first fire lit in winter, bottled and put in my mouth. And suddenly, that night at the Crosby Street Hotel came rushing back. The nervousness of it, the newness, the post-orgasmic freak-out.

"Well . . . ?"

"It reminds me of you."

"That's good enough." He placed the glass down and rolled me on top of him.

"I love this face," I said, tracing my thumbs over his eyebrows. "I love the proportions of it. I love the symmetry. I love that it reminds me of a Botticelli cherub."

He smiled. "I'm pretty certain I've never heard that before."

"Can I tell you a secret?"

"Do."

"That first night, in Las Vegas . . . I distinctly remember thinking, 'God, I just want to sit on this kid's face and pull his hair.'"

"What?" He began to laugh. "You thought *what*? That you would compare me to art and then consider desecrating it in almost the same breath is a little unnerving."

"Sorry to have unnerved you."

"And yet you made me beg you for a date . . ."

"I wanted to have sex with you, I didn't want to date you."

"I'm going to pretend I'm not offended by that . . . What made you change your mind?"

"What makes you so sure I have?"

He stopped laughing then and grabbed both my wrists, tight. "What are you afraid of? Right now, what are you afraid of?"

I didn't say anything, but I knew it was written on my face.

"Yeah," he said. "Me, too."

Oliver and Charlotte turned in shortly after, and Hayes and I resumed our high school make-out session, which led, as high school make-out sessions are wont to do, to the inevitable blow job. There was something about it that was terribly amusing to me. Because I could not remember the last time I'd snuck through someone's backyard on a balmy summer night to suck a dick in the dark. It felt almost nostalgic and it made me laugh.

"What's so funny? Why are you laughing?" he asked, his hand on the top of my head.

"I'm too old for this."

"No, really, I can assure you, you're not."

I laughed harder. "It's not the dick sucking, it's the sneaking around. It feels so nineties."

"Fuck." He tipped his head back, staring up at the stars. "I was born in the nineties."

"Shhh. Okay, stop thinking," I said, lowering my head, taking him again in my mouth.

"You were sucking dicks in the nineties?"

"No," I lied.

"Yes, you were," he laughed.

"Hayes, do you want this blow job or not?"

"I want it, I want it. Just give me a second to laugh. Please. I'm just processing this."

I sat up then. "I'm going back up to the house."

He reached out for my arms. "No, you're not."

For a second we sat like that, neither of us laughing, speaking.

"This is crazy," I said eventually. "This is completely crazy. What the hell are we doing?"

He sat up then and kissed my forehead before leaning into my ear, the smell of Scotch on his breath. "I like you, so fucking much. I don't give a damn what you were doing in the nineties. Or any-time, really . . . Please don't go up to the house. Please."

For a moment I did not move. I sat, letting him breathe into me, wanting him and knowing that we were both now in deeper than either of us had intended.

"Lie down," I said.

He did. And he remained quiet while I finished what I'd begun. And it was just us and the sound of him moaning and crickets and the ocean and summer and his dick in my mouth. And it was perfect.

He came. And then held me afterward, a wide grin plastered across his face.

"Are you happy?" I asked, borrowing his line.

"Very."

"Good. You wouldn't happen to have a stick of postcoital gum on you, would you?"

He laughed, shaking his head. "No, sorry. Have some Scotch."

"You. You're supposed to be responsible for the condoms and the gum."

"What do you bring?"

"I bring my mouth."

"All right, then." He nodded, smiling. "That seems like a fair trade."

In the morning, I went on a long run and convinced Charlotte to join me. We were evenly paced, despite the fact that she was barely half my age, and I enjoyed her company. She shared that she was about to enter her third year at Oxford, where she was studying philosophy. She'd met Oliver through mutual friends who had attended Westminster with the boys, and they'd been dating for the better part of a year.

"I imagine you've seen a lot," I said, alluding to life with the band.

She shrugged her shoulders, noncommittal. We were heading up Ocean Road, one tremendous lot after another. And passing each $15 to $20 million manse, I could not help but wonder what they had on their walls.

"Yeah," I sighed. "I probably don't want to know . . ."

"He's a good guy, Hayes. He's really sweet and respectful and responsible and . . . kind."

I let that sink in for a bit.

"He's different," she continued. "I mean, the others are all lovely in their own way, and Oliver is Oliver. But Hayes is . . . different. He's a little more mature and serious, which, you know, you've seen him, so that says a lot about the rest of them." She laughed at that. I hadn't seen her laugh much. It was beautiful on her.

"I think they all take the group seriously, but Hayes has this added pressure, because it was his idea, and he put the band together, and it was his mum who was longtime friends with their managers."

"Really?" That I did not know. Outside of our first lunch at the Hotel Bel-Air, we had not discussed the nuts and bolts of how August Moon had come to be. "Hayes's mother was friends with their managers?"

"Yes, the Lawrences. Alistair and Jane. You'll meet them eventually. They're very *daunting*," she emphasized with a clenched jaw. She sounded to me like Emma Thompson.

"He doesn't really talk about them. I know Raj and Graham."

"Graham, *blech*," she scoffed. "Graham is not particularly fond of girlfriends. Or girls at all, I presume. He and Raj are associates—or, as I prefer to call them, glorified minders. But Alistair and Jane own the company. Jane and Hayes's mum, Victoria, grew up together. And when Hayes was seventeen, he came up with this idea and made a video and a PowerPoint presentation and sold Jane and Alistair on it. They did a search to find Rory, and it went from there. It was pretty brilliant on his part, because no one had ever thought of a posh boy band."

"No. And why would you?" I laughed. It seemed far-fetched. But there was no denying the way it had caught on. The genius of it. Like bottling the appeal of a young roguish Prince Harry, multiplying it, and distributing it to the masses. With some infectious melodies, strong vocals, and clever lyrics thrown in. And just the right amount of edge.

"Yes, well, I think they all thought it would be amusing. They'd have lots of fun and there'd be lots of girls and it would be a cool way to see the world. I mean they certainly weren't doing it for the money . . . But it was Hayes's brainchild, so things tend to weigh more on him. Plus he's serious about his music."

I sat with that for a while. Replaying all our conversations about the group and the things that made him unhappy, the relentless touring and promotion, the idea of being crammed down people's throats.

When we reached Route 27, we turned around and headed back toward the ocean. It wasn't until we were bypassing our turnoff and continuing on to the beach that she spoke again.

"I *have* seen a lot." She picked up our conversation with no lead-in, as if she'd been mulling it over for the past four miles. "You are his quintessential type. You're just better at it than the others."

"What does that mean?"

"You're smarter, you're wittier, you're more sophisticated, and you don't seem to get caught up in all the bullshit . . ."

"Oh."

"You're also older, and for some reason he likes that." She'd said it plainly, but there was something there. "And, you know, your face is perfect."

The boys were lounging by the pool when we got back to the house. They'd finished playing tennis and were sitting out in shorts and not much else soaking up the sun.

"How was your run?" Hayes pulled me onto his lap, nuzzling my neck. "Mm, you're all sweaty."

"So are you. Shower?"

He nodded. "Just a second."

"What are you doing?"

He had his iPhone, poised down by his knees. "I'm Instagramming a picture of my feet."

"Are you kidding me?"

"No. They love this rubbish. Watch . . . and 'share.'"

I leaned in to see the image of his tanned feet with the pool as a backdrop. Hayes counted to ten and then pressed refresh. There were 4,332 likes. He counted again: 9,074.

"Holy shit."

"That's just my feet. Someday I'm going to put my penis on there and see what happens."

"If you could perhaps time it with the release of *Wise or Naked* so we could all profit from it, that would be great," Oliver quipped. Charlotte giggled.

Hayes turned to look at him and laughed. "I'm not sharing the proceeds from my dick with *you*. I'm saving that for my solo album."

"Oh my God, you *are* twenty, aren't you?"

"Yes." He smiled, running his hand over my back. "And you still love me. We're showering, right?"

"Maybe. Do you read your comments?"

"Sometimes." He began scrolling through. "'I love you so much. Come to Turkey.' 'Why are you so hot?' Something in Arabic. 'I wish I could show you how much I really love you. I'm not like the other fans, try me.' 'I want to lick you but your music sucks'—tell me how you really feel. 'Can I sit on your big toe?' Wow, part of me is horrified and part of me wants to check her picture. Is that bad? All right, continuing, 'Dork ass—' What? I can't say . . . It says the n-word. Why are they calling me *that*? Something in Hebrew. 'Your feet are sexy as fuck.' 'I just want to be you.' 'Hayes, if you see this, I love you.' Aww, that's sweet . . . Right then, so there you go. There's a nice sample for you."

I don't know why, but I was stunned. The immediacy of it, the fact that our moment here was playing out around the world in real time. The idea that they could communicate with him, that they were anticipating his every action. It was unfathomable, this level of adoration.

"How many likes now?" Oliver asked.

Hayes pressed refresh. "Sixty-seven thousand six hundred and forty-three."

"Show-off."

"Hey, I'm just keeping the fandom happy. If I were showing off, trust me, mate, you would know." He smiled before turning his attention back to me. "So, shower?"

There were many words I would use to describe Hayes Campbell. "Show-off" was not one of them. But his post-tennis performance that morning was undeniably brag-worthy. Because it took a certain level of skill to make me feel dirty in the shower.

After, when we were preparing for a drive into East Hampton, he headed downstairs to find Desmond. I was still in the bathroom struggling with the buttons on the back of my dress when I heard him return to the room.

"Can you do these for me?" I asked, stepping out into the suite.

But it was Oliver who looked up from the ottoman at the foot of the bed, where he was riffling through Hayes's weekend bag. "Hey."

"What are you doing here?"

"Searching for headphones. I left my Beats back at the hotel in New York. Hayes said I could borrow his."

"Do you not knock? Does no one knock here? Are there no boundaries?"

"The door was open. Sorry."

I wanted to believe him, but something in his eyes said differently.

He turned back to the bag then and fished out Hayes's headphones. "Got them. Thanks."

My eyes were glued to him as he made his way across the room. When he reached the door, he stopped.

"Do you want me to fasten your dress?"

"No, thank you."

"Do you want me to send up Hayes?"

"It's okay. I can handle it."

"Right then. Sorry I disturbed you."

As he was turning to leave, he paused again, peering at something beyond my shoulder. "Chuck Close," he said, gesturing toward the print. "Nice. Clearly, Hayes got the better setup."

He'd said it casually, but instinct told me there was more there.

Hayes, Desmond, and I whiled away a few hours touring East Hampton and Amagansett. On the way back to the house, we made a detour to a pharmacy and Desmond ran inside, leaving us in the air-conditioned car with the engine running.

"We're almost out of condoms," Hayes stated, matter-of-factly.

"We are?" I could have sworn he'd opened a box yesterday. Of how many? Twelve? It took me a moment to process. "You sent Desmond in there to buy us condoms?"

He nodded from the front seat of the SUV. "I wasn't going to send *you*, and it's not like I can be seen casually buying condoms in the Hamptons on a Saturday afternoon."

"He's your *bodyguard*, Hayes."

"Well, it is guarding a part of my body." He smiled. "I was trying to be responsible."

"Yes, I appreciate that. It's just . . . Your life is so bizarre."

An understatement. We'd spent most of the day in the car, thwarting any would-be photographers. I had not protested.

"Not that we really need them . . ." he said.

I pitched forward on the seat in order to see his face. "What do you mean, 'not that we really need them'?"

Hayes was quiet for a moment and then he turned back to me. "I know you're on the Pill, Solène."

This threw me. How he knew, what it meant, what he might have been insinuating. "You went through my stuff?"

"I've racked up quite a few hours in hotel rooms with you these past couple of months. I might have seen it in your wash bag."

"*Might* have?"

He leaned back through the gap between the seats. "Might have."

"I'm not having sex with you without a condom, Hayes."

"Have I asked you to?"

"I don't know what you do when you're not with me."

"Why is it you think I'm doing something?"

"Because you haven't convinced me that you're not."

He paused, tugging at his lower lip. I couldn't see his eyes through his sunglasses. "They test us regularly, you know."

"Who's 'they'?"

"Management. They have to do it for insurance purposes."

"Well, good for them. They can sleep with you, then."

He laughed. "All right, you've made your point."

I scooted back in the seat then. The elephant in the room. The idea that he was randomly hooking up with other people. That I had tacitly accepted it. I had thought the less I knew, the better. But maybe not.

"Fuck."

I thought I said it under my breath, but he heard.

"I'm sorry."

"No, you're not."

Desmond stepped out of the pharmacy just then and started toward the car. The stocky, tattooed ginger fellow in head-to-toe black. Desmond stood out in the Hamptons.

"Can we discuss this later?" Hayes asked.

I did not respond. Later we would have sex again and again and again, and he would manage to make me forget that at this moment I was angry.

By midafternoon we were out by the pool drinking sangria in the heat. The D'Amatos' cook had mixed a few more pitchers at our request, and Hayes, Ol, and I plowed through them with ease, while Desmond and Fergus played video games inside and Charlotte napped.

"I think I could be happy with a house in the Hamptons," Oliver said at one point. We were all three sitting in the spa, and the millennials were discussing multimillion-dollar real estate like middle-aged men in Brentwood.

"You'd never get to use it. I'm thinking London, New York, Barbados, Los Angeles," Hayes said. His pronunciation of *Angelees* always made me smile.

"I might just move in here with Dominic and *Mrs. D'Amato,*" Oliver teased. "I like what she's done with the place. Solène, did you see the Hirst in the dining room?"

"I did."

Hayes's eyes traveled back and forth between the two of us. "How did you know that?"

"Because my mother collects art, you idiot. What does your mother collect? Right, ponies."

"Fuck you, HK," Hayes laughed, splashing Oliver on the far side of the spa.

"Hayes Philip Campbell is not the culture vulture he makes himself out to be."

"Solène"—Hayes tightened his grip around my waist—"do I make myself out to be a culture vulture? Or do I mostly just sit in awe when you talk about art?"

"You mostly just sit in awe."

"Thank you." He beamed before turning to Oliver and sticking out his tongue. Lest I forget I was dating someone half my age.

"What are you? Twelve?"

"Sometimes . . ."

"All right," I laughed, "I'm getting more sangria."

I was already out of the spa and wrapped in my towel when he called out to me. "And see if they have any more crisps, please."

"Yes, Your Highness. Oliver? Anything?"

"I'll help."

Oliver followed me up to the house, snatching a towel and wrapping it around his narrow hips en route.

"I didn't know your mother collected art," I said as we headed beneath the loggia and through a set of French doors leading to the kitchen.

"There's a lot you don't know about me."

I stopped then, turning to look at him. Golden hair wet and swept back off his brow, hazel eyes piercing, serious mouth. He was beautiful, in a certain unattainable way.

"I suppose that's true."

He slipped into the pantry to find a bag of "crisps" then while I headed across the kitchen to one of the two Sub-Zeros on the far wall.

I was grabbing the pitcher of sangria from the refrigerator when I felt it: a cool fingertip tracing the span of my back, from shoulder blade to shoulder blade. And then it was gone. For a moment I could not move, and when I finally turned around he was on the far side of the room, bag of chips in hand, heading out.

I stood there, shaking. Not knowing quite how to react. Because it was so subtle he could have easily denied it. So faint, I could have imagined it. But I hadn't, and there was no mistaking his intention.

I returned to the pool eventually and dropped off the pitcher before making some pathetic excuse about needing a break from the sun and retiring to our room. He and Hayes had been laughing about something, and I could not even bring myself to look at them.

I felt sick.

Within half an hour Hayes appeared at the bedroom door. "Hey, what are you doing in here?"

"Reading," I said, barely looking up.

"You all right? I missed you." He planted himself at the foot of the bed.

"I just wanted to be alone for a little bit."

"You sure everything's all right? 'Cause I can't really leave you alone," he said, wrapping his hands around my feet. "I mean that kind of defeats the purpose of you being here." He lowered his head then, kissing my ankles, my shins, my knees.

"I can't have half an hour to myself?"

He shook his head, forced my knees open. "Nope. What are you reading?"

I held up the book. *Adé: A Love Story* by Rebecca Walker.

"A love story," he said, planting kisses on the inside of my thigh. "Is it any good?"

"Yes."

"Very good?"

"Very good."

"Is it as good as ours?"

I laughed at that. He had my attention. "Is ours a love story?"

"I don't know. Is it?" He took the book from my hands then and placed it on the night table, before peeling off the bottom of my bikini.

"What are you doing, Hayes?"

He smiled. "I brought my mouth."

The thought occurred that it might not be the most opportune time to mention Oliver's transgression.

In truth I did not know how or what exactly I would say to Hayes about what had happened. Because their relationship was already so peculiar and complicated and because what Oliver had done was relatively benign and because I did not want to be stuck in the same house with the two of them if and when things were to blow up, I kept it to myself. I managed not to be alone with him for the remainder of the weekend. And Oliver went back to being his occasionally charming, occasionally disdainful, amusing, aristocratic self. And all was well, on the surface.

———

On Sunday, Hayes and I took a long bike ride before having lunch in Sag Harbor and then returning for a swim. The others were elsewhere, and we relished the solitude.

"How is it I don't tire of you?" he asked. We were drying in the sun, our lounge chairs drawn in beside each other, cozy.

I laughed at that. "Do you tire of people easily?"

He nodded, his fingertips tracing over my back. I'd untied the straps of my swimsuit to avoid tan lines but taken care to shade my face with a large hat, and he'd managed to wedge his face in next to mine beneath it.

"But not you," he said, soft, his lips against my temple. "I never tire of you."

"And yet . . ."

"And yet?"

I said nothing.

"This is about yesterday, isn't it?"

"Here's what I'm going to say. Once . . ." I rolled into him. He reached out to finger my nipple, and I stilled his hand. "Are you listening to me?"

He nodded.

"I understand you're in this unique position, and girls are constantly falling in your lap, but you always have a choice. At some point, one way or another, you make a choice. And I'm not inclined to let this go on much longer without you making a choice. I trust you'll let me know when that happens."

He nodded again, slow. "I'll let you know when that happens."

los angeles

On the Wednesday of the second week of September, Daniel and I attended Windwood's Eighth Grade Back-to-School Night. All summer our exchanges had been civil, perfunctory, business as usual. But there was something about him that evening that I could not quite put my finger on. He was oddly charming, attentive. After the welcome and the walk-through and the mediocre coffee, he insisted on escorting me back to the parking lot. And as we neared my car, he came out with it. "Are you seeing someone?"

"What?"

"I don't know. You just seem happy."

"I can't just be happy? I have to be seeing someone?"

"That's not what I said." He smiled.

I watched him wave to Rose's parents across the lot. So polished, controlled, Hollywood. The very qualities that had drawn me in that first year of grad school. He, the cocky Columbia Law student with the intense eyes and perfect pedigree. He, who had wooed me over Viennese coffee at the Hungarian Pastry Shop on Amsterdam. How quickly I'd fallen.

"Do you remember Kip Brooker?" He turned back to me. "He left Irell a few years back to go in-house at Universal? I had lunch with him the other day . . . His wife's family has a place in the Hamptons. They summer in Sag Harbor every year. He told me he could have sworn he saw you there, at a restaurant, with one of those guys from August Moon. Like on a date. Which seems crazy, because . . ." He shook his head then, laughing. "That would just be *crazy*, right? For a million reasons that would be crazy."

I smiled at that, deflecting. "Is there something you want to ask me, Daniel?"

"I thought I already did."

"He's a client."

He stopped. He was not expecting confirmation. "A client?"

I nodded, watching him process. His poker face failing him.

"Is that his story or yours? Never mind. Sorry. None of my business. Get home safe," he said, tapping the side of the Range Rover.

I'd already started the car and was adjusting my belt when he turned back and indicated for me to roll down the window.

"That's not entirely true." His expression was stern. "I'm going to take your word for it. But on the off chance you're lying, I want to point out that your having any kind of relationship with this kid would likely kill Isabelle."

"Duly noted," I said, and closed the window.

Hayes arrived at my doorstep that Friday. In the weeks that had lapsed since our Hamptons tryst, August Moon had completed

recording their album in New York. They'd taped a bunch of footage for their upcoming documentary in London. They'd performed
on a popular TV show in Germany and accepted an MTV Video
Music Award via satellite because they were tied up recording a
charity single at home for the BBC. But Isabelle's return from camp
and the start of the new school year made it so I could not join him
for any of the above. And so when Hayes booked a ticket to visit
his first free weekend, I was thrilled. That it coincided with the
opening of our September show made it all the more satisfying.
Hayes had come to L.A. for me.

I hugged him for a very long time. And the feeling I had in his
arms—protected, safe—was one I could not remember having felt
in a while.

"One would think that you'd missed me," he laughed, his face
buried in my hair.

"Just a little."

"Are you going to invite me in? Or are the Backstreet Boys still
here?"

"Actually, the Monkees," I laughed, leading him inside.

Isabelle was at school, and then fencing. We were alone.

"So, this is home?"

"This is home." It was strange to have him in my space, his large
frame filling the threshold. I had a flash of me and Isabelle drag-
ging in our Christmas tree the previous winter and fretting it would
not fit through the door.

Hayes made his way through the entry into the great room and
its walls of glass. The Palisades, the Pacific, and points south dom-
inating the view. Catalina rising like a purple phoenix at the horizon. "Bloody hell. I am truly speechless. You live here? You wake
up to this every day?"

"Every day."

"How do you manage to leave this paradise?" His eyes were
green in the light. Oh, pretty, pretty boy.

"It isn't easy."

"No, I don't imagine it is." He turned his attention to the interiors, surveying the space: the Finn Juhl coffee table and Herman Miller Tuxedo sofa in the living room, the Arne Vodder table and Hans Wegner credenza in the dining area off to the left. "Is this your midcentury furniture?"

I nodded. "You know midcentury furniture?"

"I know you like it."

"How do you know that?"

"You told me"—he smiled—"in Las Vegas."

"You remember that?"

"I remember everything . . . especially the things you like."

I might have blushed then.

"Did you paint all these?" His attention had turned to the myriad watercolors I had mounted and framed salon-style on the far wall.

"Most. A couple are Isabelle's."

He made his way across the room to better inspect them. A mélange of landscapes and figures and still lifes. Moments I thought worth capturing. "These are beautiful, Solène. Truly."

"Thank you."

"I want one. Have you sold any?"

"No," I laughed. "It's just a hobby. I don't sell them."

"I still want one. Make me one."

"Make you a watercolor? I don't take commissions, Hayes. I do it for myself."

He did not seem altogether satisfied with that response, but he let it go and we continued on our tour. Down the corridor with the collection of mounted family photos. Most of Isabelle, a few of younger versions of me. We'd had to rearrange them all when we removed the ones with Daniel. It was not a painless process.

Hayes stopped before a black-and-white self-portrait I'd taken my senior year at Buckingham Browne & Nichols, when I was morphing from would-be ballerina to artsy Euro prep stage. An interesting phase, to be sure: long thick hair, oversized leather jacket, angst.

He reached out to touch the frame. "How old are you here?"

"Seventeen."

"Seventeen," he repeated, his finger tracing over the glass. "This. Fucking. Mouth."

I smiled up at him.

"I dream about your mouth."

"I dream about your dick. We're even."

He laughed, throwing back his head. "You can't just say things like that to me. And then . . . Okay, hurry up and show me the rest of the house."

We proceeded down the corridor, Hayes pausing at a photograph of me dancing with the Boston Ballet School, back when classes six days a week did not seem so insane. "How old?"

"Fifteen."

"Wow."

And then coming to a complete standstill before a shot of me, seven months pregnant with Isabelle, on the beach in Kona. He was silent as he pulled me into him, my back against his chest, his chin on my shoulder. We remained like that for a few moments, neither of us speaking, until he moved his hand over my belly, holding it there.

"You are so beautiful."

"Don't." I pushed his hand away. "Don't do that."

"Oh-kay . . . What . . . what am I doing?"

"Don't do the baby-fantasy thing with me."

"Is that what I was doing?" He sounded so confused I almost felt sorry for him.

"That's where it was heading."

"Oh-kay," he repeated. "I'm sorry."

He dropped it, which was wise. Because if I allowed myself to entertain any of the numerous paths I thought he might be taking in his head, I most likely would have asked him to leave and not ever come back. I could not stomach the weight of that just yet. The idea that with us there could be no happy ending.

Our tour continued: my office, the guest room, Isabelle's bedroom. My daughter was going through a Hollywood Regency phase with her fuzzy throw pillows and ornate lighting fixtures. It was all white lacquer and fuchsia with metallic accents and Moroccan poufs.

"I know this is surprising, but I haven't been in many thirteen-year-old girls' rooms," Hayes said, nosing around.

"That's probably a good thing."

Isabelle had a couple of framed graphic prints on her wall, pretty pink posters that read "For Like Ever" and "Keep Calm and Carry On." But above her desk, tacked up to the busy bulletin board, were no fewer than half a dozen pics of August Moon and the band's calendar. Her photo from the meet-and-greet was sitting on her night table.

Hayes spotted it, exhaling deeply.

"Weird, right?"

He nodded and then turned to me. "We've fucked up royally, haven't we?"

"Yeah. So now you know what I'm dealing with."

"I'm sorry. It's slightly different from this perspective."

"You think?"

"Yeah." He plopped himself down on the bed and lay back, his head on the fuzzy pink pillows. "Fuck. This is going to be ugly."

"Yes, it is."

"She'll be there tomorrow evening? What are we telling her?"

"That you're my client. That you're a friend. That's it."

"She's going to buy that?"

"Let's hope so." Daniel's words were weighing on me.

Hayes was quiet for a second, his eyes searching mine. "Why haven't you told her, Solène? You're feeling guilty . . ."

I said nothing. Guilt did not scratch the surface.

"Are you trying to protect her? Or are you protecting yourself?"

"Both of us, maybe."

The corner of his mouth curled slightly, more sorrow than smile. "Do you feel like if you just wait long enough this will be over, and you'll get away with not saying anything at all?"

"I suppose that's a possibility, isn't it?"

He held my gaze, serious. "I'm still very much here . . ."

"So it appears . . ."

"Come here," he said, tapping the duvet beside him.

My expression was beyond incredulous. There was not a chance in hell I was going to lie on Isabelle's bed with Hayes. "Absolutely not."

"Sorry." He sat up. "I suppose that's awkward."

The doorbell rang. I had not been expecting anyone. "All of it's awkward. I'll be back in a sec."

There was a fine art delivery service at the gate. I recognized them from the gallery. I had not arranged to have anything shipped, but Marchand Raphel was on the work order, so I signed for the package and led the two handlers in. The guys carefully positioned the large piece against one of the walls in the living room and cut away the cardboard packaging at my request. Josephine's name was on the attached paperwork, but when the tableau was finally revealed my heart leapt. There, in my living room, was Ailynne Cho's *Unclose Me*.

I began to shake.

"Hayes!"

It took him a moment to appear from the corridor, an impish grin on his face.

"Did you do this? Is this from you?"

"You said it was the one piece you loved."

I nodded, and then, unexpectedly, I began to cry.

Hayes saw the embarrassed handlers to the door, and then returned to me, holding me in his arms. "Shhh." He was kissing the side of my face. "It's just art, Solène," he teased.

I laughed. Through the tears and the waves of emotion and the realization that what he'd done was huge, I laughed.

"Thank you. You didn't have to do this."

"I know that. But I couldn't give up the opportunity to make you feel—what was it you said?—'everything.'"

My heart was melting. "You."

"Me?"

"This is why they love you, isn't it?"

"Who?"

"Everyone."

He smiled. "Yes, everyone."

I stood there for some time, losing myself in the seductive image. The garden, the woman, the light. The rush, the idea that it was mine. The realization: this was what it was like to be high, on art.

Hayes made his way back to the walls of glass to admire the vista. The sun was beginning to lower, casting the room in an apricot light. "Are you happy?"

"I think you know the answer to that."

"Good," he said. His eyes were still on the water, but I'd heard the change in his voice.

"When do you have to pick up Isabelle?"

"Six. We have a while."

I watched him stroll across the room.

"Is this a midcentury dining table?" he asked, his finger running along the lines of the oblong Arne Vodder. I'd got it in the divorce—the furniture, the house. Daniel got the cottage on the Vineyard. And Eva.

"It is."

"It's nice," he said.

"Glad you like it." I made my way to him at the table's head, where he was once again gazing out at the view: the lawn, the sky, the sea, the dipping sun.

Hayes reached for my hand, and then, without warning, twisted my arm, turning me away from him. He did not speak, letting my wrist loose and placing his palm firmly at the center of my back, folding me until I was bent completely over the table, the rosewood smooth and cool against my cheek.

He took his time.

His hands: climbing the sides of my thighs, lifting my skirt, peeling off my underwear. I could hear him unfastening his belt, unzipping his jeans, and then the maddening lull. My eyes were on the Cho piece, the colors blurring, evocative, while I anticipated the crinkle of the wrapper. It did not come. I felt him against me suddenly: hot, swollen.

"You're not wearing a condom."

"I'm not."

I lifted my head to look back at him, but did not speak.

"I made a choice," he said. His words sat in the air, heavy.

I didn't stop him when he slid it in. Thick, smooth, deep. The feel of him, unadorned, raw, sent me spinning. Hayes, filling me. He pulled out for a moment and waited, teasing, before gliding it back in, slow. Deeper. And then withdrawing again.

The third time he did it, he spoke, low, "Do you want me to put one on?"

"No."

"You sure?"

I could feel him at the opening, tempting. *Fuck. Me.*

"Yes."

"Good," he said, and then drove his dick in so hard and so fast, I bruised my cheekbone against the table.

In the middle of it—with his hands gripping my hips and the sound of his balls slapping up against my skin—I had the thought that perhaps this table had experienced this before. Some Danish 1950s housewife, her pale thighs banging along the smooth edge, making the most of the Scandinavian design, with a casserole in the oven and the kids upstairs in the playroom.

Hayes's hand was in my hair, yanking my head up from the table. His breath hot on my neck, his teeth on my shoulder, his dick so deep it hurt. His arm wrapped around my ribs then, his fingers grabbing me through my blouse. And just the sight of the veins in his forearm, his watch, his rings, the size of his hand, was enough. I was done.

After, when he'd collapsed atop me and I was once again lying with my face on the cool rosewood, so close I could count the striations in the buffed grain, I had the realization: this was what it was like to be fucked, on art.

———

Joanna Garel was a Filipina model turned actress turned fine artist whose Pop Art–influenced pieces centered on Los Angeles beach culture. She'd created a series of iconic lifeguard towers in mixed media that was the basis of *Sea Change*, her first solo exhibition at Marchand Raphel. The turnout was impressive. Even before my boybander was added to the equation.

That night the gallery overflowed with Joanna's photogenic multiracial family and model friends and an eclectic mix of our usual diverse clientele. And to me, it was the most lively, colorful crowd anywhere on our stretch of La Cienega. At some point early in the evening I hugged Lulit and thanked her again for birthing this idea. The desire to shake things up.

Hayes arrived to what I hoped was little commotion. I had told Isabelle that he was planning to attend, but to not set her mind on it. And yet still she spent countless hours on the phone with Georgia and Rose, scheming about what they were going to wear (jeans, not dresses) and how they were going to act (cultured, not crazy) and where they would all gather after for a full postmortem (Georgia's for a sleepover, which I encouraged for obvious reasons).

I knew he was there before he'd made his presence known. I sensed it: atoms shifting, heightened excitement, a variation in the volume. People change when they're around celebrities. First they become quiet and murmur among themselves. Then they talk louder as if they want to be overheard. They become bubbly and jovial and terribly witty. I'd seen it at Starbucks with Ben and Jen, and at the premiere for a film Daniel worked on with Will Smith. I'd seen it at SoulCycle and at yoga and Pilates. I'd seen it at Whole Foods. This kind of bizarre, forced "see, we're just like you, our lives are just like yours" behavior. But I never imagined someone so close to me would inspire it.

"Mom, he's here, he's here, Hayes is here." Isabelle found me in the kitchen, where I'd been instructing one of our servers.

"Did you say hi?"

"No, I didn't say hi. He won't know who I am. I can't just go up to him and remind him I met him once, that's so embarrassing. Please come and reintroduce us."

"I'll be right there," I promised. If she'd had any idea that only yesterday he'd been lying on her bed, she would have died.

She led me to him, in the front room, where the crowd was thickening. Where chatter was loud and wine was being swilled and Georgia and Rose were lurking off to the side, trying to play it cool while waiting for their introduction. Lulit was showing him one of Joanna's pieces: a bold lifeguard tower, shadowed by Ben-Day dots in sunset colors, rendered on a large slab of wood.

I caught his eye as I approached him, and the expression on his face was pure sex, and I knew we were not going to make it through the night without one of us fucking up.

"Hi."

"Hi." He smiled.

"You came."

"I came."

Lulit smiled knowingly. "I am going to leave you two alone, yes. I have people to flatter, art to sell. Hayes, can I get you a drink? Wine? Water?"

"No, thank you. I'm fine."

"Well, if you need anything, don't be shy. Although I'm sure this woman will take good care of you."

"I don't doubt she will."

I leaned in to kiss him the second she stepped away, one of those double-sided French cheek kisses, which was something I'd never done with him before and which felt so awkward and foreign that we both started to laugh. But I could feel it: people watching him, watching *us*. Including the newly minted teenager just beyond my shoulder. The one who would later sleep at her friend's house, completely oblivious to the fact that her mother was engaging in unspeakable acts with one-fifth of the world's greatest boy band, just down the hall from her pink-and-white bedroom. Keep calm and carry on, indeed.

"Hayes, do you remember my daughter, Isabelle?"

"Isabelle. I believe I do."

"Hi, Hayes." Isabelle was divided between offering up the biggest smile of her life and hiding her braces.

"How have you been?" He hugged her, and she visibly turned to mush, her arms folding in at her sides, her hands not knowing quite where to go.

Oh, if she knew . . . If she knew . . .

"I can't believe you're here."

"I'm here." He placed his hand atop her head. "I think you're taller. Are you taller?"

She nodded, beaming up at him.

Something fluttered in my chest. Something like betrayal.

"And you brought your friends?" Hayes continued, sticking to the script.

Rose and Georgia had sidled up to us. I reintroduced them to their idol and watched as they fawned.

"Congratulations on your VMA," Georgia blurted.

"We were really hoping you would perform," Rose chimed in, flicking her red hair over her shoulder. According to Isabelle, she'd had it blown out earlier that day, signifying just what a big deal this evening was.

"They teased us and made us think you were going to be there, but you weren't really there, so it was just a whole lot of Miley."

"Ah, yes, Miley." Hayes smiled.

"My mom doesn't approve of that video," Rose said. "She says she's a bad influence and she's putting ideas in our head."

"Is that what Miley's doing? Okay, then you should probably listen to your mum. And stay away from construction sites and such."

"But it's a great song," Isabelle added.

"It is a great song."

"Are you guys still recording your album?" Georgia asked. How they managed to know everything going on in these guys' lives and still live their own was fascinating to me.

"We've just now finished it. They're still doing some mixing, but we've done our bit."

"I can't wait to hear it." Isabelle smiled, her hand hiding her mouth. The ring from Eva was twinkling on her middle finger. She had not taken it off since camp.

"I can't wait for you to hear it."

I took my cue when Georgia crossed her arms over her breasts (dear God, when had that happened?), cocked her head, and very seriously said, "So, Hayes, are you into contemporary art?"

I gathered this was all part of their "act cultured" plan and so I politely bowed out.

"I'll be wandering about, should you have any questions," I said. "If you can't find me, check my office."

He smiled, nodding. Rakish Hayes with his silk scarf, his gaggle of pubescent girls, his perfect hair, his fetching smile. "I will," he mouthed. It was a promise.

Josephine had assembled a playlist for the opening, and Ed Sheeran's blue-eyed alternative hip-hop acoustic soul pumped throughout the gallery. It was the perfect complement to Joanna's serene pieces. Pop Art done in unexpected muted shades of sun, sea, and sand.

"Your boyfriend." Lulit approached me in Gallery 2, the middle room. "Wow."

"Please don't call him that."

"He's killing me with the puppy dog eyes. The way they follow you around the room. What did you do to that poor boy?"

"I have no idea," I said, waving off a server with a passing tray. "We just . . . *click*. It's terrifying actually." I turned my body into her and away from those surveying the art. "You know why he's not drinking anything? Because he *can't*."

Lulit's eyes widened, and we both started to laugh. "Oh, Solène. That's *bad*."

"Yes, I'm aware of that. I have no idea where this is going. I'm just enjoying the ride."

"I bet you are . . . You are like the poster woman for reclaiming one's sexuality."

I laughed at that. "I didn't know I'd *disclaimed* it."

"I think it was lying dormant, and now it's back in full force. Lest anyone think we women of a certain age were no longer sexually viable."

"Yes." I smiled. "Lest anyone think that.

"I'm going to give him a few more minutes and then I'm going to save him from the girls. And then I'll get him to take some pictures, yes?"

"Yes." She nodded, stroking her neck. Her hair was pulled back, and the thin straps of her dress accentuated her delicate bones. "Daniel is going to lose his mind."

"Yes, well, Daniel fucked up, didn't he?"

I was navigating the sea of bodies filling our space when I bumped into Josephine chatting up a guest. She stopped me, grabbing my elbow.

"Great show. Great turnout."

"Yes, I'm very happy. You guys worked hard. Awesome DJ-ing, by the way."

"I made sure not to put any August Moon on the mix." She smiled.

"Probably wise."

She introduced me to the guest she'd been chatting with, an early-thirties male with a man-bun and one of those lumbersexual beards. I did a quick check of the condition of his shoes and fingernails. These days, it was getting harder to tell who the potential buyers were.

The hipster excused himself to look at a piece, and Josephine leaned into me, furtively. "I assume you got your package."

"I did. Thank you."

"He wanted to surprise you. You have no idea how difficult it was to not mention it all this time. And the look of disappointment on your face when you realized it was sold . . ."

That Saturday night in July, at the *Smoke; and Mirrors* opening, I'd noticed a mark on our master list indicating the piece had been purchased. When I asked Josephine who the buyer was, she threw out some name I'd never heard.

". . . I so wanted to tell you then."

"I'm glad you didn't."

"So," she said, sipping her Pellegrino, "I guess this means the *Access Hollywood* thing is true? I mean, you don't have to say anything. But he's *here*. And that piece was fourteen thousand dollars."

"I know how much it was. Thank you."

"And then that video in the Hamptons . . ."

I froze then. "What video?"

"TMZ. It's not . . . It wasn't a big deal. Just footage of him in an SUV with his bodyguard. And you're in the back. You're turned away from the camera. It's fuzzy, and you can't see your face, but it's your hair, and I recognized your dress. The white one with all the little buttons up the back. I love that dress."

I stood there for a moment, unable to speak. The idea that we, that I, had been caught. We weren't even doing anything. And I felt guilty.

"No one's mentioned it," Josephine said eventually.

I nodded, slow. "I appreciate your discretion. Get the guy with a bun a drink. He may buy something."

They had not moved very far. Although the number of guests who had gravitated to Hayes's general vicinity had appeared to multiply, the girls were still surrounding him. They had positioned themselves strategically before *SexWax*, Joanna's nod to Warhol's *Campbell's Soup Cans*. The canvas featured a brazen image of the popular surf wax with its iconic logo. "Mr. Zogs Sex Wax," it said. "Quick Humps, The Best for Your Stick." Lovely.

As I neared them I could see Rose tossing off a joke with her attitudinal stance, and Hayes laughing, and I feared where their conversation had turned.

"May I borrow him for a second?" My voice sounded off to me, the side effect of my worlds colliding. The revelation of TMZ. I just needed to get through the night.

"Hayes, I need to introduce you to someone. Ladies, I'll bring him right back. Promise."

Hayes excused himself graciously and followed me through the crowd.

"Sorry about the girls."

"Oh, it's fine. They're very sweet. She's very sweet, your daughter."

"Yes," I said. And then: "I hope you'll remember that when we're breaking her heart."

"Oh bollocks!" he said, which actually made me smile. "Very much looking forward to that. All right, so to whom am I being introduced?"

"No one. I just wanted you to myself for a little bit."

"Ooo, that sounds naughty."

We made our way into Gallery 2, which was marginally less crowded. I could see the artist, Joanna, across the way, radiant and ebullient, a vision in a black minidress. She was laughing loudly, the crowd in her hand.

"Okay." My attention returned to the boy a half step behind me. "Just look very serious and act like we're talking about art."

"Can we talk about this dress?" He smiled.

"No."

"Can we talk about your arse in this dress? Because that's kind of like art."

I laughed. "No, definitely not." I stopped him in front of one of the larger pieces. *Low Tide at No. 24*, acrylic on linen. "I want you to act like you really like this."

Hayes's eyes scanned the print. "Oh, I do quite like it."

"Even better. Act like you're interested in purchasing it. I'm going to go to my office and return with some information on the piece, and then you are going to follow me into my office, as if you're planning to buy it."

He nodded, slowly. "Oh-kay. I see you've thought this through."

Hayes cocked his head then, eyeing me closely. "What happened to your face?" His hand gestured toward my cheekbone.

I stood there, staring at him, looking for signs of recognition, but nothing was registering. "Really? The table."

His eyes widened and his jaw dropped, and I wasn't sure if he was going to laugh or cry. "Oh, Sol." He'd never called me that before. "Why didn't you say something?"

"It's okay. I'm fine."

"No, it's not okay. I'm sorry." He leaned in as if to kiss it.

"Don't."

"I'm sorry," he repeated. "No more tables. Promise."

"I liked the table," I said, and then turned and walked away.

Minutes later we were in my office, the door securely locked.

"Now can we discuss this dress?" He did not waste time, his hands moving over the material, my waist, my hips, my ass.

It was a clingy jersey halter dress in smoke gray. Paired with my four-inch black Alaïa Bombe "fuck me" sandals with the embellished ankle strap. He did not stand a chance.

"What is it you wanted to say about it?"

"It's very . . . nice," he said, lowering his mouth to mine, his hand traveling up over my abdomen and reaching in the top of the halter.

"I did not bring you in here to do this."

"Didn't you?"

"No. I just wanted to smell you."

"Really?" He smiled. "Just smell me? That's all?" His mouth was on my breast. I could hear voices outside the door. Ed Sheeran: "Don't."

"You. Are like a fucking drug. Hayes Campbell."

He pulled away after a minute and stepped back, smiling like the Cheshire cat. "Go ahead. Smell me, then."

I took the opportunity to inhale him. His neck, his throat, his ridiculous silk scarf. I reached into his perpetually unbuttoned shirt and ran my hands over his smooth chest, his perfect erect nipples. I could live here.

"I have gum," he said.

"Gum, but no condoms."

He smiled then, sheepishly. "I have condoms."

"You have condoms *here*?"

He nodded.

"Yesterday, then . . . Were you just testing me?"

"I was *enjoying* you."

It hit me intensely, the memory of it. The feel of him.

There was laughter in the corridor. Familiar. It might have been Matt.

He leaned into me then and whispered in my ear. "Can I just bend you over this desk, please? For like a second?"

It was not like him to ask.

I looked at him as if he were crazy. And then I heard myself say: "You have two minutes."

"I can be done in two minutes." He smiled.

"Do *not* get anything on my dress."

"Won't. Promise."

Six minutes later we were back out in the gallery and no one was the wiser. At least I wanted to believe that.

"Will you do me a huge favor?" I asked him as we made our way into the crowd. "There's a photographer here from Getty. I would love to get a shot of you with Joanna. But if you feel uncomfortable doing that, I completely understand."

I hated asking him. I hated everything it insinuated. I did not want him to think for one second that I was taking advantage of our relationship and his celebrity to sell art.

"Solène." He grabbed my wrist then, pulling me into him. "Why wouldn't I do that for you?"

I turned to look at him, aware that he was touching me in this very public space. The boy who I had just let fuck me in the office.

"I came here for you, right?"

"You came here for me. You didn't come here for Marchand Raphel."

"I came here for *you*," he repeated. "And last I checked, that was a huge part of you."

We shot him along with Joanna and her husband before *Low Tide at No. 24*. Hayes insisted on there being a third person in the photograph because Joanna was "far too beautiful" for him to be pictured alone with her.

"They'll assume I'm sleeping with her," he had said when I questioned his reasoning.

"What? Who are 'they'?"

"The press. The fans. The world."

"She's like twice your age, Hayes."

"Yes, well, clearly that doesn't stop me, right?" He smiled, salacious, chewing his gum. "Do you want to sell art, or do you want a scandal?"

Evidently, Hayes knew what he was doing.

Joanna's husband was a chiseled Jamaican-Chinese model who had apparently spent some time at the gym and whose dimples rivaled those of Hayes. It only sweetened the photo op.

The photographer, Stephanie, posted a dozen photos of them on Getty Images the evening of the opening. By Sunday, they'd been picked up by numerous sources, including *Hollywood Life* and the *Daily Mail*, and by the following week they'd run in *Us Weekly*, *People*, *Star*, *OK!*, and *Hello!*. By then, our *Sea Change* show had long sold out. And the demand for Joanna's work had far exceeded any of our expectations.

paris

In October, there was Paris.

Lulit and I went each year for the FIAC art fair, which typically overlapped with my birthday. When Hayes proposed to join us, I did not decline. That he was so intent on making it memorable awed me. The way he scheduled his TAG Heuer photo shoot to coincide. The way he booked the penthouse at the Four Seasons Hotel George V and insisted I stay with him instead of at the apartment in the 17th that we typically rented. The way he upgraded my and Lulit's tickets from business class to first without either of us being the wiser—a lovely surprise greeting us at the Air France check-in. "I wanted you to be well rested when you arrived," he cooed later, over Dom Pérignon in our hotel room. It was the most indulgent working holiday that I could recall, filled with wine and art and turning leaves. And like all time spent with Hayes, it passed too quickly.

He arrived from London Tuesday evening, hours after I did, having just returned from four days in the Dolomites, where the guys were shooting the music video for "Sorrowed Talk," their planned first release from *Wise or Naked*.

"I've missed you, I've missed you, I've missed you," he gushed. He was lying beside me, postcoital, propped up on one elbow, his fingers tracing my cheekbone.

And to me, it was clear: he was falling.

"I can't do these long breaks. I think you're going to have to quit your job, sell your gallery, and just travel around with me for the next few years."

I laughed at that. "And what am I supposed to do with my daughter?"

He shrugged, smiling. "Daniel? Boarding school? I suppose we could always get her a room, hire her a proper tutor . . ."

"Yes, that sounds doable."

"Truly. What thirteen-year-old girl wouldn't want to come on tour with August Moon?"

"What mother in her right mind would allow her thirteen-year-old girl to go on tour with August Moon?"

"Hmm . . . Point taken."

I saw Isabelle's face clearly then as she bade me farewell the previous morning. Her wide blue eyes, her sweet smile. Clueless. She'd made me a card: "Have the Happiest Birthday ever!"

And I knew, no matter how delicately the news was delivered, it was going to shatter her.

I was going to shatter her.

Hayes was smiling, his fingers outlining my lips. "So plan A, then . . . Daniel? That's not an option, I take it?"

"That's not an option."

"What if I quit the band?"

His voice was soft, so soft I was afraid to acknowledge it. For a moment, the two of us lay there in silence. The question hanging in the air. And then, without saying more, he rolled into me, kissing the corners of my mouth, his hand at my neck, my throat.

"I need more of you."

"I don't know that there's more of me to give."

"That's not a good enough answer."

I smiled, my legs wrapping around his waist, my hands in his hair. "What is it you want from me, then?"

He positioned himself. We'd become lax with the condoms. "Everything."

I spent all Wednesday with Lulit on the second floor of the Grand Palais, where our booth was situated for the Foire Internationale d'Art Contemporain. The VIP viewings began at ten a.m., and from that moment on our day was jammed with esteemed collectors and dignitaries, the crème de la crème of the art world. Each visitor slightly more fabulous and well-heeled than the next, speaking myriad languages, all slightly high in the presence of art. And once again I was reminded why I loved what I did. Because to be surrounded by such varied, intriguing types—to be a part of a community where it was admired for bending, nay, *expected* to bend the rules—was, for me, to be at home.

Hayes spent his day in a studio shooting portraits with a watch.

On day two of the fair, the first day it was open to the public and no fewer than 18,000 visitors filed through, Hayes's shoot ended early, and he surprised me by dropping by the Grand Palais shortly after five. In a world of iPhones and texts, it was such a shock to see him pop into our booth unannounced, it took a full three seconds to register who this handsome stranger was, and it made me wonder how others saw him. His notable height, his hair, his eyes, his jaw, his broad mouth; black jeans, black boots, and a three-quarter-length dark suede coat. Even if he weren't famous, he'd be difficult to overlook. And the fact that for this moment he was mine . . .

"What are you doing here?"

"I wanted to see what you do when I'm not with you . . . And I thought perhaps you might like some macarons." He smiled, proffering a Ladurée bag.

I hugged him then. Tightly. And in that brief moment I did not care who saw us. Or what they might have thought. "You know, you're acting suspiciously like a boyfriend."

He laughed at that. "As opposed to . . . ?"

"As opposed to someone who just 'really, really, *really*' enjoys my company."

"Ha!"

Lulit approached us from across the booth where she'd been communicating with a Chinese collector. "Well, to what do we owe this great honor?" She kissed him in the double-sided French way, and with her it did not look awkward.

"I thought I'd see what the hullabaloo was about."

"But the lines must be crazy. Did they make you wait in line?"

Hayes shook his head, an amused expression on his face. As if he'd ever in his life had to wait in line for anything.

"Thank you, again, for your very generous upgrade."

"You're quite welcome. And I brought macarons. You're to share them." That last part he directed at me.

"You're not rushing off, are you?"

There had been nonstop foot traffic at the fair all day, but that late in the afternoon there was a bit of a lull and so I offered to give Hayes a quick tour, starting with our booth: the canvases by Nira Ramaswami, the sculptures by Kenji Horiyama, the mixed-media works by Pilar Anchorena. At turns haunting, inspired, political.

Anders Sørensen, our long-standing art preparator who was responsible for installing our fair booths, had flown in from Oslo at the beginning of the week to set up. We'd sold seven pieces alone during the private viewing, and Anders had already rotated out the sold works and reinstalled the booth. If we managed to sell all eighteen pieces that we'd shipped for FIAC, it would be a banner week. I explained all this to Hayes.

"So your mission here is to sell as much art as possible?"

"It's not just about the sales." We were circling the corridors of the second floor, surveying the other midsized galleries. "The fairs are an opportunity to make connections, see what new artists are emerging, how their work is being received. And it's great exposure for our artists and the gallery. Not all those who apply get in."

"Who decides where they put your booth?"

"There's a committee. The larger, blue-chip galleries are always on the main floor. Better foot traffic."

"Is that something you aspire to? A larger gallery?"

I smiled up at him. I loved that he had questions. I loved that he cared.

Daniel had never been fond of the art world. The proverbial camel's back had broken four years earlier at MOCA's annual gala, *The Artist's Museum Happening*, where he was content to schmooze with the likes of Brian Grazer and Eli Broad but had little desire to peruse the actual exhibit. When I'd asked him what he thought of the show, he'd swilled his wine and said it was "overrated and self-indulgent," and I wondered how I'd managed to marry someone so fundamentally different from me. I'd spent that evening fighting back tears and knowing it was over.

"I kind of like where we are," I said to Hayes now. "If we had an operation like that, we'd have additional gallery spaces in New York, London, Paris, or Japan. Not so easy to manage as a single mom."

He thought about that for a moment but said nothing.

We descended to the main level. There was so much I wanted to show him, so many spaces and bodies to navigate, that even in three-inch Saint Laurent booties, I was moving fast.

"Don't lose me," he said at one point, reaching for my hand. But when he gauged my reluctance, he dropped it and laughed. "We're going to discuss this eventually. But just . . . don't lose me. There are a lot of people here."

"I won't. Promise."

There *were* a lot of people, although very few in his target audience and so I assumed he would be safe. But I did not know what it felt like to be him, to imagine that at any moment the throng could change and that panic might ensue, especially in the absence of a Desmond or a Fergus. I had no clue what it was to live with that reality.

I slowed my pace and walked beside him, and tried not to think about how people perceived us. Assuming they were paying attention at all. But the thought occurred that maybe we did not have to be holding hands. Maybe our chemistry was palpable enough.

"Are you going to show me what you love?" he asked.

"I'm going to show you what I love."

I led him to two stunning works by Danish-Icelandic artist Olafur Eliasson. *The New Planet*, a large rotating steel-and-colored-glass oloid. And *Dew Viewer*, a cluster of myriad silver crystal spheres creating multiple reflections. Both mesmerizing, memorable.

"There's quite a lot of us in there," Hayes whispered into my ear before the *Dew Viewer* installation. "All the little Hayeses and Solènes . . . like two hundred, at least."

"At least."

"I like us multiplied," he said, soft.

"I'm not sure what you're insinuating."

"Nothing." He smiled. "Nothing at all."

On the way back through the main corridor, we popped into Gagosian, where I introduced Hayes to my friend Amara Winthrop. It was Amara I'd met for breakfast at the Peninsula the morning August Moon did the *Today* show and made me and everyone else in midtown Manhattan fifteen minutes late. But if she recognized him there in the Grand Palais, she did not let on. Even though I'd used his first and last name and presented him as my "friend." Not my "client." I was trying it on for size.

"You're looking fabulous, as usual."

I watched as Amara reconstructed her chignon. She wore a fitted peplum blazer over a pencil skirt. The tailoring impeccable, likely British. In grad school, she was the blonde from Bedford Hills who'd intimidated us all.

"Yes . . . well, you know the drill: multiple degrees, and it still all comes down to your legs. But must sell art, right?"

I smiled at that. Lulit and I had lamented the same on numerous occasions. "Yes. Must sell art."

"You're still coming to dinner tonight, yes?"

"I am."

"Dinner?" Hayes cocked his head.

"I told you about it. It's my one business dinner this week."

"I think I conveniently forgot."

There were two young women, early twenties, circling one of the John Chamberlain sculptures near the front of the booth. It was clear to me they'd recognized Hayes, as they'd kept sneaking looks in our direction. Hayes managed to ignore it.

"She keeps abandoning me," he told Amara. Which pretty much laid out . . . everything.

She took a second to compute and then responded, "Well, then, you should come."

He looked to me, a wry smile forming. "Maybe I'll do that."

"*Pardon.*" One of the young women finally made her approach. "*Excusez-moi, c'est possible de prendre une photo?* We can take a picture?"

"*De l'art? Oui, bien sûr,*" Amara replied.

"*Non. De lui. Avec Hayes.*" She had that adorable way the French had of not pronouncing the *H.* "You can take a picture with us, 'Ayes, please?"

Hayes obliged them, while Amara looked on, visibly confused. And when he returned to the conversation with "So, tonight . . ." as if posing for photos with total strangers who knew his name was not completely out of the ordinary, Amara stopped him.

"Oh. You're somebody, aren't you?"

"Somebody? Yes." He smiled.

"Okay, I'll figure it out. But yes, you should come. It's a fun bunch. Bring him." She turned to me before looking back toward my "somebody." "Make her bring you."

We had a late reservation at Market on Avenue Matignon. There were ten of us, and they gave us the large table in the back room. It was secluded, sleek, warmly lit. And following a dalliance and a shower at the hotel, I was happy Hayes had joined us. I feared he might be slightly out of his element. But surely all that fine breeding and three years as a world-class celebrity had to amount to something.

When we were still dressing at the George V, I received an amusing text from Amara:

Just googled your boy toy. WTF? How'd you swing that???
If you don't want to come out with us old artsy-fartsy types,
I will totes understand. I probably wouldn't either. But I'm
going to need details later. Many. Xoxo

But at the restaurant, she maintained her discretion. It was a lively group: Amara; Lulit; Christophe Servan-Schreiber, who owned galleries in Paris and London; the painter Serge Cassel, one of Christophe's artists; Laura and Bruno Piagetti, collectors from Milan; Jean-René Lavigne, who was with Gagosian's Paris outpost; Mary Goodmark, an art consultant from London; and us.

There was more wine than I could keep track of, and we were loud. The Italians especially. Hayes and I sat on the banquette side of the table, our backs to the window, flanked by Christophe, Lulit, and Serge. He managed to hold my hand the entire night. And I did not stop him.

"So how do you know Solène?" Christophe asked my date. We'd been there for the better part of an hour and were working our way through the shared appetizers: scallop tartare with black truffles and black-truffle-and-fontina pizza. Half of the table was discussing the sale of an Anish Kapoor the previous day for an alleged two million dollars. The others were trading war stories of art fairs past, Mary and Jean-René filling us in on what we'd missed at Frieze London. Which left Hayes fielding questions from the revered art dealer.

He grinned, turning toward me. "Solène"—his voice was deep, raspy, full of innuendo—"how do I know you?"

His fingers slipped between my knees then, and I could feel myself getting wet. It took so little with him.

He smiled and turned back toward Christophe. "We're very good friends."

"Are you a student?"

"No," he laughed.

"An artist?"

Hayes shook his head. "A budding collector."

"Have you seen anything special yet at the fair?"

"Hmm." Hayes contemplated for a bit, and I feared he'd retained nothing from this afternoon. "The Basquiats were particularly compelling," he said finally. "Angry, deranged. But he always seems to be that way, doesn't he? His demons evident in his work.

"There were a couple pieces in Solène's booth by Nira Ramaswami that I was quite keen on. Very poetic. Melancholy. And the Olafur Eliasson installations. You could lose yourself in those. Truly . . ."

If I could have buried myself in his lap and sucked his dick right then and there, I would have. Who was this person, and what had he done with my art neophyte? At best, I had expected him to regurgitate some of my interpretations, but these were all his own thoughts.

"Sì, mi piace molto. I love this, the Basquiat," Laura spoke up from across the table. "How you can feel . . . il dolore. Come si dice?" She turned to Bruno beside her, her black bob swinging. Laura had alabaster skin and generous lips. She wore a gorgeous tomato-red dress, its deep neckline showcasing her swan-like throat.

"Pain," Bruno said. He was older than Laura, more salt than pepper, with a distinct jaw and a villa on Lake Como.

"*Sì*. You feel the pain. I love."

"I don't need to feel the pain," Lulit contributed. "I appreciate that most artists are a little crazy—no offense, Serge—but I don't always need to feel that in the work. Sometimes I just want to look at it and be happy."

"Like Murakami," I said, "in certain doses."

"Like Murakami, yes." She smiled. "There's so much negativity in the world, sometimes I need art to just lift me."

Hayes was swishing his Cabernet Sauvignon around in his glass, in a manner that was slow, hypnotic. "Maybe there *is* pain in Murakami's work, but we just don't feel it because it's his minions who carry out his genius."

We all turned to look at him then, intrigued.

"What is it you do?" Christophe asked. He had one of those accents you could not quite put your finger on. A French father, British mother, Swiss boarding schools. An international soup, quite common in the art world.

"I'm a singer-songwriter. I'm in a band."

"What kind of music?"

"Pop, mostly."

Serge, Jean-René, and Lulit had continued on the negativity thread and begun discussing the disturbing rise of anti-Semitism in France over the past year and the large number of Jewish people who were migrating as a result.

"*C'est horrible*," Jean-René said, leaning in from his far end of the table. "*C'est vachement triste, et ça va continuer à se dégrader, c'est sûr. Si personne ne fait rien, ne dit rien . . . On va attendre jusqu'à quand? Comme la fois précédente? Non, pas question!*"

"Pop music, that's nice," Christophe continued, ignoring the weight of the conversation at hand. "And do you have gigs?"

"I do. We do." Hayes nodded.

"And do you play . . . what . . . like clubs?"

Amara spoke up from across the table. "Oh, Christophe, he's

humoring you. Hayes is in that pop group August Moon. They've sold a gazillion albums and have quite a following. Of teenage girls mostly."

"That *is* you! I thought it was you!" Mary nearly spit out her wine. "I saw you boys on *Graham Norton* the other day. You were *so* charming. You made all the girls *so* happy. My nieces are going to flip."

"Really?" Christophe was amused. "Are you famous? Is he famous, Solène?" He leaned across to me.

"In certain circles," I said, squeezing my date's hand.

"But clearly not this one," Hayes laughed.

"Boy bands are like the Murakami of the music world." Amara grinned, pleased with her observation. "No one focuses on the pain behind the genius. We can just look at you and be happy . . ."

Hayes contorted his face for a moment. "In certain doses?"

"In all doses." She smiled.

"Thank you for that. That was awfully kind. I think . . ."

She nodded, sipping from her Vittel. "There's a lot of good in what you do. You wouldn't have that following otherwise. I mean teen girls and all their angst and craziness, that is the most difficult age to make happy . . ."

"Besides middle-aged women," Mary added.

"Besides middle-aged women," Amara laughed, "and you've clearly cornered the market."

"No pressure," he chuckled.

I squeezed his hand again. It was good for him to hear that his art was appreciated, especially in this judgmental crowd. Although, in truth, it probably should have come from me.

"And how do you know so much about art?" Christophe continued.

Hayes smiled, his hand sliding to my knee again. "I have an exceptional teacher . . ."

I could not get him home fast enough. I could blame it on the wine, on Paris, on him spouting informed opinions on Murakami and Basquiat, but in the end it might have just been the knowledge of what he was capable of. Of the magic I felt when I was with him.

"You were *so* charming, Hayes. You made all the girls *so* happy . . ."

We were in the elevator en route to the eighth floor when I quoted Mary, pressed fully against him, my mouth on his neck.

"I did. I *do*."

"Why don't you show me . . . how you make the girls so happy?"

He chuckled, salacious. "Here?"

"Here." My hand slipped in the opening of his coat, finding his belt.

"No."

"No?" It was not a word I was used to hearing from him.

"There are cameras here."

I looked up into the corners of the elevator. He was right. And it struck me, the idea that I'd never given them much thought, and that Hayes had a very different awareness of privacy.

"I assume you don't want your daughter seeing how I make you happy."

"No. Probably not."

"Are there cameras *here*?" I asked when we'd reached our floor and were approaching the door to the penthouse.

He was fumbling in his pockets for the key card. "Typically, yes."

"That's too bad, then." My hands found their way back to his belt, quickly unfastening it, the clasp of his pants, his zipper.

"Fuck," he laughed, grabbing my wrist. "Was it something I said? Was it the truffles?"

"Yes." My fingers slid into the front of his pants. Hayes and his perfect dick. "The truffles."

"Fuck," he repeated, closing his eyes. We remained there for a moment, in front of our closed door, me jerking him off in our semi-private hallway of the George V. Cameras be damned.

"You're going to get us into trouble."

"*I* am?"

"*You* are." He stopped me finally, brandishing the key card and pulling me inside.

Hayes shut the door behind us and threw me up against the wall, hard. "Where were we?"

"Truffles."

"Truffles." His mouth was on mine as he wrestled off my coat. His hands moving over the surface of my dress, hiking up the hem.

"I wasn't done."

"Weren't you?"

I shook my head, freeing myself from his grip, dropping to my knees in the narrow foyer.

We didn't even make it to the living room.

"Bloody hell . . ." His hands were in my hair, his coat still on, his pants around his calves. Hayes, in his happy place.

But as much as I'd come to adore his reaction, as much as I'd come to adore *him*, I hated that the act gave me so much time to think. And always my mind went to dark places. What the hell was I doing with someone so young? And how in God's name had I ended up here, on my knees in a five-star hotel, sucking some guy in a boy band's dick? And dear Lord, please don't ever let my daughter do this. The things you never see coming.

"Fuck, fuck, fuck, Solène." He stopped me before he came, pulling me up from the floor and pinning me once again to the wall. "Is this what Paris does to you? We're going to need to come here more often . . ."

"I'm okay with that."

"I can tell," he slurred, his fingers sliding into my panties, sliding into me, easy. "Fu-uck."

"That's an awful lot of 'fucks.' Even for you."

He smiled, peeling off my underwear. "Are you counting?"

"Maybe."

"Don't."

He did three things seemingly at once then—lifted me off the floor, thrust his dick inside me, and placed his wet fingers in my mouth—and suffice it to say, I forgot every dark thought I had had two minutes prior.

Somewhere in the throes of it, with my arms around his neck and my legs around his waist and my dress twisted and bunched around my torso, I came to the realization that in all our years together Daniel had never fucked me like this. Not even in the beginning. He wasn't this strong, he wasn't this big, he wasn't this uninhibited, and he certainly wasn't this passionate. And I got the feeling that for all Hayes and I had already done, there was still so much more of him he had yet to reveal.

We came. And I had a vague awareness of hearing myself cry out and him pressing his fingers against my lips before we fell to the floor.

"Fuck." He was laughing, lying prostrate in the foyer. His pants still around his ankles, his coat and shirt and boots still on.

"What's so funny?" I crawled on top of him to kiss his dimples, to feel his warmth.

"*You*. You. Are. *Loud*. Mrs. 'I've Never Been a Screaming Girl.'"

I was still catching my breath. "Did I say that?"

He nodded, his eyes closed. "In New York. At the Four Seasons."

"How do you remember that?"

"I told you: I remember everything."

He was quiet for a moment, his hand playing in my hair.

"And now I'm always going to remember how much fucking noise you made at the Four Seasons in Paris."

I laughed. "Great."

He nodded again, drowsy. "It *was* great. It was *better* than great. I like you loud. Happy Early Birthday, Solène Marchand . . ." He drifted off for a second, and when I kissed him, he whispered, "I'm falling in love with you. I'm just going to put that out there, because I can. Because you told me I couldn't if I was sleeping with anyone else, and I'm not, so there you have it . . ."

"Shhh." I put my finger over his mouth. "You're talking in your sleep."

"I'm not sleeping," he said, his eyes still closed.

We were quiet for a long time, there on the floor, until I could feel his semen seeping out of me, dripping between my thighs. All the little Hayeses and Solènes . . .

"How do you suddenly know so much about art, Hayes?"

For a moment he didn't respond, and I was certain he'd passed out, but then he smiled, faint. "I read a book."

"You read a book?"

He nodded. "*Seven Days in the Art World.* I thought I should probably learn something about what you do . . ."

And in that instant I was thankful that he was half asleep. Because asleep, he could not see me cry.

On Sunday, after two full days of killing time, Hayes became restless.

"Please stay," he begged from his position strewn across the bed, where he was watching me dress for my fifth and final day at the fair.

It was a quarter after eleven, and I had to be at the Grand Palais by noon. "You'll have me all day tomorrow. Promise."

"Not good enough. I want you now."

I laughed, zipping my skirt. "Again?"

He smiled, resting his cheek on his folded arms, his hair fluffy and in disarray, a pair of black Calvin Klein boxer briefs his only attire. "I just want to be around you. Don't go. Please."

I finished putting on my earrings and Hayes's borrowed watch before making my way over to him, cradling his face in my hands. "You are very, very, very irresistible. You know this. But I have to work. Please respect that."

He lay there, allowing me to muss his hair and kiss his lips, without responding.

"I'll text you later, okay? Okay?"

He nodded. This was Hayes, vulnerable.

That afternoon the Grand Palais felt slightly more cavernous than usual, and I could sense it in the air: the end of a beautiful thing. We had two pieces remaining unsold, and Lulit and I were already talking about Miami in December. The installation, the parties . . . It wasn't quite half past three when I looked up to find Hayes striding into our booth.

"Do you know what today is?" he began the conversation. No greeting, no kiss.

Lulit and I exchanged looks.

"Sunday? October twenty-sixth? The last day of the fair?"

"It's the last day of your thirties," he said.

"Shhh," Lulit laughed. "No one says that stuff out loud."

"Sorry. It's true . . ." He paused while a French couple who'd been admiring one of the Kenji Horiyama sculptures exited the booth. "So . . ." he continued, making his way over to me, "I'm taking her."

"You're what?" Lulit said.

"I'm taking her," Hayes repeated, his hand encircling my wrist. "May I take her? I'm taking her."

"Hayes, I'm working."

"She's working."

"It's your birthday, it's *Paris*." His angelic face broke my heart just a little.

"I know and I appreciate that, but we have all day tomorrow. We have tonight."

"If I buy something, will that make a difference?" His eyes were scanning the walls.

"I don't want you to do that."

"What if I want to do that?"

"I don't want you to do that," I repeated.

Lulit caught my eye then, and the expression I read on her face left me cold. She was entertaining his offer. Knowing full well that he would go to extremes to close the deal. Her eyes said it all: *Go. Sell. Art. To rich white men.*

"No." I shook my head.

"What's still available?" He turned to Lulit. "She said there were still two left. Which ones are they?"

"There's a Ramaswami. And one of Kenji's sculptures."

"Which Ramaswami?" he asked, and Lulit gestured accordingly.

Nira Ramaswami's work, typically oil on canvas, detailed the plight of women in her native India. Forlorn figures in fields, young girls at the side of a road, trusting brides on their wedding day. Stirring, passionate, dark eyes and solemn faces. They had always been compelling, but the Delhi gang rape in December 2012 brought about a surge of interest in the subject matter and she was suddenly in high demand.

"This one?" Hayes's eyes lit up. "I like this one."

Sabina in the Mango Tree.

"It's not cheap."

"How not cheap is it?"

"Sixty," Lulit said assertively.

"Thousand?"

"Thousand. Euro."

"Fuck." Hayes paused. His eyes going from Lulit to the painting. Of all Nira's pieces in the fair, it was the most uplifting, hopeful.

His hand was still encircling my wrist. "If I buy it, will you let me take her?"

"No. Hayes, do *not*. I'll be done at eight."

"Will you let me take her?" he repeated to Lulit.

She inclined her head, ever so subtly.

"Good. Done."

"Hayes, you're being ridiculous. I'm not going to let you do this."

"Solène. It's already done."

I stood there, stunned. "This feels a little like slavery. White slavery."

"Except I'm buying your freedom, I'm not buying your services. Don't overthink it."

We made our way through the throngs on the first floor and out onto the street, Hayes leading me by the hand the entire time. It felt so open and obvious, and all I could think was how the European art world would be talking about the fact that I'd abandoned my partner to engage in a patently inappropriate affair.

There were girls when we stepped out next to the Champs-Élysées. Many. It was Sunday afternoon, after all. And when Hayes took a moment to don his sunglasses and a gray knitted cap, I stepped away from him and crossed my arms.

"Are you just going to pretend we're not together?" he asked as we made our way to the taxi queue.

I laughed, uneasy. I did not want a TMZ repeat.

"Whatever."

There was a family in line ahead of us with two young daughters and a son. They recognized Hayes immediately and after much squealing and cooing in Japanese, they wrangled a photo out of him. As usual, he was amiable.

I stayed just off to the side, with the teenage son, bundled against the wind.

In the cab, Hayes rattled off some address in the Marais to the driver, and we rode in silence down the Champs-Élysées, through the Place de la Concorde, and along the Quai des Tuileries, continuing east.

At some point, I reached for his hand on the seat and he pulled it away. "You're angry? With me? After what you just did, you're angry with me?"

He was staring out the window at the Seine, the Musée d'Orsay, and points south. The light was beautiful at this time of day. Even through the gray, everything was tinged gold and russet with the changing leaves. It dawned on me that I had not seen the late-afternoon sky in almost a week.

For a while, Hayes did not speak. And when he finally did, his voice was soft. "I'm angry at myself. I just wanted to spend the day with you."

"I know. And I appreciate that. But you can't just blow in making these grand gestures, like you're in a Hugh Grant movie. You can't . . . *buy* me . . . or my time."

He turned to me then, gnawing at his bottom lip. "I'm sorry."

"And I told you I had to work, and you didn't respect that. Which is completely selfish and rude. And entitled."

"I'm sorry," he repeated.

"You can't always get what you want, Hayes."

He held my gaze for a minute, not saying anything. We were whizzing past the Louvre on the left.

"Do you even *want* that painting?"

"It's beautiful."

"It *is* beautiful. But that's beside the point. Purchasing art shouldn't be something rash, or manipulative. It should be this pure thing."

He smiled faintly. "You're a bit of an idealist, you know."

"Maybe."

He was quiet again, but he reached out and hooked his pinky finger around mine on the car seat, and that tiny motion was enough.

"Why don't you want to be seen with me?" His question took me by surprise. "Why? Why are you so uncomfortable? What are you ashamed of? What do you think will happen when people find out? We're together, are we not?"

"It's complicated, Hayes—"

"It's *not*. I like you. You like me. What does it matter what anyone else thinks? Why do you care?"

"How do you *not*?"

"I'm in a *boy band*. If I cared what people thought of me, then I've clearly entered the wrong line of work.

"Seriously, Solène, why do you care? I mean I want to protect your privacy because I don't think Isabelle should find out this way. But if there's another reason you feel uncomfortable being seen with me, then I need to know what that is."

I was quiet as the taxi snaked past the Hôtel de Ville and into the Marais. Parisians out on the streets in droves.

I so wished I could not care, about the million and one things that were holding me back from completely falling for him. "I don't know where to start," I said.

"Start from the beginning."

Just then the cab pulled to a halt, and our Arab driver announced, "*Trente, Rue du Bourg Tibourg.*"

"*Oui, merci, monsieur,*" Hayes said, pulling out his wallet. His British-accented French, oh so charming.

We stepped out of the taxi and into the narrow street before Mariage Frères, the renowned teahouse. Of course he was taking me to tea. It was four o'clock, after all.

"Mariage Frères!"

"You know this place?"

"I *love* this place. My dad's mom used to bring me here. And lecture me about being French. A hundred years ago . . . before you were born."

He smiled wide, taking my hand and leading me inside. "I knew there was a reason I picked you."

"*You* picked *me*?"

He nodded. We made our way back to the restaurant area of the shop and waited to be seated. Hayes gave his name. Apparently, he'd made reservations, which I found amusing, that all along he'd had the audacity to believe he was going to pull off this quasi-kidnapping.

"Why did you pick me, Hayes?"

"Because you looked like you wanted to be picked."

I laughed, uneasily. Our fingers were still entwined. "What does that mean?"

"That means exactly what you think it means."

He let that sit there for a while, saying nothing else.

The host seated us quickly, a small table toward the back. But the room was well lit, and there was no hiding who my date was. It might have been his height, his hat, his sunglasses, but heads were turning. Again.

"The best part," Hayes said, leaning into me, after we were seated and given our menus, "was that you had all these adorable little rules that were completely arbitrary."

"You don't forget anything, do you?"

"I don't. So don't make me any promises you don't plan on keeping."

I wasn't sure if he was saying it to be clever, but it stayed with me for a long time.

"So tell me," he continued, "tell me why you don't want to be seen with me. Is it the group? Is it the age difference? Is it the fame thing? Is it not having gone to university? Is it all of them combined? What is it?"

I smiled at the list he'd imagined in his pretty head. "Not having gone to university?"

He shrugged. "I don't know how your mind works. Arbitrary, remember?"

I took a moment to drink him in. His hair sticking in twenty-one directions since he'd yanked off his beanie. His Botticelli face.

"I am entirely too old for you, Hayes."

"I don't think you truly believe that. I mean, do you like me? Do you not have fun when we're together? Do you feel like I have a problem following the conversation?"

"No."

"Then I don't think you really believe that. If you did, you wouldn't be here. I think you care what other people might be thinking, or saying, and that's what's fucking you up."

I paused. "How do you not care?"

"Do you know how much *shit* gets said about me? Do you know how many fucks I give? Zero."

I sat there, watching him finger his sunglasses on the table.

"Do you know what they've said about me? I'm gay, I'm bi, I'm sleeping with Oliver, I'm sleeping with Simon, I'm sleeping with Liam, I'm sleeping with all three at the same time. I'm sleeping with Jane, our manager, who is attractive, but no. I've slept with at least three different actresses I've never even spoken to. I have ruined no fewer than four marriages on three different continents, and I have at least two kids . . . I'm *twenty*. When the *fuck* would I have crammed that all in?"

I started to laugh.

"I wish I was making this up, Solène, but I'm not. Which is why you can't believe everything you read on the Internet. Oh, and Rihanna may or may not have written a song about me. Because we may or may not have had sex . . ."

"*Did you have sex with Rihanna?*"

He gave me a look then that I could not quite decipher. It seemed equal parts *How dare you think I did?* and *How dare you ask me?*

"Does Rihanna even write her own songs?"

"You're missing the point here."

"I'm sorry. Go on."

"I'm really happy when I'm with you. I get the feeling you feel the same way. And if that's true, I don't think you should give a fuck about what people may or may not think of our age difference. Furthermore, if our ages were reversed, no one would bat an eyelash. Am I right? So now it's just some sexist, patriarchal *crap*, and you don't strike me as the kind of woman who's going to let that dictate her happiness. All right? Next issue . . ."

Our waiter came to the table then, and naturally neither of us had looked at the menu.

"*Encore un moment, s'il vous plaît,*" Hayes said, dismissing him.

When he'd parted, Hayes leaned forward, grabbing both my hands. "I think when we go home, you need to tell Isabelle the truth. I don't think we can do this again without telling her. I don't think it's fair to her. And I want to do this again."

"We're covering a lot today."

"I'm trying to get it all in before you turn forty." He smiled his half smile. "Plus when we're at the hotel I can't seem to manage a proper conversation because I have a hard time thinking about anything but fucking you.

"So . . ." He sat back, opening his menu. "Fancy a tea?"

After, outside, heading north on the narrow street, Hayes wrapped his arm around me, protective.

"Let's find a *tabac*," he said. "I want a cigarette."

I looked up at him, amused. "Oh-kay . . ."

"I didn't have sex with Rihanna," he announced, and then he grinned. "But not for want of trying. Apparently, I'm not her type."

"You're not bad enough." I smiled.

"I'm not bad enough."

"You're bad enough for me."

We spent the early evening wandering through the Marais and over to the Île Saint-Louis, where we strolled down the Quai de Bourbon to the Place Louis Aragon, the western tip of the island that looked out over the Seine and the Île de la Cité and Notre-Dame and all the things about Paris that were magical to me. We sat there huddled on a bench, drinking in the view and each other, until our appendages were numb. It was the perfect place to watch the sun set on my thirties. And it very well may have been worth 60,000 euros.

Later that night, Hayes and I slipped into the bar at the George V for a drink and some inspired people watching. The room was insufferably old-world: cherrywood panels, stenciled parquet floors, velvet drapes. Charcoal drawings of foxhunts and eighteenth-century-style portraits gracing the walls. There were various couples dallying over thirty-dollar cocktails. Curious pairings, unexpected. Perhaps not unlike us. We surveyed it all from our perch on the chintz sofa beside the fireplace.

For all its pomp, Hayes seemed decidedly at home in the stodgy bar, swilling from his Scotch like one of the landed gentry. He was so poised and comfortable in his skin; so *natural*, it was beautiful to watch.

I assumed his family's country home, somewhere in the Cotswolds, was not too different from this. And for a minute I deigned to imagine what that life would look like. A life with him. Weekends in the garden and corgis and sheep. Dinner parties in London during the Season. And then, just as quickly as I'd entertained it, I shook it off. What the hell was I thinking?

"Is this a trend?" he said. We'd been there for the better part of an hour, listening to the band's music drift in from the Galerie. Standards mixed with watered-down contemporary pop, "Mack the Knife" and Pharrell's "Happy."

"Is what a trend?"

"*This.*" Hayes angled his head, gesturing subtly to the rest of the room. Among the clientele, there were no fewer than seven mixed-race couples. And five of them were comprised of sixty-something white men with forty-something Asian women.

"It's kind of par for the course in California."

"This *exact* age spread? It's a little peculiar, no?"

I shrugged, sipping from my champagne cocktail. "Eva, Daniel's girlfriend, is Asian. Half." I had not made it a habit of discussing Eva. In all the months we'd been together, I'd mentioned her half a dozen times in passing.

He squeezed my hand. "Sorry. For bringing that up. Does it bother you?"

"It bothers me that she's young."

"How young?"

"Thirty."

Hayes chuckled. "Thirty is not that young."

"Shut up. It is."

"Well, look at it this way: You've won, right? Because I'm con-siderably younger than that."

I smiled at him. The thought had not crossed my mind. I'd never set out to get back at Daniel so much as I'd set out to get on with my life. It was not a competition. But that was part of the beauty of Hayes being twenty. That occasionally we saw the world completely differently, and at times it was refreshing.

"Hayes, you know when you're forty, I'm going to be sixty, right?"

"I love it when you talk sexy," he laughed.

"Just stating a fact."

He took a sip of his drink then and leaned into me. "You under-stand that you're going to be attractive well into your fifties."

"*Well* into my fifties?" I laughed. "That old?"

"Yes." He smiled. "Michelle Pfeiffer . . ."

"What about her?"

"In her fifties. Still fucking sexy. Julianne Moore, Monica Bellucci, Angela Bassett, Kim Basinger . . . Not saying they're age appropriate for me. Just saying those women aren't going to stop being sexy anytime soon."

I sat there, drinking him in. His cheeks flushed, his hair stand-ing on end. His young face in this very grown-up room. "You carry this list around in your head?"

He smiled. "Among other things."

"Have you ever been in therapy?"

He laughed, loud. "No. Are you trying to tell me something? I'm surprisingly well-adjusted. Have *you* ever been in therapy?"

"Yes."

"Hmm . . ." He cocked his head. "Interesting . . ."

"How old is your mother, Hayes?"

He paused for a moment, and then: "Forty-eight . . ."

Shit. It was uncomfortably close. Although certainly not surpris-ing. "Do you have a picture of her?"

He picked his iPhone up from the coffee table and began scrolling through. Eventually he handed it over. It was the two of them, in what I gathered was the countryside. Hayes was wearing a Barbour jacket and Hunter Wellies and looked ridiculously English. She, Victoria, was suited in full riding regalia. She held her helmet in one hand, and the lead to a handsome horse in the other. Hayes's head was turned to face her, and the look in his eyes was one of complete and utter adoration.

She was beautiful. Tall, reedy, with porcelain skin and an unruly ponytail of wavy black hair. She had his wide smile, his dimples, his eyes, although the crow's-feet were more pronounced. Her features were slightly softer, but there was no mistaking this was his mother.

"Who's the horse?"

He smirked. "That would be Churchill. And I'm quite sure she loves him more than me."

I laughed. "Now, *that's* something for your future therapist."

Hayes collected the phone from me and stared at it before closing the image. Quiet.

"What is it about you and older women, Hayes Campbell?"

He took the time to empty what was left in his glass and sign the check, a wry smile spreading across his mouth. "Who have you been talking to?"

"No one."

"You were Googling."

"You told me not to. Remember?"

He bit down on his lip, shaking his head. "Nothing. There's nothing about me and older women."

"You're lying."

He started to laugh. "Let's go upstairs."

"I'm not letting you off that easy."

His sigh was audible. "I like all kinds of women."

"You like *older* women. You have a definite type."

"Are *you* my type?"

"I'm guessing so."

He smiled, sinking back into the couch. "You think I meet plenty of hot, almost forty-year-old divorcées on the road?"

"I don't know. Do you?"

He snorted, crossing his arms in front of his chest, defensive. It was not his typical stance.

"Tell me about Penelope," I said.

"What about her?"

"Where did it happen, the first time?"

"Switzerland."

"*Switzerland?*"

He nodded. "Klosters. I went with Ol's family on a ski holiday."

I started to laugh. "The family invited you to ski in Switzerland, and you fucked their daughter?"

"To be fair, she fucked me."

For a moment, neither of us spoke. He sat there, guarded, a cryptic smile on his perfect face. And all I could think about was sitting on it.

"Okay. Let's go upstairs."

I turned forty. And the world did not end. The firmament did not move. Gravity did not suddenly forsake me. My breasts, my ass, my eyelids were all pretty much where I'd left them the night before. As was my lover. In our big, big bed, his head on my pillow, his arm draped over my waist, clinging. As if maybe he were afraid to let me go.

It was indulgent, as birthdays go. There was pampering and lovemaking and foie gras and a two-hour stroll along the Seine and autumn in the air and Hayes. Adoring, attentive, kind Hayes.

In the early evening, while I prepped for our celebratory dinner, he watched me from his perch against the counter in the master bath. The room, like everything else in the penthouse suite, was luxurious. Exceptionally appointed, flawless marble, an infinity tub. Although Hayes would not give me an exact figure, I knew it was costing him thousands of dollars a night. Which was absurd, despite the fact that TAG Heuer was picking up half the tab.

He stood there in black dress pants and a white shirt still unbuttoned, his hair blown dry and uncharacteristically neat. Gone were the boyish curls.

"What are you thinking over there?"

He shook his head, smiling. "I was thinking that you putting on makeup was somewhat redundant."

I laughed, applying eye shadow. "It's not a lot."

"I like when I can see your skin. I like your skin."

"My skin likes you." This was not untrue. It may have been Paris, or the change in climate, but it seemed to me that I was glowing.

He smiled, absorbing the process. The liner, the curling, the mascara. "You're unfolding the flower again."

"Am I?"

He nodded. "Even though you're covering yourself up . . . Watching you do it reveals more of you."

I put the mascara wand down then, meeting his eyes in the mirror. Thankful that, despite all the reflective surfaces in this gleaming *salle de bains*, the lighting design was particularly warm. It made my lingerie considerably more forgiving. Although I was not going to focus on that, because forty did not look terribly different than thirty-nine.

"Who are you, Hayes Campbell?"

He smiled, his hands burrowing in his pockets. "I'm your boyfriend."

"My twenty-year-old boyfriend?"

"Your twenty-year-old boyfriend. Are you okay with that?"

I grinned. "Do I have a choice?"

"You always have a choice." He'd appropriated my words, which I found amusing.

"Then, yes . . . I am *very* okay with that."

"Come here."

I inched over to him. I had grown to love his "come here" and where it often led.

He took my wrists in his hands then, his thumbs on my pulse points. "No watch?"

I shook my head, holding his gaze.

"Just as well," he said, leaning in to kiss me. And then I felt it, a slight pinching on my right wrist.

Eventually, he pulled away and I glanced down to discover an exquisite gold cuff bracelet adorning my arm. A one-inch band of delicate filigree work, Indian in design, intricately wrought and trimmed with pavé diamonds. Arguably the most singularly beautiful piece of jewelry I had ever seen.

"Happy Birthday," he said, soft.

My eyes met his. There were a thousand and one things I could have said, but none of them would have been quite right. And so I wrapped my arms around his neck and held him, close. For a very long time.

When we finally parted, I saw it—just beyond his shoulder, and in every corner of the room. Us, multiplied.

malibu

It was not supposed to happen this way. Our dalliance was supposed to be easy and casual and *fun*. It was not supposed to entail me wringing my hands about how and when exactly to break my daughter's heart. But that is how I spent most of November. When the group's first single from the new album was released and it felt as if suddenly they were everywhere. On the radio, on the TV, on a massive billboard on Sunset that made me simultaneously giddy and nauseated every time I drove past. Hayes, six stories high. When Isabelle was listening to "Sorrowed Talk" on repeat and I could not share with her that Hayes had given me six additional tracks from *Wise or Naked* for fear that she would tell her friends and somehow they might be leaked. Apparently this—leaking an album—was a *thing*. And I could not share with *anyone* how somehow their songs had gone from feeling like harmless pop ditties to inspired, earnest compositions. His words, his voice, affecting me in ways I could not have foreseen, profound. None of this was supposed to happen.

They were performing at the American Music Awards. They were scheduled for several days of press leading up to the show, and Hayes arranged to arrive earlier than the rest of the group and rent a house in Malibu for a few days before heading down to the Chateau Marmont to stay with the others.

I'd had every intention of breaking the news to Isabelle before then, but at each turn my attempts were thwarted.

"There's something I've been meaning to tell you," I said. We were hiking in Temescal Canyon the Sunday before Hayes's arrival. She was leading.

"Me, too." She smiled back at me, eyes alight.

"You wanna go first?"

"I kind of like this guy, but he barely knows I exist." The words spilled out of her mouth so quickly, it took me a second to register.

And then I panicked. She'd been raving about him since the *Sea Change* opening. "Who?"

"Avi Goldman. He's a senior. He's on the soccer team. He's like perfect."

Oh, sweet relief. "That's great, Izz."

"It's not great, Mom. He sees me, but he looks right through me." She was walking faster now, the narrow path winding. "It's like I don't even register."

"That's likely in your head, peanut. You can always introduce yourself, say hi."

"It won't matter. He only dates cool, pretty, popular girls. And I'm like . . ." She shook her head, trailing off.

"You're what?"

"I'm an eighth-grade fencer with braces."

"Are you trying to tell me that's not cool?" I smiled up at her.

She stopped walking suddenly, her eyes welling with tears.

"Oh, Izz, I'm sorry . . . It's not going to always be this way. I promise you. You will not always feel this way."

"You can say that, because look at you."

I hesitated then. I did not want her making comparisons. "What is he, Avi? Seventeen? Eighteen? Boys that age don't always have the best judgment. They don't necessarily know what they want or what's best for them. And even if he did, Izz, he's not exactly age appropriate. Your father and I would never agree to that." The irony of this was not lost on me.

"I know. I just hate feeling invisible."

I hugged her then, close. "You will not always feel invisible, peanut. I promise."

She calmed down, and after sometime we began walking again. "So what's your news?"

"You know what? It can wait."

And so it was that Hayes was coming to Los Angeles and I had failed him in the first thing he'd asked me to do. And then I failed in the second.

He was flying in on Sunday and picking me up en route to the house in Malibu, and we were going to shack up there for the next three days, cut off from the rest of the world.

And so I'd planned for Isabelle to stay with Daniel. "I need a couple of days to decompress," I'd said to him, vague. But on Sunday morning he called to tell me he was flying to Chicago last minute for a deal and that he could not take Isabelle after all.

I was irate.

"Are you kidding me? We made arrangements."

"What do you want me to do, Sol? I didn't *choose* this. Have Maria come." His voice on the line sounded distant, removed. The idea that he would suggest our housekeeper move in for three days, as if she did not have other responsibilities, boggled the mind. But Daniel had grown up with live-in help. Daniel wrote the book on privilege.

"Maria has kids of her own, Daniel. I can't ask her to sit on a school night."

"What about Greta?"

"I checked with Greta. She's working."

"What is it you're doing? Where are you going?"

I hesitated. I was not ready.

"Fuck. Is this the kid? Are you planning something with that kid? Solène . . ."

I did not answer.

"Look," he said after a moment, "I'm sorry. I would tell you to just drop her here, but . . . Eva's sick. And I don't think you'd be comfortable with that arrangement anyway. I'll be back on Tuesday—"

"Forget it," I said. "Forget it."

Hayes, as I expected, was not so understanding.

Landed.

He'd texted shortly before three-thirty.

Need to talk. Change of plans. Call me.

Will do.

And then, much later:

Fucking paps. Sorry. Ringing you soon.

"Hi." He called after what seemed an eternity.

"Hi, yourself. How was your flight?"

"Long." His voice was hoarse, raspy.

"Are you alone?"

"Yes. Why? Are we doing phone sex stuff again?"

I laughed. "No. Just wanted to know where you were."

"I'm in the car. I'm coming to get you."

"About that . . ." I said, and then I told him. That Daniel had flaked, that Daniel knew, that I could join him in Malibu for the evening, but that I could not stay because Isabelle would be home alone. And that I could come up during the day on Monday, but in the evening I would have to return again.

He was not happy. "*What?* What kind of rubbish is that?"

"I'm sorry."

"I've been on a bloody plane for eleven hours and you're telling me you're not coming?"

"I'm coming. I'm just not staying."

"Can't she sleep at a girlfriend's or something?"

"It's a school night."

He paused; I could picture him at the end of the line. Fingers pulling at his hair. "Fuck Daniel."

"I know, I'm sorry. I'm really sorry . . . And Hayes, you can't pick me up here. Isabelle is here and I don't want her to see you." This last bit I whispered, from my hiding space, tucked away in the confines of my bedroom closet. This is what it had come to. "I'll just meet you in Malibu. Okay?"

He took a moment to respond, and even in his breathing I could hear the frustration. "*You still haven't told her?* Solène, what are you waiting for?"

"I tried. I couldn't—"

"You *promised*—"

"I know. I *will*."

"The longer you wait, the more it's going to hurt her."

It landed.

The line went quiet for a second, and then: "Fine. I won't come in the house. But I'm picking you up. Meet me out front. I'll be there in thirty minutes."

Isabelle unwittingly watched me dress for my date with Hayes. I had told her I was going to cocktails and dinner with a couple of clients. That I would not be home too late, but that she should probably not wait up for me. And I had left it at that.

"You look beautiful," she said, her blue eyes wide, drinking in every detail.

I'd chosen a long black silk shirtdress with a deep neckline, equal parts alluring and demure. This I had learned from my unfailingly French mother: to be both a lady and a woman.

"You don't look like a mom," Isabelle observed.

"What does a mom look like to you?"

"I don't know." She smiled. "Cartier Love bracelet? Lululemon?"

I laughed at that, her referencing the staples of private-school carpool lanes.

There were so many things I wanted to teach her. That being a mother did not have to mean no longer being a woman. That she could continue to live outside the lines. That forty was not the end. That there was more joy to be had. That there was an Act II, an Act III, an Act IV if she wanted it . . . But at thirteen, I imagined, she did not care. I imagined she just wanted to feel safe. I could not blame her. We had already shaken her ground.

"*Am* I a mom?" I asked her then, kissing her forehead.

She nodded.

"Well, then, this is what a mom looks like."

For someone who'd just gotten off an eleven-hour flight, Hayes was remarkably dewy. Poreless skin, the faintest hint of stubble lining his jaw. And yet I would not let him kiss me until we'd cleared the driveway. Just in case.

"You are incorrigible," he said. He'd pulled over the car near the bottom of the hill, in the shade of an avocado tree.

"*I* am?"

"*You* are."

"Really?"

"You've fucked up everything." He was kissing me then, one hand at the back of my head, the other between my knees.

"Do you want to just take me back home then?"

"I *should* . . ." His hand had found its way beneath my "you don't look like a mom" dress, no time wasted.

"Is this your hello?"

"This is my hello."

"Hello, Hayes." I trembled. His fingers, pulling aside my underwear.

"Hello, Solène."

There was a song playing that I did not recognize, the smell of new leather, sleek lines on the dash. Where did he get this car? Did someone like Hayes Campbell just walk into Budget or Enterprise and ask for an Audi R8 Spyder? Was he even *old* enough to rent a car? So many questions. His rings, cool against my skin. His fingers.

"Did you miss me?" I spoke after several minutes, my breathing erratic.

"Not at all," he slurred, his breath hot in my ear. "I quite enjoy being six thousand miles away from you. Especially when I come to town and you can't manage to get a fucking sitter." He withdrew his hand then suddenly and turned back toward the steering wheel. "Where am I going?"

It took me a moment. "Whoa. Oh-kay . . . Make a right on Sunset and then take it all the way down to the PCH."

He didn't say anything after that, but he reached out to hold my hand while he drove. And we remained that way, all the way up the coast.

———

Hayes's people had found him a 5,500-square-foot sleek, contemporary house on the cliffs with heart-stopping views and retractable walls of glass and a chef's kitchen and designer everything, and the fact that we were just visiting saddened me. Because for a moment I allowed myself to imagine what life could be like if we played house there. And maybe I could sell my half of the gallery and send Isabelle to Malibu High School and spend my days painting watercolors and making love and being happy. And then I attempted to picture Hayes as Isabelle's stepfather and I started to laugh.

"What?" he said.

We were in the master suite and I was drinking in the view from the oversized window seat while he was riffling through his luggage.

"Nothing. I . . . It's perfect here."

"It is."

"Is it for sale? Do you know?"

"I don't," he said, curt. "I'm jumping in the shower. We have reservations for Nobu at seven-thirty. That leaves about an hour to do the things I want to do to you. Don't go anywhere."

At Nobu, we dined under the stars. A luxuriant feast of sushi and sake and Hayes's fingertips playing over my palm at the table. He filled me in on developments in his schedule. The album being released in December to coincide with the documentary, *August Moon: Naked*. The film premiere scheduled for New York. The tour that would begin in February, last a little over eight months, and take him to five different continents. I tried not to think about it all because much of it translated to time apart. And the thought of that made me miserable.

No fewer than nine people stopped by our table. Those who knew him, or claimed they knew him; three fans. Hayes was gracious at every turn, but I could see it wearing away at him.

"I probably should have picked someplace more low-profile," he said. "But it's Sunday. And it's November. I assumed it would be quieter."

"It's still Nobu."

He was silent for a moment, staring out toward the water. A splattering of stars, a half-moon, a seamless black horizon.

"What if I quit the band?"

"I thought you said that was impossible."

"It's not impossible, it's just . . . *complicated*."

"What would you do if you quit?"

"I don't know." He turned back to me then, and reached out to finger my bracelet. The cuff he'd given me in Paris. I had yet to take it off. "I'm just tired. I want a break."

For a moment neither of us spoke. I watched his fingers tracing over the filigree. His movements slow, hypnotic.

"Why did you get into this business, Hayes? What were you expecting from it?"

"I liked writing music. And I thought . . . I had something to say. I'm a solid songwriter, and I have a decent voice. It's not one of those once-in-a-generation voices like Adele, but it's decent. And I knew I had a good face and that was only going to last for so long, but if I grouped it together with a handful of other good faces with decent voices it might be more compelling. I'd have a better chance of getting my music heard." He looked up then, meeting my gaze. "And it worked. But I've no desire to write happy pop stuff anymore . . ."

"A lot of your stuff isn't happy. It's ironic or tongue-in-cheek. Smart."

"It's still . . . *safe*. I don't want to be so safe."

He was quiet for a moment. The sound of the ocean lapping the shore beneath us, another party's laughter.

"But I also have this opportunity now that I didn't really foresee, of being able to affect people and hold their attention. And to not use that for some good, for something bigger than just performing songs, would be a bit of a waste. The chance to do something noble. I'm still figuring it out."

"You know you're only twenty, right?"

He grinned. "So you keep reminding me."

"You have so much more time to do whatever it is you want to do. Just enjoy this for what it is, because you're not always going to have it.

"And you have the rest of your life to redefine yourself, if ever you get tired of being 'Hayes Campbell, pop star.'"

He smiled, slow, leaning in across the table. His eyes a muddy-blue in the candlelight. "If I kiss you here, are you going to be okay with that?"

"I don't know," I said. "Why don't you try it and see?"

We got back to the house close to eleven. All the indoor lights were off, and so I assumed Isabelle was sleeping.

"So what's the plan?" Hayes asked, pulling into the driveway, killing the engine.

"I'll drop her off in the morning, and then I'll come back up to you."

"This is rubbish, you not spending the night. You know that? I'm going to be very lonely in that big house all by myself."

"You'll manage."

"Barely."

I laughed. He leaned over to kiss me, and we went at it for a couple of minutes. It felt a little like being eighteen again, there in the car, his hand pressed to my cheek, the faint taste of alcohol. And Hayes, being Hayes, had one hand up my dress in very little time.

"Don't." I grabbed his wrist. "My daughter is inside. I need to go."

"Just give me a minute . . ."

"You really like doing that, don't you?"

"I like just knowing that I can."

"Tomorrow," I said, opening the door.

He smiled his half smile. "I like you."

"I like you, too."

"Come back to me," he said.

"Tomorrow."

The house was completely quiet when I entered, which was odd. Typically Isabelle left the television on when she was home alone after dark. Something about the silence put me on edge.

Hayes's Audi had just peeled away, and I could faintly hear the gears shifting as he descended the hill. Likely driving too fast. Boys and their toys.

I was tiptoeing down the hallway, my shoes in my hands, when Isabelle's bedroom door flew open without warning.

"Oh God, you scared me," I started. "I thought you were sleeping."

"Where were you?"

"What are you still doing up, Izz? It's late."

"Where were you, Mom?" she repeated, urgent. She was dressed for bed: a T-shirt, flannel pajama pants, her thick dark hair in a ponytail. But there was something off about her face, her eyes.

"I told you, I had dinner with a client . . . a couple of clients." I was trying to remember the story.

"Were you with Hayes?"

Fuck.

"Who?"

"Hayes Campbell. Were you with Hayes Campbell?" She was not asking it gently. She was not being polite. She *knew*.

And suddenly I could feel the black cod with miso threatening to make a reappearance. "Yes. He's a client of mine. We had dinner."

"A *client*? Don't lie to me, Mom. I saw you. You were *kissing* him. I *saw* you." Her tears were welling. And I could feel it, her pain, in my knees.

This is not how it was supposed to happen, in the confines of the narrow corridor with the walls closing in and her childhood photos taunting me and me playing defense. Not this way.

"Izz . . ." I'd begun to sweat.

"Oh my God. Are you *dating* him?"

"I'm not—"

"*You're dating him? You're dating Hayes Campbell?!*"

"Honey, I'm not *dating* him. We're . . . we're friends." God, what a crock! I was standing there with his sperm still swimming inside me, and attempting to convince her otherwise. And my daughter could see right through me.

"Gross. Gross. Gross, Mom." She was visibly shaking. "That is so gross! How can you be dating Hayes Campbell? You're *old*! You're like *twice* his age!"

If she'd wanted to hurt me, she'd succeeded.

I reached out for her shoulder, and she pushed me away. Her tears were pouring, and I got the impression that if she could have hit me, she would have.

"Why didn't you tell me? Were you just not going to tell me?"

"Isabelle . . . I'm sorry."

"I love him."

"You don't love him, Izz. You love the idea of him."

She looked at me, her eyes wild with fury. "I. Love. Him."

"Okay," I said. "Okay."

She began to ramble, snot running from her nose, her lips catching on her braces. "I heard the car, because the TV wasn't on, so I heard the car, and I looked and it looked like him, but I was thinking, 'No way.' There was no way that was him, because he was supposed to be in London until later this week when they come for the AMAs, and *Ellen*, but it *really* looked like him and I searched it, and there are paparazzi shots of him landing at LAX today. And it's him. It's *him*. And he's in our driveway and he's kissing you. He's kissing *you*. He picked *you*. And I hate you. I hate you I hate you . . ."

The way she'd said it, like it was a competition between us, made me numb. "Izz, I'm sorry."

She shook her head, crazed. "Did you . . . ? Are you . . . ?" She trailed off, unable to articulate.

I did not know what sordid thoughts she was entertaining. But they were probably accurate.

"Oh God. How could you do this to me? How could you? Oh my God, this isn't really happening!"

"Isabelle." I reached for her again, and she recoiled.

"Don't touch me. Don't touch me. What kind of mother *are you*?" she spat, stepping back into her pink-and-white bedroom. Ripping my heart.

"Izz, you're making a much bigger deal out of this than it is—"

"Don't come in here," she said, slamming the door. Locking it. "Don't come in here."

I sat there. Outside of her closed door, for an hour. Listening to her sob and destroy things. And there was nothing I could do. Keep calm and carry on.

"I'm sorry, Izz. I'm sorry," I kept repeating. But to her, it meant nothing. I'd waited until it was too late. And as Hayes had predicted, it was ugly.

She did not talk to me for a week.

On Monday, she went to school, looking as if she'd gone twelve rounds in a boxing match, she was that swollen. I insisted she stay home, but she refused: she did not want to be around me. I don't know what she told her friends.

On Tuesday after school, she packed a bag and waited for Daniel to pick her up. When I pleaded with her again, and apologized again, she turned to me very coldly and asked, "Did you have sex with him?" And when I could not answer her, she started to cry.

———

She would not return until Sunday, when Daniel insisted on bringing her back. She had up to that point not responded to any of my calls or texts, but had no other option because Daniel was leaving town again. He dropped her off that afternoon, and when I attempted to hug her, she let me, although she did not hug back.

"I missed you," I said, inhaling her. Her shampoo, her sunscreen.

She nodded, and then made her way into the house.

Daniel was in the driveway, pulling bags out of the trunk of the BMW. I moved to help him.

"Hey."

"Hey," he said.

"Thanks for bringing her."

He shook his head, irritated. "It's been a very fucked-up week."

"I know."

He shut the trunk then and finally looked at me. "I warned you. I fucking warned you. Jesus Christ, Sol, what were you thinking?"

I did not respond.

"Seriously. *What the hell were you thinking?* He's a *kid*. Have you lost your mind?"

My temples throbbed. For days my head had hurt, and my thoughts had been dark and slow and muddled, like being stuck inside a Turner painting.

"You know what, I'm not going to have this conversation with you. Not now. Possibly not ever."

"No. You *are*. Because our daughter is a complete and total mess right now, and I fucking warned you this would happen, and this is not just about you . . ."

It killed me to hear this, to know that he was right.

"She's been listening to Taylor Swift's new album on repeat and saying that she finally understands her pain," he continued. "I don't even know what that means . . ."

"She's hurting, Daniel. Her heart's broken."

"Because of this Hayes kid? Or because of *you*?"

That stung.

For a moment he was quiet, staring out at the street. "My God, Sol," he said, low, "what are people going to think?"

It struck me: the fact that in the midst of all this he was thinking about appearances and judgment. It was base and unappealing. And I had to wonder if this is how I'd come across to Hayes. Caring about how things looked and what people thought and not what truly mattered.

A couple of hikers were descending the hill, and Daniel paused until they were fully out of earshot.

"How did this even happen?" he asked. "How long has this been going on?"

I didn't answer. My mind was off in a thousand different places, a dozen different hotel rooms. New York. Cannes. Paris.

"Are you in love with him? My God, what am I asking? He's like eighteen."

"He's not eighteen."

"You *have* to end this."

"Please don't tell me what I *have* to do."

"You *have* to end this. It's like my wife is Mary Kay Letourneau."

"I'm not your wife, Daniel."

He froze then, realizing his error. It took him a moment to collect himself, and then: "I mentioned it to Noah, and Noah already knew. How the fuck did Noah know? Have you been talking to Noah?"

"No."

"Then how the fuck did he know?"

I shrugged. "I don't know. Soho House . . ."

"*Soho House?*"

I watched him processing, as if in slow motion. The sun glaring in his eyes.

"That was *him*? That was *him* who came over to our table at lunch? Were you fucking him then? Were you *fucking* him when he came over and introduced himself?"

"Daniel . . ."

"You've gotta be fucking kidding me."

"Please, stop."

"Eva's pregnant. We're getting married," he spat.

If he had punched me in the face, it would not have hurt more.

"I was waiting for the right time to tell you, but it never came. I'm sorry."

He stood there for a moment, not knowing quite what to do. And then he got into his BMW and drove away. Leaving me, once again, with the baggage.

On Monday, the day after August Moon performed "Sorrowed Talk" on the American Music Awards and walked away with four trophies, Hayes came to visit.

I had spent much of the previous Monday and Tuesday at the house in Malibu, crying. He'd held me and comforted me, and not once did he reprimand me for having waited so long. And then he expressed the desire to talk to her when things calmed down.

"I think it will only make things worse," I'd said. We were sitting on the balcony, staring out at the waves, the rolling hills behind us.

"I don't think it will. Part of what's alienating her is that I don't quite seem real. Like I'm the bloke in the poster and, to her anyway, I'm not tangible. She's put me on some pedestal where I can't possibly live up to whatever it is she has in her head. And she needs to see that I'm just kind of normal and human."

"You? Normal? Human?"

He smiled. "Sometimes . . ."

And so, Monday afternoon, when I was still reeling about Daniel and Eva's news, and when Isabelle was still punishing me with monosyllabic exchanges, Hayes showed up at the house. I had not given Isabelle warning. Because I did not want her to prepare or overthink it. I just wanted her to *be*. She was sitting on one of the lounges in the backyard, doing her homework, a blanket wrapped around her narrow shoulders.

"Izz, someone's here to see you."

She glanced up, and her expression when Hayes stepped out revealed what to me seemed the full extent of everything a thirteen-year-old girl could feel. Love and betrayal and heartbreak and expectation and disappointment and fury and lust and hurt. And the fact that it all fell on his shoulders worried me. But if he was daunted by it, it did not show.

"Hi, Isabelle," he said, sitting beside her on the lounge. His voice raspy, comforting, familiar.

She smiled at him, faint. And then she started to cry.

Hayes, apparently, was used to girls crying around him. Girls crying because of him. I watched as he wrapped his arm around her shoulders and tucked her head into his neck, and repeated, over and over, "It's okay, it's okay," while stroking her hair. And it was like magic. Everything she would not allow me to do for her, she accepted willingly from him. And he sat like that, still with her, for a very long time.

"You all right?" he said eventually.

She nodded. "You came all the way here to see me?"

"I heard you were upset."

Isabelle looked over to where I was standing by the sliding doors. She started to say something and then stopped. "You guys were really good last night," she mustered instead.

"Thank you. Did you see me almost trip? That was classy." He was quiet for a moment and then: "So . . . this is weird, right? I know. It's kind of weird for me, too."

"Except you don't have all my albums, and pictures and stuff. You never stayed up late watching my videos and planning how you were going to marry me and my friends. So no, it's not weird for you in the same way."

"All right." He smiled at her. "Point taken." And then, after a very long pause: "I really like your mum."

Isabelle did not speak. She was avoiding eye contact, fingering her friendship bracelet, the lone survivor from summer camp. The others had all unraveled.

"I'm sorry that upsets you, but it kind of just *happened*. And sometimes you can't plan these things."

He allowed her to sit with that for a bit. Not forcing the issue. He was so good at this. And in that moment I recalled our conversation in the bar of the George V. *I'm surprisingly well-adjusted*, he'd said.

"But look, it's just me, right? And I'm here. And I'm kind of in your mum's life. Which means I'm kind of in your life. For the time being, anyway. And I'd really like for us to be friends."

I could sense my eyes welling.

"I know right now you feel like shit . . ."

Isabelle smirked.

"Sorry," Hayes apologized, "like crap. But when you're feeling better, if you're up for it, we have a movie coming out next month and they're premiering it in New York, and I would really love for you to come. And maybe you can bring a friend or two. But you have to promise me you won't cry. No crying on the red carpet. Can you do that?"

She giggled, hiding her braces with her hand. I hadn't seen her smile in eight days.

"You also have to promise you're going to be nice to your mum. Because she never wanted to hurt you, and it's killing her that you're so sad. All right? Can you promise me that?"

"Yes."

"Good," he said. "What are you working on?"

"Math."

"Maths? Ech. I sucked at maths."

She laughed at that.

"I am sorry that you are being subjected to that . . . torture. I'm very sorry." He reached into his pocket. "Fancy a stick of gum?" He offered it to her, and while she was opening the wrapper, he glanced over his shoulder at me and stuck out his tongue. Still my Hayes.

Later he joined me in the kitchen, where I was making tea.

"That was amazing. How did you do that?"

He smiled, shrugging. "I'm good with people."

"Was that on your list?"

"Probably. I'm like . . . a fixer."

"A *fixer*?" I laughed.

He nodded, watching me pour the hot water. "I'm like the one they send in to calm down all the crazed hyperventilating fans."

"I thought you didn't do well with women who freak out."

"I *don't* do well with women who freak out. But I can handle girls." He smiled, easy.

"Thin line . . ."

"Sometimes." He moved toward me then, wrapping his arms around my waist. "And, you know, I make all the girls *so* happy . . ."

"Apparently," I said, kissing him.

"And occasionally, I make their mums happy, too."

"Very . . ."

"Very."

miami

Things were not perfect. I did not kid myself into believing that Isabelle would miraculously be okay with the idea of Hayes and me, just because Hayes had willed it so. But I had hoped she would ease into it. Make her peace, gradually. Like she had with the divorce. But she had been younger then, less sensitive, less likely to view things as a personal affront. It had been surprisingly easy to rationalize with her. Now everything was the end of the world. Battle Hymn of the Teenage Girl.

"Do you want to talk about it?" I asked, at least once a day.

"No," she said each time, slipping into her room. "I'm okay." And then the door would close and the Taylor Swift would begin.

We were not yet out of the woods.

Daniel broke the news to her about Eva. According to him, she'd sobbed and wailed that everything was changing. And he'd agreed that it was, but that we would never love her any less and that she would always be our firstborn. She would always be the first best thing that had happened to the two of us. She would. She was.

That Sunday evening, after he'd dropped her off, she came into my room and curled up on my bed like a snail and cried. And the fact that she let me comfort her was progress. The fact that she let me hold her and breathe her in and marvel at the beauty of her was its own sweet reward.

"I'm sorry," she said eventually. Her voice hoarse, broken. "I'm sorry about Daddy. I'm sorry about Eva. I'm sorry about everything."

My heart ached for her. Her world was shattering, unrecognizable, and there was little I could do to fix it. I lay there, my body curled around hers, wondering at how we'd gotten here. Our family so fractured and rearranged. Like the faces in a Picasso.

"I love you," I said.

She nodded, threading her fingers slowly in between mine. "I love you, too."

"We're going to be okay, Izz. We're going to be okay."

We spent the first week of December in Miami for Art Basel. On the flight out, Lulit gave me a stern talking-to.

"You're not leaving me this go-round," she said. "We're a team. No afternoons off to go gallivanting with your boyfriend."

"Okay." I nodded.

Hayes was in New York that week doing the press junket for *August Moon: Naked*. But he was slipping out on Thursday to spend the weekend in South Beach.

"I know you're totally into each other, and I know you don't see him that often, but I need your help," Lulit continued. "I need you. I didn't get into this to do it by myself. We're a team. We work well as a team. We have *fun* as a team."

"Okay," I repeated. "I get it."

She was right. We had fun. Miami was one nonstop party: cocktails and dinner and ridiculously late nights. Having Matt on hand made juggling the workload that much easier. We wined and dined and schmoozed and sold art. And it was good.

I booked an ocean view suite at the Setai while the rest of the team set up camp in a rental. I knew Hayes would appreciate the relative calm and privacy. He showed up in Miami on Thursday evening, a little weary from the onslaught of press. Interviews, photo shoots, answering the same questions over and over. If you weren't doing this, what would you be doing? Would you ever date a fan? Have you ever been in love? What's your favorite word for boobs? Soft-shell tacos or hard?

"It's such mindless drivel," he said, watching me dress for dinner. "Kind of makes me envy my mates at uni."

"Who I'm sure envy you . . ."

"Because I'm in South Beach with the world's hottest gallerist?" He smiled.

"Yes," I laughed. "Because of that."

He paused then, taking a deep breath. "So I have something of interest to tell you . . . My parents are coming to the premiere."

I spun to look at him. He was reclining on the bed, long legs crossed, hands folded behind his head, completely at ease. A pose incongruous, I thought, with the subject matter at hand.

"Fuck." It was barely a whisper.

"It's okay, I've already prepared them."

"You told them how old I was? You told them about Isabelle?"

He nodded slowly.

"Did they freak out?"

"Define 'freak out' exactly . . . No, I'm playing with you. They did not freak out. They were surprisingly . . . okay."

" 'Okay'?"

"Okay," he repeated, a small smile on his lips. "It's going to be okay."

But I doubted that. Highly.

We decided to skip the flurry of industry parties that night and went to a late dinner at Casa Tua on James. We'd only just arrived at the restaurant and were snaking our way through the candlelit tables in the courtyard garden when someone called Hayes's name. I turned to find him stopped alongside a table of what looked to be three young models. Accompanying them was a middle-aged gentleman. Perhaps an agent, a father, a predatory paramour. It gave me pause. Was this what I had become? Middle-aged?

The girl closest to Hayes was fine-boned, blonde, beautiful. Her thin hand was wrapped around his wrist. "Amanda," she was saying. "We met at the Chateau a couple of weeks ago."

I watched him register, smile. "Amanda. Yes. Hi. How are you?"

"Wonderful," she said. Of course she was. She had flawless skin and a smattering of freckles over her delicate nose. And she was young enough that she could get away with going out at night in South Beach with not a lick of makeup.

"We were just talking about you," she cooed. "I believe you know my friend Yasmin." She gestured to the girl seated across from her.

A brunette, slightly older, vaguely ethnic, large wide-spaced eyes and a pornographic mouth.

Hayes took a moment, placing her, and then he nodded, slow. "I do."

"Hi." Yasmin smiled, flicking her hair.

"Hi." He grinned. He'd fucked her. That much was apparent.

It was in the shift in his body language, and the way she refused to hold his gaze. And it struck me, that I was able to tell so quickly, that I knew him that well. My boyfriend.

I had not, for the most part, expended much energy worrying about the women of Hayes's past. Because the past was the past. And since September, I had tried not to worry about the women of the present, because he promised me there were none. He'd asked me to stay off the Internet and not read tabloids and to trust him, and for the most part I did. But all I had was his word.

"Do we need to use a condom?" I had asked him earlier that evening. It had become something of a ritual.

He had cocked his head, wily. "I don't know. Do we?"

"I'm asking *you*."

"Have you done something you're not proud of?"

"No," I'd said. "But I'm not the one in a band."

"If I do something I'm not proud of, I'll let you know," he'd said, flipping me onto my stomach.

"I'm *trusting* you, Hayes."

"I know you are."

But there, in the garden of Casa Tua, beneath the stars and the sprawling trees and the Moroccan lanterns, the reality hit me. That there had been many, that there would always be, that they would be everywhere. Hayes's conquests. Creeping, entangling him, like ivy.

"Are you here for Basel?" Amanda asked. She'd pronounced it *basil*, which was irksome.

"Yes," Hayes said.

"Cool." Her skinny fingers were still encircling his wrist, serpentine. "Where are you staying?"

He paused for a moment, his eyes scanning the faces at the table and then landing on me. "With a friend . . . I'm sorry, I'm keeping her waiting." His attempt to untangle. "Good to see you. Yasmin. Amanda. Enjoy your dinner." He waved at the others and pulled away.

Later, over the burrata and a bold Cab, Hayes felt the need to explain himself. "So, Amanda . . . She's Simon's friend."

"I didn't ask."

"I know you didn't. But I didn't want you wondering."

"And Yasmin? Simon's friend, too?"

He swished his wine in his glass. "No. Yasmin wasn't Simon's friend."

"Yeah, that was evident."

"Sorry . . . It was a long time ago."

I nodded, swilling from my wine. "I thought you didn't like models."

He laughed. "I'm pretty sure I never said that. Who doesn't like models?"

"Oliver."

Hayes grew serious, fast. "Yes, *Oliver*. He knows his art and he's too sophisticated for models."

The way he'd said it surprised me.

He reached out then and grabbed my hand on the table. "I don't have a problem with models. They are, for the most part, quite pretty. But given the choice, I'd rather be with someone who's lived a little, has something interesting to say, and isn't just eye candy.

"Do you know what girls like that talk about? Instagram and Coachella . . . That's good for like a night. Which was what Yasmin was. A night."

My eyes were on his hand holding mine. His long, thick fingers. His two rings: silver, patterned, one on his ring finger, one on the middle. He switched them up so often.

"I thought you loved Instagram," I said.

"I do Instagram because our team makes us. You know what I like about you? That you've never been to Coachella and the only thing you Instagram is art."

"You were looking at my Instagram?"

"Maybe . . ." He smiled, coy. "I'm thinking about taking a page out of your book and segueing into artsy photos."

I laughed. "What? No more body parts? No more 'Hayes, can I sit on your big toe?'"

He shuddered. "That's really . . . I don't quite have the words for what that is. Sometimes our fandom scares me."

"Yes," I said. "Me, too."

I awoke the next morning to a phone vibrating. The shades were drawn and I could not determine the time, but it felt early. Too early for the phone. After numerous rings, Hayes answered, annoyed. There was a pause and then he bolted upright.

"No. Fucking. Way."

"What happened?"

He looked to me, eyes wide. His hair was unruly and his voice croaked, but his smile was glorious. "It appears I've been nominated for a Grammy."

August Moon was in the running for Best Pop Duo/Group Performance for their song "Seven Minutes." The ballad, which Hayes alone had written with one of their producers, was also up for Song of the Year. It was, in every way, a big deal.

We dined at the Bazaar at SLS that night with Lulit, Matt, our artist Anya Pashkov, and Dawn and Karl Von Donnersmarck, a couple of New York collectors. The mood was decidedly festive.

"Your life, Hayes, will be even crazier if you win?" Lulit said over cocktails, her pitch rising at the end. As if at the last moment she'd decided to make it a question.

"Oh, we won't win. Boy bands don't win Grammys. This alone is huge. I'm rather chuffed." He beamed. "It might earn us a bit more respect. But still, we are pretty much at the bottom of any respectability charts."

Dawn laughed loudly, raising her glass. "I love that you're so good-humored about it. And you, Anya, kudos to you."

Artnet had posted a favorable write-up on Anya's installation that morning. *Invisible* was a conceptual video exploring how women of a certain age cease to be seen. How society sweeps them under a rug, ignores them, discards them once past their prime. She'd curated a series of portraits of women middle-aged and older, spliced with media images and common advertising tropes, and layered a soundtrack above of real women speaking about their experiences, their fears, their insecurities. It was painfully, brutally honest.

"My friends and I discuss this all the time. It's like you cease to exist," Dawn continued. Dawn was a patrician blonde, New York born and bred. Tall, capable. If she was older than me, it was not by much. "How many times do you find yourself in a room or at a party and you're thinking, 'Am I here? Can anyone see me? Hello!'"

Karl, quiet, bookish, wrapped his arm around her, smiling. "I see you, hon."

"You know what I mean, Karl." She turned to me then. "Like the guys who typically talk to you on the streets . . . Not the cat-calling construction workers, but the doormen who generally say 'Good morning' . . . That just stops. It stops. Do I no longer warrant a 'Good morning'? There's something very disturbing about them not even registering you anymore. Like *shit*, when did this happen?"

Hayes was holding my hand beneath the table. He squeezed it suddenly, and I looked over to him, wondering what it was he'd read on my face. The uncertainty of it all. The idea that my own invisibility might be around the corner. Around the block. Miles away. But still, inevitable.

"It's groundbreaking what you're doing, Anya," I said.

"Thank you, Solène." She was sitting across from me, nursing a vodka tonic. Anya's features were sharp, memorable. Fair skin, black hair, red lips. She had a few years on me, but she seemed to have it figured all out. While I was still reeling from the news about my ex-husband's pregnant fiancée and trying to hold together a heartbroken teen while bedding her twenty-year-old idol, Anya was taking on the future of womankind.

"We sent out press releases to the women's magazines in addition to the usual art publications because they're in a unique position," I continued. "Sure, some are partly to blame, but they have this opportunity now to kind of turn it on its head. To further the discussion. The fact that we continuously equate beauty and desirability with youth. That we beat ourselves up instead of embracing the inevitable. And these are *women* running these magazines. Why do we do this to ourselves?"

"Because we've been brainwashed," Lulit said, sipping her mojito. "But this is the beauty of art, right? We hold up a mirror to ourselves and say, 'Who the hell have we become?' That's what we do."

I looked to her then, my partner in crime, my best friend. "That's what we do."

After dinner, the others decided to head over to Soho House for a party where the Roots' Questlove was spinning, but Hayes assumed it would be too much of a scene and so we opted out.

"I'm seeing him next week. We're doing *The Tonight Show*," he said, as if that were a normal thing.

"What a thrilling life you lead." Dawn smiled. We were standing by the valet, waiting for their Uber. "Well, you two have fun. I'm going to go be invisible at Soho House."

I laughed at that. "You're not invisible, Dawn. You're wearing Dries Van Noten."

"Ha!" She threw back her blonde head, her punchy floral dress in high relief. "Thank you for noticing! Thank you for seeing me."

"I see everything," I said. "That's my job."

"I love that you love what you do," Hayes said, sometime later. We were tucked into a corner of the Setai's courtyard bar—low lights, reflecting pool, palm trees. The vibe more Mooréa than Miami.

He was sipping from his Scotch. Laphroaig 18. "What do Isabelle's friends' mums do? Do they work?"

"The majority of them, no."

"My mum didn't go back to work after I was born. She rode horses and did charity stuff and . . . had lunch," he laughed. "I don't know *what* she did, come to think of it. I don't know *how* she filled her days."

"Would you describe her as a good mum?"

"I guess so. I turned out all right. I mean, *you* like me."

"I *do*." I smiled. "Do you think she was happy?"

"I don't know. Maybe. Are *you* happy?"

"Right this moment? Yes."

He was quiet for a minute, watching me. "Do you think you'd be as happy if you weren't working?"

I shook my head. "Maybe if I'd gotten married and had kids older, I would have felt the pull to settle down. But I had all this education and energy and desire and there was more life to live than that. And now it's so much of my identity. And yeah, sometimes I feel guilty that I wasn't the mom serving hot lunch at private school. But who's to say that would have made me a better mom? I probably would have just been restless and unhappy. And resentful."

He nodded, his fingers tracing over my cuff. "Yeah, I get that."

"If you hadn't done this, what would you be doing?"

"Ha! Press junket questions. I'd be at Cambridge with half my year, sleeping in the same five-hundred-year-old college four generations of Campbells have slept in, playing football, chasing skirts, rowing, and having a grand time."

"Interesting," I said. I could not picture him doing any of that. "Hard or soft-shell tacos?"

He laughed. "Soft."

"Ever been in love?"

"No."

I stopped. It was not what I was expecting. "No?"

He sipped from his drink, placed the glass on the table before us. "No."

"Never? Really? Wow."

"Do I strike you as someone who's been in love?"

"You strike me as someone who knows what he's doing."

"I've had some good teachers. Some of whom have said, 'Don't fall in love with me.'" He let that stand in the air, accusatory.

"Did I say that? I'm sorry."

"It's okay. I didn't really listen to you anyway." He said it with no pretense. His hand had found its way beneath the table, to my knee, to the scalloped lace hem of my dress. "I've thought I was in love. Turns out I was wrong."

"Penelope?"

"Penelope."

My mind paged through the times he'd said he was falling, at the Chateau Marmont, at the George V. I was weighing them differently now, those proclamations. I'd written them off as infatuation. Things a young boy might say. But perhaps he'd been revealing more of himself all along.

A sultry breeze blew up from the ocean. The air was moist, balmy. Hayes's fingers slipped beneath my hem and I flinched. For a long time neither of us spoke. He held my gaze as he forced my knees apart, uncrossed my legs, pried open my thighs.

There was another couple on the banquette not far from us. A group of Basel types across the reflecting pool. We were not alone. And yet I did not stop him.

"I take it we're done talking about Penelope . . ."

He chuckled, sly. His fingers pressed up against me, inside me. "We are very done talking about Penelope."

He leaned into me then, his mouth near my ear, his breath hot on my neck. The thought occurred that I would miss this when he moved on. When he was with someone ten years my junior, and I was somewhere invisible. I was going to miss his hands.

This.

His thumb on my clit and my heart in my throat and the humidity enveloping us like a blanket.

When I thought it might happen, that I might come right there in the courtyard of the Setai, he stopped, pulling away. I reached for his arm. "Where are you going?"

"I'm not going anywhere," he said. And then he took his hand from between my legs and rubbed his wet fingers over my mouth. My lips, my tongue . . . I sat, speechless.

He smiled his half smile, took a swig of Scotch, and then kissed me. Deep.

"You," I said, when I found my voice.

"Me."

"You. Are so fucking dirty."

He leaned in again to suck on my lip. "Am I?"

"Can we go back to the room now?"

"Not yet." He was smiling when his hand returned between my legs, his fingers slipping beneath my underwear, sliding up inside of me, effortless. "You. Are so fucking wet."

I sat there for another minute, lost in him. And then I grabbed his wrist. "Pay the bill," I said, "and then meet me upstairs."

"Okay."

It took him longer than I would have liked to arrive at the suite. But the sight of him at the bedroom entrance—black dress shirt slightly unbuttoned, glass still in hand—gave me such a rush, I forgot to question where he'd been.

"Candles?" he said, taking in the room, taking off his boots. "Were you hoping for something romantic?"

"Actually, I was just hoping you'd bring your mouth."

He smiled at that. "I bet you were."

From my position on the bed, I watched him make his way toward me, his body long, lithe, beautiful. He took a moment to hook his iPhone up to the speakers. Then, as the music started, some evocative baseline I did not recognize, he took a sip of Scotch and drank me in.

"Are you going to make me wait, Hayes Campbell?"

He grinned, setting down his glass. "Maybe. Just a little."

The vocals kicked in then. A haunting, familiar voice. Bono. Although nothing I'd ever heard before. Raw, sexy, disjointed lyrics.

"U2?"

"U2."

Hayes joined me on the bed, took his time unzipping my dress. His fingers warm against my flesh. A driving guitar, his hands unclasping my bra, his mouth on my breasts. His tongue . . . He lowered himself, eventually, index finger running along the waist of my panties, from hip bone to hip bone and back. Bono's voice, lulling. *Sleep like a baby, tonight* . . .

He paused for a second, his eyes finding mine, and then he bowed his head, took the material in his teeth, and slowly, slowly pulled them off. When he'd succeeded in getting them down to my ankles, he sat back and crossed his arms over his chest. His expression almost smug.

"What? What are you thinking?"

"I want to see what you do when I'm not with you."

It took me a minute to register his request. "Now?"

"Now. Show me."

When I got to our booth at the fair just before eleven the following morning, Matt was already there poring over his laptop. Lulit had yet to arrive.

"You want the good news or the bad?" he greeted me.

"No 'Good morning'?"

He smiled, pushing his glasses up onto his face. "Sorry. Good morning. Good news: We're going to sell a lot of art today."

We'd been doing well thus far. Glen Wilson's installation *Gatekeeping* was striking. Salvaged chain-link fences, with large-scale portraits woven throughout the steel mesh, symbolic of the gentrification transforming the artist beach community of Venice. The pieces representing the remnants of once-affordable properties and their displaced residents. It was political, powerful art.

"So what's the bad news?"

"You're a blind item," he said, positioning the laptop so I could view the screen.

"A what?"

"Jo just sent this."

The browser was opened to a website I didn't recognize. Blind gossip something or another. At the top of the page there was an item titled "Naked Lunch."

Which pretty boy with a penchant for mature women has been moonlighting as a collector in South Beach this week? Is he fulfilling his artistic desires or that of his amorous dealer?

I stared at it for a moment, trying to compute. It seemed so esoteric to me, random. "Is there a photo?"

"No."

"Is my name up there?"

"Not yet. But it's a matter of time before someone guesses."

"How did Josephine know it was us? It could be anyone."

Matt sighed, shutting the window. "The clues: *Wise or Naked*, August Moon, *Petty Desires*. It's all in there."

"Fuck," I said. We'd been so careful. So lucky. "Who reads that thing?"

"Pretty much everyone who cares about gossip," he laughed. "Sorry."

I nodded. It was bound to happen. "'Amorous dealer.' Great."

Matt smiled. "It could have been much less favorable. Lulit doesn't know. We don't have to tell her."

"Okay," I said. "Maybe that's best."

My pretty boy friend showed up sometime after two, wanting to see me, to see the fair. There was something of a lunchtime lull, and so we slipped away with Lulit's permission.

"This dress," he said as we meandered through the neighboring booths.

"What about it?" It was a cream-colored crepe shift. Sleeveless, short.

"It's rather . . . *wee*."

"That it is." I smiled over at him.

As always I was aware of the eyes on Hayes. Poufy curls, skinny jeans, boots. A walking exclamation mark. But for the first time, and I wasn't sure if it was just my imagination, it seemed that people were looking at *me* as well.

When we finally snaked our way over to the Sadie Coles booth to see Urs Fischer's *Small Rain* installation—a thousand cartoonish green plaster raindrops suspended from above—I leaned into him. "We're a blind item."

"You and I?"

"No, you and some other chick you were with the last couple of days in Miami." I paused. "You weren't with some other chick the last couple of days in Miami? Right?"

He smirked. "I'm trying to imagine when I would have squeezed that in. Perhaps when you passed out after your eighth orgasm? I slipped out and headed over to Soho House to see what trouble

I could get into. By the way, that, I think, might be our new record. Although I can't truly take credit for the first two because
you were pretty much on your own . . . Can we do that again,
tonight?"

"Can we not discuss this here?"

"You're being very short with me." He smiled. "Almost as short
as this dress."

"I'm a little on edge."

"Because of the blind item?"

"Yes."

He nodded slowly. "Can I give you some advice? Ignore it. It's
going to get worse. It's going to get really bad."

I turned to him. "What do you mean? How bad is it going to
get?"

"It's going to get bad."

Up until now I had assumed the worst that could happen was
Isabelle finding out and losing her mind. And I had barely survived
that. I could not envision how anything could possibly be more
traumatic. Clearly, I had just been naïve.

"That's it? That's all you're going to give me? You're just going
to send me out into the world with your psychotic fans and tell me,
'It's going to get bad, just ignore it'?"

He smiled, but there was something sad in his eyes. "Solène,"
he whispered, taking my hands. "There's no instruction manual
for this. We make it up as we go. Here's the deal: I don't talk about
my private life. Ever. I don't release statements. I don't comment
on it. I don't discuss it in interviews and I don't address it on social
media. You can choose what you want to do, but I find that's the
best way to deal with it. Otherwise, you're just giving them fodder.
Let them speculate. People are going to say a lot of things. Most of
them will not be true. And much of it will not be nice. But you
have to be strong enough to not acknowledge or address any of it.
If you can ignore it completely, that would be best. But if you can't,
you just have to remember that these are people who don't know

you and don't know me. And for the most part they're just making things up to sell advertising. Got it?"

I nodded.

"And whatever you do, never ever, ever read the comments."

"Okay."

"You look terrified." He smiled.

"Because I *am*. I wish you'd told me all this before."

"Before when? Before you started falling in love with me?"

"Who told you I was falling in love with you?"

"It's just a hunch."

"It was the eight orgasms that gave it away, wasn't it?" I deflected. My eyes were threatening to tear. There, among raindrops the size of pears, in the middle of Art Basel. "Fuck, Hayes."

"Shhh." He held my head, kissing my cheek. "It's okay. One day at a time. Today we ignore the blind item."

"Today we ignore the blind item."

When we returned to our booth, Lulit was in the midst of showing the *Invisible* installation to a curator from the Whitney. They were deep in conversation about Anya's work: part of a larger series of striking black-and-white portraits shot with either extremely high or low exposures, so her subjects, all women, were either blown out or reduced to shadows, both effectively rendering them near invisible.

"Lulit is sounding *very serious*." Hayes came up behind me, close.

I shushed him. There were a handful of others admiring Glen's gates. Matt had evidently stepped away.

"You know," he said, low, "I adore you both, but you are not the women to sell this whole invisible rubbish. Have you looked at yourselves?"

It took me a moment to register what he was saying, the audacity.

"I know you probably mean that as a compliment, but I'm not taking it that way."

"I'm just saying, it is quite likely that people will think you are taking the piss."

"That we're what? Taking the what?"

He smiled, adorable, even when infuriating. "Like mocking them. You are the two least invisible women in this entire convention center."

"I'm not sure that's true. But if it were, for the reasons you're insinuating it is, it would give us more impetus to support this project."

He was quiet for a bit, mulling the idea.

"You realize that we are currently the only gallery of our size owned by two women? If we're not the ones to back this, I don't know who is."

I was proud of that fact. That Lulit and I had managed to make it work despite the odds. That we'd garnered a certain amount of respect, success in the ten years that we'd been doing this. That we'd birthed this idea—to fight for the underrepresented, the underappreciated—and we were winning.

"I did *not* know that. That kind of makes you hotter."

I laughed at that. "Okay, go away. I need to work."

He drew me into him, both hands on my hips. A motion that was decidedly suggestive. "Tonight I think we should go for nine."

"I think you need to leave."

"I think you need to lose this dress."

"*Go.*"

" 'Look how sexy I am. But for the rest of you who are not so sexy, here's this wonderful installation that addresses all your insecurities.' "

"Get out of here, Hayes. Being a woman is a complicated thing."

"I bet it is." He leaned in to kiss my nose. "Have a good day. I love you. Good-bye."

"What did you say?"

"Nothing. I didn't say that. Fuck. I didn't say that. Good-bye." His face was red as he backed out of the booth. And for a fleeting moment I considered following him. Anywhere.

"What is it you're doing?" Lulit approached me shortly after the curator from the Whitney had departed. "This Hayes thing. What are you doing, Solène?"

I looked at her, not understanding. Was she not the one who'd fully endorsed this? Who'd told me to go and get my rock star?

"I thought this was just going to be a fling," she said, soft. "Like for the summer . . . I thought it was temporary and you were having fun and that was great. And *important*. For you . . . to move on, and grow. But it's now like serious, and you're completely falling for him, and it's affecting your decisions in not the best way. And he's *twenty*, Solène. *He's twenty*."

I was speechless.

"And he's going to fucking break your heart and I can't sit and watch that happen again. And don't tell me it's just sex. Because it's not just sex anymore. I've seen the way you look at each other . . . It's not just sex."

I wanted to be angry with her. I did. But I was terrified that everything she had said was right.

On Sunday, after a late brunch in the Design District, Hayes and I returned to find no fewer than two dozen young girls congregated outside at the front of the Setai.

They'd found us.

We managed to evade them by looping two blocks down to Eighteenth Street and using the beach entrance at the back. There were a handful of fans lingering there as well, and Hayes stopped and took a few photos. And then, just as we were about to maneuver our way through the gate, one of them asked, rather politely, "Is that your girlfriend?"

I felt it, every single hair on my arms and the back of my neck standing up. I spun to look at him, which was probably a rookie move. Hayes waved to his fans and smiled. "You guys have a good day, all right?" And then he shut the gate and it was over.

"Crisis averted?" he asked.

"Crisis averted."

We were meandering back through the sultry lobby when I spotted her: a striking brunette, with olive skin and exquisite bones. She looked to be early thirties, slender, sexy. Not the kind of person you could overlook, and yet Hayes did not seem to see her. He was doing that thing that celebrities sometimes do, purposefully avoiding eye contact with strangers so they wouldn't assume they had permission to start a conversation. I'd seen him do it before, in crowds, in public spaces. Shutting out the world. This time, his iPhone was the distraction.

But I noticed her right away. I saw her see us, see Hayes, and then I watched as a million emotions washed over her face. She looked away quickly and then turned back, as if drawn against her will. Her eyes scanning, scrutinizing, looking away again. And then I understood. She was too old to be a fan. She knew him. She *knew* him.

"Do you know this woman who's riveted by you?"

He looked up, his eyes landing on her just as she glanced over. I watched it register on his face. The recognition, the history. He'd slept with her. He might have even loved her. Whether or not he would call it that.

"Fee," he said. "Yeah."

She smiled faintly, and he, we, made our way in her direction.

"Hey," he greeted her, slightly flustered, leaning in to kiss her cheek. "Fee."

"Hayes." She said it slowly, the hint of an accent.

"How are you?"

"Good. I'm good."

"That's good." He was tugging at his hair, uncomfortable. "Um, Solène, this is Filipa. Fee, this is my friend Solène."

She smiled at me, her eyes missing nothing. And likewise, I found myself assessing her, wondering, reading between the lines. Whatever it was going back and forth between them, it was intense.

Is this how it would be, were I to randomly bump into him years from now when at least one of us had moved on? Would he be anxious and awkward and pulling at his hair? Would my eyes betray both my desire and contempt? I saw my face in hers and it scared me.

"Are you here in town for a while?" she asked.

"Just a few days."

"Work?"

He shook his head. It was painful to watch.

"Um, I need to check in with Matt," I said, excusing myself. I wanted to give them a moment alone.

But even from my perch a few yards away, where I was scanning aimlessly through emails, I could feel the weight of their conversation. Of them. And it struck me, how much she looked like me. How he had a type. How perhaps we were all versions of this Hayes Campbell ideal. Yasmin, too.

Eventually, they parted and Hayes collected me to head up to the room.

He didn't speak until we were in the elevator. "Sorry about that. That was . . ."

"Yeah, it was kind of obvious what that was."

He sighed, and then reached for my hand, squeezing it.

When we got to the suite, Hayes made his way out onto the balcony, where he stood staring at the ocean for a good ten minutes before finding his way back inside to me.

"So, Fee . . ." he said, clearing his throat.

"I don't need to know," I said.

"I need you to know . . . Full disclosure: I kind of fucked up her marriage."

I looked over from where I was standing near the bedroom entrance. "You *kind of fucked up her marriage*? Either you did or you didn't."

He paused, tugging at his lower lip. We were back to that. "I did."

"I thought you said those were just rumors."

"Most of them are. That one wasn't."

I took my time processing. "Just so I'm aware, are we going to continue to bump into people who you've fucked . . . up?"

"That's not fair."

"Isn't it?"

"You're not jealous . . ."

"I'm not jealous."

"I like you."

"I don't doubt that . . ."

"I'm here with *you*."

"That's not the point."

"What's the point, then? I'm confused."

"Never mind," I said, because I wasn't sure. And the point may have very well been that I wasn't sure about anything. That I wasn't sure about us. That the idea that this would continue to happen, always, might have been more than I signed up for. That I wasn't ready to exert the energy in comparing and competing, and maybe, just maybe, I'd made a mistake.

"Perhaps I hadn't thought this through," I said.

"What does that mean? Why are you saying that?"

"I know you want me to think of you as just Hayes, but every time we step outside, you are also Hayes Campbell. And that comes with a lot of baggage, and some of it is harder to carry than others."

He stood there, watching me, the vast Atlantic behind him. "Are you saying you don't want to do this?"

"I'm saying when we're alone in our little cocoon, it's perfect."

"And when we're not?"

"And when we're not, it's less so."

I could see him growing angry, frustrated. "What are you doing, Solène? Are you trying to push me away?"

"I'm not trying to push you away."

"Well, then, what are you doing? None of this should come as a surprise to you," he said. "You knew what I did. What I do. You knew getting into this."

"I know that."

"It's complicated, yes. There's baggage. But there's a lot on your end, too. And I've accepted that . . . and I'm half your age." He let that sit there. Stinging. "I'm going for a walk," he stated, terse.

He seemed to have taken the air out of the room with him, because suddenly I could not breathe. His absence, stifling.

I knew I was wrong. My way of coping. To distance myself before the inevitable. In some ways, I had done the same to Daniel. I had pushed. And now he was getting married and fathering someone else's child. And that could not be undone.

It would cost me nothing to push Hayes away. To not have to think about random women in hotel lobbies. And reptilian models. And the numerous fans who would have eagerly taken my place. To be rid of all of that. His fame, cumbersome, like a fucking steamship. I wondered then who he would have been without it.

The door flew open, and Hayes came charging in. It had been minutes.

"I can't even go for a fucking walk!" His eyes were wet, his voice quaking. "I forgot my sunglasses and I haven't a hat and I can't even go for a fucking walk!"

He hadn't a hat.

I would have smiled at him if I did not think it would upset him more.

"I fucking hate this," he said before I could speak. And I wasn't sure if he was referencing our spat or his inability to walk out on it without being recognized.

"I know what you're doing, and I'm not just going to stand here and let you push me away. You're trying to push me away."

"Maybe," I said.

"Why?"

"You're a rock star—"

"I'm a *person*. First and foremost. And I have feelings. And I know this career comes with a lot of baggage, but don't write me

the idea *of* you   239

off just because I'm in a fucking band. It's what I do, it's not who I am. It doesn't—what is it you say?—it doesn't *define* me.

"What happened?" he asked. "It was going well."

"It stopped being just sex."

"It hasn't been just sex in a long time, Solène." His words hung there, heavy like the Miami air.

"Where are we going with this, Hayes?"

"Where do you *want* to go with this?"

"Where do *you* want to go with this?"

"I want to go all the way." In that moment he sounded so sure of himself, despite his tears. So certain of the possibility of us.

I was still. Quiet.

"You afraid?" he asked.

I nodded.

"So am I. But I'm all right with that. If I get hurt, I get hurt. It happens, right? Someone always gets hurt. But I don't want to miss out on us because I was afraid."

new york, ii

It started off small.

Rose's parents would not let her come to New York for the boys' premiere. Her father argued that she'd be missing two days of school, which was true. But I'd seen them pull her out a full week before spring break so they could make the most of their Kenyan safari, and I knew it had less to do with their concern of her being truant than my current relationship status.

On Twitter, I gained eleven new followers, none of whom I personally knew and all with anonymous handles like @Hayes_curls17 and @MarryMeCampbell. There was one random message in my notifications from an @NakedAugustBoyz that read: "Are you the one?" And for some reason, that simple question seemed terribly intrusive, personal. As if she'd reached out from wherever she was, and touched me.

And then, on my Instagram, beneath a photo I'd posted from Miami, of one of Glen Wilson's pieces, someone with the peculiar handle @Holiwater had posted: "Hayes?" And nothing else.

Hayes had once explained how a certain subgroup of their fandom had fantasized all these perverse relationships between the guys. "They 'ship' us," he'd said. "Like they think I'm having a relationship with Oliver or Liam or Simon, and they combine our names and they invent all these scenarios, and it's very entertaining but it's also quite crass." And so I knew any handle with the name "Holi" in it was a "shipper" of Hayes and Oliver.

"That's the most insane thing I've ever heard," I'd said when he'd informed me. "Why would teenage girls fantasize about you having sex with your friends?"

"Absolutely no idea," he'd said.

But I was still clueless as to how any of his fans might have identified me, and then I made the mistake of revisiting the blind item. And to compound it, I read the comments. All 128 of them. The majority of which had accurately named Hayes. There were no fewer than a dozen posters who had recalled his photo at Joanna Garel's opening and inferred that it had to have been someone at Marchand Raphel. The rest was cake.

We arrived in New York late Tuesday night. The boys had shot *The Tonight Show with Jimmy Fallon* earlier in the day after a handful of interviews, their PR in overdrive in anticipation of the movie and album release. Hayes was exhausted but putting on a brave face.

"Text me when you're close to the hotel," he said, on the phone, shortly after we'd landed. "There are a slew of fans out front and I'm going to send someone down to meet you and the girls."

"What's a 'slew' exactly?"

He laughed. "A little less than all of them. But you'll be okay, I promise."

He was not exaggerating. There were easily over a hundred and fifty girls outside of the Mandarin Oriental, at eleven p.m., on a school night, in December. Where were their mothers?

"Oh my God." Georgia's face lit up on seeing the swarm. "How cool is this?"

Isabelle turned to me, and I could see the panic in her eyes. "Are we going to walk through that? Do they know who you are?"

"Yes, we're going to walk through it. No, they don't know who I am. We'll be fine." I tried to say it as convincingly as possible.

Then, like clockwork, as the car pulled up in front of the entrance on Sixtieth, I spotted Fergus exiting the building with a bellhop in tow. I'd never been so happy to see a familiar bald head.

"Well, hello there," he greeted us, opening the car door.

The fans were barricaded on either sides of the entrance, but the hum of their excitement and squeals of "Who's that?" and stomping of their feet and singing of "Sorrowed Talk" en masse was still unsettling.

We had almost made it safely to the entrance when a voice off to the side called "Solène," and I turned to see whom I might have known who was also staying at the Mandarin Oriental. And then it dawned on me: I knew no one.

Someone yelled, "That's her!" and there was a collective gasp and flashes were going off, and I realized in that moment that my life as I knew it was over.

The girls would not sleep.

Hayes had booked us adjoining rooms on the forty-sixth floor and then came by to make certain we were settling in. Two hours later, they were still on a high, giggling and plotting and cooing over their good fortune, and I could not effectively slip out of my room to meet him in his suite on the floor below.

"I'm knackered. Just wake me," he'd texted. "Just crawl into my bed and do things . . ."

It was almost two when I finally made it to his room, and at that point I would have been happy to have him just hold me, and inhale him while he slept. But Hayes evidently had other plans.

"Hiiii."

"I thought you were knackered."

"I'm knackered, I'm not dead," he said, wriggling out of his underpants.

"They ID'd me."

"Who ID'd you?"

"Your fans."

He smiled then, pulling off my T-shirt, pushing my hair out of my face. He was not completely awake. "It's okay. You're safe here. You're safe here in my bed."

"And when I leave?"

"And when you leave . . . if I've done my job . . . you'll be happy."

In the morning, Isabelle and Georgia went for a swim in the hotel pool while I ducked out for a long run. I bundled up, donned a set of headphones, and timed my departure with a group of German tourists, and none of the fandom seemed the wiser. And that hour or so alone was heaven. Up Central Park West, cutting in at Eighty-sixth Street, twice around the reservoir, and home. The air cold, crisp, perfect. I'd missed this. New York.

In the thirty-fifth-floor sky lobby, while waiting for an elevator post-run, I encountered a guest at the front desk who was having problems with his room key.

"This key card is a bit dodgy. Could you perhaps switch it for me?"

I smiled on hearing his accent: British, posh, desirable.

He ended up riding in the elevator with me. He was tall, rakish, a thick head of salt-and-pepper hair. Maybe fifty, if that.

"Good run?" he asked once we'd pressed our respective buttons.

"Very. Yes."

"Where did you go?"

I told him.

"You did all that? This morning? Bloody hell, that shows dedi-
cation. Perhaps if you'd given me a wake-up call, I would have come
with you."

I laughed at that. He had kind eyes, an inviting smile.

"I didn't get the wake-up call, I'm afraid."

"Tomorrow . . ." I teased.

"Tomorrow," he chuckled. "Room 4722. I'll be waiting."

"All right."

"If my wife answers, just hang up."

"Okay," I laughed. "Will do." We'd reached the forty-sixth floor.
The doors were opening.

"You're beautiful," he said suddenly, as if he could not help himself.

"Thank you."

"You have a lovely day."

"You, too."

I was still smiling when I got to my room. The idea that I could
be pouring sweat and still attractive/attracted to middle-aged busi-
nessmen in hotel elevators. Perhaps it was the Lululemon.

I'd barely gotten my sneakers off when the girls came barging
in, hysterical. They were yelping and jumping and speaking over
each other. Apparently, they'd had the distinct pleasure of
bumping into one Simon Ludlow and his personal trainer at the
pool. And after they chatted him up and explained who they
were, Simon had invited them to join him for a quick jaunt to the
Apple Store and lunch before he had to begin prepping for this
evening's premiere. And could they pretty please, with icing on
top, go?

"Absolutely not."

"Mom, his bodyguard is going to be there."

"I don't care, Isabelle. Simon is twenty-one years old. Why is he inviting you to lunch?"

"It's just pizza."

"Actually, he turned twenty-two last month," Georgia added, as if that would somehow help their case.

"No. *No.*"

"Mom, *please.* He only invited us after I told him you were my mom. He was just trying to be nice. *Please.*"

"He's like the sweetest one," Georgia said, and at that point I realized they were wearing makeup. What the hell?

"He might even be gay," Isabelle added. Her attempt to soften the blow?

Georgia threw her a look. "He is not gay. Simon is like the *least* gay."

"He's not the *least* gay."

"There's a *least* gay? Who's the least gay?"

"Rory," they said in unison.

"Okay, I can't deal with this right now. I'm going to have a shower and think about it and then I'll let you know. But don't get your hopes up. And take off that makeup. No one is going anywhere with makeup."

"Okay," Isabelle said. "But we're supposed to meet him in the lobby at eleven-fifteen. So could you kind of shower fast?"

I was trying to remember everything I knew about Simon. Whether he'd struck me as a potential rapist, child molester, predator. But the only image I had of him was as a jocular blond who liked age-appropriate models. Regardless, I texted Hayes.

Simon invited the girls on an outing to the Apple Store.
Please advise.

Totally safe.

Really?

Really.

Also, did you know there was a LEAST gay guy in your
band?

Lol.
Rory.

Great. I want to ask where you fall on that list, but maybe I
don't really want to know . . .

?????
You haven't been complaining.
Stop getting ur intel from 13 yr olds.

By ten after eleven we'd all congregated in the sky lobby, with its
sweeping view of Columbus Circle, the park, midtown. The girls
were near jumping out of their skin, and at the same time trying
to keep their cool. And I had still not made up my mind.

"*Please*, Mom."

"Do you not trust me?" Simon smiled, all broad shoulders, cleft
chin, and blond chiseled perfection. Did they just make them like
this in England? How was it they all found one another? "Your girlfriend doesn't trust me, Campbell."

His candor threw me. I was not yet in the habit of referring to
myself as Hayes's "girlfriend," especially in front of Isabelle.

"I made a promise to Georgia's mom," I said.

This was true. Earlier in the week, when I'd swung by Georgia's house to pick up her bags, her mother, Leah, had asked about
Hayes. I told her the truth. She high-fived me, and I laughed, but
vowed to keep her daughter under lock and key.

"She'll be fine," Simon said. "Trevor will be with us the entire
time."

I looked over to see Trevor standing watch near the elevator

bank. Tall, all-powerful Krav Maga Trevor. Ready to take on the
tsunami of fans below.

There were a group of girls congregating in the sunken lounge
not far from us. Fans who'd somehow figured out the boys' schedule and booked rooms at the hotel. Security detail was keeping
them at bay, but I could see them in my peripheral vision, whispering and giggling and capturing everything on their camera
phones. Later, our exchange, inaudible from a distance, would end
up on YouTube.

"They'll be okay, Solène," Hayes said, reassuringly, his hand at
the base of my spine.

But they weren't *his* kids.

My eyes moved from Hayes to the girls to Simon and back
again.

"Trevor," Desmond called over to him. He'd been surveying the
activity in the lounge, never more than twenty feet from Hayes. "I'll
go with them. You stay here. You all right with that, Solène?"

I nodded, touched by the kindness of his gesture.

"Thank you!" Isabelle hugged me. "You're the best mom *ever!*"
The girls were near exploding as they headed with Simon toward
the elevators. I imagined what they were going to tell their friends
in L.A. Poor Rose and her judgmental parents. Missing out.

"Thank you," I said, wrapping my arms around Desmond. I
could not recall ever having hugged him before.

"No problem," he said. And then: "Don't break him." He gestured toward Hayes.

"Just his heart." I smiled.

"Not even that."

I watched him take a few paces toward the group near the elevators before I called him back. "Des, they're thirteen."

"Got it."

"Treat them as if they were your own daughters."

"Absolutely," he said.

It wasn't until they had parted that Hayes threw me a bemused
look. "What precisely do you think is going to happen at the

Apple Store?" he laughed. "What kind of animals do you think we are?"

"They're virgins, Hayes. I've seen you in action. I know how persuasive you can be."

"Really?" He took my hand, leading us to the elevators that went up to the rooms. He seemed to not care that we were being watched, recorded. "Well, for one, I'm pretty sure you weren't thirteen when I met you. Nor a virgin. And still . . ."

"And still?" An elevator arrived and we waited for the passengers to exit before stepping into the empty lift. The doors closed. Alone.

". . . and still I was very respectful. I did not force you to do anything you were not comfortable doing. Not once. And now you're like: 'Anal? Sure.'"

I laughed, uneasy.

This was something new. The "when in Miami" that I thought was going to stay in Miami, but apparently not. And evidently something that once required a year of marriage and much coaxing could be negotiated with two glasses of Scotch and an "I promise I'll be gentle." Fucking millennials. *Fucking* millennials.

"There are cameras in here," I whispered.

"The cameras don't have mics," he said, completely assured.

I thought about it: Solange Knowles pummeling Jay Z, and that football player knocking out his fiancée, and I realized, indeed he was right. No mics.

"I'm pretty certain I didn't say 'Sure.'"

"Actually, I think you said 'Please.'" He smiled, coy. Dimples. "You like me an awful lot."

"Don't push your luck."

He moved toward me then, reaching to hold my head in his hands. "Please," he repeated, before kissing me on the mouth. So soft, so tender, I might have forgotten where I was.

"Cameras," I whispered when we parted.

"I don't care who sees us," he said. And then he kissed me again. "We've got about two hours. Let's go do something dirty."

The doors were opening. There were two security guys I did not recognize on his floor. Different from the ones who'd done the night shift. I'd stopped trying to keep them straight. Staying in a hotel with Hayes and staying in a hotel with August Moon were two completely different things.

"Thank you, Simon Ludlow," Hayes said, stepping out of the lift. "Your check is in the post."

I froze, realizing what he'd said. "Did you . . . Did you arrange with Simon to take the girls?"

He was holding the doors open, waiting. "Maybe."

"Hayes. That is totally inappropriate."

"Is it?"

"You *paid* him?"

"He owed me."

I could not help but laugh. "You are so fucking bad. You are the worst."

"And that is why you love me," he said. "Two hours. The clock's ticking . . ."

The crowd at the Ziegfeld Theater for the premiere of *August Moon: Naked* was unlike anything I'd ever seen. There were thousands of fans swarming in every direction. Fifty-fourth Street completely closed off. Traffic at a standstill on Sixth Avenue and Seventh. A red carpet that extended a full city block, bleacher upon bleacher of photographers and press. Extensive security detail. For five guys who were schoolboys just a few short years prior, "playing football on Green," I imagine it was overwhelming.

We arrived nearly two hours after the boys. Their time occupied with photo ops and walking the press line and engaging with their fans. Hayes had warned me that he would be consumed with promotional duties and suggested I would probably be happier if I brought a friend, and so two weeks earlier I'd called Amara and asked how she felt about being my wingwoman.

"Are you kidding me?" she'd laughed, on the phone. "The

opportunity to cross that off my bucket list? Star-studded premiere of boy band documentary? Check. What are we wearing?"

The theater was huge, the crowd chaotic. Industry types and Brits and contest-winning fans and celebrities with their teen daughters. My own was on a momentous high. She and Georgia had been floating since their trip to the Apple Store. Replaying every moment of their afternoon. Everything Simon did, said, laughed at. They'd already experienced the unthinkable. The premiere was just icing.

It went quickly. The film was surprisingly well done: beautifully shot reportage of the band's meteoric rise. Concert footage, intimate portraits, a compelling, almost wistful look at Augie mania in all its fervent glory. Much of it shot in artistic black and white. A series of flawless frames lingering on skin and lashes and lips. By the end I'd determined that she, the director, must have loved them all.

Amara agreed. "I feel like I just watched a ninety-minute Herb Ritts music video. Is it bad I want to lick them? Their skin . . . Did we not appreciate our skin when we were that young?"

"I don't think we did."

"Youth," she laughed. "Wasted."

I did not see him until the after-party. The guys, all seated together, were swarmed and swept up so quickly when the credits began to roll that there was no penetrating the thick wall of security and sycophants. But in the car, on the way over to the Edison Ballroom, he texted.

Where are you? Why aren't you with me? I miss you. I need you.

Ditto.

What'd you think? Did you like it?

Loved.

xo

Find me. When you get to the party, find me.

I did. But it was no simple feat, in a sprawling two-story hall with atmospheric lighting and nine-hundred-plus guests. We navigated through the crowds and the waitstaff and the cocktail tables and the potted trees dripping with white lights, part sexy speakeasy, part winter wonderland. The DJ was blasting "All the Love," the group's next scheduled single. There was a large screen above the stage playing looped clips from the documentary, and I was keenly aware that everyone was there to celebrate my boyfriend, more or less.

At some point near the center bar, someone called my name, and I turned to find Raj. I had not seen him since Cap d'Antibes. He greeted me with a warm hug and introduced himself to Amara and the girls. And he was so affable and familiar I realized that for better or worse Hayes had likely been filling in some people on aspects of our relationship all along.

Raj led us through another level of security to the private booths off to the side. Each with its own reserved place card: "Universal," "WME," "Lawrence Management," "Liam Balfour," "Rory Taylor," "Oliver Hoyt-Knight," "Simon Ludlow," and there, tucked in the most secluded corner, "Hayes Campbell." He was standing with his back to me, engaged in conversation with a gentleman I did not recognize.

Raj called out to him, and the look on his face when he saw me made my heart smile. Surprise and happiness and wonder. As if he were seeing me for the first time. As if we hadn't spent the afternoon doing naughty things.

And yet, despite the fact that I could read every emotion washing over his features, I was beside myself when he took my head in both his hands and kissed me. Before my kid, before my friend, before his businesspeople, before his fans, before every single fucking person in the Edison Ballroom.

"Hi," he said.

"Hi." I beamed. He, in his Tom Ford suit and dazzling smile. "So . . . I guess we're public?"

"I guess we're public." He leaned into me, his thumbs flicking over my earlobes, his voice low. "You look insanely beautiful."

"Thank you."

It was sublime, my dress. Lanvin. Midnight blue silk, draped, gathered, fitted, hitting me at the knee.

"Red lipstick?"

"I thought I would switch it up."

"It just makes me want to do things to your mouth," he said.

"As opposed to all the other times when you don't?"

He laughed, withdrawing. "Hello, ladies!"

I looked on as he greeted Amara and the girls and introduced us to those in his booth: friends of his parents, a couple of reps from TAG Heuer, a publicist. Ever the host, he busied himself making certain we were all taken care of, pouring me and Amara flutes of champagne and the girls cranberry juice, even though he was drinking water.

"Fucking Graham," he muttered to me, "he's been on me and Liam like a hawk. Oh, girls." He turned to Isabelle and Georgia. "Have you met Lucy Balfour? She's Liam's little sister. She's thirteen. She flew all the way from London with her mum and dad and she's miserable because she says she has no one here her age to hang out with. And when I pointed out that there were quite a few thirteen-year-old girls here, she complained that they were all 'crazed, immature fans.' And then I said, 'Well, you haven't met my friends Isabelle and Georgia, because they are certainly not that.'"

My girls were beaming. So very sweet in their dresses.

"Come, let us find Lucy!"

"Where the hell did you find him?" Amara asked. We had stepped away from the booth and were navigating a path toward the main floor. "He is really quite perfect."

"I know," I said. "He is."

"Jesus. How did you do it? I'm out here on Tinder, and I'm miserable . . ."

I nodded, empathetic. Amara was a few years older than me and had never been married. She had never wanted kids. But she had also never wanted to be alone.

"And with all these online dating services," she continued, "so much comes down to your photos, your physical appearance, your face. Tinder is purely your face. It's people swiping left and right in reaction to your face. And my face is changing. And people re-act to it differently. Men react to it differently. I used to be a hot young blonde, and I'm not anymore. Although I still think of my-self that way on the inside," she laughed.

"I think of you that way." I smiled. It seemed to me that all my friends were going through this. The self-definition crisis.

"But I'm not. On the outside anyway. And it's like I have this shifting identity. I'm not who I used to be. And ten years from now I might be somebody else altogether. Even if I never become some-one's mom or change my career or move to Idaho. My identity is different because the world responds to my physical appearance differently. And their response inadvertently changes how I see my-self. And that's kind of . . . crazy."

"It is," I said. "But we redefine ourselves. We evolve. That's what people do."

"But I want to evolve because *I* evolve. I don't want other people to choose when that happens for me."

She had a point. And I had to wonder if I was evolving. Or if this thing with Hayes was just one giant step back. Never mind how people were viewing it.

The DJ was playing Justin Timberlake, king of the boy band graduates. Justin, who had somehow settled down and was about to become a father. Clearly, he'd evolved.

"I think aging is hard for everyone." Amara swiped a red bliss potato with crème fraîche and caviar off a passing tray. "But it's definitely harder for women. And I think even more so for beautiful women. Because if so much of your identity and your value is tied up in your looks and how the world responds to your physical appearance, what do you do when that changes? How do you see yourself then? Who do you become?"

I paused, attempting to process all of it. Hayes was on the screen. His features blown up to ridiculous proportions, and the symmetry still, like art. His beauty clearly defining him. "I think I'm going to need more to drink."

She laughed, popping the potato in her mouth. "Don't worry. You have a couple more years left. Things don't really start falling apart until forty-two."

We spotted each other at the same time. He was engaged in conversation with two fetching twenty-somethings who were clearly smitten. But he waved and I inclined my head, and then he dismissed them before making his way over.

Oliver.

"This one is so fucking cute," Amara said under her breath as he approached.

"Let it go. He's trouble. But he does know his art."

"Murakami." She smiled. "You can just look at him and be happy."

She'd said it casually, a throwback to an earlier conversation. But something about it resonated. Finding joy in art.

"Solène Marchand." Oliver grinned. That he knew my last name threw me.

"Oliver Hoyt-Knight. This is my girlfriend Amara Winthrop. Amara, Oliver."

He greeted her before turning his attention back to me. "Hi."

"Hi." I leaned in to kiss his cheek. And it wasn't until he reached out for my waist that I realized I'd made a mistake.

"You look stunning," he said in my ear, low.

I pulled back, and made a point of announcing loudly, "You clean up quite nicely yourself."

He laughed.

"That's a joke, Amara. Oliver always looks like this. When you first learn to tell them apart, you learn that Oliver is the dandy one."

He was wearing a charcoal-gray three-piece suit, a dark tie, a coordinating pocket square. Posh sex on a stick.

"Who told you that? Beverly?"

"Is she your wardrobe person? Yes, then, Beverly."

His hand was still on my hip.

"Also, we look nothing alike," he said, hazel eyes piercing.

"Where's your girlfriend?"

"She couldn't make it. Exams."

"I'm sorry."

He let loose my waist then, sipped from his glass. "It is what it is."

Amara spoke suddenly, and the fact that I'd nearly forgotten she was there was telling. "Dominic and Sylvia D'Amato are over at the bar. I'm going to say hello."

It took a second to register: the owners of the Hamptons house. *Mrs. D'Amato.*

"You know them?"

"Please. They practically pay my mortgage." She winked. And then I remembered: the Hirst, the Lichtenstein, the Twombly, the Murakami. Gagosian repped them all.

"Oliver, pleasure . . ." Amara said. "Solène." She gave me a funny look. "You okay if I leave you for a minute?"

"I'm okay," I laughed, downing my champagne.

"So," he said once she was gone, "are you having fun?"

"Yes."

"Are you being taken care of?"

"I am, thank you."

"Yes, I heard." He smiled, swilling again from his drink. "Thinner walls than you would think at the Mandarin Oriental."

I froze, allowing it to sink in. The ease with which he'd transgressed. As if he'd reached out once again and touched me. "If I'd known you were listening, I would have made an effort to call your name."

He laughed. It was not the response he was expecting. "Well, maybe next time I can watch."

"Me? . . . Or Hayes?"

Oliver tensed. "What do *you* think?"

"I think it says something that I'm asking you to clarify."

He stared at me for a moment. And then he smiled. It hurt that he was so good-looking, and still managed to be such an ass.

"Well, you know where to find me. When you're ready for an upgrade . . ."

"I love your audacity, Oliver. I'm going to be nice to you, because I know how much you mean to Hayes. And because I like Charlotte. And because you're cute. But I'm not going to let you cross the line . . ."

He paused, smiled, swilled from his glass. "I think you already have."

"Ollie!" A voice called from off to the side.

He looked over, and I followed his line of sight to a striking young woman approaching us in a peacock-green dress. I took her for a model, but then thought she seemed far too self-possessed. And he seemed far too adoring.

"Hey." She hugged him, mussed his hair. He kissed her cheek. And then I realized.

"Solène, do you know my sister, Penelope? Pen, this is Solène. She's a friend of *Hayes*." It seemed to me he said it pointedly, but I could not be certain as to why.

She was stunning.

She had her brother's height and arresting hazel eyes, but the similarities ended there. She was sexier than I'd pictured, riper, darker, fuller lips. A young boy's wet dream. I wanted to high-five Hayes's fourteen-year-old self. I imagined his joy. And then it dawned on me that *she* may have very well been the prototype. The original Hayes fantasy.

"Pleasure," she said, extending her elegant hand.

I could feel her assessing me and then remembered that I was not supposed to know their story and could not openly assess her in the same way.

"Are you from New York?" she asked.

"Los Angeles," I said, and she nodded.

"Did you like the film?"

"Very much . . ."

There was something unnerving about being in her presence. Knowing who she was and what she'd represented to Hayes. And the idea that she knew him. She knew his mouth, she knew his dick, she knew his hands. She knew what I was going back to at the hotel. She *knew* him.

This seemed to be happening over and over again.

"Did *you* like it?" I asked.

"It was *fun*." She smiled. "They're a *fun* bunch."

"Yes," I said, turning to look at her brother. "That they are."

"Ha!" Oliver smirked. And as much as I might have wanted to, I could not hate him. Because he had that *thing*. That cocky thing I fell for. Every single time.

"Liam, especially," Penelope continued. "He's quite rascally, that one."

I nodded, taking her in. Round breasts, narrow waist. I wondered if she'd slept with Liam, too. Lanky Liam with his darling freckles, angelic voice, and winsome smile. And then I realized how outrageous that sounded. But it was all a wee too incestuous for me. I needed to get out of there.

"If you'll excuse me," I said, "I have to check on my daughter. Penelope, it's been a pleasure. Oliver, I'll see you around."

I found Hayes back up near the booths, engaged in conversation with a bunch of women I did not know. They could have been publicists, industry execs, ex-girlfriends, fans. I'd stopped caring.

His face lit up when he saw me, and he managed to remove himself from his admirers. "Where did you run off to? You okay?"

"Penelope is here. I just met Penelope."

"Yeah . . ."

"Did you *know* she was going to be here?"

"I found out yesterday."

"Were you *not* going to tell me?"

"I didn't want you to worry unnecessarily." His hand was by my face, tucking my hair behind my ear, subtly transmitting our relationship to all.

"Have you seen her yet?"

"Briefly. In the theater." He reached out for my wrist, fingering my cuff, familiar. "Solène . . . It's been over for a long time . . ."

"I understand that."

He was quiet for a moment, and then: "I'm sorry you keep bumping up against my past."

I nodded. It was something I had not had much experience with. When I married Daniel, there were only fourteen girls that he'd slept with, and they were all on the East Coast. Except for that one in Capri.

"Come," he said. "My mum and dad are over there. I want you to meet them. Have you had a sufficient amount of alcohol?"

"Probably not."

"Let's get you some more champagne then, and we'll go meet my parents."

They were standing over near Hayes's table. I could see her face in profile as we approached. She had lovely bones and flawless skin, and she looked like the boy I had come to love, and that, in itself, was unsettling. She was laughing at something and I could see her dimples, and for a moment I thought I might not be able to go through with it. But Hayes called to them and they both turned around and there was no time to run. Not that my feet could have moved if I'd willed them, because standing next to Hayes's mother was the rakish Brit from the hotel elevator.

The air left my lungs.

"Mum, Dad, this is Solène," he said proudly, his hand at the small of my back, encouraging, protective.

"Victoria." She took my hand in hers, warm. Warmer than I'd expected. "It's a pleasure."

"Likewise," I said.

"Ian," Mr. Campbell said, never breaking character, his two large hands pumping mine. "Lovely to meet you, Solène."

"My pleasure." I might have smiled a smidge too wide. Blame it on the awkwardness, the champagne, the fact that I'd openly flirted with Hayes's father.

I thought back to the first time that I'd met Daniel's parents at their house on the Vineyard, and how daunting they'd seemed to me then. It felt like I was there again. Except these people were technically my generation. And I knew they were likely thinking, *What the fuck are you doing with our child?*

"Our son is quite fond of you," Victoria said.

"Is he?" I turned to him, and the way he was looking at me brought to mind his expression in the photo he'd shown me with his mum and Churchill. So much adoration and awe. That it was directed at me was staggering.

"He's pretty wonderful, your son." I hoped I was not giving too much away. "You must be very proud of him."

"We are," Ian said. "Did you enjoy the film?"

"Very much, yes. It was artsier than I expected."

"It was. Hayes says you're in the art world?" Victoria was twirling the string of pearls around her neck. Her dress, black, classic, I recognized as Chanel. Of course.

"I am."

"A gallerist?" Ian asked.

"Solène's gallery is in this fantastic industrial space. And she and her partner solely represent artists that are women or people of color, which is pretty extraordinary on their part."

"That's rather noble," Ian added.

"Noble?" Hayes laughed. "It's *tremendous*."

"Hayes says you have a daughter?" Victoria took it upon herself to change the subject.

"Yes. Isabelle. She's here with a girlfriend, flitting about somewhere."

"They're with Lucy Balfour. They hit it off quite well."

"How old?"

"Thirteen."

"Thirteen." She smiled knowingly. "It goes by quickly."

Ouch.

"Campbell!" Rory Taylor was leaning in over the velvet rope. All gussied up, but still every bit the bad boy. He was tan, dark hair slightly disheveled, stubble, black suit, black shirt partially unbuttoned, chest tats peeking out. Was that a butterfly? A bird? "Sorry to interrupt. Hi, Mrs. Campbell, Mr. Campbell, Solène . . . Hayes, they want us to come up to the stage. Some introduction thing."

"All right. I'll be back. Don't go too far." He kissed me. In front of his parents, he kissed me. And part of me wanted to crawl under the fucking booth and die.

"So *you're* the girlfriend?"

Sometime after the band and the director and a handful of studio execs had officially thanked everyone for coming out and posed for a bunch of photos onstage, I ran into Ian near a side bar.

I was three champagnes in and looking for my fourth. "I'm the girlfriend."

"Wow. That's impressive. Even for him. However did he . . ." He trailed off, shaking his head. "Never mind. I'm not sure I want to know."

I don't know why I hadn't seen it before, but it was all there: Hayes's nose, Hayes's jawline, Hayes's hands, Hayes's fingers . . .

"So, I take it we're not running tomorrow," he laughed.

I shook my head, smiling. "Probably not . . ."

"Yes, that's probably for the best."

I could see Hayes across the room, whispering something in Simon's ear, laughing. His hand dwarfing the mouth of his glass. He'd managed to get himself something besides water, Graham be damned. What were they discussing? I wondered.

My attention turned back to Ian. "Was that your real room number, 4722?"

Hayes's father smiled, then swilled from his glass. "I'm not going to answer that question."

"Yes," I said, "that's probably for the best."

Toward the end of the night, when Amara had parted and the girls had returned to the hotel under the supervision of Liam's parents, Hayes and I sat together in one of the booths. We were alone, but it felt false. The velvet rope, Desmond standing a few feet away with his back to us. Like exotic animals in a cage.

"You know tonight changes everything, right?"

"Because I've met your parents?"

"No." He smiled. "Because there are people with cameras here. And press. People are going to talk. And it's going to be more than a blind item."

"I know that."

"And it's going to be more than one or two fans calling your name outside of a hotel. It's going to feel really different. I'm just warning you."

"Are you trying to say it's too late to turn back?"

He laughed, kissed me. "It's definitely too late to turn back." His hand had found its way to my knee beneath the table. "Jane and Alistair are giving me dirty looks from across the room."

"Are they?"

Hayes inclined his head to the ballroom floor, where, sure

enough, his managers, a commanding couple, were in conversation with some record people but clearly staring daggers in our direction. Hayes put on one of his megawatt smiles and waved. "Hello, Jane and Alistair, I know I'm going against your boy band playbook by consorting with someone completely age inappropriate in a public setting and we're going to lose a bunch of young fans in the Bible Belt. Sorry."

I laughed, grabbing his waving hand. "Stop that."

"Do you think they can read my lips?"

"I think they can read your cheeky attitude."

He turned to me then. "I like you."

"I know you do."

"Thank you for coming. It really meant a lot to me that you were here." He smiled slowly, his hand reaching to stroke the side of my face. "I more than like you. You know that, right? I'm not going to say it right now . . . but I do."

We sat there for a bit, disappearing in each other.

I spoke first. "I'm really proud of you . . ."

"For putting on a suit and showing up?"

"For all of this. None of this would have happened if it weren't for you, and your idea."

He squeezed my hand and smiled. "It might have been a wee selfish on my part. Plus, it's not exactly rocket science, is it?"

"It's art. And it makes people happy. And that's a very good thing. We have this problem in our culture. We take art that appeals to women—film, books, music—and we undervalue it. We assume it can't be high art. Especially if it's not dark and tortured and wailing. And it follows that much of that art is created by other women, and so we undervalue them as well. We wrap it up in a pretty pink package and resist calling it art."

Hayes was quiet, processing.

"That's part of why I do what I do . . . to push back on that, to combat it. And that's why you should be a little more proud of what *you* do . . ."

I could see him searching for a response. The start of a smile playing over his lips. "Remind me again. How did I find you?"

"My ex-husband bought you in an auction."

He laughed, his head angling back. His jaw. "We probably should thank him then."

"We probably should . . . Let's go back to the hotel. We can thank him properly there."

"Yes." He smiled. "Let's."

anguilla

They were eloping. Daniel and Eva. They'd made plans to do it in Maui the week after Christmas. Evidently Daniel liked his women pregnant in Hawaii. At least he'd had the decency to choose a different island.

He'd informed me the Saturday after we returned from New York. Straight, no chaser. "It's going to be a tiny ceremony, and I'd like Isabelle to be there."

"Of course," I said, attempting to hide all emotion.

We were in the kitchen. He, standing with his arms across his chest, looking ever awkward. His eyes roaming the space, the unfamiliar postcards and photos tacked to the fridge. This was no longer his home.

"She says she had a great time in New York . . ."

"She did."

"Did *you* have a good time?"

I paused at my spot before the stove where I'd been stirring risotto. Was he trying to parse out information about Hayes and me? Or was he genuinely interested in my happiness? "I did. Thank you."

"So . . . this is really a thing?"

"This is really a thing."

He nodded, leaning back on the island, stroking his chin, watching me.

"What, Daniel? What do you want to say?"

"I want to know how you see this playing out. Even if she says she's okay with it, I want to know how having a boyfriend that famous is not going to fuck up our daughter. And when he ends it and breaks your heart, and is photographed with some nineteen-year-old model on the cover of *Us*, I want to know what you think it's going to do to Isabelle to watch you go through that."

The risotto was boiling. There was nothing to say.

"I want you to be happy, Solène. I do. But not at the expense of our daughter."

By Sunday, four days after the premiere, things had begun to change. Drastically. I logged on to Twitter for the first time since New York and found I had 4,563 followers. Up from my previous high of 242. I thought perhaps it was an accident until I saw my notifications, which were too many to count, too much to process. I began to scroll through them, against my better judgment and Hayes's advice, and was shocked by what lay within.

Fuck u, u fucking bitch.

You're pretty but you're old af.

wtf is all this shit about you and hayes can you just confirm
something so i can go on with my life, thanks

When he cums does he scream "Mommy"?

u r so pathetic. I'd be so embarrassed if you were my mom. I bet
your daughter hates your guts

Don't listen to all those bitches, Solne, they're just jealous. You
seem nice.

hi December girlfriend

What does he see in you? I can't imagine your old ass is worth it.
What are you, 50?

Holi is real. Holi is real. Holi is real. Holi is real.

Instagram was no better. Whoever held the account @Holiwa-
ter had returned to comment on every one of my photos of the past
two and a half years with her signature inquiry: "Hayes?" Another,
@hayesismynigga, had written "bitch," "salope," "connasse" over
and over and over again. And yet another, @himon96, took the opportunity to write in all caps on at least a dozen photos "VINTAGE
VAGINA."
When Hayes called from his place in Shoreditch that night,
the sprawling loft that I had yet to see with the Nira Ramaswami
and the Tobias James gracing the walls, I tried not to let him hear
the anxiety in my voice. The band was both dropping the album
and premiering the movie in London on Monday, and I knew he
was already overwhelmed. But immediately he sensed something was off.
"What's wrong?"
"Twitter."
"I'm sorry, Sol. I'm sorry."

"They're animals."

"Not all of them."

"Just the ones who write on my page?"

"I told you not to read the comments. They can be really toxic. I'm sorry."

I thought about closing both accounts, switching them to private settings, blocking every hateful Augie. But in the end, I just put down my phone and walked away. They could not reach me if I did not let them.

On Tuesday I arrived at work shortly before ten. The others had already arrived, but the gallery was strangely quiet. I was going through my emails in the office when Lulit slipped in and shut the door.

"Hey. How are you feeling?" It was an awkward greeting.

I looked up from my computer, aware that something was amiss.

"I'm fine, thanks. Why?"

She braced herself, crossing her arms, leaning up against her desk. I knew her well enough to know that this was her confrontational pose. "Our voicemail was full when Josephine got in this morning," she started. "Our voicemail is never full. About a third of them were hang-ups, a third of them were press wanting to know if you could confirm whether or not you were dating Hayes Campbell, and a third were very rude girls leaving explicit comments. And that's just on our main line."

"Oh," I said.

"*Oh?*"

"I'm sorry."

"Solène—"

"I know. I know what you're going to say, Lulit . . . I'm sorry. I'm sorry they're calling. I'm sorry it's bleeding over into my work. I'm sorry."

She was quiet for a moment, staring off to the side. Who knew what was going through her pretty head?

"What are you going to do?" she spoke eventually. She'd asked it as if it only pertained to the phone calls, but I knew she meant about everything.

"I don't know," I said. "I don't know what I'm going to do. Tell Josephine to tell them 'No comment.'"

In the end, it did not matter whether or not Hayes and I commented because the tabloids picked up the story, what little of it they actually knew, and ran with it. And although I did not once search for material online, I'd heard the news from Amara. There was a series of shots of us exiting the Edison Ballroom that ran in *Us Weekly*, and *People*, and *Star*.

"You look exquisite," Amara said Wednesday morning on the phone. "He's leading you by the hand. His suit jacket is over your shoulders. He's turning to look back at you. You're smiling at each other and you both look ridiculously in love."

"Shut up. Don't say that."

"Sorry. It's true. It's a great shot. You should see it."

"I don't want to see it," I said. I was in traffic on the 10. Running late after my SoulCycle class. My in-box overflowing with old friends and acquaintances from out of the blue: "Hey, I see you have a new boyfriend." The day already weighing on me. And Hayes, a million miles away.

"You look like the Kennedys."

"You mean if John-John had dated his mom?"

"Yes, exactly," she laughed. "Shit, I've gotta go, it's Larry. Hang in there. Beware the wrath of teenage girls."

That evening, I got caught up on a phone call with Hayes, who was in Paris and flying to Rome the next morning, and I was late picking up Isabelle from fencing. Again. He'd made arrangements for us to spend a week in Anguilla over the holidays. He'd wanted to surprise me, but quickly discovered that negotiating Christmas trysts with a woman who had a teenage daughter and an ex-husband in the picture was not for the faint of heart.

"Well, if this was easy, then it wouldn't be worth it, would it?" he'd said, which made me laugh.

"You like me complicated, don't you?"

"I like you complex. I don't like you complicated."

"I like you every way possible," I said, and I could hear him smiling.

"Woman, I have to go to sleep. It's bad enough I'm in Paris and you're not here. Don't tease me."

I was still thinking about him and the lure of a week in the Caribbean later that night when Isabelle called me from her room, a distinct panic in her voice.

"Mom! Mom!!"

I found her seated at her desk, her laptop opened, an amateur handheld video playing on YouTube.

"What is that? What are you watching?"

"Us. You."

It took me a moment to register what I was seeing. A group of people in conversation from a distance. A vast well-lit space. And then it came together. The lobby of the Mandarin Oriental. The morning Simon took the girls to the Apple Store. Hayes and I had our backs to the camera. The others were facing us, their features coming in and out of focus. I couldn't make out any of our conversation, but it did not matter. The girls doing the recording had included a precise play-by-play.

"Is his hand on her ass? Holy shit, his hand is on her ass. Are you getting this? Shhh, I'm getting it. His hand is totally on her ass. Shhh. Did she just say 'Mom'? Did she call her 'Mom'? Oh my God, is that her daughter? No way! Holy fuck, that's her *daughter. Duuuude, your mom is fucking Hayes Campbell.* Whoa. Sucks to be her. Um, she just got into an elevator with Simon, I don't think she's hurting right now. But still, imagine your mom is fucking Hayes Campbell. That's like the fanfic that writes itself. She probably gets to call him 'Daddy.' 'Hey, Daddy.' 'Hiiiiii, Daddy.' 'I have an itch that needs scratching, Daddy.' 'Daddy, why don't you—'"

"Turn it off. Turn it off turn it off turn it off!" I slammed the laptop shut so forcefully, Isabelle's canister of markers flew off the desk. "Ignore it, Izz. Ignore it. No one's looking at that."

"Really?" She looked up at me, her eyes welling. "Because apparently it already has thirty-four thousand views."

I was shaking. "Please don't watch that. Promise me you will not watch that."

"It's out there, Mom."

"It's out there, but we don't have to let it in here. You have to promise me, Izz." I stooped to her level, taking her hands in mine. "You have to promise me that you will not search for those things. You will not go looking for those things. You will not Google. Because it's only going to hurt you. It's only going to hurt *us*. Those people don't know us. They don't know you. They don't know me. They don't know Hayes. They're going to say some really hurtful things and we just have to ignore it. Okay?"

She was crying now. The tears rushing. Her pain, palpable.

"Promise me, Izz. Please. Promise me."

"Okay." She nodded. "Okay."

But I knew it in my heart: there was no ignoring this.

Isabelle and I spent Christmas with my parents in Cambridge. Technically it was not my year to have her, but since Daniel was taking her to Maui for the second half of the holiday, he conceded Christmas. Coparenting was a complicated thing.

My mother and father fawned over Isabelle. They adored her and encouraged her in a way that I had not felt they'd done for me.

She was free to have her flaws, to be a little too loud, a little too dramatic, a little too American. And I think they found her amusing. Like a piece of Pop Art in a collection of Realists. They'd been much less forgiving with their own daughter.

In my parents' house there were reminders of my failures. There, in the library, amidst my father's numerous honors and awards and my mother's whimsical sketches. My wedding invitation, which my mother had mounted and encased in a shadow box frame with hydrangea petals from my bouquet. "Professor and Mrs. Jérôme Marchand request the honour of your presence at the wedding of their daughter Solène Marie to Mr. Daniel Prentice Ford . . ." They'd had them printed in French as well. There was my acceptance letter from Harvard. That not so much a failure as a reminder of my father's disappointment. And the numerous photos of me as a would-be ballerina.

For all these reasons I'd delayed telling them about Hayes. Because I knew there would be judgment. But now that it was out there in the public, I could no longer put it off.

"I'm going to tell you something, but you have to promise you'll keep your criticisms to yourself."

It was twilight, two days before Christmas, and my mother and I were strolling on Newbury Street, awash in its holiday glow. It had been raining on and off, with temperatures in the forties. The chill penetrating my coat, cutting to my bones. I'd lost five pounds since New York. It was not intentional.

"*Eh, pffft,*" my mother said, making that typically French gesture of disdain. "*C'est parfois difficile.*"

"It's not difficult, Mom. Just try it."

"Okay, *alors. Vas-y.* What is it?"

"I'm seeing this guy. He's in a band." I'd begun to make a concerted effort to no longer refer to Hayes as a "boy." If not for his dignity, then for mine.

"A band?" she repeated. "Does he do drugs? Does he have tattoos?"

"No." I smiled. "No drugs. No tattoos."

"Is he poor?"

"No." The idea was amusing to me, Hayes struggling. "It's a fairly successful band. The premiere Isabelle has been talking about was for his group."

"*C'est quoi, leur nom?*"

"August Moon."

She shook her head. "Never 'eard of them."

I laughed, my breath visible in the air. A car drove by us then, honking its horn. It struck me as a nostalgic sound, gridlock, wheels rolling over cold wet pavement. Winter in the city.

"Is he an idiot?"

"No, Mom. Give me some credit. He's smart. He's educated and charming . . . I think you would like him actually. He's British. He comes from a good family. He's kind . . ."

"So what is the problem then?"

I hesitated for a moment. "*Il a vingt ans.*"

"*Vingt ans?*"

I don't know why I thought telling her his age in French would lessen the blow. Evidently, I was mistaken.

"*Vingt ans?!*" she repeated. "*Oh, Solène . . . Ce que tu es drôle!*"

It was not the response I had been expecting. I *humored* her? Well, I suppose it was better than disappointing her, disgusting her, disgracing her. All of which she had let me know, in no uncertain terms, that I had done at some point or another. Maybe, in her old age, she was softening.

She was quiet for a moment, stopping to gaze into the window at Longchamp. And then when she resumed walking, she turned to me and said, "Well, this is just sex, right?"

I looked at her, speechless, although I should not have been. This was my mother after all. She was nothing if not blunt.

"You cannot fall in love with him," she continued. A warning. "Solène? You *cannot* . . ."

I said nothing.

Her face fell. "You have already fallen in love with him. *Dis-donc!*" She shook her head.

Now she was disappointed.

To my mother, falling in love was a bad thing. Not because I could get hurt, but because, to her, I was giving up my power. What a bizarre notion that was. That I could not completely open my heart and still be strong. That I was no longer in control of the relationship if I wasn't in control of my feelings. And as if any of that actually mattered.

"*Vingt ans,*" she repeated, sighing. We were passing the Church of the Covenant as we neared Berkeley Street. "*Eh bien* . . . Well, maybe you are more French than I thought."

And then I saw it, at the right corner of her mouth . . . the hint of a smile.

Anguilla was a magical place. A tiny slip of an island in the Lesser Antilles. Sleepy, subtle, even in its peak season. Hayes—or, more accurately, his assistant, Rana—had found us a secluded villa on the south shore with breathtaking views of Saint-Martin. Limestone, teak, exquisitely appointed. We had staff, we had security, and we had four bedrooms and seven days to ourselves.

"Do you like it?" he said. We were in the great room with its retractable glass doors opening to the terrace, the infinity pool, and a majestic panorama of the Caribbean.

"It'll do."

He smiled, squeezing me from behind. "Are you happy?"

"I am very happy."

We stood like that for some time, his body pressed up against mine, his nose buried in my hair, soaking in the moment, the tropical breeze, the seascape, serenity.

"Come," he said eventually. "Let's see the rest of the place."

We wandered through the various wings of the villa to see the additional bedrooms and their en suite baths, each with its own remarkable view. Outdoor showers and bathtubs perched on balconies, and Hayes took it in with the eagerness of a child.

"I assume we're going to christen these all. Is that the plan?"

He laughed, nodding. "You know me far too well."

"Well, I didn't think we were coming here for the golf."

When we entered the third bedroom, with its cool stone floors and its walls of glass, I noticed, set up along the south wall, an easel and, accompanying it, pencils, paper, a pack of newly purchased Holbein watercolors, and Kolinsky brushes.

"What is this? Did you see these? Hayes . . ."

He was standing in the doorway, still. And then I understood. He'd arranged for it.

"The light is incredible here," he said. "I thought you might want to capture it."

I turned to him, enveloping him, my heart full.

"You."

"Me?"

"You like me."

He paused for a moment, upsetting our usual back-and-forth.

"I *love* you," he said. Without qualifiers, without conditions. He allowed it to sit there and wash over me. Warm, like the Caribbean sun.

"You don't have to say anything," he said; apparently, I hadn't. "Just know that I do."

On Monday, having sufficiently christened all the rooms in the house, we ventured out to explore the island. And sitting beside him, in our rented jeep, the wind in our hair, his arms bronzed and beautiful maneuvering the stick shift, driving on the left side of the road, felt like some kind of teenage fantasy realized. The boyfriend I never had in high school. And as trite as it sounded, I was content to live in that moment. Me, with my middle-aged self.

We spent the afternoon at a small whisper of a beach called

Mimi's Bay on the east end of the island. We'd whiled away an hour at the Anguilla Heritage Museum earlier, and Mimi's was a stone's throw away. It was secluded and required a drive up a barely navigable dirt road and a hike through brush to get there. Our entire MO on this trip was to not be identified. And when we arrived on the strip of white sand and found ourselves alone, Hayes high-fived me. Who knew he'd find such joy in escaping his celebrity?

"Remember the first time I was at your place and you told me not to do the baby-fantasy thing with you?"

It came out of nowhere. After swimming and sunning and downing the picnic lunch Hyacinth, our cook, had prepared, we were prostrate on our blanket, soaking up the late-afternoon sun, and he brought it up. *The baby-fantasy thing.* He'd managed to remember the exact phrasing.

"Did you just not want me to talk about it? Or did you not want me to imagine it at all?" he continued.

"Both."

He turned to face me then, taking my hand. "Why does it scare you?"

I could not answer him. I could not tell him that still, even with my heart wedged open and him burrowing inside, even with him professing his love, *still* there could be no happy ending. That this teenage fantasy I was living out in my head was just that.

He repositioned himself, placing his head on my chest. "Are you just not going to discuss this with me? Are you just going to leave me wondering?"

"I'm forty, Hayes . . ."

"I know how old you are, Solène. And I imagine I know what's running through your head . . ."

"You're so young." My hand was in his hair. His thick, beautiful hair. "You have your whole life ahead of you. Don't rush it."

He was quiet for a second, staring up at the sky. "Would you ever have another baby?"

"I don't know . . . It would have to be the right circumstances. And it would have to happen pretty soon . . ."

"Did you and Daniel ever want another one?"

"At one point, yeah . . . but I also wanted to work. And he didn't want me to do both."

He took hold of my hand, squeezing it. "I would let you do both."

It tickled me. That he was so infatuated he was incapable of thinking straight. That he just wanted to make me happy.

I loved him.

I had yet to say it, but I loved him.

On Wednesday, New Year's Eve day, we chartered a fifty-two-foot speedboat to go island-hopping. Hayes nixed St. Barth and Saint-Martin because he wanted to avoid the paparazzi at all costs, so we kept it to a tour of Anguilla and its surrounding islands. We had lobster, we had champagne, we had each other, and we were happy. At some point in the afternoon, our captain, Craig, moored our boat just off the coast of Dog Island, and Hayes and I swam in to explore. It was an uninhabited islet that was so serene and raw in its beauty, we did not want to leave. The sand like talcum, the water an unfathomable blue.

"Let's buy this place and live here and grow old together," Hayes said. We were lying on the beach staring out at the sea.

"Like *The Blue Lagoon*?"

"The what?"

I laughed. That he did not get my pop culture references.

"What? Why are you laughing? Was that a movie?"

"Forget it."

"Am I too young?"

"You're not too young," I said. "You're perfect."

Later, when we'd swum back out to the boat and were lying on the sun pads in the back, our captain otherwise engaged, Hayes was taking liberties. There were a handful of other boats that had anchored near us, including the sleek catamaran that we'd spotted earlier in the day at Shoal Bay, but none were close enough to detect him tracing the triangles of my bikini top with his finger. His touch at once faint and deliberate.

"Why are your bones all sticking out? You haven't been doing some crazy juicing thing?"

I watched his hands descend over my ribs. Drops of water from his hair falling and pooling between my breasts. "No. But it might have something to do with the fact that your fans are calling me at work."

"Are they?" He stopped. "I'm sorry. Are you *talking to them?*"

I shook my head. "They're just leaving messages. Letting me know how they feel about me."

"I'm sorry," he repeated. "I can't imagine Lulit's happy."

"No. Lulit is very much not happy."

"You should talk to them. Tell them I say hi. Tell them I send my love. Tell them, 'Hayes says, "All the love,"'" he snickered, his fingers moving once again, traversing my belly, dipping in my navel.

"Are you just trying to make me laugh?"

"I'm trying to make you laugh. I'm sorry. I know you didn't sign up for this . . ."

"I signed up for lunch."

"Lunch, and some polite fingering?"

I laughed. "I thought that's what lunch *was.*"

"It's code, actually."

"It's boy band speak?"

"Not all boy bands. Just ours." He repositioned himself, maneuvering on top of me, spreading my legs. "Dinner is something completely different."

"Dinner is anal?"

"No, that's dessert."

I smiled, my hands exploring his back. Smooth, broad, firm. "I'm too old for this."

"You keep saying that, but clearly you're not."

He lowered his head then to my hip bone and undid the string of my bikini bottom with his teeth.

"You. And your mouth."

"You like my mouth . . ."

". . . so fucking much."

He undid the second string. And I remembered we were not alone on the boat.

"Can you see Captain Craig?"

He was pushing aside the fabric, his fingers unclosing me. "This isn't Captain Craig's first boat ride. He's not coming back here. I can assure you."

I stopped breathing in that moment that he lowered his head. Anticipating his arrival. Knowing how quickly he could make me come.

He did not disappoint. His lips wrapping around my clit, so wonderfully precise. That sucking thing he did. "Hiiii."

"Hi. So is this dinner, then?"

"No." He shook his head, letting me feel his tongue. "This is tea."

I laughed, my hands in his hair, the sun beating down on us, the water lapping at the sides of the boat. His mouth.

Far into the future, when I thought of Anguilla, this was the moment I would think of. Whether I wanted to or not.

We stayed in on New Year's Eve, forgoing celebrations at the Viceroy and Cap Juluca, to avoid the crowds, the madness, the cameras. "I just want it to be the two of us," he'd expressed on the boat ride back into port. "I just want to be with you. Always."

———

Late Thursday, I'd installed myself before my easel on the wrap-around balcony outside of our suite, capturing magic hour and the mountains of Saint-Martin, indigo spires against a salmon sky. Hayes was in the bedroom going over his tour itinerary. They were heading to South America in a month's time, and he wanted me to join them.

"At least Brazil. And Argentina," he said, stepping out onto the balcony. "We have days off in between and we can explore." He wrapped his arms around my waist, nuzzling my neck. "I'm sure that's your dream holiday, right? Buenos Aires with me and the lads."

I laughed at that, the idea of me and the five of them. And then I paused, setting down my brush. "I don't trust your friend, Hayes."

"Who? Rory?"

"No, Rory is harmless. Despite being the least gay." I smiled. "Should I not trust Rory?"

"I wouldn't say he's *harmless* . . ."

"I don't have a problem with Rory," I said.

He pulled back then, turning me to face him. He knew. "What did Oliver do?"

I told him. Most of it.

"Why didn't you tell me? Why didn't you tell me when it happened, Solène?"

"Because I didn't want to make it a bigger deal than it was . . . than it is."

He sighed, wrapping me in his arms. "I'm sorry."

"I'm okay. I can take care of myself."

"Oliver is smart. Oliver is one of the smartest blokes I know. But he can also be a prick and that's not always the best combination.

"He's like . . . the closest thing I have to a brother . . ." he continued.

"I know . . ."

". . . and all that entails."

"I know," I repeated.

"He's competitive, and he'll push. But he's not *dangerous*. He's not going to hurt you."

I paused, taking him in, his eyes changing colors in the setting sun. "But he would hurt *you* . . ."

Hayes nodded, slow. "Maybe," he said. "Maybe he would."

On Friday, our last full day on the island, we spent the day by the pool, me reading, Hayes penning lyrics in his leather journal. His expression intense, focused; one hand pulling at his lip, mind elsewhere. The staff all disappeared directly after lunch, and we skinny-dipped before making love on the pool stairs and cuddling on one of the lounges. Bob Marley serenading us. He fell asleep in my arms, and in that moment he looked so lovely that I disentangled myself and went to fetch my sketch pad and pencils from inside.

I drew him, naked, lying on his stomach, a peaceful expression painted on his boyish face. His beauty was so exquisite it was unnerving. And I knew, even then, that I was capturing something unspoiled and consummate. And that youth was fleeting and in the blink of an eye Hayes would no longer look like this. He would lose his hair or grow hair in places I'd rather him not, his muscles would atrophy, his skin would lose its suppleness, its flawlessness, its glow . . . He would no longer be the Hayes I fell in love with.

But in that moment in time, he was still perfect. And he was mine.

We were changing planes Saturday in San Juan when the spell was broken. Hayes had arranged for an airport handler to meet us and usher us through customs before we had to separate for our respective flights. We'd just rechecked our bags and were killing time in the priority lounge when it happened.

"Fuck," he said, louder than he normally would in a public setting. I looked across to where he was seated tucked away in a corner. His eyes were on his phone, a pained expression on his face. "Fuck."

"What? What happened?"

He covered his face with his hand and sat like that for thirty seconds while I imagined the worst. Finally, he looked up over at me and for an instant I thought he might cry.

"Hayes, what?" I moved in closer to him.

"I love you," he said, soft. "I'm sorry."

My heart had begun to race. "What are you sorry about?"

"I'm going to show you something, okay, but you can't freak out because there are people here." It was barely a whisper. I may as well have been reading his lips.

"Did someone die?"

"No."

"Did you get someone pregnant who's not me?"

He almost smiled then. Almost. "No."

"Okay," I said. "I can deal with it, then."

But I couldn't.

On his phone, he'd pulled up a celebrity gossip blog, and there in big, bold colors was a photo of the two of us, on the back of the speedboat at Dog Island, and there was no mistaking what was going on.

My stomach lurched. I began to shake, my hands clammy, my head reeling. This was what an anxiety attack felt like, wasn't it? This terror. I could not breathe.

"Oh my God. Oh my God."

"Shhhh." Hayes was holding my arms, his forehead pressed to mine. "I'm sorry, Sol. I'm sorry."

"Who has it? Where is it?"

"It's everywhere."

"Who sent it to you?"

"Graham."

Graham. Of course. "Is that the only picture?"

He shook his head.

I began to cry. "Isabelle . . ."

"I know." He kissed my forehead. "I know."

But he could not, because he was not a parent. Because he was a celebrity, and in some strange way he'd asked for this. Or at the very least, he was prepared for it. It was not out of the realm of normalcy for him. This intrusion, this parasitic creature that fed off of him and every little thing he did and broadcasted it for the masses. This fandom that leeched.

I wanted to hit him. For being so fucking stupid. For exposing us like that. But what good would it have done? It's not as if he were solely to blame.

"Who took them?"

"I don't know. Someone with a really good lens . . . Do you remember seeing anyone, any boats, following us?"

I thought about it. The catamaran. It had been there at Shoal Bay. It could have been that one. It could have been anyone.

"Does it matter? My life is completely ruined now. My parents are going to disown me. Daniel is going to take Isabelle away. Lulit is going to offer to buy out my share of the gallery. It's over. My life is over."

"It's not over, Solène. Don't be so dramatic."

"But you are really, *really* good at eating pussy, so maybe it was worth it."

He laughed, kissing my wet cheeks. "I love you. I'm so sorry this happened. I love you."

"Yeah . . . That's what all the boys say."

"No, they don't," he whispered. "No, they don't."

aspen

By the time I touched down in L.A., it was, as Hayes had con-
firmed, everywhere. I was greeted by nineteen new voicemails,
thirty-three texts, and forty-two emails when I powered on my
iPhone. And without looking at any of them, I powered it down.

Daniel was not scheduled to bring Isabelle back until tomorrow.
So I went home, turned off the landline, crawled into my bed, and
cried.

And cried.

It wasn't until eleven the next morning that I turned on my

iPhone again and found no fewer than a dozen messages from Hayes awaiting me. I called him immediately in London.

"What the hell, Solène? Where are you? Where the fuck have you been?" He was panicked, incensed. I could not recall ever hearing him so angry.

"I'm here. At home. I had the phone off. What's wrong?"

"You didn't think to check in after you landed? You couldn't send a message or anything?"

I was quiet. My head pounding, my face swollen, my mind scrambled. Had I done something wrong?

"You cannot . . . Fuck . . ." His voice was quaking. "You cannot just fall off the face of the fucking earth like that. You can't. I don't know if something's happened to you. I don't know if you've done something. I don't know if there are fans outside of your house. I don't know anything. You can't just fucking disappear."

"I'm sorry," I said. "I just didn't feel like dealing."

"Well, you *have* to deal . . . *with me*," he said, and I realized he was crying. "Look, we're in this together, and as it is, I feel responsible. And if I can't reach you, I don't know if you've gone and done something completely stupid or if you're hurt . . . You're six thousand fucking miles away. You got on that plane emotional and then you just . . . disappeared. You can't do that to me."

"I'm sorry."

He was quiet for a moment, his breath heavy in the receiver. "Call Lulit," he said finally. "She's on her way over there. Call her and tell her you're okay."

"You called Lulit?"

"Just call her," he said. "And call me back."

"Okay . . . I'm sorry."

"I love you. Don't do that again."

As much as I'd hoped to, I could not avoid the inevitable. The humiliation, the disgrace awaiting me at what I assumed would be every turn. It started with Lulit, who was relieved but not terribly warm when I reached her on the phone.

"I just want to know that you're okay."

"I'm okay. I mean, I haven't turned on my computer yet or listened to any messages, but I'm okay."

"Call me if you need anything," she said.

"I will. And thank you, for getting out of your bed on a Sunday morning to do a wellness check."

"Your boyfriend was very insistent. I told him you were not the suicidal type, but he would not take no for an answer . . ." She drifted off, and then: "I think he loves you."

"I know," I said. I imagined she wanted to ask what my plan was, what I was thinking, how much longer could I let this go on. But she bit her tongue. And that, for Lulit, was no small thing.

My mother, who could not hold her tongue, lectured me in rapid-fire French. She used words I'd never heard from her mouth, and I'd heard quite a bit. She closed her tirade with her customary "*Je t'adore avec tout mon cœur.*" But telling your daughter "I love you with all my heart" is much less effective after just having called her "*une pute.*"

Amara checked in to make certain I was not falling apart. To assure me the photos were not that bad. "They're blurry. You can't see your face. You can't really see his. You can't see any detail." And then, finally, to make me laugh: "It could have been so much worse, Solène. You could have been the one going down, and he could have been the president."

The brief levity she had brought to the situation died the second Daniel and Isabelle arrived. My daughter could barely look at me.

She walked in tan and taller and beautiful, and she would not look at me. Worse yet, she would not mention it.

"Was Hawaii amazing?"

She nodded, fiddling with her backpack. We were in the entry, Daniel still retrieving bags from the car.

"Was Eva's dress nice?"

"Yeah."

"Did you do your hair yourself?" I reached out to tuck a wayward lock behind her ear, and she tensed.

"They did it at the Four Seasons. I'm going to my room."

"Okay . . . Okay."

Daniel summoned me outside once he'd brought in the luggage. And we stood there, beside the BMW, the relentless California sun glaring, mocking, like a joke. Just once I wanted the weather here to not be perfect. Just once I wanted it to mirror my mood.

"Congratulations," I said.

He nodded, slow. "Thanks." His hair was lighter, almost blond, the lines around his blue eyes soft. He looked rested.

"So you're married again?"

"I'm married again." He was twisting the shiny platinum band on his finger with his left thumb. It was narrower than the one I'd placed there. The moment still clear. The invitation mounted in a frame.

"I didn't bring you out here to discuss this—"

"I know you didn't."

"This is appalling, Solène. This is so . . . *fucked up*. I don't think you realize how big a deal this is—"

"I do."

"I know it's not my place to tell you how to live your life, but I'm still Isabelle's father. And when you do dumb shit like this, it has consequences."

"'Dumb shit'? Is that what it is?"

I watched him stew for a second. His thumb flicking his ring.

It grated on me. That no one would question him moving on. Him marrying and impregnating someone more than ten years his junior. Because that's what divorced men in their forties did. His stock was still rising. His power still intact.

Daniel had become more desirable, and I somehow less so. As if time were paced differently for each of us.

"Do you really think this is in the best interest of Isabelle?" He'd put it out there. *Best interest.* It was a legal term, and there was no mistaking his use of it.

"Are you *threatening* me?"

"I'm not threatening you, I'm just saying . . ."

"What exactly are you saying?"

"I think she's been through enough."

"And you're pinning that all on me. You're pinning the divorce on me. You're pinning Eva and your baby and your marriage on me."

"None of this would have happened, Solène, if—"

"If what? If I'd just stayed home and been happy? Fuck you, Daniel."

For a moment he did not say anything, just stood there, staring out toward the street, the hikers in the distance. "I'm sorry I wasn't enough for you. I'm sorry our family wasn't enough." It hit. Hard.

"Figure out what you're going to do about this guy, before it destroys your relationship with your daughter."

It was a miserable week. I tried to focus all my energy on the Ulla Finnsdottir show that was opening on Saturday, but it was not easy. Not with the barrage of social media. The 423 new friend requests on Facebook from people I did not know, many of whom appeared to be twenty-something boys. The numerous vile messages on Twitter:

Why r u still around bitch? I thought you'd be gone by now. It's January.

skanky whore cunt. Aren't you someone's mother? Act like it.

Why don't you just kill yourself and save us the hassle?

Stop fucking with Simon's boyfriend.

Die. Die. Die. Die. Die. Die. Die.

The lengthy missives on Instagram: the questioning of my worthiness; the intra-group fighting among Augies; the damaged, the deranged. "Famewhore. You're only after his money. You're not even that pretty." "Be nice to her. If she makes Hayes happy, shouldn't that be what matters?" "I'm angry okay. I'm angry that I've been supporting him for 3 fucking years and then a fucking old bitch comes and ruins everything . . ." "Step off hayes" "Every time I cut myself I think of you. Hope your happy."

And even those that were written with the best of intentions scared me, scarred me. "Just remember when you hold his hand, you are holding the entire universe. Please don't break him."

In the end, I froze all my accounts.

We hired security for the opening on Hayes's suggestion. It was a larger turnout than we'd ever had previously. There were myriad girls crowded on the sidewalk in front of the gallery and a handful of paparazzi, who I'm guessing were disappointed to learn that my boyfriend was on the other side of the Atlantic. It was a huge nuisance, but we sold out the show in record time. And Lulit could not complain about that.

On Sunday, Georgia came over to hang out with Isabelle. They locked themselves in her room, and I could hear them laughing, and it sounded to me so sweet, so rare. And I wondered what it was Georgia had said or done to finally bring my daughter around.

Earlier in the week, I'd approached her. When the photos, albeit somewhat sanitized, ran in *Us Weekly* and *People* and the others,

I could no longer just pretend it was not happening. I could not imagine the toll it was taking on her at school.

"I need to talk to you about what's going on," I'd said, sitting on one of her Moroccan poufs.

"I don't want to talk about it . . ."

"I know you don't, Izz. But it's kind of a big deal and I don't want you to have all these emotions bottled up inside. I can only imagine what's going through your head."

She looked over to me from her perch on her bed, beneath the "Keep Calm and Carry On" poster, and beside the nightstand where our meet-and-greet photo used to lie. She'd shredded it back in November.

"You're an adult," she said. "He's an adult. You can do whatever you want, right? It's not my business."

It was not the response I was expecting. She sounded so mature, so altered. My little bird.

"I'm sorry it's so public, Izz. I'm sorry it's everywhere. That was never my intention."

She shrugged. "He's famous. That's what happens when you're famous."

I nodded, slow. Who had she become? Wise and jaded.

"Hayes is really special to me, Isabelle. He makes me happy. And those people out there, the media and fans and whoever . . . they're going to make it sound ugly. And what Hayes and I have is not ugly. I need you to understand that."

She nodded then. "I'm trying, Mom. I'm trying."

Leah came to pick Georgia up at the end of the girls' playdate. She arrived with a bottle of Sancerre and chocolaty chocolate-chunk cookies from the Farmshop. "Let's go admire your view," she said.

We sat out on the patio, wrapped in blankets, watching the sun dip. I wanted to believe the bearing of sugar and alcohol was a friendly gesture, but I feared that as a former attorney and now president of Windwood's parent association, she might have different intentions.

"So . . . are they asking us to leave the school?"

She smiled. "No."

"Are they giving me a slap on the wrist and saying 'Please don't engage in sex acts with almost-minors in public places'?"

Leah laughed. She had warm nut-brown skin, her daughter's curls. "Solène, you were on a private boat in the middle of the Caribbean. That hardly counts as a public place. In fact, I'm pretty sure that's what the Caribbean was made for. Guys in the music industry have been having sex on boats in the Caribbean since the dawn of time. Mick Jagger, Tommy Lee, Diddy, Jay Z . . ."

I smiled. "You just assembled that list yourself?"

"Yes. And now, Hayes Campbell . . ." She grew serious then. "No one is talking about it."

"You're lying to me."

"I'm telling you the truth. No one is talking about it. And if they are, they won't be for long. In the ranking of scandals at L.A. private schools, yours rates pretty low. There are parents sleeping with other parents, and tenth graders going to rehab for porn addiction. There are eighth graders sexting and English teachers behaving inappropriately with underage girls and toxic crumb rubber on elementary school soccer fields. This is nothing. It's cunnilingus on a boat. It's not murder."

I smiled at that. But as light as Leah made it sound, I knew things were not as breezy for my daughter.

"Has Georgia mentioned it to you at all? What's going on at school . . . what Isabelle might be going through . . ."

"Barely. You know this age: secretive . . ."

I nodded, my eyes fixed on the water. "I want to know what the other kids are saying. To her. I assume they're saying something."

"Have you asked her?"

"She doesn't want to talk about it."

Leah nodded, picking at her cookie. "Does she have someone else she can talk to? Professionally?"

She'd said it tentatively, but I bristled at the implication. I did not want Isabelle to have to return to therapy because of this. Because of *me*. Because that would mean I'd failed her. And I would end it before it came to that.

"No," I said. "I'm not ready to go there. Yet."

Hayes came into town the last week of January. The guys had a bunch of press and meetings leading up to the Grammys and then they were heading to South America to embark on the *Wise or Naked* world tour. And there seemed to be no way to stop it. Time.

On Thursday night we celebrated his birthday with a festive dinner at Bestia. The restaurant was in an industrial space in the Arts District downtown. A converted warehouse turned foodie mecca. We were tucked away at the back of the patio. Hayes and I, the rest of the band, Raj, Desmond, Fergus, and a pretty redhead who answered to the name of Jemma and clung to Liam's arm.

It was a fun evening: the cocktails, potent; the lights, low; the food, divine. The boys were loud and happy, and after so many phone calls fraught with tension, it was lovely to see Hayes once again at peace and comfortable in his skin.

He did not let go of me, his hand touching some part of my being throughout the night. I turned to him at one point when his thumb was tracing the inside of my wrist.

"You missed me," I said, low. My face at his collarbone, inhaling his scent.

"I missed you. Is it obvious?"

I nodded. "You're very touchy-feely. Even for you."

He tipped my chin up to his face then and kissed me. As if we weren't in a crowded restaurant. As if we didn't already stand out as the table with the current most visible band in the world. As if we were not just in every tabloid on six continents blasted for our public display of affection. He kissed me as if none of that mattered.

"Don't leave me . . ." he said.

"I'm not going anywhere."

". . . ever."

When I didn't say anything, he kissed me again and repeated it: "*Ever.*"

"Okay," I said. And at that point I could not be certain as to who was more intoxicated.

Late in the night I slipped away to the restroom, and on exiting I encountered Oliver in the adjacent vestibule. We had until that point exchanged very few words.

"Well, you seem to be hanging in there." He smiled, coy.

"Excuse me?"

"I just assumed you'd leave our boy after those photos."

I paused. It was the way he'd phrased it. "Well, you assumed incorrectly."

"Clearly."

The vestibule was narrow, dimly lit. I could smell the gin on him.

"Where's Charlotte?"

"It's over. We're through."

"I'm sorry to hear that."

"Yes, well . . . She ended it."

"Can you blame her?"

He laughed. "Oh, Solène . . ." He was drunk. "Did Hayes ever tell you what he said when he first saw you in Las Vegas? Did he?"

I didn't respond. Somehow I knew where this was going.

"'I just want to fuck her mouth.'" He said it slow, soft. "Did he tell you that? 'Did you see that mum? I just want to fuck her mouth.'"

I stood there, not moving. Feeling his closeness in the tight space.

"What's wrong, Oliver? Do you just not want him to be happy?"

He shook his head then, and there was something in his eyes that seemed to me sad. "You have no fucking idea, do you?"

"No," I said. "I don't."

But I'd begun to wonder.

On Friday morning Hayes and I flew to Aspen for four days to celebrate his birthday. I'd booked us a luxury suite at the Little Nell, a swank resort at the bottom of Ajax Mountain. The property was elegant, serene. Our suite decorated in soothing grays with multiple fireplaces and cozy throws and pristine views. The perfect winter hideaway.

In the late afternoon, after massages and lovemaking and a walk around town, Hayes decided that he wanted a "proper tea." He rang up room service, and I listened as he requested a "spot of Earl Grey and something sweet like scones or digestive biscuits, if you have any," and my heart ached. My sweet, sweet boy, so far from home.

"Well, that was a first," he said, hanging up the phone. We were in the living room, peeling off our layers. Snow falling outside on the terrace.

"What was a first?"

"He just called me Mr. Marchand."

I started to laugh. "You didn't correct him? You didn't say, 'It's Mr. Doo to you'?"

He smiled, pulling me into him, his hands and nose still icy. His cheeks, red. "No, I quite liked it. '*Mr. Marchand.*' It's *rather sophisticated.*" The last bit he stressed with an upper-crust accent, mocking his own people, as it were.

"Think I'll try it out for a few days, see if I like it enough to make it a permanent thing. You know, in case we get married." He kissed me. "I'm going to go warm up in the shower. Don't hesitate to join me."

I watched him make his way back into the bedroom. His broad shoulders in flannel, his jeans clinging to his ass. How the fuck had I gotten so lucky? How, in this great world, had we found each other? And how, I wondered, when the time came, was I going to let him go?

I made my way eventually to the master bath. Hayes was in the steam shower. I could smell his soap, his grapefruit body wash. He traveled with his own toiletries because he said he spent so much time in hotels, it was his way of holding on to his identity. Of remembering who he was.

He turned when I opened the glass door, his eyes brightening. I'd removed everything. "Hiiii."

"Hi yourself." I stood there, drinking him in. All of him.

And feeling everything.

And then I said it. "I love you."

Hayes froze, a confused look on his face, water streaming down his long torso. "Are you saying that because I'm naked?"

"No."

"Are you saying that because it's my birthday?"

"I'm saying it because I love you."

He was quiet, weighing the moment. And then he smiled, wide. "What took you so long?"

I laughed. "I was just making sure it was you, and not the idea of you."

"Come here," he said, pulling me under the stream of water. His hands pushing my hair from my face, his mouth on mine, his penis stirring against my groin. "Would you mind saying that again so I know I didn't imagine it?"

"I love you."

"Yeah." He smiled, all dimples. "That's what I thought you said."

On Saturday morning, Hayes awoke early to go to the gym before we hit the slopes, his body still on Greenwich Mean Time. I watched him dress from the comfort of the bed: his shorts, his girlish headband holding his hair off his pretty face, his #BlackLivesMatter T-shirt.

"Hayes Campbell, political activist?"

He smiled, grabbing his headphones from the dresser. It was still dark out. "Hayes Campbell, concerned citizen of the world. Your country, as much as I adore it, can be a bit fucked up when it comes to race . . ."

"You don't say?"

"I do. That's one of the things I love about you: that you're giving these artists a voice.

"I read an interesting piece in *The New York Times* this week on Kehinde Wiley—is that how you pronounce it? And he's kind of *fascinating*. But it just made me proud of you. And I know I gave you a hard time about the *Invisible* installation, but I've been thinking about it a lot since our conversation in New York—about how we value some art more than others—and really, I think what you do is amazing."

I lay there staring at him. Every time he opened his mouth, I liked him more. It had taken Daniel much longer to not view my work as some kind of self-indulgent charity project. In many ways, I'm sure he still did.

Hayes made his way over to me then, leaned in, kissed me. "I love this mouth. I'll be back in a bit."

"Oliver said something interesting the other night . . ."

"Did he?" He tensed.

"He said the first time you saw me, that night in Vegas, you said to him: 'Did you see that mum? I just want to fuck her mouth.'" I allowed it to sit there. "Is that true? Did you say that?"

He was quiet for a moment, contemplating. "Mm, that sounds like something I might have said . . . But in my defense, I was a twenty-year-old lad. We can be crass."

"Hayes . . ."

"Fucking Oliver . . . Oh, come on. What did you say when you first saw me? To yourself, what did you say?"

"Probably something like, 'Oh, he's cute.'"

"Really? Hmm . . . Because I clearly remember a conversation with someone saying, and I quote, 'God, I just want to sit on this kid's face and pull his hair.'"

I smiled at that.

"I don't know," he continued, "but that sounds an awful lot like fucking my mouth."

"It sounds more delicate my way."

"*Delicate?* Delicate mouth fucking?" He smiled. "Right. You're insane, Solène, and that is why I love you." He kissed me again before heading toward the door. "Let me know when you're up for some delicate mouth fucking. I'll be back."

I awoke in the middle of that night to Hayes's mouth traveling the length of my spine. His lips, tongue, soft, descending. To my ass and between my legs before I could properly recall where we were. My screams, stifled in the pillow. And when he was done, he flipped me over and did it again.

And I wasn't certain if it was the thinness of the mountain air, but everything felt so heightened and intensified that I could not be sure whose birthday we were celebrating. Hayes's tongue unfolding me. His fingers, long and thick, and so very familiar. The way he explored me so completely, as if each time was the first. As if he were *enjoying* it. I could not get enough. My ass lifting off the bed to meet him. My hands in his hair, gripping his skull. My nails in his scalp. Jesus fuck.

I came so hard it seemed to me the entire room was spinning.

"Shit," he said, smiling up at me. "That wasn't very delicate, was it? My apologies."

Hayes wiped his face with the back of one hand and grabbed both my wrists with the other, pinning them above my head.

And before I could recover, his dick was pushing up inside of me. And as always, that first thrust was everything. I marveled at it: the way he fit me. Thick. Perfect. Like no one who had come before him. As if all my life I'd been walking around with a Hayes-shaped vagina and never knew. The idea made me smile. But then, completely unexpected, I started to cry.

He stopped moving, his free hand brushing my hair from my face. "Are you all right?"

I nodded.

"Are you sure?"

"Yes."

"Why are you crying? It's a little disconcerting when we're having sex and you're crying." The heel of his palm slid over my cheek.

"I'm sorry."

"Why are you crying, Solène?"

"Because . . . I love you. Because this is perfect and I don't want it to end." It was the most honest I'd been with him. It was the most honest I'd been with myself.

"Are you ending it?"

I shook my head.

"Then there's no reason to cry. I'm not going anywhere." He started moving again. So. Fucking. Deep.

"It ends every time you leave. Every time I go back to my life and my fucking computer, it ends."

"Well, we'll get you a new computer, then." He smiled. "Look at me. *Look at me.* It's just us. It's just you and me in this relationship. Fuck everything else."

The fact that he could say that to me with my arms pinned above my head and his dick gliding in and out—the fact that he held my gaze the entire time, never wavering, never losing his tempo, the fact that I could smell myself on his face—was so unbelievably sexy. I did not want it to end.

I did not want it to end.

When he was close to coming, he leaned in and bit down on my lower lip so hard that I anticipated the taste of blood, but it never came.

"You. Are fucking everything to me," he said. His breath coming in short spurts. "I'm not going anywhere."

Afterwards, when I was reveling in the joy of my third orgasm and he'd passed out beside me, his body slick with sweat, I thought long and hard about what he'd said. It was just us. Fuck everything else.

———

In all the months of slipping off to various locations, Hayes and I had never flown in and out of the same terminal together. We had never departed and arrived as a couple. It was something I'd not made note of until we touched down at LAX Monday evening.

"It's going to be crazy out there," he said as our plane was taxiing. "Just a warning."

"Like photographers?"

"Photographers, fans, all of it. It's Grammy week. It's going to be bad."

"Okay," I said.

But "all of it" did not quite capture the madness. We had no fewer than three airport escorts who met us at the gate and accompanied us to baggage claim, and the entire time, walking at a relatively fast clip, we were hounded by a handful of paparazzi. Hayes walked one pace ahead of me, clinging to my hand, protecting me from the brunt of it. And what struck me most was not the intrusiveness of the experience, but the running commentary spewing from the guys with the cameras. "Hey, Hayes. Happy Birthday, Hayes! How does it feel to be twenty-one? How was Aspen? Hi, Solène. Did you get a lot of skiing in? You gonna go out drinking tonight? What bars you gonna hit? You excited about the Grammys? You're looking good, man. I love your work, dude. I love the new album. Your girlfriend is very beautiful. What do you think of Rory's new tattoo?" Dear God. Who were these people?

And then, as we exited into the chaos of the baggage claim, the full scale of Hayes's celebrity hit. There were over a hundred girls squealing with cell phone cameras and throwing themselves in his path attempting to take selfies and yelling his name and falling down and crying, and it was terrifying. The paparazzi's flashes, blinding. I spotted Desmond with our driver, and even his familiar ginger head did not alleviate my panic. They were touching him and pulling at him, and he was squeezing my hand harder.

And they were at turns euphoric, diplomatic, and violent. "Get the fuck out of the way." "Make a path." "Hi, Solène." "You're so pretty, Solène." "Guys, let them through, please." "Happy Birthday, Hayes!" "Can you sign my face?" "There's a girl on the floor." "OhmyGod!OhmyGod!OhmyGod!" "Can I get a picture, please?" "Let them through!" "Happy Birthday!" "HayesHayesHayesHayesHayes." "Let him go!" "He doesn't want to take your picture. Just let him go!" "Get off of him!" "They're gonna think we're animals!" "Move, bitch!" "Hayes, I'm so sorry about this." "You guys, let him go. Jesus fucking Christ!"

By the time we got into the back of the Escalade, I was hyperventilating. And he was as cool as a fucking cucumber. "I'm sorry. I'm sorry," he said. "I'm sorry."

It took me a minute to catch my breath, to gather my wits, to assess that I had not been physically harmed. "Yeah," I said. "It's just you and me in this relationship. Fuck everything else."

beverly hills

The Fifty-Seventh Grammys were scheduled to take place the following Sunday evening at the Staples Center. The guys were performing "Seven Minutes," their nominated single. Their week filled with press leading up to the awards show and the tour, including a day in Santa Barbara shooting an exclusive interview with Oprah. And by that, I was a little impressed.

Things at Marchand Raphel were once again busy after the holiday lull. Hamish Sullivan Jones, the curator from the Whitney Museum, was coming to town and had scheduled a visit at Anya Pashkov's studio to see more of her *Invisible* collection. The fact that he was still interested was noteworthy. If we could land Anya an exhibition at the new Whitney with all its expectation and hype, it would be a coup. At the same time, Lulit and I were organizing our pieces to be shipped to New York for the Armory Show the first week of March.

It felt good to be back in the groove of working. To not put too much energy into the offensive voicemails and the occasional fans who showed up at the gallery randomly during the day, hoping to get a glimpse of their idol. Josephine solved our problem by hanging a "By Appointment Only" placard on the door. She fielded questions from the media with her rote response: "I'm sorry. It's the Marchand Raphel policy to not comment on any of our associates' private lives." They seemed to buy that.

On Friday evening, after a day of interviews and a rehearsal at the Staples Center, Hayes dropped by the gallery to see the Finnsdottir exhibit and say hello. Matt and Josephine seemed so charmed with his genuine affability, you would have thought his celebrity hadn't put us all out. That we hadn't received death threats.

Lulit was a tougher nut to crack.

"So," he said, sidling up to her in the kitchen where she was brewing a cappuccino, "I met Oprah."

"I heard."

"And I got a tour of her Montecito house . . ."

I watched him as he crossed his arms and leaned back on the counter, smiling, smug.

"She's recently redone it and she's got quite an art collection . . . but I think it's missing a few key contemporary pieces."

"Ha!" Lulit said, the hint of a smile. "Did you tell her that?"

"I *did*. And I told her I knew just the women to sell it to her. She has a few African pieces and she does all this charity work in South Africa, and so I specifically told her about you . . ."

"No, you didn't."

"I *did*. And she said, 'Have her get in touch with my people.' So . . ." Hayes dug into the pockets of his jeans and withdrew his wallet before proffering a folded sticky note. "Oprah's people. They're expecting your call."

Lulit stood there with a goofy look on her face and then turned to me in the doorway. I shrugged.

"You're pulling my leg," she said.

"I promise you, I'm not. And you know who Oprah is very, very good friends with?"

Lulit and I looked at each other and smiled. "The Obamas."

"The Obamas," Hayes said. "And last I checked, Sasha was still prime August Moon age."

"Shut up," Lulit laughed.

"And you thought your best friend dating a guy in a boy band was going to lead to nothing but trouble."

"I never said that."

Hayes cocked his head and rolled his eyes before walking out.

"Fuck, he's good." She smiled at me.

I nodded. "He's good."

After, we scooped up Isabelle from her fencing class, and the look on her face when Hayes walked into the gym was priceless.

"That's quite a getup." He smiled. "You look like a Musketeer."

She laughed. A big, bright, confident laugh. She'd gotten her braces off two weeks prior and she was sharing it with the world.

"Holy fuck." Hayes turned to me. "*That's your mouth.*"

I gave him a look, and he turned away, and we never spoke about it again.

We made a quick detour to the Whole Foods in Brentwood, and no one stopped him to request a photo or an autograph or his time. And watching him openly pick out wine while Isabelle sifted through the cheese selection made me content in a way I had not been in a long time. The idea that maybe this could work.

We dined at home: ratatouille and rack of lamb. The three of us seated around the oblong table, the lights of Santa Monica twinkling in the distance. Hayes, at turns amused by Isabelle's tales of middle school, and seemingly enamored, stealing glances at me, wistful. When Isabelle got up to clear her plate, he leaned forward, his hands flat against the rosewood.

"Do you know what this table makes me think of?" His voice was low, raspy.

"Yes."

"Good," he said. "So long as you're thinking of it, too."

Following dinner, when Isabelle excused herself to FaceTime her friends, I took the opportunity to lure him into my office on the pretense of checking my availability for the South American tour dates. But the second he stepped into the room, I shut the door.

"I have something for you. I wanted to give this to you before Aspen, but it wasn't ready."

Hayes raised an eyebrow, curious, as I handed over the large flat package that had been propped up against the far wall.

"Did you get me something for my birthday? You didn't have to do that."

"It's small."

"It doesn't feel small. Is it art?"

"Open it."

I watched him carefully unwrap the brown paper to unveil a float-mounted watercolor. Sunrise, as viewed from our bedroom in Anguilla. For a moment he did not speak, his eyes taking it in, and when he finally looked up at me, they were smiling. "You made this."

"I made this."

"You're giving it to me?"

"I'm giving it to you. *I made it for you.*"

"It's beautiful, Solène. It's perfect." He set the frame down before taking me in his arms. "I love it. It's the perfect gift."

We stood there for a long time, losing ourselves in the painting, in the moment.

"I don't remember seeing you do this one, in these colors. They're extraordinary."

They were. Teal waters, charcoal mountains, the sun bursting apricot beneath a lilac sky. "I did it one morning when you were still sleeping. I thought the colors would complement the pieces you have in London."

He stared at me for a minute, an inscrutable expression on his face. He reached to tug on his lower lip, and then: "Do you remember the house where we stayed in Malibu? It's for sale. I looked at it yesterday. I thought you should know."

It was loaded. What he was telling me. What I was taking from it. What he'd intended for me to take from it.

"Oh," I said.

He laughed, uneasy. "Do you think that's insane?"

"Maybe. A little."

"Yeah. I thought so, too. But not so insane that I'm not considering it."

August Moon did not win their Grammys, but that did not put a damper on our celebration. I skipped the actual awards show, and joined Hayes and the rest of them at the Ace Hotel downtown for the Universal after-party. It was crowded and loud and full of little clusters of sycophants swarming the likes of Rihanna and Katy Perry, and Sam Smith basking in the win of his myriad trophies.

The guys, whose live performance went flawlessly, were all on a high. Rory, whom I passed entering the ornate theater, literally. His eyes glazed, his face buried in the neck of some Victoria's Secret Angel. Liam talking animatedly with a young singer I did not recognize. Green eyes dancing, pouty lips, freckles. As adorable as he was, he was never going to be the sexy one. Simon and Oliver were at the band's reserved table, deep in conversation, when I arrived.

There were a handful of pretty girls standing around the perimeter, waiting to be acknowledged, eager puppies in sequins and spandex. I leaned in to greet the guys, and Simon rose to hug me, but Oliver did not budge.

"Are you not going to say hi?"

"No. I was told I'm not to talk to you anymore. So I'm not talking to you."

"Okay." I smiled.

"Nice dress," he said, and Simon laughed.

"You can't stop yourself, mate. You're a fucking mess."

They were both a wee inebriated.

"I have no idea where your boyfriend is. He ran off. Champagne?"

I found Hayes eventually, on the other side of the theater, talking to a model. For fuck's sake. Young, thin, wide-spaced eyes. She looked to be Brazilian, or Portuguese. Some exotic ethnicity that was completely his type. And for a second I felt it in my gut, the impulse to turn and run. But he looked up and his expression on seeing me was so completely smitten, if he'd felt an ounce of guilt it did not show.

"Hi. You're here."

"I'm here."

He took my head in his hands and kissed me, and he smelled of citrus and amber and Scotch. And all was forgiven. Almost.

"You look amazing," he said, low.

"Ditto."

"This is Solène." He turned toward the model. "And I'm sorry, what was it you said your name was?"

"Giovanna." She smiled. Her teeth were not perfect.

"Giovanna," he repeated. He turned back to me, a wide grin on his face. "Giovanna was just telling me how many Instagram followers she has."

I tried not to laugh as Hayes did his best to disengage and bid his new friend adieu.

"What are you doing?" I said when we were heading back across

the space, weaving through the crowd and potted oversized bon-
sai.

"I was killing time until you got here."

"With eighteen-year-old models?"

"I was avoiding Rihanna," he laughed. "Stop. You're walking
too fast. I want to look at you."

I turned to face him. He looked ridiculously sexy, even for him.
Black suit, sheer black shirt partially unbuttoned, long silk scarf
draped around his neck. Hair, elegantly disheveled. The fact that
he was still wearing a light dusting of makeup from the show didn't
even bother me.

"Hi," he said, again.

"Hi. I'm sorry you lost."

He shrugged. "It happens. Where did you get this dress?"

"Balmain," I said. "A few years ago."

It was easily one of the sexiest things I owned. An intricate lace
top, a high-waisted, studded fitted skirt ending just above the knee,
my Isabel Marant bondage shoes. Daring, black, rock-and-roll.

I turned and continued heading toward the table, still pissed
about the model.

Hayes's hands were on my hips, pulling me into him. His mouth
at my ear.

"Bloody hell, I just want to fuck your arse in this dress."

I laughed. "Who the hell *are* you?"

"I'm the guy who gets to fuck your arse in this dress."

His words stopped me. There, in the middle of the theater at
the Ace Hotel. Surrounded by music execs and wannabe starlets
and Grammy winners. My rock star boyfriend pushed up against
my back.

"You wanna go *now*?"

"I want to go now," he said. "There's a *GQ* and Armani party
in Hollywood, and we have to swing by there because I have to
show my face. And then we're going to stop by Sam's party in Bel-
Air because I told him we would. And then we're going to go back

to the hotel so I can fuck your arse in this dress . . . Are you okay with that?"

"Do I have a choice?"

"You always have a choice."

"Do you have lube?"

He laughed. "We'll improvise."

His hand was spanning my abdomen, pressing me into him. All of him.

"Okay. Call our driver."

"Done."

Later, much later, when Hayes was passed out in a signature suite at the SLS Beverly Hills, I lay awake, watching him sleep. The night had passed in a blur of champagne and music and sex. It was going to hurt in the morning. It was already hurting now.

My eyes scanned the room, plush and slick with Philippe Starck touches and an overabundance of leather ottomans. The floor-to-ceiling mirror facing the bed was anything but subtle.

"Who chose this place?" I'd asked when we arrived, sometime after one. Two? "I feel like a hooker."

"You're going to feel even more like a hooker when I'm done with you," Hayes said, making me laugh.

He was rough. And fun. And I loved everything about it.

At one point, when he was lying above me, inside of me, his chest against my back, his arms splaying mine, fingers entwined, he brushed his mouth against my ear and said, low: "Do you feel like you could be my mother now?"

There was a faint knocking in the hall. A knocking and a whimpering of sorts. I looked over to see if Hayes had heard it, but he was snoring, oblivious. His postorgasmic slumber.

I grabbed a robe and peeked out the peephole but could not

make out much, a lone figure in the corridor, knocking on the door across the hall. A girl.

"Liam, please open the door," she was saying, soft. "Please. I'm so sorry. I screwed up. Please open it."

She continued to knock and whimper, and Liam's door did not open, and finally, I cracked ours.

"Are you okay?"

She was young. Very. Brown hair, big doe brown eyes, sullied with makeup. She was crying.

"My phone is dead and I don't have a charger and my girlfriend has my wallet in her bag but I can't find her and I just want to go home."

"Okay," I said. "Okay. What do you need? Do you need me to charge your phone?"

"Please."

My eyes were scanning the corridor for security, but there was none. "How did you get up here?"

She shook her head. Her dress was mature beyond her years. Red, Herve Leger. A lot of effort for a little girl.

"Did you come up here with someone?"

"Simon," she said, wiping her eyes. She was clinging to a set of keys and what looked like a student ID.

"Where's Simon now?"

"In his room. Sleeping."

"Which one's Simon's room?"

She pointed to the suite next to ours.

I was confused. "Then why are you knocking on Liam's door?"

She shook her head, and the tears started to fall again.

"Okay. Okay. Give me your phone and I'll charge it and we'll find your friend and get you a ride home."

Hayes was stirring in the bedroom. "What are you doing up? Who are you talking to?"

"There's a girl, in the hallway. I don't know if she's a fan or a groupie or what. But she's young, and she's out there, and she's crying."

"Well, get Desmond to deal with it."

"I don't know where Desmond is. It's four o'clock in the morning, Hayes. There's no security out there."

"Fuck." He rolled over, burying his head under the pillow.

"Oh-kay. I guess I'll take care of it then."

"She's not your problem. Don't get involved."

"She's someone's daughter, Hayes."

"Everyone is someone's daughter, Solène. Don't get involved."

I returned to the girl in the hall once her phone was charging. "Where's your friend? The one you came with?"

She shrugged. "She disappeared with the drummer."

"Who's your drummer?" I turned back into the suite. Hayes was now up, in the living room, in his underwear, looking for his phone.

"Roger," he sighed. "He's a good guy."

"Yeah, they're all good guys." I stepped back into the hallway. "Where do you think she could be now?"

"The last text I got from her said she was going home. And I told her to go because I was with Simon and he said he'd get me a ride . . ."

"But he didn't."

"But he didn't . . ."

"And you ended up with Liam?"

She started crying again.

I was trying to imagine how it had played out, and every possible scenario was ugly and seemed very un-Simon/un-Liam like to me. But what did I know? How well did I really know these guys? And how crazy was I to have trusted my daughter with them? I excused myself and rejoined Hayes in the suite.

"Desmond isn't answering his mobile," he said. "Neither is Fergus."

"She's a mess. We can't just leave her there. Let's just let her sit in here until her phone charges and she finds her friend and we can put her in a cab and send her home."

He shook his head, his eyes wide, his hair sticking in sixty-nine directions. "She can't come in here. She's freaking out. I told you I don't do well with women who freak out."

"Is she a woman or a girl? Because she looks like a girl to me."

"She's borderline."

"Hayes, that's someone's daughter."

"I understand that. But she can't come into this room." He said it with such conviction it alarmed me.

"I'm just going to make sure she's okay and call her an Uber."

"She *can't* come into this room."

"Who *are* you?"

"Right now? I'm Hayes Campbell. And I can't have that girl's DNA in my room."

"Are you kidding me?"

"Look at me, Solène. I'm completely serious right now. I cannot have that girl's DNA in my hotel room. I don't know what happened with Simon and Liam, and I love them like brothers, but I cannot get involved."

"Fine. Fine. I'll take care of it. But tell your friends they can't *fuck* underage girls and leave them crying in the hallway."

His hands were at his head, pulling at his hair. "See. This is why I don't mess with anyone under thirty."

"That's because you have mommy issues."

He cocked his head. "What?"

"You heard me. Just go. Go back in the bedroom. Go lie down in your own DNA. I'll take care of it."

"How old are you? Be honest with me," I said to the girl, back out in the hallway. She'd eaten off most of her lipstick and I found myself wondering whose dick she'd sucked.

"Sixteen."

Shit. "How old did you tell them you were?"

She paused. "Eighteen."

Fuck. "You are *not* supposed to be here."

"I know. I just want to go home."

"Do you need to go to a hospital?"

"No."

"Are you sure? This would be the time to go if you're going to go." I felt awful throwing Simon and Liam under the bus. Where was Desmond and why wasn't he handling this?

"I'm sure. I'm okay. I just need to go home."

I sighed. "Okay, I'm going to call you an Uber."

"Thank you," she said, looking up at me, her brown eyes smeared with mascara. Like a baby panda. What the hell had they done to her?

"You look really familiar to me," she added then. "Do you have a kid at Windwood?"

My heart stopped. Fuck. "What's your name, honey?"

She told me.

"Where do you live?"

"Brentwood."

"I'm going to go inside for a second. Stay here. Don't move. Okay?"

Hayes was lying in bed, texting like a demon when I returned to the bedroom.

"How is she doing?" he asked.

"She fucking goes to school with Isabelle."

"Holy shit."

"Ya think?" I'd located my purse and was tearing through my wallet. "I'm giving her cash for a cab. I can't have an Uber car on my account taking a sixteen-year-old girl back to Brentwood. How the hell did I end up here? I did not sign up for this. This is not cool, Hayes."

He sighed deeply, placing down his phone. "I called the front desk. They're sending someone up to make sure she's okay, and they're going to put her in a courtesy car and take her home."

I spun to look at him. "Did you really do that?"

"I really did that."

"Thank you."

He nodded. "You're welcome. Will you come back to bed now?"

In the morning, things were not pretty. My head ached, my body ached, I was no longer twenty-four. Hell, I wasn't even thirty-five.

We showered and ordered up room service, and then got back in bed. The shared realization that we were running out of time. That he was leaving. That things would not be the same. I was starting to get a feel of what life on tour might be like for him. And I did not like it.

"I'm sorry about last night," he said. His voice was craggy, his eyes red, but he was still beautiful to me.

"She was young."

"I know. I'm sorry."

"I want to believe that if that were Isabelle, you would have helped her. You wouldn't have left her out there in the hallway crying at four in the morning."

Hayes sighed. "Obviously I would have helped Isabelle because I *know* Isabelle. But there are so many, Solène. There are so many. And I can't know them all.

"Come here," he said. He pulled me into him, tucking me into the crook of his arm. "I'm going to tell you a story, okay. But don't say anything until I'm done."

"Okay . . ."

"Two years ago, we were in Tokyo, on the *Fizzy Smile* tour. We were staying at the Palace Hotel, like on the twentieth floor. Incredible views. And after our show, this girl came back to the hotel with me. She wasn't super-young. Like twenty-three or something. When we were done, I said to her, in the most polite way possible, 'This was lovely, but I have a very early wake-up call tomorrow and it would probably be best if you didn't spend the night.' And she looked at me like she didn't understand what I was saying. I mean it's possible she *didn't* understand what I was saying, because I speak like five words of Japanese: 'hello,' 'please,' 'good luck,' and 'thank you for the fish.'"

I looked at him dumbfounded.

"Although I didn't say that. I promise. But those *are* like my only five words. Anyway, she insists on staying and I tell her no and then she gets out of the bed and walks to the other side of the room and I think she's getting her clothes, but then she opens the door to the balcony and walks out there, completely naked, and she manages to climb up onto the fucking railing and threatens to pitch herself off. And she's sitting on it, facing me, but leaning back and she's crying hysterically, like not playing a game or teasing, she's bawling, and all I could think was, HolyFuckHolyFuckHolyFuckHolyFuck. And I couldn't scream for help because I thought it would just set her off, and I couldn't call or text anyone because my mobile was back in the room, and I couldn't leave her, and all I could do was plead with her to come down and it was the longest, most horrific seven minutes of my life. And then finally, finally, I get her off the railing and lure her back into the room and into bed and then I just held her until she stopped crying and fell asleep, which took like two hours, and at that point I texted Desmond and he came and got her the fuck out of there."

For a moment I was speechless. And then a random thought came to mind. "Seven minutes."

He nodded, slow. "Seven minutes, yeah."

"Do people know what it's about?"

"No one knows what it's about. Well, maybe Desmond . . ."

"Oh, Hayes, I'm sorry."

"Yeah, well . . . It taught me to be a little more selective about who I bring back to my hotel room."

I was quiet for a moment, respectful. "I thought it was about falling in love."

He shook his head. "It's about falling."

On Tuesday, the boys headed out to Bogotá. And I went back to work.

south america

Friday morning, on my way to Marchand Raphel, Hayes called from Colombia.

"It's crazy here, Sol. Our security is at a level I've never seen. There are about two hundred of them, and they're armed. Like military specialists. They follow us everywhere."

"What are they protecting you from? Fourteen-year-old girls trying to kiss you?"

"Yes," he laughed. "Exactly."

"Seriously."

"Kidnappers. Apparently that's a problem."

"Be safe, okay."

"*You* be safe. I have armed guards following me to the loo. I think I'm good."

The phone signaled then. The gallery. I told Hayes I would call him back, and switched over to a frazzled-sounding Lulit. "Are you on your way in?"

"Yes, we've got Cecilia Chen at ten."

Cecilia was an established photographer and director of art films. Caribbean born, New York bred, she'd spent the last twenty years in Paris building up a portfolio of exceptional work and was now looking to relocate to Los Angeles. She'd come recommended by one of our current artists, Pilar Anchorena. Cecilia also happened to be black, Asian, and female, the holy triumvirate of Marchand Raphel. Lulit and I were looking forward to meeting with her.

"It's been canceled," Lulit said then, "but just . . . hurry."

"What's wrong? Did something happen?"

"Everything's okay. Just waiting for you."

But she had not been truthful. There were two police cruisers in front of the gallery when I approached, and immediately the hairs on the back of my neck stood up. Three officers had congregated in front of our building, talking, milling, one writing in a notepad, a fourth seated in one of the cars. Things were not okay.

I parked in my spot behind the gallery and entered through the back door.

Lulit, Matt, and Josephine were all standing in the kitchen, their faces solemn.

"What happened? Was there a burglary?"

They looked at me. Funny. But not talking. Matt sipped from his espresso.

"*What happened?*"

"We had an incident," Josephine said. "It's not a big deal. It's just graffiti."

"Then why are the police here?"

Lulit took a moment to respond. "They're taking it pretty seriously."

"They're taking what pretty seriously?"

Without speaking she grabbed my hand and walked me through the gallery, to the front entrance and out the door. There, on the lower part of the white brick wall that had been blocked from my view by the police cars, spray-painted in large black letters, were the words DIE WHORE.

"Oh my God. OhmyGodOhmyGodOhmyGod. Is this for me? Is this about me? Is this because of me?" My head was spinning and I could not feel my legs. "I think I'm going to be sick."

"Let's go inside," Lulit said, taking me by the arm.

"I'm going to be sick."

"You're not going to be sick. You're going to be fine."

I'd begun to shake. "Those fucking fans. Those fucking crazy fans."

"All right . . . Let's get you a glass of water. Jo, can you get her some water? They're going to want to ask you some questions, but it's okay."

"It's not okay."

"It's going to be okay. They've photographed it. They've dusted for prints. They're going to check the camera footage. It's probably just a couple of teenage girls. It's going to be okay."

"It's not okay, Lulit."

"Look at me. *Look at me. It's going to be okay.*"

She led me back into our office and sat me down, and I could not keep my water from sloshing out of the glass, I was shaking so.

"Who called the police?"

"Josephine did. She told them what was going on, the phone calls, the threats. They came immediately."

Josephine was flustered. "I know you said to use discretion, I know you said 'No comment,' but I thought this was a pretty big deal. I'm sorry."

"No. You did the right thing." My mind was racing. "Are they going to paint it? Can we paint it? Can we get rid of it before the press gets ahold of it? Oh my God, I can't believe I'm even saying this.

"Those fucking . . . *bitches*," I said. And then I started to laugh. We all did. "It's not funny. I feel like I'm in high school. Except I never even got to date the cute guy in high school. Can't I just enjoy this? It's not fair."

"I say we find those bitches," Matt said, "and then we beat their asses. Who's down? We've got box cutters in the back."

If ever I had doubted my team, I appreciated them anew that morning. The way they rallied for me. They were so calm and collected, and they went about the rest of the day as if I had not potentially put us all in danger.

"Thank you," I said to Lulit, later that afternoon, in the office.

"For what?"

"For not saying 'I told you so.'"

She laughed at that. "Hey, even I could not have dreamt up this. I just told you to use a condom."

"Hmm." I smiled. "You did."

Lulit peered into my eyes for a minute and then frowned, shaking her head. "Whatever. It's *your* vagina."

Isabelle had a sleepover at Rose's. The girls' friendship had been strained since November, and I knew it had everything to do with my romance with Hayes. The idea that my daughter's relationships were unraveling because I had found love seemed like a cruel and poorly timed joke. And yet another reminder that it wasn't "Just us. Fuck everything else." Rose had invited both her and Georgia that night to watch *Friday the 13th*, and Isabelle was thrilled to be back in her good graces. I dropped her off in Westwood and returned to the house alone, still a little on edge from that morning's incident.

I'd only just stepped in and was sorting through the mail when I came across the package: a large padded manila envelope, with no return address, postmarked from Texas. I did not, to the best of my knowledge, know anyone in Texas. But that did not stop me from ripping it open and reaching inside. The second I touched it, I recoiled, horrified. I knew, without looking, precisely what it was. And for the second time that day I was shaking and sweating and feeling physically ill. Because there in the package was an enormous dildo. There was a note accompanying it. "Go fuck yourself," it said, "and leave our boy alone."

They'd found me. Somehow. They'd tracked me down and discovered where I lived and violated me in such a way that it felt as if they were in my house. I could hear panting as I rushed to put on the alarm and every light, and it took me a moment to realize the panting was mine. All the glass doors facing our cherished view were black and foreboding, and even when I turned on the patio lights I could not be certain someone was not there lurking. And it felt foolish to be so unnerved by what I was certain were teenage girls, but I could not rationalize it away. The fear.

I tried calling him. Over and over. But of course he did not answer. He was onstage in Colombia, drowned by the screams of thirty-five thousand girls. How could I expect him to pick up his phone?

I had the inclination to call Daniel, but then remembered he was against this all along. And the idea that he would leave his twenty-seven-weeks-pregnant wife on a Friday evening to come and check on me, when Isabelle was not even here, was absurd.

And it hit me then, how alone I was.

I called my mom and cried. And she listened to me blubber about being scared and torn, at the same time elated that I'd found someone who had taken the time to know me, and all the little things that made me so very happy. And how I did not want to let him go. And for the first time in as long as I could remember, it seemed to me she did not judge.

"C'est ça, l'amour, Solène. Ce n'est pas toujours parfait. Ni jamais exactement comme tu le souhaites. Mais, quand ça te tombe dessus, ça ne se contrôle pas."

Love, she said, was not always perfect, and not exactly how you expected it to be. But when it descended upon you, there was no controlling it.

Hayes called in the middle of the night. The show had gone well, he said, but he was alarmed by my numerous messages.

"What happened?" His voice was hoarse, froggy. It was almost two their time. In the morning they were flying to Peru.

I told him everything.

"Oh, Sol," he said when I was done relaying the extent of the day's lunacy. "I'm so sorry."

"It's harassment, Hayes. I'm being sexually harassed . . . And I know it's probably harmless young girls, but it doesn't feel like it. It feels threatening. It feels real."

He was quiet for a moment, and then: "What kind of security do you have there? At home?"

"I have an alarm system."

"Do you have cameras?"

That seemed extreme. "No."

"You need cameras."

"Hayes, this is crazy. They're *girls*. I don't need cameras."

"You need cameras. I'll pay for them. I'll have Rana ring you in the morning and she'll get it all sorted."

"Hayes . . ."

"You should have cameras, Solène. Why didn't your ex-husband put in cameras? You're a beautiful woman and a thirteen-year-old girl living alone in the hills. You should have cameras."

"I love you," I said.

"I love you, too. Get some sleep. I'll call you when we get to Lima."

In the morning, when I picked up Isabelle from Rose's, she was not her usual chipper self. I expected tales of horror movies and late-night girl talk, but on the car ride home, she was solemn. It was becoming more and more customary.

"What's wrong?" I asked. We were winding west on Sunset, approaching the 405. Isabelle was gazing out the passenger window, her face blank.

For a while she did not speak, and then, without diverting her attention, she said, "I don't like people talking about you."

"Are people talking about me?"

She nodded, quiet.

"Are your *friends* talking about me?"

She didn't answer.

"I'm okay with people talking about me, Izz. People talk. That's what they do. And we live in a world, a city, obsessed with celebrity . . . and people talk. And much of what they say is not true. So we just ignore it, okay? I don't care what they say, because I know who I am. *You* know who I am. And we don't let them define who we are for us."

I caught her out of the side of my eye, wiping a tear that had fallen on her cheek, her gaze still fixed out the window.

"Hey." I reached for her, our fingers interlocking. "I'm okay. We're okay. We're going to be okay."

If I said it enough, perhaps I would actually believe it.

She spent the afternoon in her bedroom reading. And the few times I checked on her she seemed so melancholy it hurt my heart. But I did not press her, because talking about it seemed only to upset her more. So I left her alone.

And then I went against Hayes's advice and all the rules I'd laid down for my daughter and myself and I got online and searched my own name. Because I wanted to know. What I was up against, what they were saying, what others were consuming without my knowledge. I wanted to know the worst of it.

There was much to behold. Tabloid gossip and myriad blog posts and speculation. How we had gotten together, how long it had been going on, how serious it was, how many years there were between us. *Daily Mail* and Perez Hilton and TMZ. Fake Twitter and Instagram accounts with variations of my name spewing lies and filth. Fan-run websites and Tumblr pages with cruel memes. The one that would stay with me longest was "Solène Marchand: Mother, Fucker." And photos. Far beyond the boat excursion in Anguilla and shots of us leaving the Edison Ballroom, we'd been caught a dozen-odd times. Outside of the Ace Hotel, the SLS, LAX, Bestia, Whole Foods, Nobu—places I did not even recall seeing photographers. And it had been going on for months. There I was: boarding the boat in Saint-Tropez, exiting the Chateau Marmont with him in my car, leaving the London, standing in the taxi line outside of the Grand Palais, waiting by the valet in Miami, returning from my run in Central Park. All those moments when I assumed I was still anonymous, invisible—captured.

And suffice it to say, the things they said—the fans especially—were not kind. Biting, caustic, insulting, offensive. Sexist, ageist, awful. I had to wonder which of these things Isabelle's friends were repeating to her. And how long she could attempt to ignore it. Because, I gathered, she could only internalize it for so long before it destroyed her.

And I realized then that part of the problem with Hayes's "no comments on his personal life" policy was that he would not defend my virtue. He had the luxury of living in his cocoon because the fandom would always protect him. They worshipped him. They adored him. There is no telling what they would do for him. And in the most extreme cases, I feared what that meant for me, and my family.

I flew down to Buenos Aires the following Sunday to meet up with the band. In my absence, they'd performed in Peru, Chile, and

Paraguay, with sightseeing detours to Machu Picchu and Chile's Lake District. Hayes had been enthusiastic at the beginning, but his excitement had started to wane.

"It's a little stifling here," he'd said via phone, late Saturday night from Paraguay. "It's been nearly impossible for us to get out because the crowds have been so deep. We go straight from the airport to the hotel and from the hotel to the venue and then back, and all the things that I'd hoped to see I'm not seeing. In Santiago, there were about seven hundred fans outside of the hotel and they refused to disperse. The other night they sang through all three of our albums, beginning to end. With Chilean accents. It was quite charming. But loud. And I got no sleep."

"*Métro, boulot, dodo,*" I said.

"What's that?"

"It's a French saying. You get up, you go to work, you go home, you go to sleep. It's kind of what the rest of the world does. Not what you signed up for, huh?"

He laughed at that. "I guess not, no."

By the time I reached the Four Seasons in Buenos Aires, it was almost eleven-thirty on Monday morning and the guys had already departed for their sound check. It was just as well, because I relished the opportunity to take a much-needed shower and crawl into our bed and sleep.

I awoke some hours later to Hayes's body sliding up against mine, his arm wrapping around my waist, drawing me into his warmth. Like being in a womb. His breath soft at the back of my neck.

"You came back to me," his lips buzzed my ear.

"Of course I did. Liam."

He laughed.

"Wait. Whose room is this?"

"Mr. Marchand's."

"Crap. I might be in the wrong room."

He smiled, rolling me over to face him. "Hiiii."

"Hi."

"You want to come with me to an August Moon concert to-night?"

"It depends . . ." I said.

"It *depends?*"

"Do I have good seats?"

His finger was tracing my cheekbone. "You can sit on my face."

"Okay. In that case I'll come."

The Estadio José Amalfitani was a massive stadium in the Liniers neighborhood of Buenos Aires that held just shy of fifty thousand people. August Moon had managed to sell it out two nights in a row. We arrived a few hours before showtime and already thousands of girls had lined up in the large thoroughfare leading to the structure. More fans than I had ever seen congregated in one place. The band and their entourage traveled by caravan: nine vans interspersed with motorcycle police. The cavalcade winding its way through throngs of screaming girls. Barriers holding back crowds near the hotel and the stadium. This was what Desmond had been referring to when he talked about Peru being crazy. This unimaginable level of idolatry and pandemonium. It was hard to wrap one's mind around. I sat there in the van, holding Hayes's hand and watching the madness unfold on either side of us, wondering what was going through his head. How did one even begin to process something like this? How?

He leaned into me then, sensing my anxiety. "You'll get used to it, Sol."

He said it so reassuringly, but I knew—I could never get used to this.

Inside, beneath the stadium, was a maze of winding tunnels. Utilitarian rooms and dank corridors that went on and on. The guys were set up in a series of large dressing rooms: wardrobe, hair and makeup, catering, a space for their band. I watched them prep and dress and psych one another up and carouse with their stylists and their handlers, and they struck me as young again, frenzied, like high school boys before a big game.

In the final minutes before they went on, when the guys were lining up and the crowd was so loud the ceiling seemed to be shaking, Hayes took me aside and handed me a box.

"Open this," he said, "before we go onstage." He was fiddling with the power pack at the back of his jeans and its accompanying belt.

"You bought me a gift?"

"Just something I promised I would get you . . . a very long time ago." He leaned in and kissed me then, before backing up down the long corridor, security detail flanking his sides. "I love you. Enjoy the show."

I watched him follow his bandmates around the bend until I could not see him anymore and he was sucked into the reverberating walls and the chants of fifty thousand girls. And only then did I open the box. Inside was a pair of noise-reducing headphones and a note:

I told you there'd be a next time.

And so it was that I was just one of the many females in Buenos Aires that night crying over Hayes Campbell.

I fought my jet lag to make it to the hotel gym the next morning, and on the way back up to the room, I found myself alone in an elevator with Oliver. Even before the doors closed, I could feel the tension.

"How was your workout?" he asked. Like Hayes, his voice was gruff after a show.

"Fine, thank you."

"Good." He stood directly across from me on the opposite side of the lift. Long arms folded across his chest, eyes piercing. "You look good."

"Really?" I laughed. "All wet and sweaty?"

"All wet and sweaty." He smiled. "Is that how he likes you?"

I stiffened. And then I remembered we were in an elevator and there were cameras and he would not touch me. Here.

"I thought you weren't supposed to be talking to me," I said.

"I think the ban was lifted."

"Did you lift it yourself?"

He shrugged.

"Why do you insist on fucking with me, Oliver?"

"Because I can." He smiled, sly. "Because you let me. Guys will try to get away with as much as they think they can get away with. Even if it means screwing their friends. Ask your boyfriend. He wrote the book."

And in that moment I knew. He knew about Hayes and Penelope. He was just biding his time.

The doors were opening on the seventh floor. One of the band's security was standing watch. Omnipresent.

"I do find it sweet that you're rather loyal. You get points for that," Oliver said, stepping out. And then, just before the doors closed, he turned back to me. "Because most of the others . . . weren't."

I did not bring it up with Hayes immediately. Partly because I was being selfish and I wanted us to enjoy each other's company without anything dark or subversive hanging over us. And partly because I did not want him to hurt. They were living in such close quarters, performing together every night. The very nature of their success made it imperative that they get along. But at the same time, I did not want Hayes to be blindsided. And I remembered what he'd said in Anguilla. That, given the chance, he thought Oliver would hurt him. And knowing that, I could not put it off for long.

On Wednesday, we flew private to Uruguay. Hayes and I sat toward the back of the jet, along with Simon and Liam, and when he excused himself to go to the loo, I took the opportunity to scold them.

"Are we in trouble?" Simon smirked when I said I wanted to bring up something serious.

"You could be." I lowered my voice, leaning forward over the table. "Remember the girl at the SLS Hotel the night of the Grammys? The one you left out in the hallway? I don't know what happened. I don't know that I *want* to know what happened. I'm not accusing you of anything. I'm just telling you that she was sixteen years old and in California that's illegal and you need to be aware of that."

Simon sobered. "She was eighteen. She said she was eighteen."

"She lied."

"Which girl?" Liam looked confused.

"The girl in the red dress," Simon said.

"The UCLA girl?"

"She said she went to UCLA."

"She lied," I repeated.

"She had that UCLA thing. Like a school ID . . ."

"And a key chain," Liam added.

I stared at them both. "She. Lied."

"Fuck." Simon's hands were pulling at his hair.

For a long time I didn't say anything, watching the two of them squirm.

Eventually Simon spoke: "Why are you looking at me like that?"

"Like what?"

"Like a disappointed mum."

"Because I *am* a disappointed mum. I trusted you with my daughter—"

"I didn't touch your daughter—"

"I know you didn't. But you need to be more careful. You realize if her parents find out or she tells the wrong person, it's over, right? This, all of this, will be over and you'll end up in jail. You realize that?"

Simon nodded, glum. Liam did not respond. He sat there, chewing on his plump lips, nervously twisting his hair. He looked to me like a little boy. And yet . . .

"Liam? Do you understand what I'm saying?"

"Yes."

"Don't let it happen again."

"I need to tell you something. And it's going to upset you a bit, but I think you need to hear it."

It was late afternoon and the band had returned to our hotel in Montevideo after having taped a talk show in town. The fans outside were so loud, I could hear them singing from our suite on the fourth floor. "Undressed," from the *Petty Desires* album. The lyrics twisted, titillating.

"Are you ending it?" Hayes asked. He was lying on the bed, resting. His head was throbbing, he'd said.

They were at that point nine dates into the tour. There were sixty-six remaining.

"If I were, do you think I would start it that way?"

He smiled faintly, his hand reaching for mine. "I'm not sure. Sometimes I can't read you. What is it?" he asked. "What is it you want to say?"

"Oliver . . ."

"Fucking Oliver . . . What did he do now?"

"He's fucking with me, Hayes. He's fucking with *you*, for a reason. I think he knows."

"He knows what?"

"I think he knows about you and his sister."

He propped himself up on his elbows then, his eyes searching mine. "Did you bloody say something?"

"No."

"Did you say something, Solène?"

"No. I would never do that to you. But something is up with him and I'm not going to be his pawn, Hayes. I'm not going to let him play me against you. That's *your* issue."

"Fuck."

"I'm sorry. I just thought you should know."

Friday evening found us in Brazil. Hayes and I were in our suite at the Hotel Fasano in São Paulo, getting ready for dinner, when Isabelle FaceTimed me.

"Are you having so much fun? Is it amazing?"

"It's a little crazy," I said. "There are fans everywhere. They really, really, really love them here."

"More than they love them in the States?"

"I don't know. I have nothing to compare it to. Hayes," I called to him in the bathroom, "do they love you here more than they do in America?"

"Maybe," he called. "I think they're more enthusiastic here. But then again I can't really understand what they're saying. Who are you talking to?"

"Isabelle."

"Hiiii, Isabelle." He stepped out of the bathroom in black Calvin boxer briefs. And nothing else.

I shook my head, shooing him back inside. "FaceTime," I mouthed.

"Byyyye, Isabelle."

"I miss you, peanut. I miss you a ton."

"I miss you, too," she said.

"How's Daddy?"

"He's good. He's here. Do you want to talk to him?"

"No. Does he want to talk to me?"

"Probably not."

"Okay," I laughed. "I love you. I'll talk to you tomorrow, okay."

"Love you, too. I hope you're having fun. *Bisous.*"

It was the way she said it. I could not help but feel guilty. "*Bisous.*"

I returned to the bathroom to watch Hayes dry his hair and brush his teeth and do all the little Hayes things that I'd come to know so well.

"What?" he asked after several moments had passed. "Why do you look like that?"

"What am I doing here?"

He wiped his face and placed his towel on the edge of the sink before turning toward me. "You're keeping me company. Come here."

I made my way into his arms.

"You're missing your daughter?"

"I'm missing my life."

He didn't say anything then. He buried his face in the top of my head and kissed me. But he didn't say anything.

That night, we had a late dinner in one of the hotel's restaurants, along with Rory, Simon, Raj, and Andrew, the group's new tour manager, a tall, striking thirty-something Brit with smooth, dark skin and piercing cheekbones.

"God, where do you find these people?" I'd said to Hayes upon first meeting him.

Hayes had laughed. "Beverly, our wardrobe person, calls him Idris."

"To his face?"

"No, not to his face. But it's caught on, and now all the women on tour refer to him as Idris."

Afterwards, when we were all at minimum two caipirinhas in, the guys decided they wanted to check out a club in the Itaim Bibi neighborhood. With a population of eleven million, São Paulo was massive and the only city I could recall visiting where the skyline seemed to stretch the entire length of the horizon. I did not pretend to know where we were or where we were going. I resisted at

first, because I took it to be a fishing expedition for Rory and Simon, who'd been talking about Brazilian models for at least two
countries now. But when Petra, the group's hair and makeup artist, arranged to come with us, I acquiesced.

And once again it was the coordinating of security and sched-
uling of a caravan and I suddenly understood what it must be like
every time Obama decided to go for a burger.

Fuchsia lights, house music, and beautiful wealthy people reigned
at the club Provocateur, where the crowd parted like the Red Sea
and they escorted us to a sectioned-off area and the alcohol
flowed like water. Raj immediately ordered three bottles of Cris-
tal, and the servers delivered them with sparklers, as if we needed
more attention. It took no time for a bevy of pretty young things
to flock to our area and Rory and Simon were in their element
and I was old and someone's mother and six thousand miles from
home.

"What are you thinking?" Hayes said. We were seated in our
booth, his hand between my knees.

"Nothing."

"You're lying to me. I know you far too well. Let's dance for a
bit, and then, if you want, we can go."

"We just got here."

"I want you to be happy," he said.

"I am."

"Are you sure?"

"I'm sure."

And so we danced. And we drank. And we did not leave until
close to three. Rory and Simon with two girls apiece. And I was
not sure if they were wing women or what, but they certainly
seemed committed. There were some high-level machinations as
we slipped out through the back entrance to pile into our ride, and
the girls left separately and took a cab to the hotel, where Trevor

met them in the lobby, and it all felt so sordid and rehearsed, I wondered who they thought they were fooling.

"I'm sorry I'm keeping you from having two girls tonight."

Hayes laughed. "Is that what you're doing?"

We were back in our suite, on the sixteenth floor. Hayes was seated on the Knoll-style leather sofa, and I was standing above him, my hands on either side of his shoulders, my knee between his legs.

"You should be out there having fun."

"Do you think I'm not having fun?"

"You're twenty-one."

"I know how old I am." His hands were moving over the skirt of my dress, slipping beneath the hem, traveling up the backs of my thighs. He was drunk. We both were.

I kissed him. He tasted of rum and lime and sugar and happiness. And I wanted to lock it away and remember it forever.

His hands moved to my shoulders, and with little effort he peeled off my spaghetti straps and unhooked the back of my dress, freeing my breasts.

"What would I do with four boobs anyway if I only have one mouth?"

I laughed. His tongue was already at my nipple. "I think you'd figure something out."

"Probably. But it wouldn't be as fun without you."

I was quiet then, listening to my own breath, smelling his hair. He had one hand on my breast and the other had returned to beneath my skirt, ascending, expertly tugging off my thong.

His eyes met mine. "See, right now I would just be learning their names and trying to keep them straight. I already know your name. We can skip all the formalities."

I smiled, untangling myself from him, kneeling down and undoing his belt. He watched me, his eyes glazed, a half smile playing over his lips. I unfastened his pants and undid the zipper, and his penis was so unfathomably hard it seemed to me even larger than it was when we'd had sex earlier. And it was large then. There was something so appealing about the head cresting out of his underwear. Like a gift.

"Fuck, I love you," I said, reaching into his pants.

"And see, that would be weird coming from the two girls I did not know," he snickered.

"I love this dick."

"I know you do."

"I'm going to miss this dick."

"It's not going anywhere."

"It's going to Australia when I go to New York."

"But then we'll wait for you in Japan. I promise. Are you crying? Fuck, don't cry."

"I'm not crying," I said. But I was.

"You're not allowed to cry with my dick in your mouth . . . Solène." His hand was in my hair. "That's not cool. That's really going to kill it for me."

I laughed, wiping my eyes. "I'm sorry. Okay. Let's do this."

He came quickly. And I found myself appreciating the pineapple-and-mint juice he'd had at lunch.

"I fucking love you," he said, after. His hands at the sides of my face, his mouth on mine. "You're going to come to Japan, right? You promise?"

"I promise."

"You're not going to change your mind."

"I'm not going to change my mind. I promise."

Hayes wrestled out of his pants and hiked up my skirt, pulling me onto his lap. His thickness sliding into me. No recovery time necessary. And as inebriated as I was, I was glad I had the where-withal to retain all that happened that night. Because I knew, in my heart, that we would not last. And because every moment of it was extraordinary.

I did not hear how the fight started.

Sunday evening, we were backstage at the Estádio do Morumbi, a stadium that held no fewer than sixty-five thousand attendees. It was the guys' second night playing to a sold-out crowd in São Paulo. They'd already been through hair and makeup, and a meet-and-greet. Following their vocal warm-up, they were hanging in one of the dressing rooms, waiting to go on. Liam was doing push-ups, and Rory was strumming his guitar and sucking on a lollipop, and Simon and Hayes were chatting about something or another, their voices alternating between low whispers and loud guffaws. Oliver was standing not far from them. He'd been reading up until that point and had just put down his book. How he went from zero to sixty with fifteen minutes to showtime was beyond me. And as always there was the hum: the stomping and shrieking of the fans, the bass of the opening local band, the vibrations in the walls.

I had managed to tune it all out while composing work emails from my spot in the corner. It had come to be my ritual: attempting to run a business from backstage. And then I heard it, the shift in tone.

"Yes, Hayes is very good at keeping secrets. Aren't you, Hayes?" Oliver had said.

"What does that mean?"

"I think you know what it means."

"Do you have something you want to say to me? Then say it," Hayes spat.

There was a measured pause, and then: "I knew, you bastard. I knew."

My hairs bristled. They were doing this. Now.

"It was a long fucking time ago."

"That's not what I heard," Oliver said. "I heard it was as recently as last year . . ."

The room fell quiet. Rory stopped strumming; Liam ceased to move. And I realized two things: none of the others knew what was going on, and I knew less than I thought I did.

"Who told you that?" Hayes said, slow, sharp.

"Don't worry about it, mate. Just know that I know."

"Who fucking told you that?"

Oliver turned to face him then, direct. "*She* did."

"No, she didn't."

"She *did*. She said, and I quote, 'Yeah, I shagged him, it was no big deal.'"

There was a second where I saw my boyfriend flinch. The slightest twinge in the corner of his left eye. I couldn't be certain as to whether the others saw it, but to me, it said everything.

"She didn't say that."

"Really? You want to ring her? Ask?"

"Fuck you."

"Fuck me? You sleep with my sister and you have the nerve to say fuck me? Fuck *you*, Hayes. Fuck you and your always getting your fucking way."

"All right, enough." Simon stood, wedging himself between them. Arms outstretched, making the most of his rower wingspan. "We're onstage in fifteen minutes. Everyone just fucking calm down."

But I could see Hayes still smarting, and I knew that was not going to happen.

"Really?" he said, taunting. "Was it *me* getting my way? Or your sister getting *hers*?"

Oliver's eyes narrowed. And then, unexpectedly, he began to laugh. "Hayes Campbell. Doesn't play well with others."

He was turning away, a smug smile on his aristocratic face, when Hayes spoke. His voice low, but clear enough for us all to hear:

"At least not in the way you'd *like* me to."

There was a moment of quiet while we were all registering what Hayes had said, and then it happened in a flash. And I think none of us was more surprised than Oliver, the elegant. He spun around, his arm whipping back and then flying over Simon's shoulder, catching Hayes in the center of his perfect face. It wasn't skilled or pretty, but it had the desired effect. There was a popping sound and then blood . . . everywhere.

"Fuck!!"

"Holy shit!!!" Rory jumped on the other side of the room.

"Fuck! Fuck!! Fuck!!!"

"Raj!!!!!!" Liam yelled. A bit like a girl, I thought.

"Holy shit!"

"What the fuck?" Simon pushed Oliver in the chest, and he stumbled back onto the floor. "What the fuck are you doing?"

And Hayes, in the middle of it all, both hands to his nose, eyes wide and unbelieving, and the blood dripping down his forearms and his chin, onto his Saint Laurent shirt. And his boots, his favorite boots.

"You fucking hit me? You little bitch."

I jumped up and grabbed a towel from the stack over by Petra's table and went to him. "Tip your head back."

"This fucking hurts."

"I know, honey. I'm sorry. Come, sit. Liam, go find Raj or Andrew and tell them we need a medic. Rory, get us some ice. Now!"

Simon helped us over to the couch along the near wall, rolling a towel to support Hayes's head. When he was done, he stepped back, watching me, a wry smile on his chiseled face.

"What?"

"You're like the hot mum I never had."

"Really? Not the 'disappointed mum'?"

"Campbell." He leaned over Hayes and gave him two thumbs up. "It's like the MILF fantasy and the nurse fantasy rolled into one."

"Simon . . ."

"Also, high-five on Penelope."

"Simon, *go away*. And change your shirt. There's blood on your shirt."

"Change it for what? It's not like we can go on without him."
He spun around to nail Oliver on the other side of the room. "You
are in so much fucking trouble, HK."

Andrew appeared then at the door with Liam and three security detail. "What the bloody hell happened?"

For a second no one spoke. Oliver stood with his arms crossed
looking contrite. Simon shook his head. Hayes's eyes were closed.

"Apparently, Hayes shagged his sister," Liam said. And that was
all he said.

Andrew's look was incredulous. "Today?"

"Fuck," Hayes said.

"I think a long time ago," Simon volunteered.

"And they chose to fight over it *today*? There are *sixty-five thousand* girls out there who have paid good money and are screaming
your names and waiting for you to go on in fifteen minutes, and
this happens *now*? Are you *mad*?"

"No," Hayes said, his voice muffled by the towel. "No more so
than usual."

August Moon went on without Hayes. Oliver had managed to frac-
ture a bone in his nose, which swelled quickly, efficiently rendering
Hayes's voice useless for the next several hours. The show started
almost forty minutes late, the guys scrambling with their vocal
coach to see who would take which solos and which, if any, harmonies could possibly be rearranged in such little time. They pulled
it off. Between the fans singing along loudly to everything, and
screaming in the moments when they weren't singing, Hayes's
absence was not a total deal breaker.

"Maybe we're just better as four," he said.

"Don't be silly. They need you. They're not the same without
you. This is your brainchild, remember?"

It was later that evening and we were back at the hotel, rehashing
the night's events: the hours in the hospital, the agreed-upon story

that he'd tripped and fallen during a rehearsal, the decision to hold off on realigning anything until he saw a specialist back in the States.

"Isn't that a little excessive?" I'd asked him in the examining room, when we had a moment to ourselves, Raj stepping out for yet another call, Desmond and two other security guards directly outside the door.

"They're taking it very seriously," he'd said.

"Who? Management?"

"Management and . . ." He'd paused for a second. "Lloyd's of London. It's insured, my face."

I could not help but laugh. "Of course it is, Hayes Campbell. Of course."

But back in the hotel with his face swollen and changing colors, he'd become melancholy.

"Fucking Oliver . . ." he muttered for the thousandth time.

"You *did* sleep with his sister, Hayes. What did you expect was going to happen?"

He grunted in response. We were lying in bed, his head propped on a pile of pillows, a latex glove filled with ice straddling the bridge of his nose. He looked ridiculous and yet still darling to me.

"Why would she tell him?" I asked.

"I don't know." He shook his head. "Maybe she thought it had been so long that he wouldn't care. Or maybe she was mad at me and it was her way of getting back . . . I don't know."

"I'm sorry."

He squeezed my hand.

"Why didn't you tell me it was still going on?"

"It's not *still* going on."

"You slept with her last year."

"It was before you. Does it matter?"

"You'd made it sound like it hadn't happened in years . . ."

He sighed, deep. "It was once last year, Solène. Once. Over the Christmas holiday. It was before I even met you. And evidently, 'it was no big deal.' I don't hold anything you did before me against you, do I? All the dicks you sucked in the nineties . . ."

"There weren't many dicks . . ."

"Whatever. It was *before* me. I don't care. Likewise, you shouldn't care about Penelope." He shut his eyes then, and for a moment neither of us spoke.

I lay there listening to the whir of the air conditioner. A siren rang in the distance, the pitch unfamiliar—a reminder that I was in a foreign city, far from home.

"What happened with you two, Hayes?"

"You know everything, Solène. There's nothing more to tell."

"Not Penelope. Oliver."

His eyes opened and strained to look at me. "Nothing."

"I'm not going to judge."

He was quiet for a long time and then he repeated it. "Nothing."

I wished I could have believed him. "Okay." I nodded. "Okay."

"You once asked me about my biggest secret," he said, soft. "I told you what it was. Any others . . . are not mine to tell."

In the morning, we flew to Rio. Hayes's face an inspiring palette of purple and blue. And while the rest of the guys snuck out to see a couple of the sights, we stayed behind at the hotel, icing.

On Tuesday, the band played to a crowd of forty thousand at the Parque dos Atletas. Petra was able to cover the green under Hayes's eyes, and the show went off without a hitch. His fans and his bandmates—Oliver included—were happy to have him back. In that last beat before heading toward the stage, they did their customary huddle, and I witnessed Oliver pat his back and whisper something into his ear. Hayes smiled and squeezed Ol's shoulder, and to the outside world they seemed okay. And for now, maybe that was enough. This facade. And maybe I would never know what happened. Maybe part of me didn't want to.

On Wednesday, I flew to New York, and the guys scattered to the corners of the globe. They had five whole days to themselves before reporting to Australia for the next leg of the tour.

japan

I thought there would be a joy in getting off the plane unencumbered. I thought I'd have a newfound respect for the ability to come and go as I pleased, unrecognized, the anonymity that I'd taken for granted. I thought there would be an exhilarating sense of freedom. But there was not. And perhaps it was coming down from the tour high, but everything to me felt bleak, dichromatic, insurmountable . . . like a Wyeth landscape.

It might have been all the travel or the lack of sleep, but New York to me seemed sad. I arrived at the Armory Show Thursday morning, after a ten-hour flight and a quick shower at the Crosby

Street Hotel. And nothing was quite right. Matt and Josephine had flown in early in the week to assist Anders with the setup of our booth at Pier 94. Lulit had arrived the day before. We were featuring five of our artists. Already our sales had exceeded expectation, but I could not manage to focus. I could not help but feel as if I were walking around in a fog, with some essential part of me missing. And I kept getting lost in thoughts of him.

I'd woken the day before in Rio with Hayes's arms wrapped so tightly around me, I could not breathe. And I knew he sensed, even in his dreams, that it was ending, and he did not want to let me go. And I think he feared that me leaving Brazil was me leaving for good. I think we both feared it.

I'd untangled myself and kissed him and stroked the side of his bruised face and whispered a thousand times over that I loved him. And that I would join him in Japan. I promised. I promised.

And to have been uprooted from that and transplanted to Manhattan selling art on a Thursday felt off-kilter. Inside, I feared something was dying.

That evening I went back to the hotel, the site of our first tryst, and I got into my bed and everything came flooding back. How he was still such a stranger to me then. How nervous I'd been. How he'd touched me and unfolded me and gifted me his watch. "Thanks for giving me the pleasure," he'd said. As if he were the only one benefitting. As if I'd done him a favor.

On Friday, we received news that Anya Pashkov had been offered a solo exhibition at the Whitney. I celebrated with the rest of our team, going out for cocktails at the end of the day, but I was there in body only.

It was on the cab ride back to Soho when we crossed through Times Square that my heart stopped. There, several stories high, was a billboard with the new TAG Heuer campaign. Hayes in black and white. Soulful eyes, generous mouth, stunning. They had captured him so beautifully, I began to cry.

The campaign debuted in a variety of publications that first week of March: *Esquire*, *GQ*, *Vogue*, and *Vanity Fair*. There were three different ads that ran, each photo more breathtaking than the next. And just like that, Hayes Campbell had successfully separated himself from the rest of his boy band. He'd redefined.

"They're perfect," I said to him that night on the phone.

"You're just saying that because you're my girlfriend."

"I bet I could find twenty-two million people who would agree with me on Twitter."

He laughed at that, his voice muffled. He'd been treated by a renowned plastic surgeon in Beverly Hills earlier that day. It was an outpatient procedure, and Raj was in charge of post-op duties while Hayes convalesced at the Hotel Bel-Air. I hated knowing that he was in L.A. without me.

"I love you," I said. "I wish you were here."

"I am," he said. "In your heart."

On Saturday, Lulit and I had dinner with Cecilia Chen, our potential client whom we'd had to reschedule the day the gallery was vandalized. She was in New York for the show, and so we met up at Boulud Sud near Lincoln Center. I liked her. A lot. She'd lived in Paris long enough that all the good things had rubbed off on her. Her accessories, her insouciance, the way she flicked her wrist. We were just winding up with cappuccinos, and discussing the work of Tunisian-French director Abdellatif Kechiche, when a portly middle-aged man approached our table. At first, I assumed he must have known Cecilia, or perhaps even Lulit, but when he shifted his weight, I noticed beyond his shoulder two tween daughters holding cell phones and I knew.

"Excuse me," he said. "Are you Solène Marchand?"

I nodded, albeit reluctantly.

"I'm so sorry to interrupt your meal, but we're here visiting from Chicago, and my girls would love to take a picture with you."

I don't remember saying yes, although somehow it happened. I do remember the expression on Lulit's face: bewildered, admonishing, torn. Cecilia looked on confused.

"You're even prettier in person," the girls said. "Tell Hayes we love him."

When they'd parted, I attempted to return to the conversation as if nothing had happened, just as I'd seen Hayes do a million times. But Cecilia was not having it.

"What was that all about? Are ten-year-olds suddenly collecting art in Chicago?"

"Her boyfriend's a musician," Lulit interjected before I could say anything. "He has a following."

Musician. It was rather diplomatic of her.

It was not the first time that week it had happened. No fewer than half a dozen teenage girls had stopped me on the streets. Random visitors kept popping into our booth pretending to look at the art. I felt it, eyes, everywhere. I did my best to ignore it and hoped it would not affect my work. I was trying to do that now.

We returned to the topic of French contemporary cinema, and my boyfriend did not come up again. But I had seen the expression on Cecilia's face, that very Parisian look of disdain. And I knew that moment had changed everything.

Early Sunday morning, the day I was to fly out, Amara met me at Balthazar for breakfast. The French bistro was a block from my hotel and just loud enough that I did not have to worry about people eavesdropping on our conversation. Because that had become something I was concerned with—privacy.

We'd been talking about her. She'd met someone, on Tinder. They'd been dating for three months and she was cautiously optimistic.

"He's young," she said, smiling.

"How young?"

"Thirty-five . . ."

I laughed at that. "That's practically over the hill where I come from."

". . . and he doesn't want kids." She sipped from her latte. "Lucky me, right?"

"Lucky you."

"Does Hayes want kids?"

It was a completely benign question, and yet the absurdity of it struck me. I placed down my utensils and began to laugh. "What the fuck am I doing? I can't believe you asked me that. And it wasn't a joke. He's twenty-one years old. He doesn't know what he wants. I mean, yes, he says he wants kids, but . . . Oh God, what am I doing?"

Amara was quiet for a moment, watching me, and I had to wonder what she was seeing: a woman on the verge of losing her mind.

"What are you thinking?" she said after a minute.

"I spent ten days with him on tour in South America, just following him around. We go from city to city. From the hotel to the stadium and back to the hotel. There are walls of screaming girls everywhere and we are constantly surrounded by security. They pace our floor. We can't go anywhere by ourselves. We can't sightsee. We can't have a casual dinner at a restaurant. We can't go for a walk. We can't do anything without an entourage and bodyguards, and this is his life for months out of the year. *Months*. I can't do that."

She nodded. "Do you love him?"

Crap. I was going to cry. Here. In Balthazar. Under the gold lights and the oversized French mirrors. My avocado and poached eggs on toast were getting cold. "I love him."

"Okay, then."

"But I don't know that that's enough. I think Isabelle is miserable. She's not herself. His fans are stalking me. They defaced our gallery; they send death threats, dildos to my house. Not to mention the harassment on social media. I don't know that I can do this . . ."

"What are you most afraid of?"

"Everything." I smiled, but it felt forced. "Isabelle having a nervous breakdown. And it being my fault. Getting older. Getting old. My boobs, my upper arms, my ass. All of it. Eventually he's going to take a good look at me and be like, 'Bollocks! You're forty!'"

Amara laughed. "That's a good accent you do."

"Thank you." My thoughts got drowned out in the hum of the restaurant. Laughter, the clinking of silverware, the scraping of bistro chairs on tile. "But even if everything were perfect . . . even if the harassment stopped, and Isabelle grew to accept it . . . how would it happen? What, we move in together, we cohabitate, we have a kid, we get married? He goes on tour, I run a gallery? How crazy is that?"

Amara shrugged. "I don't think there are any real answers. I think you just do it."

I sighed, pushing away my plate. I'd had all of seven bites and my appetite was gone. "You know what I'm most afraid of? I look at Daniel and Eva having a baby, and I think, I can't give him that. I'm already old. By the time he's ready to have kids I will be too old. What am I saying? He's twenty-one. He's in a boy band. I can't have a child with a guy in a boy band. How insane would that be?"

"It's not just 'a guy in a boy band,'" Amara said. "It's *Hayes*. It's Hayes. And you love him."

My heart caught in my throat. I could feel the tears welling.

"And he *adores* you . . ."

"I know . . . But that's bound to end, right? One day he's going to wake up and realize I'm twice his age. And he's going to freak the fuck out and leave me."

Amara reached out to squeeze my hand on the table. She was quiet for a long time, and then: "He might not."

"He might not," I conceded. "But he might."

I arrived in Los Angeles that evening. Only hours after Hayes had departed for Australia. And yet it was probably for the best, because I wanted nothing more than to curl up with my daughter and hear about her life. She was not her usual excitable self, but she filled me in on school and fencing and the musical she'd been cast in and her crush on Avi, the soccer-playing senior. ("Do you think he'll notice me now since I don't have my braces anymore?" "How could he not?") She seemed to be functioning, normal. Eighth grade.

And so I tried not to let the other things bother me. The pile of mail I'd received without return addresses or addresses I did not recognize—letters and cards and packages—I placed unopened in a box, on the instruction of the detective who was assigned my case after the vandalizing of the gallery. They were monitoring my mail to see whether a pattern of threats had been sufficiently established to be legally considered stalking. Apparently one dildo was not enough.

On the following Tuesday after I'd gotten back, we received the news from Paris: Cecilia Chen had decided to go with someone else. She claimed that Cherry and Martin, another reputable midsized gallery, was a better match. "They're slightly less flashy," she said, "and that appeals to me."

Marchand Raphel was many things, but flashy was not one of them. And I knew then that she'd gone and Googled me, and my boyfriend, and based her decision on that.

"Solène." Lulit cornered me as I was leaving the office that evening.

"I know what you're going to say," I said, "and I'm sorry—"

"No, you don't," she cut me off. "What I was going to say is: I like Cecilia, a lot. I think she would have been great for us. I think we would have been great for her. But I like you more. And I want you to be happy."

Her tone, her voice, her expression were all so sincere, in that moment I remembered everything I loved about my best friend, and I began to cry. "It's tearing me apart. I love him so much. And it's tearing me apart."

"I know it is," she said, wrapping her arms around me. "I know it is. It's okay. We'll figure it out. We'll make it work."

But again, I could not imagine what that would look like.

I was still hurting when I arrived at Isabelle's school to pick her up after her rehearsal that evening. But I did not want her to see it, so I covered, as I usually did, and pulled up to the carpool area with a smile.

She was standing far off to the side when I approached. There was a cluster of older girls to one side of the entrance, laughing and texting. And I was happy she was not with them.

Isabelle climbed into the car and slammed the door before I'd even shifted into park. "Drive."

"Hey, peanut. How was your day?"

"Drive, Mom. Just drive."

"Oh-kay . . . No 'Hello'? What happened?" I looked back over toward the older students as we peeled out. "Do you know those girls?"

"I do *now*."

"What happened, Izz?"

"Nothing, Mom. Just a bunch of girls from the Upper School who wanted me to ask you if you could get a picture of Hayes Campbell's penis for them. You know, typical teenage stuff."

My stomach lurched. "They said that?"

"No, actually, they said 'dick,' but I thought I would edit it for you to be polite."

I pulled the car over then, frazzled. "Oh, honey, I'm so sorry."

"But as long as you're happy . . ." She began to cry.

"Oh, Izz . . ."

"Please keep driving. Please don't stop here. Please don't stop until we get home."

"Okay," I said. "Okay. Okay."

It wasn't until we got on the 10 that she added: "And remember that guy Avi, the one I think is really cute? Well, he finally spoke to me today . . ."

I nodded, my mind elsewhere.

"He came up to me in the hall just as I was going into Life Skills, and said, 'Tell your mom I turn eighteen next month.' So yeah, that's how my day was."

"Izz . . ." I could barely find my voice. "I'm so sorry . . ."

She was shaking, the tears streaming down her face. Everything she had held back for so long, released.

"We can talk to the head of school."

"And say what? What are you going to say? What is she going to do? Send out a school-wide email warning against teasing Isabelle Ford about her mother's indiscretions? What is she going to do, Mom?"

I had the sensation that I might vomit. There, in the car. The bile rising, my knuckles white against the wheel. I'd begun to sweat. There was no place to pull over.

"How long has this been going on, Izz? Why didn't you tell me?"

"Since January. Since those stupid pictures from Anguilla. But I know you're happy and I know you love him. And he's really nice, and you deserve to be happy. Because Daddy's happy. And I don't want you to be alone."

"Oh, Isabelle." My heart was wrenching. These were the thoughts that had consumed my daughter. "We can change schools," I said. "You don't have to go back there."

"But I *like* my school," she cried. "I like my school. And *where* would I go? Where would I go to school with other thirteen-year-old girls who *don't* know Hayes Campbell? Zimbabwe?"

Traffic had come to a standstill on the PCH. Construction. The sun was setting over the Pacific, purple and perfect. And once again I cursed California for having weather that did not mirror my mood.

I leaned over the divider to hug her, my own tears falling. "I'm sorry, Izz. I'm so sorry."

"I know you told me to just ignore it, and I've been trying, I have. But I can't. I can't, Mommy. I can't."

I held her, and sobbed with her, and breathed in her hair until the traffic started to move. And I knew.

I knew.

And all the other things, they did not matter.

That night, after I made Isabelle a bowl of hot chocolate and she calmed down enough to fall asleep, I called Hayes in Australia. It was three in the afternoon and they'd just arrived in Adelaide. And the second I heard his familiar gravelly voice I began to cry.

"What happened?" he asked.

"I can't do this. I can't do this to her."

"*What happened?*"

I told him. About Cecilia first, and then Isabelle. And for a long time he did not say anything.

"Are you there?"

"I'm here."

"I'm sorry," I said. "I'm sorry."

His breath was heavy. "Can we not discuss this right now? Can we not . . . Can we not make any decisions right now? Can we just deal with this when we get to Japan?"

"Are you not listening to me? Have you not heard anything I've said?"

"I heard you. What do you want me to tell you? 'It's fine, let's just end it'? I'm not going to say that. I love you, Solène. I'm not just going to give you up without a fight."

I was quiet then.

"And I'm like eight thousand miles away from you. I can't do anything from here. I can't . . . Fuck. *Fuck*. You promised me you'd come to Japan."

"I know I did."

"You *promised*." His voice was quaking.

"I know."

"Please just come, and we can figure it out then. Please. Please."

Windwood's spring break was for two weeks at the end of March. Georgia's family had invited Isabelle to join them on their annual ski trip to Deer Valley. I let her go. That it happened to coincide with the Japan tour dates did wonders for alleviating my guilt.

On Saturday afternoon, after Isabelle had safely departed, Daniel came by the house to sign the school's annual tuition contract. He did not bring up Hayes and we managed not to argue.

"Make sure you email me your itinerary," he said. We were standing in the driveway: he, leaning against his car; me, pulling letters out of the mailbox.

"I will. As soon as—" I froze. There in my hand was a large manila envelope. No return address. Postmark: Texas.

I dropped it, shaking.

"What's wrong? What is it, Solène?"

I could not speak.

"What is this?" Daniel picked up the package from the ground. I could see the phallic outline in his hand, taunting.

"Don't open it."

"What *is* it, Solène?" He tore open the envelope and looked inside. "Did you order this?"

"Yes. Yes, I typically order dildos and then cry when they arrive."

His tone shifted, the realization settling in. "Did someone send this to you? What the hell? Solène? Did someone send this?"

I did not respond. He reached into the envelope, withdrew the note enclosed, and read it. "What the fuck? Solène, who sent this?"

"A fan."

"A *fan*? What kind of *fucking fan* sends this? I thought they were all sweet little girls like Isabelle."

"Most of them are. Some of them are not."

"How long has this been going on?"

I told him.

His face fell. "Why didn't you say anything? Why didn't you tell me?"

"I didn't want to bother you. I didn't want your judgment. It's okay, I'm taking care of it."

"You didn't want my *judgment*? Solène. I *care* about you. I'm always going to care about you. Something like this happens, it's serious. You need to tell me. Fuck my judgment."

I stood there, wiping away the tears with the back of my hand. I did not want him to see me suffering. I anticipated it: the great big "I told you so."

But instead, he wrapped his arms around me and held me close. It had been so long. I found myself searching for something familiar.

"I'm sorry," he said. "I'm sorry."

When he got into the BMW, he still had the envelope in hand.

"I have to give that to the detective."

"I'll hold on to it. I don't want this reminder in your house. It's disturbing as hell." And with that, he flung the package into the backseat and pulled out of the driveway.

I arrived in Osaka Monday evening. I did not have a plan other than to love him as profoundly as I could. And then let him go. It seemed to me my only true option.

We lay in bed that first night in our suite at the Imperial Hotel. Close, clinging, postcoital, my fingers tracing his face. We were not talking about it. Us.

"So this is the new nose . . ."

"It's the old nose. Just 2.0." He smiled.

I held his chin in my hand, tipping his face in one direction, and then the other.

"Well?"

"It's pretty perfect."

"Botticelli?"

"Botticelli." I smiled.

"He actually made it one percent more symmetrical than it was before. He could have gone for a whole three percent, but we weren't sure if it would visibly affect the symmetry of the rest of my features."

"You realize how ridiculous this conversation sounds, don't you?"

He smiled, his lips curling, his hands at my waist pulling me on top of him. "You mean when there are still girls missing in Nigeria? Yes, I absolutely do. But you yourself said it was art, so . . ."

I kissed the tip of it, delicately. "It's art. All of you is art."

"That's why you love me," he said, soft. As if he were reminding me.

"That's why I love you."

Tuesday afternoon following the boys' sound check at the Osaka Kyocera Dome, Hayes and I slipped out of a service entrance at the back of our hotel with Desmond in tow, and strolled through the adjacent Kema Sakuranomiya Park. Whoever scheduled the *Wise or Naked* tour was brilliant enough to coordinate their Japanese dates with peak cherry blossom season, and our hotel happened to abut the Okawa River and the blossom-laden promenade that lined it.

We walked hand in hand, with Desmond a few paces ahead of us. Feigning normalcy. Hayes in a gray fedora and Wayfarers, almost unrecognizable.

"So there are a few big producers who are interested in meeting with me," he said after we'd been walking for several minutes, drinking in the scenery, the canopies of pink. "To discuss potentially collaborating. Partially because of the Grammy nom, but also the TAG Heuer campaign."

"That's great. Who?"

"Jim Abbiss, who's done a ton of brilliant stuff. Paul Epworth, who's tremendous. Both have worked with Adele. And Pharrell . . ."

"*Seriously?* That's *huge*. And you're just telling me now?"

"Well, they didn't specify meeting with August Moon. Just me. Which is a little awkward."

"Hayes." I stopped walking then. "That's a big deal."

"I know," he said. I could see it in his eyes, the excitement.

"Are those guys less pop?"

He smiled, bright. "They're less *safe*."

Wednesday morning, when the guys were whisked off to do a radio show, I went for a long run on the promenade. I returned to the hotel through the riverside entrance, and en route to the elevators I passed Oliver in the airy lounge. Evidently, the guys had finished early. He was seated at a table beside the wall of glass, his back to me, deep in conversation with a woman I did not recognize: Japanese, early thirties, smartly dressed, refined. Her body language read slightly stiff, but Oliver seemed unusually comfortable, and as I rounded the bend I could see his face. He looked, to me, happy.

Thursday found us in Tokyo at the Ritz-Carlton. I watched the band's press conference from the back of a full room. Yearning to see Hayes as the rest of the world did. In addition to their publicist, whom I had met briefly backstage in Osaka, there were two other women who accompanied them, dressed chicly in head-to-toe black, clinging to their note cards and microphones. And as the questions began I realized two things: these women were August Moon's translators, and one of them was the woman from the lounge at the Imperial Hotel.

There was a sense of pride I felt watching the guys. For all their competitive boyishness behind closed doors and boisterous antics onstage, they were surprisingly poised. They were witty and charming and gracious. I tried to remember what impression I had of them that first night at the meet-and-greet. How skilled they were at engaging their fans. How at ease in their bodies. So damn likable. And none of that was lost in translation.

In between the "*konnichiwa*s" and the "*o-genki desu ka*s" and the "*arigato*s," there was the adaptable "*ganbatte*," which Hayes and Rory had taken a particular liking to, and which, I learned, translated to the sentiment of "do your best, try hard, good luck." An encouraging greeting, if ever there was one.

Hayes and I ducked out to visit the Mori Art Museum and explore the Roppongi district under Desmond's watch later that afternoon and returned unscathed. I considered it a blessing.

In the hotel's sky lobby on the forty-fifth floor, we bumped into Oliver and Reiko, the translator. They appeared to have either just finished cocktails or were meeting up—it was not entirely clear. But what *was* clear was that they were heading out together at the same time. We stood by the elevator bank with them making small talk. I don't know why I assumed they'd be going down, but when the up elevator arrived, the two of them stepped in behind us, and Hayes and I gave each other looks like teenagers who had happened upon some delicious piece of gossip. We rode together in silence, and when the elevator slowed as we approached the fiftieth floor, Oliver's stop, Hayes leaned forward, put his hand on Ol's shoulder, and said loud enough for us all to hear: "*Ganbatte*."

"Wow. Is that a thing?" We were giggling once the doors closed.

"It *will* be in about five minutes."

"Did you know about this? How long has it been going on?"

"In Ol's head, about three years. This is the first time she's responded."

I was amused. Good for Oliver. "Your friend . . . is very, very complex."

"No." Hayes smiled. "He's complicated."

We arrived at the fifty-first floor and acknowledged the security detail on our way to the corner suite. Hayes was futzing with the key card.

"You nervous?"

He smiled, pulling me into him and pressing me up against the door. "Does that feel nervous to you?"

He kissed me, and then he grew serious. "You can't fucking leave me. You can't fucking leave me, Solène."

It jarred me. That he'd been carrying it with him, just below the surface. Beneath all that pop star charm and charisma, he was hurting.

"Let's go inside," I said.

But inside was no better. Even with our breathtaking view, the lights coming on all over Tokyo and Mount Fuji on the horizon, we were trapped in some surreal world where everything looked perfect and yet still we could not make it work.

"I don't want this to end," he said.

"I don't want it to end either."

"You're letting them win. You're letting them end us."

I didn't say anything.

"I promised myself I would never let them do this. I would never let them dictate my happiness. And you're allowing them to do this to us . . ."

"Hayes, it's not just about us anymore."

"I know. I know . . . it's Isabelle. I'm sorry." The tears were falling. He wiped his face. "Fuck. I'm fucking crying like a little girl. Okay. I'm going to be okay. I'm going to have a shower. And you're going to join me. And we're going to have sex. And then I'm going to be okay."

I smiled at that. Through tears, I smiled. "Okay."

On Friday night, August Moon played the first of four shows at the Saitama Super Arena to a sold-out audience of thirty thousand. It seemed there was no end to the amount of fans who would fork over all their allowances and babysitting money and Bat Mitzvah loot to see the guys perform over and over again. Hayes had once told me that five hundred dollars was not out of the ordinary for floor seats. It boggled the mind.

We left the arena as we always did, running at a decent clip to get everyone into the vans or buses and out of the lot before the fans exited the stadium. The girls would still be singing "That's What She Said" or "Tip of My Tongue," one of the encore numbers, long after the guys had cleared the stage. Their voices traveling through the night, bright, blissful. It was a lot of fucking power. I tried to imagine what it would take to give that up. But I did not have the gall to ask him.

Late Saturday, after the show, the lot of us congregated in the Ritz lobby. The guys wanted to go out clubbing with what seemed a third of their entourage. It was a big bunch and they were loud, and while Raj was coordinating with drivers and security, Hayes and I decided to bow out.

When they departed, Hayes made his way from the bar over to the baby grand in the corner. I followed, sitting beside him on the narrow bench.

He began to play, his fingers moving over the keys, fluid. A melody I had not heard before. It was at once delicate and haunting, raw. And I felt it almost immediately, my insides seizing. It was personal.

"Is that something you wrote?"

For a moment he did not answer, and then: "Something I'm writing."

"What's it called?"

"'S.'" He said it plainly, no eye contact, no break in the music.

"Just 'S'? Are there words?"

"Not that I'm ready to share."

I sat there numb while he played for a minute more in silence. Then, very abruptly, he stopped.

"I think we should probably go upstairs now."

"I think so, too."

As the days passed, I was increasingly aware that our emotions were scattered. We went from laughing to crying and back again so frequently it became our new normal. On Sunday afternoon, we went shopping in the Omotesandō-Aoyama area. We'd started at Céline, where I found a classic box bag in gray. I decided to treat myself, and when I asked the saleswoman to ring it up, Hayes proffered his credit card.

"What are you doing?" I asked.

"I'm going to get it for you."

"No, you're not."

He raised an eyebrow. "Don't be silly."

"Hayes, you're not."

"You're really not going to let me buy it for you?"

"I'm not going to let you buy it for me."

He stood there, looking at me for a long time, a bewildered expression on his face. "Oh-kay," he said eventually.

I watched the saleswoman package the box, tying it all up with a bow, just so. When I turned back to Hayes, his eyes were brimming.

"What?"

"You make it so fucking hard not to love you," he said, soft. He lifted the neck of his T-shirt to wipe his cheek, and it seemed like something a young boy would do. His abdomen bared for a split second: the faint line of hair descending below his belly button, the crease traversing his groin. There was nothing about his body that I did not know, and that both comforted me and made me profoundly sad.

I wrapped my arms around his middle and held him close. "You, too."

We followed Desmond over to Alexander McQueen, just a little ways down. Hayes had on his sunglasses, but no hat, and although he turned several heads, only two people stopped him for selfies.

I trailed him through the sleek new store, pristine white marble and gloss, as he picked up two scarves and a shirt. We were upstairs toward the back, in the men's section, when Desmond approached us.

"We 'ave a bit of a problem."

I could not recall ever having heard him say those words, and it alarmed me. He walked us to the front side of the store, where through the floor-to-ceiling windows we could see a swarm of girls gathering below, at least fifty. The second they saw Hayes's face, their screams pierced the air.

"Shit. Where the bloody hell did they come from?"

"I've no idea. I'm going to get the driver to come around, but they're multiplying fast."

I could hear a commotion below on the first floor and feared some of them had already forced their way in, like locusts.

"Stay away from the glass," Desmond said. "I'm going to check with security and make sure they lock the doors."

There were a handful of other customers on the upper level, and I could feel them eyeing us, curious. One salesgirl, perhaps realizing who Hayes was, approached and bowed.

"Um, I'm probably going to have to leave in a bit of a rush," he said to her, sweetly. "Could you ring these up for me, please? *O-negai shimasu.*"

"*Hai.*" She bowed and took his credit card.

"It's like a tour bus just deposited them, out of nowhere. Are you freaking out? Don't freak out." Hayes reached to tuck a lock of hair behind my ear. "We're safe in here."

He had no sooner said it than a dozen girls came running up the marble staircase, camera phones at the ready, squealing, "Hayes!" Their behavior on seeing him was so oddly not Western. There was none of the grabbing or pawing that I'd become used to, but more of a delighted jumping and respect of his space. They did not physically have to touch him; it was enough to be near.

Desmond had called in for backup, and we waited another twenty minutes or so before Fergus arrived with two additional guards.

Outside was chaos. The crowd had grown to terrifying proportions. Girls in all manner of Harajuku dress, Minnie Mouse bows, and schoolgirl knee-highs. Fanboys with purple-dyed hair. I did not see how we were going to reach our car without being trampled. But the guards sandwiched us, and we moved through the throng like salmon swimming in the wrong direction. Perhaps it was because I did not understand anything they were saying besides "HayesHayesHayesHayesHayes," but their voices were so high-pitched and cacophonous, it sounded to me like cats mewling. Cats in heat, grating, earsplitting. And I would hear it in my dreams for a long time to come.

"Don't fall," Hayes said to me, as if it were something I was considering.

There was shoving and pushing and pulling and the feeling of the world closing in on me, the fear of asphyxiation. And then finally we made it into the car. And still I did not feel safe. Our driver was yelling, "*Sagattute! Sagattute!* Move back!" They were banging on the windows, hard.

Hayes hugged me close, and buried my face in his chest.

"You're okay," he said. "We're okay."

But I was not.

We did not talk about it when we got back to the hotel. We lay side by side in our room with the view of Mount Fuji and simply held each other.

On Monday morning, the day of their last concert in Tokyo, the day before I was leaving, Hayes worked out with Joss, their trainer. When he returned, I was in the living room answering emails, finalizing arrangements for Frieze New York. Without saying a word, he showered, got dressed, and then sat down before me.

"I don't know how to say this," he said, soft. "I don't know where to begin. But I love you so completely and the idea of you leaving is fucking breaking my heart. And I know . . . I understand every reason why you're doing it, but it still doesn't make sense to me. It doesn't make sense that we can't make it work."

"Hayes . . . I'm sorry . . ."

He'd begun to cry. "Why? Why can't it work? What if we're just quiet about it? What if we just go back to not saying anything?"

"We've never said anything," I said. "We've never said anything and look what they've done to us. I don't want to hide, Hayes. I don't want to feel like everything's a secret. I just want to live my life. And I can't do that with you right now without it destroying Isabelle."

"You said you wouldn't leave, Solène. You said you wouldn't leave."

"When? When did I say that?"

"At Bestia. At my birthday dinner . . ."

I was wracking my brain to remember. God, how he locked everything away.

"What if I quit the band?"

"You're not going to quit the band, Hayes. It's such a huge part of who you are. At your core. It's this extraordinary part of you. It's this *gift*. And you're good at it and you love it. People spend their whole lives searching for something like that.

"You have to be true to yourself. You can't just do this for me. Otherwise it will eat away at you and destroy you and you'll *resent* me. And I don't think either one of us wants that."

He was staring at me, his eyes wide, but I couldn't be certain anything was registering.

"And this is not going to last forever. Boy bands don't last forever, so enjoy it. Because eventually you outgrow it. You move on. And someone will quit. And someone will get someone pregnant. And someone will go solo. And someone will come out. And someone will marry a questionable blonde and get a reality show. And it will be over. And you'll never get this time back. So *enjoy* it."

He sat there, quiet for a minute, the tears spilling, his nose running. "So that's it . . . You're not even going to fight for us . . . You're just giving up . . ."

"I'm not giving up, Hayes. But . . . we're in such different phases of our lives. And I can't do this. I can't do this to Isabelle. I can't do this to myself. I can't follow you around the world. I'm not twenty. I have a career and I have a kid and I have responsibilities. And I have other people who need me—"

"*I need you.*" There was a desperation in his voice that startled me. "*I need you*, Solène. I need you."

I could feel it then, his heart breaking. And something inside of me unexpectedly shattered. Something I was not even aware existed. And I did not know what hurt more: my pain, or knowing that I'd caused his.

"You can't fucking leave," he cried. "You can't fucking leave."

I moved to wrap my arms around him then, and I held on to him, as tight as I could, for a very long time.

When he'd stopped sobbing, I wiped his face, pushing his hair back from his forehead. His beautiful forehead. There was nothing about him that I did not love.

"You are going to be okay," I said. "I know it hurts, but you are going to be okay. You have to know that. You have to *believe* that. I am not the only person you're going to love."

He nodded, slow. His eyes swollen, red. What damage I had done.

"How did we get here?" I heard myself say. "This was only supposed to be lunch, remember? This was only ever supposed to be lunch."

"You," he said, his voice frayed, foreign.

"Me?"

"You. You let me unfold you."

home

It hurt.

Those first few weeks, when I was trying to hold it together and occupy my time and my mind and convince myself that I could return to functioning normally. But I could not. And it would hit me at the oddest of times: on the off ramp at La Cienega, or picking up birth control pills at the pharmacy, or struggling to click in my shoes on my bike in spin class, and I would feel it in my gut—his absence—and I would start to cry.

When he went from calling and texting me several times a day to not at all, I assumed he'd moved on. That he was having too much fun in Bali or Jakarta or wherever he was. That he was living his life and enjoying his youth, like I'd told him to. And I had only myself to blame. I felt it then, my insides coming undone.

The last Saturday in April, I skipped the annual fund-raiser for Isabelle's school, which was a first. But I could not go out and socialize and pretend that everything was fine when my heart was bleeding. I lied and told her I was coming down with something, and retired early. Yet sometime in the middle of the night, when I had assumed she was sleeping, she came into my room and climbed into my bed. Her arm wrapping around me, her breath warm at the back of my neck.

"Mommy? Are you crying?"

I was.

"Because of Hayes?"

I nodded.

"I'm sorry. I'm so sorry."

She held me and allowed me to sob until it seemed there were no more tears to shed. And I marveled at how this had happened, how we had traded places.

When I had calmed somewhat, I rolled over and turned toward her, and I could see it on her face: the mess I must have been. Hollowed and swollen and wan. And not like her mother. She had never seen me like this. Not even during the worst of Daniel. I had hid it so well.

She was quiet, reaching out to trace her hand along my cheekbone; over the road map of broken capillaries, I imagined. "I'm sorry that you hurt."

"It's okay, Izz. I'm okay."

She nodded. And then just as quickly she shook her head and began to cry. "You're *not*. I know you're not."

It was unexpected, her declaration. "I *will* be."

"I'm sorry that I couldn't ignore it," she said, her voice quaking. "I'm sorry that I wasn't strong enough . . . For *you*. For *him*."

"Oh, Isabelle." I reached for her hand, lacing my fingers between hers. "It's not your fault. This is not your fault. There are a thousand reasons why we wouldn't have worked . . ."

She stilled then, biting her lip. Her very French mouth. "Did Hayes know that?"

"I think he did. I think deep down he did."

"Do you think he's hurting this much, too?"

I nodded. "Yeah . . . I do. But he's going to be okay.

"Love is this very precious thing, Izz. It's this precious, magical thing. But it's not *finite*. There's not a limited amount of it out there. You just have to be open to allowing it to find you. Allowing it to happen." I was not entirely sure that I believed this, but I needed *her* to.

"And for a long time I closed myself off to it, because it was easier and safe . . . But I wasn't necessarily happy.

"And Hayes is young. He has many, many years ahead of him. And he's going to fall in love again. And again. Even if he doesn't realize that right now, he will. Hayes is going to be okay. Promise."

She was quiet for a long time, her breaths deep, even. "What about you?"

I managed to smile. Despite the tears, and the thrumming in my head and the wrenching in my chest, I managed to smile. "I'm going to be okay, too."

It was late the following Thursday when I heard from him again. Out of nowhere, shortly after midnight, he texted.

Open your door.

I thought it might have been a prank. They were supposed to be in Europe. But sure enough, he was there, on my doorstep. His eyes were swollen, and my first thought was that he'd been in another fight with Oliver. And then I realized he'd been crying.

"What are you doing here? What are you doing here, Hayes?"

"I had to see you." His voice raspy, low, brought back every sweet memory. My happiness, my love.

"What about the tour? You just *left*?"

He was looking beyond me, into the house; lost, it seemed. "We have three days off."

"So you flew here? Hayes, I can't . . . You can't be here."

"Please let me in. Please, Solène." His eyes were brimming. He looked to me at once young and old. His tortured face a harsh reminder that I'd destroyed us. *I'd* done this. *I'd* done this.

I stepped aside and shut the door behind him. "Isabelle is here. She's sleeping."

"I won't wake her. I promise."

"Hayes, we can't do this . . ."

He wasn't listening to me. His hands were in my hair, at my neck, caressing the sides of my face as he inhaled me, and kissed me, thoroughly, passionately, completely.

"What are you doing? We can't do this." Even as I said it, I was aware my body was communicating otherwise. Melting into him. His hand beneath my T-shirt. The feel of his skin on mine. His mouth. Hayes Campbell. Like a fucking drug.

"I love you. I fucking love you so much. You cannot leave," he whispered. "Tell me you don't feel this, Solène. Tell me you don't want this . . ."

I shushed him. My finger on his lips. "You're going to wake Isabelle."

He stopped, his eyes peering into mine in the half-light. Pleading. And before I'd registered what I was doing I had taken his hand and led him down the hall.

It happened fast, the first time.

I did not regret it. Not feeling his weight on top of me, and his hips between my thighs, and smelling him—familiar. His mouth moving over mine, and his fingers gripping my hair, and his dick . . . filling me. Fulfilling me.

We came quickly, and at the same time. And we might have been both laughing and crying when I said, "This is not setting a precedent."

"It's not." He smiled, shaking his head.

"I'm serious, Hayes. We can't do this again . . ."

"We can in two more minutes." He curled himself up beside me with his head on my chest, his fingers interlaced with mine, and I felt it: happy. "I missed you, so fucking much," he said, soft.

"I missed you, too. But I'm serious: this can't become a habit. I don't care how far you've flown, or how long it's been—we can't do this again. Do you understand that?"

He did not respond.

"Hayes?"

"I heard you."

My hand was in his hair, his coveted hair. "If you keep coming back like this, you're never going to move on, and you *have* to move on."

We were both quiet. His phone vibrated on the nightstand, and he ignored it.

He propped himself on one elbow, gazing down at me, his fingers tracing my eyebrows, my cheek.

"Why? Why do I have to move on?"

"Because I can't be your girlfriend. And I'm not going to be one of your friends you fuck . . ."

"Do you think I could ever think of you that way?"

"I don't know."

His fingers were outlining my lips, trailing down over my chin, my neck. "I could never think of you that way, Solène. I didn't think of you that way in the beginning, I'm certainly not thinking of you that way now."

I was quiet. His phone was vibrating again, unanswered. His hand was descending across my clavicle, my breast. The tip of his middle finger drawing circles around my nipple.

"What are you doing?"

"I'm just loving you for a few more minutes before you kick me out." His voice cracked and I realized he was crying. Again.

"I'm not kicking you out just yet, Hayes."

He nodded. A tear fell onto the side of my face and he kissed it away. "Sorry."

His phone vibrated once more, and he reached over to silence it.

"You're quite popular tonight."

Whether or not he'd registered what I'd said, he did not respond. His fingers had returned to my chest, descending, traveling over my belly to my navel and back up again.

I stilled his hand then with my own and, without saying a word, guided it down between my legs.

For a second, he resisted. "You said no."

"Now I'm saying yes."

"You're very confusing. You realize that, don't you?"

I nodded. God, his fingers. "You're already here."

"So if I'm already here, it's fine. But if I'm not already here, I can't come back?"

"Exactly."

"Well then, I just won't leave, then . . ."

The second time he was controlled and focused, intense. He was unusually quiet, and it felt to me that every movement was a concerted effort to win me back. His thrusts, slow and deep, our hands clasped above my head, his gaze holding mine, never wavering. He wanted me to feel it, all of it. And remember it. And I would.

"Look at me," he said when I was coming. "Look at me, Solène." And the moment was so unbelievably charged, I started to cry.

Afterwards, he held me in his arms, close, ignoring his phone, which was still lighting up on the nightstand.

"Who keeps calling you?" I asked once I'd regained the ability to speak.

"Jane," he said, low. "I quit the band."

"What?!" It was quite possible I had not heard him correctly. "You what?!"

"I quit the band."

I sat up, alarmed. "What do you mean you quit the band? Why would you do something like that?"

He looked up at me, confused. "Because," he said, "it was the one thing that was keeping us apart."

Funny how I'd waited for this for months, it seemed. And when it finally came, it had the complete opposite effect on me. Nothing about this was good.

"Oh no. No no no no no." I grabbed my T-shirt from the other side of the bed, pulling it on. "You're not going to do this. This is a mistake."

"It's not a mistake," he said, sitting up. "What are you doing?"

"You're going."

"I'm not going."

"You're going. I'm going to go to the bathroom, and when I get back, you're going to go."

When I emerged, he was still sitting on my bed, naked. His expression, lost. "You're freaking out. Why are you freaking out?"

"You can't quit the band, Hayes."

"I did it for us."

"I understand why you did it, but you can't. I don't want you to do it for us. You need to stay in that band. You're going to get on the phone right now, you're going to call Jane, and you're going to tell her you're coming back. Tell her you made a mistake and you're coming back."

"I'm not going back."

"You're going back. I am not going to let you squander this opportunity, this gift, for what? Sex?"

He looked at me, shocked. "This is not just sex, Solène. I *love* you."

"I know you do."

"I thought you loved me, too."

"That doesn't matter."

"Of course it matters."

My head was spinning. My heart, racing. Nothing seemed clear. "What is this, Hayes? What do you think is going to happen with us? Do you think we're going to move in together? Get married? Have kids? Are you going to be a stepdad? Drive Isabelle to fencing practice and visit her at summer camp in Maine? Think about it. *Think about it.*"

"I *have* thought about it."

"Then you have to realize how crazy it sounds. Nothing about us makes sense."

"Don't say that." His eyes were welling. Crap.

"You're young, you have your whole life ahead of you . . ."

"Stop saying that."

"It's *true*. You think you know what you want now, but it's going to change a million times before you reach thirty. You're not going to be the same person ten years from now. Five years from now, even. You're not."

"Stop," he said.

"I'm not going to let you do this. I'm not going to let you throw this opportunity away for something you think you want right now. And I'm not going to be the fucking Yoko Ono of August Moon." I was crying. I did not recall at what point it started, but it had. "I don't want the wrath of your fans. I don't want this pressure for us to make this work. I don't want the guilt when it doesn't. You need to call Jane and tell her you're coming back. *Now.*"

There was a thump against the far wall and I feared we'd woken Isabelle.

"Fuck. Put your clothes on. You have to go."

He sat there, seemingly stunned.

"Now." I grabbed his underwear from the floor. His black jeans, his T-shirt. His boots. "Now."

"I can't believe you're doing this."

I stopped for a second, peering into his eyes, haunted. "This was never going to be forever, Hayes . . . You need to move on."

He reached for my arms. *"I'm not going to stop loving you, Solène. I'm not ever going to stop loving you."*

"It's a choice. You make a choice."

"You don't honestly believe that."

"Put your clothes on. You have to go."

I watched him dress. Crying.

"Why are you doing this? Why are you pushing me away?"

I could not speak. My chest, crushed. My heart, hemorrhaging. And I thought perhaps this is what it felt like to drown.

I led him back down the hall. Past Isabelle's room, past the photos of me pregnant, of me doing ballet, of me at seventeen figuring out who I was supposed to be. And out into the night air.

"You love me," he said. "You loved me. You said you loved me. Why are you doing this?"

And I realized, then, that there was only one way to truly let him go. "Maybe it wasn't you," I said. "Maybe it was the idea of you."

He stared at me for a minute, silent, his eyes red, wide. And when he finally spoke, he seemed to me broken. "You're lying," he said. "You're lying to me. You're trying to push me away. Again. And I don't know if you're just trying to convince me. Or you're trying to convince yourself. But either way, I know you're lying."

"You have to go, Hayes."

The tears were falling, rushing, easy. "Tell me. Tell me you're lying, Solène."

"You have to go."

"Tell me you're lying."

"Please. Go."

"Fuck. I love you. Don't do this to us."

"I'm sorry," I said. And I stepped back in the house and shut the door.

He went back to the band. And from what I could tell, nothing came out in the press about him having ever left. He'd missed a show in

Sweden due to the "flu," according to their management. But I knew better.

He called me. In the beginning, every day. Multiple times. Although I would not answer. And he texted. At first often, and then every few days or so. It went on for months. These little messages that would paralyze me. And to which I resisted responding. Because I had made a choice.

I miss you.
I'm thinking of you.
I still love you.

And then one day, they stopped.
Long, long before I had stopped loving him.